In the Heart of the Country

By Derek Bickerton

Published in the USA by Aignos Publishing, Inc.
54-253 Kaipapau Loop
Honolulu, HI 96717
www.aignospublishing.com

Printed in the USA

Edited by Zachary M. Oliver
Cover art provided by Carlos Aléman
Design by Liang-Han Yu

13-digit ISBN: 978-0-9904322-8-9
10-digit ISBN: 0-9904322-8-9

This book is fictional; the story and characters herein are not meant to portray any person who ever existed or who has ever been purported to have ever existed.

Chapter One

In the half-light of earliest morning the big boat rode sluggishly upstream. At this hour most captains and their crews would still have been comfortably sleeping, moored to the bank, with a watchman on guard and lanterns set out to deter bandits, crocodiles and hippopotami. But not the captain of the Sobk. He had not gotten to where he was by idling about. Moreover the Nile at this time of year (a couple of months before the flood came) was running low, care had to be taken not to go aground on sandbanks, passage time was correspondingly lengthened. And time was money.

So, with a brisk northerly breeze filling the single big square sail, and three men a side pulling long broad-bladed oars, the Sobk edged its way upstream, keeping to the deeper channels even when this meant tacking from one side of the river to the other. Crewmen stood by the ropes, ready to lower sail whenever, during one of these crossings, a northbound vessel bore down on them, for the north-bounders, in the grip of the current, and going faster still if they had oars working, took precedence—there was no way they could slow down or even turn at the speed they were going.

The Sobk, fifty feet in length, eight feet in beam, had a

capacity of around four hundred tons. Below deck, its hold was laden with silver and bronze ornaments, glassware, bales of linen sheets and clothing, rolls of papyrus, huge earthenware jars of wine and olive oil, all the riches of Alexandria, bound for the upper Nile cities, for the Meroitic kingdom beyond, for the Nubian and Ethiopian kingdoms beyond that—for who knew how far those things might be traded and retraded, down into the unknown lands of men who had two heads or who walked upside down. On the deck, under a low roof made of matting, lay the passengers, most still asleep on their reed mats, huddled in their cloaks against the chill of the river night, their pathetic bundles of belongings under their heads to serve as pillows and to deter thieves. Some were waking now, stretching, coughing, moving to spit over the sides, for the captain, one of the few who owned his own boat, but whose boat was all he owned, took what seemed to many of them a ridiculously hard line on cleanliness, and had been known to expel passengers by force for fouling his ship, throwing their baggage and the balance of their fares after them.

The sun finally cleared the low hills on the further bank, and glancing towards the bows the captain saw that the girl, Leila, was already awake and leaning on the low bulwark, gazing eagerly upstream. Her big day, he thought with wry amusement. By noon, if there's no hangups, we'll drop her off at Atripe. End of the line for her. End of her life, if you ask me. Shut up there with a parcel of old hens, no man between her thighs, no babies to suckle, ever. And everyone under the thumb of that lunatic Shenoute. Christians! You couldn't figure them out. Our God is a jealous God, they said. Not like all the other gods, who got along just fine with one another, having statues in each other's temples, being carried along in each other's processions. No, their God had to put everyone else's down.

Live and let live is my motto, the captain said to himself. Wonder if she realizes this ship's named after one of those gods? Probably wouldn't have sailed in her if she'd known.

For his boat was named after Sobk, or Souchos, as speakers of Greek called him—crocodile god of Arsinoe, the captain's home town. On the god's feast-days he would decorate its bows with garlands and pour libations of the finest oils and wines into the river, not so much because he believed the god would reward him for this as because he feared what might happen if he did not. He had owned the Sobk now for eight years and had good luck with her, what fool would risk changing that? If he died tomorrow he could still afford a third-class embalming job. A couple more years like this and he could afford a second-class embalming job and still leave the Sobk to his sons, not that the lazy bastards would profit from it, but he would look bad if he didn't. For that was how the world kept going—men worked, took women, bore sons, left them property, and the sons went on, worked, took—

'Hard to starboard,' he said to the steersman; his quick eyes had spotted the north-bounder, distant yet, but bearing down unbelievably fast and too far over. 'Drop sail,' he shouted to the men by the masts. The ropes slackened, the spar that held the lateen sail aloft came down in a series of short rushes, the sailors keeping time with rhythmic shouts. Immediately the Sobk began to lose way, in a moment she would begin to drift backward with the current, the steersman would need to keep the tiller bar hard over to stop the bows swinging out into the northbounder's path.

As the Sobk slid backwards, the other vessel came riding triumphantly past them. On its deck, Roman officers, helmeted, plumed, their equipment glittering, gazed with frosty-eyed scorn on the humble deck passengers of the Sobk hawking, spitting and scratching themselves as they roused from slumber. The captain stood stiffly to attention until the vessel was safely past him. He despised himself for doing this, but could not help it. With a jug of wine in his belly he might boast of his pride in Egypt, a country that had ruled the world when Rome was a dunghill in some Etruscan farmer's back yard, and express his contempt for the Roman administrators, a bunch of effete bisexuals who were already letting that world slip through their limp fingers. But he knew in his heart they still had power, a totally arbitrary power subject to no restraining hand, power that could reach out and snatch a man's life for any reason or for no reason at all.

'Up sail! Lively, now, lads!'

The other vessel was receding. Two or three passengers, little more than kids really, were jumping up and down in the stern of the Sobk, giving the departing Romans the finger, whooping and catcalling. There was nothing the Romans could do about that, once they had fallen astern. Not all their power could reverse the Nile's flow, and the youths knew it. But the Romans weren't even looking, they had turned and were going below deck, their helmets vanishing one after another, to a breakfast of grilled larks' tongues prepared by odiously subservient slaves no doubt, the captain thought bitterly and quite inaccurately as the Sobk labored to make up the ground she had lost. Crestfallen, their energy spent, the youths subsided again into their peasant indifference. Nothing really mattered. Nothing ever changed.

In the bows, Leila dreamed of the White Monastery. Soon, soon, in a matter of hours she would be safe there, free from all the sufferings of the secular world. She had had a hard time of it these last few months, ever since she had been kidnaped by the bandits. No one had believed her story, of course. Not her father, who promptly beat her, nor her mother, who shrieked and threw herself about, nor the priest of the village, who came to stare owlishly at her, h'm-ed and ha-ed, then exorcized her, just to be on the safe side. Her family believed she had a lover and had simply made the whole thing up to conceal her vices. Examine me, she had pleaded, just examine me and you can prove I'm still a virgin.

But inspecting the intimate parts of his parishioners, the priest demurred, was no work for one in holy orders, so she was handed over to a cabal of elderly Christian midwives, who pawed her over in the most shameful and humiliating fashion. Reluctantly, almost regretfully, they pronounced her still intact. That's it, her father said, now we can marry you off to young what's-his-name before you get into any more nonsense. When she humbly refused, repeating that she had vowed her body to Christ, her family threw her into an empty granary, barred the door, and swore they would not let her out until she consented.

They had not cleaned out the granary properly and for several days she survived on raw grains that were left there and water that her little sister poured under the granary door—water that Leila retained by building a small dam of mud and lapping the resulting puddle like a dog. Then news of her plight somehow reached the priest. He came round, and there followed a long and sometimes rancorous argument in which the need of respectable Christian landowners to increase their influence by judicious marriages was weighed against the right of virgins to serve their Savior. The extreme methods the family had used to abridge this right were scarcely referred to, although the priest did once dare to hint that, much as he respected the absolute authority of menfolk over their households, the Savior might not have wholeheartedly approved of starving a daughter to death.

And that was the reality that faced them: Leila had sworn that if she could not serve Christ as she had promised, she would still ensure her salvation by heading for heaven the shortest way. When the corn ran out, that would be it. Her father wavered for a few days after the priest's visit, then caved in. She should go to the White Monastery, if that was what she wanted. Not with his blessing, that was too much to expect, but at least with the fare for a southbound vessel and enough extra to feed her until she got to Atripe. After all, he could hardly let her walk there or go donkey-back like a poor peasant. He was a rich peasant.

So here she was, having taken passage on the Sobk, how many days ago she could not remember, it seemed like forever. And before that her father had passed up a couple of boats because there was no one on board who would keep an eye on her. But the priest knew and would vouch for the captain of the Sobk as a man who, although a pagan, would not tolerate any kind of evil conduct aboard his boat. Moreover, there was an old monk among the passengers, one Bios, who had lived in the White Monastery under both Shenoute and his predecessor, Pjol, and who was now returning after a visit to the Archbishop of Alexandria. He came up alongside her now; he was no longer afraid of her, as he had seemed to be at first, although surely anyone his age should long since have passed beyond any carnal thoughts.

'God be with you, Leila.'

'And with you too, Father Bios...It won't be long now.'

'No, not long now,' the old monk agreed out of a mouth from which a majority of teeth had long departed. 'We'll soon be there, soon be there, little sister, not long now.' He had a tendency to go on repeating the same remark over and over unless you stopped him. Leila stopped him.

'Father?'

'Yes, little sister.' His eyes blinked as though it cost him an effort to hold the eyelids open.

'The story you were telling me...about the holy Abbot Shenoute...'

'Story?'

'Yes, You know, about the boy. The boy who was

tormented by demons.'

'Ah, yes. The boy.' A vague light of remembrance glistened in the old monk's rheumy eyes. 'Yes, they so tormented him that he made a vow. He vowed that if his father should come to the monastery to visit him, he would go back with his father into the world.'

Bios paused. When the pause had gone on long enough, Leila realized he thought the story was over. 'And then, Father?' she prompted him. 'What happened then?'

'Oh, then...Then the holy Abbot Shenoute, that righteous man, knew instantly what he was thinking. And he called the boy to him and said, "Is it true that if your father comes, you will go back with him into the world?" The boy was embarrassed, he just laughed and hid his face. So our righteous Father said to him, "Truly, I will send you to your true father."'

'And what did he mean by that?' Leila asked.

The old monk seemed not to hear her. 'The young boy fell sick,' he went on, 'and the brothers said to Abbot Shenoute, that man of God, "He is in great pain, Father, will you pray for him?"'

'And the Abbot made him well again?' Leila asked eagerly.

Bios broke into an ecstatic smile. 'Oh, better than that' he said. 'Far, far better than that. Our father the prophet, who foresees everything, said to them, "What concern is he of yours? He wants to go to his father." And sure enough, on the seventh day, the boy fell asleep at the ninth hour, and they took him and buried him.'

'He died!' Leila was shocked. 'But then of course, the Abbot brought him back to life...'

The old monk gazed at her in bewilderment. 'Did someone tell you that?'

'No...No, I just thought...'

'If they told you that, they've got it all muddled up. Not that he can't bring people back from the dead, no, of course he can, he has, indeed he has...One time the corpse of a glassblower was found lying out in the desert…'

Leila knew that if she let him go on she would never hear the end of the first story. One tale would loop into the next, endlessly, that was how things were when you got so old. 'The boy,' she insisted. 'You were telling me about the boy.'

'You don't want to hear about the glassblower?'

'No. I mean, yes, but not right now. Tell me about the boy first.'

Bios blinked at her. 'Boy? What boy?'

'The boy who wanted to go to his father!'

'Aha!...That boy. Well, our father the holy prophet Shenoute called all the brothers together and said to them,

"Believe me, brothers, today there went to God a soul that has no stain. He wanted to go to his father and he is already with his father." His heavenly Father, he meant. So we all went away extremely edified.'

And the monk, Bios, a blissful smile on his features, fell silent. Leila stared at him. 'Father. are you quite sure you've got it right?'

Bios was indignant. 'Of course I'm sure! I was there, wasn't I?'

'But you don't think it was...well, a bit...'

Now it was Leila's turn to fall silent. She could not explain the chill that had fallen on her when she heard that story. She thought of the boy, silly, foolish no doubt, younger than her, writhing in agony for seven days. And had the Abbot, the holy Abbot...? Was it possible? No, it was unthinkable – the monk was senile already, he must be the one who had muddled things up. He was going on talking now, oblivious to her feelings:

'And he speaks with Our Lord, regularly, did you know that? Oh yes! His disciple, the blessed Father Besa, has heard them! And our abbot the prophet Father Shenoute sees Him too! In the flesh!...Well, as it were in the flesh. No one else in the monastery is holy enough for that, no one...'

And he went on to tell other stories about Shenoute,

many of which he had told before, more than once. Leila found her attention wandering. She thought once more of the bandit who had saved her from the other bandits—the one with the wild, reckless face and the flute tucked into his belt. But for him, she wouldn't be here now, on the brink of achieving her dream. And she didn't even know his name! But every night from that night on she had included him in her prayers. Had they worked? Had he abandoned his life of evil, was he perhaps even at this very moment approaching the gate of a monastery somewhere? Perhaps if she prayed earnestly, God would answer her questions in a dream or a vision. But no, it was vainglorious even to hope for that. She would have to pray, fast, keep vigil, mortify her flesh for years before she could become worthy of gifts like that.

Passing her on his rounds of the vessel, for he was forever looking to make sure everything stayed in place, the captain noticed that her rather ordinary little face, flushed by some inner feeling, looked almost beautiful. He sighed, and shook his head. Such a waste! He stopped, for he was a kindly man, and said, 'Round the next bend, look straight ahead of you and you'll see it.'

She turned, startled. 'What's that, sir?'

'The White Monastery, of course.' And, nodding to the old monk at her side, the captain went on.

'Is that right, Father? Are we nearly there?'

Bios, who had been dozing against the bulwark in the hot sunlight, blinked his pale eyes at her and nodded. She could hardly contain her impatience. The stony landscape either side of them moved with such slowness! Then at last, as they rounded a low bluff, there it lay, spread out in front of her.

But it was immense! Not so much a monastery as a village, a small town, even. Low whitewashed walls and flat white roofs stretched in every direction, with here and there the dome or cross of some chapel rising above them. Around the compound, as far as the eye could see, stretched cultivated fields growing flax, vegetables and corn; here and there she could pick out the bent backs of men working in the fields. 'They're all monks?' she asked.

Bios shook his head. 'Not all. Seculars live here too. Separate from the monks, of course.'

'And where do the women live?'

'Oh, way out on the south side.' Bios gestured vaguely. 'Quite a walk, I'm afraid.'

'I can't wait to get there!' Leila cried, clapping her hands.

The captain came by again. 'There's no freight for here,' he said, 'and you're the only passengers. We're not going to moor, we'll just pull in to the bank and you can jump ashore. It's quite safe. The crew will help you.' He looked directly into

Leila's eye for a moment, and in a voice too low to be heard by the old monk he said, 'Good luck, girl. You may need it.'

She had no time to worry about what that might mean. With its oars raised and its sail half-lowered, the Sobk was bumping along the sandy, friable bank, knocking crumbling chunks of it off into the water as she went. A couple of sailors jumped ashore and trotted alongside the boat, their hands extended. Another crewman caught the old monk by the collar and swung him to them, while a fourth tossed the worn leather bags that contained their few possessions onto the bank. Leila, not wanting the sailors' hands to touch her body, jumped lightly onto the bulwark, but the deep gap between boat and bank yawned at her feet and although the distance was short, she felt suddenly panicky and automatically stretched out her hand to the monk. A look of shocked horror crossed the old man's face, and he recoiled as if she had threatened him with an asp. But she had already launched herself, and when he jerked nervously back from her, she stumbled and half fell.

A sailor grabbed her, but not the lustful monster his features had led her to expect. 'You all right, miss?' he asked, raising her gently, gazing at her with concern.

'Yes...thank you,' she said in a breathless voice.

'Just don't be so impatient next time, eh?' the sailor said, grinning, and with a wave of his hand he and his companion jumped back aboard, the steersman leaned into the tiller bar, the sail went rattling up again and the Sobk drew away from the bank, headed upstream. The vessel had been home for several days now, and even in her excitement Leila felt a small twinge of sadness as she watched it pull away. But the feeling passed almost instantly, and she turned to Bios with a joyful face, forgetting or at least forgiving his momentary withdrawal from her. After all, there was nothing personal in it. She was a woman .

'Isn't it wonderful? We're really here at last!'

'Yes, praise be to God,' Bios said, 'and don't forget to thank Him, sister, for bringing us here in safety.'

'Amen, father Bios!' They stood on the bank in silent prayer for a few moments, then picked up the bags with their possessions and set out towards the White Monastery. They proceeded slowly. Bios could do no more than shuffle, and even at that he was obliged to make frequent halts. Leila would have liked to offer him a hand, but had sense enough not to do so. Instead she loitered along at his side, scuffing her feet in the dust, chafing at the delay. The path had no trees, not a drop of shade: the noon sun burned down on them until she began to feel dizzy. But within minutes she was reproving herself. She would have to curb her feelings, learn how to acquire patience and humility if she wanted to succeed in her new life.

Finally Bios pointed ahead of them and said, 'There, that's the women's gate. I cannot accompany you further. Knock on the shutter at the side there, and they will speak to you.' He did not say, 'They will let you in.' but in the excitement of the moment it did not occur to her that that might mean anything.

'Will I see you again. Father?' she asked, for although he had been tiresome at times she had grown fond of the old monk.

'Not in this life. I'm afraid,' Bios said. 'No men are allowed within the women's walls—only the Elder Brother.' He did not see fit to mention the corollary to this: that once inside she would never come out again. 'But in the life to come...' he added wistfully.,

'In the life to come, then,' Leila said shyly, feeling uncomfortable, and sad too, for Bios might enter that life any day now, while she, Leila, surely had many years left in this one. 'Pray for me, Father,' she added impulsively.

'Oh, I will, I will...God be with you and keep you, sister.' And the old monk shuffled away down the path.

Leila turned to the women's gate, feeling suddenly lost and alone, helpless. The gate—door rather than gate, an arch of bolt-studded timber fitting so tight that the crack where its halves joined was barely visible—loomed over her. The angle of the wall blocked the breeze, the air stifled her, her soul longed for the cool darkness she could only imagine within those walls. Timidly she rapped on a wooden grille that adjoined the door. Nothing happened. She had a sudden terrifying vision of being left out there alone in the blazing sunlight, for ever. She rapped again, more forcefully, and this time the grille opened a crack and a woman's voice, creaky, harsh as a crow's, asked: 'What do you want?'

Leila blushed, suddenly tongue-tied. 'I ... I've come to... I mean 1 want to be a, a, to live in your—'

'We don't know you. Clear off.'

Leila was dumbfounded. 'But...but...I...'

'What's the matter with you?' the voice demanded testily. 'Don't you understand Egyptian? We don't just let in any stray harlot wandering the desert. And besides, we're full up.' The grille slammed shut with a crack that re-echoed in the narrow space outside the gate, fading slowly into the all-embracing silence.

Leila stood there, distraught. This was something she had never dreamed of. She had to get in! There was no life left for her outside these walls! Her family would never take her back if she returned to them. But for the few copper coins she had left, she was destitute. She had nothing to sell but her body, and before she profaned that temple, she would fling herself into the river, praying God to forgive the lesser sin of suicide, committed only to avoid the greater one of unchastity. In her imagination she was already there, poised on the bank where she had disembarked, ready to leap, when she remembered the letter that the village priest had given her. She pulled the rolled sheet of papyrus from the hollow between her breasts where she had been carrying it, and beat insistently on the grille until it was opened.

'You again?' the voice from the shadows croaked, spitting malice. 'All right, I'll call the Mistress of Novices and we'll soon see who's...'

Leila did not bother to speak; she simply thrust the letter through the grille. The voice stopped abruptly. She heard a muttering sound, as if the woman inside was mouthing the syllables of each word in the letter. Then there came a grunt, silence, another grunt. 'Are you a virgin?' the voice asked.

'It tells you in there I am.'

'I don't care what it tells you in there! This letter was written three weeks ago. Are you still a virgin?'

'Yes I am.'

'Can anyone vouch for that?'

Leila, near tears, choked back the sob in her voice and said, as calmly as she could, 'The monk, Bios, of your monastery, was with me all the time on the river. He left me only now.' There was a sullen 'Hmph!' from within. Then the voice said, 'All right. You are allowed to enter. Not the monastery itself, you understand. Just the gate-house, here. You are a novice now. You will remain in the novitiate for a period of three months. You will be on probation during that time. Every word, every thought, every move you make will be watched, to make sure that you measure up to our standards. And only then, if you do measure up, and if you renounce all your worldly goods, and if you swear the Sacred Oath of the White Monastery—only then will you be admitted. D'you understand all that?'

'I understand,' Leila said in chastened tones.

'You understand what?' the voice snapped.

'What you just told me,' Leila said, puzzled.

'Idiot! What kind of novice d'you think you'll make? When you address me, you address me as 'Mother'. You show respect to your superiors. At all times....Now. Let's start again. Do you understand all that?'

'Yes I do, Mother.'

The voice sighed, resignedly. 'Then see you don't forget it...You can come in now,' it added, grudgingly.

The door yawned. Inside, just as Leila had anticipated, it was dark, cool, silent as the grave. Above the worn stone floor, in the foot or two of light that penetrated the gloom, dust-motes floated, golden. She plunged into the darkness, the silence, like a diver into a pool. The door creaked shut behind her.

She had finally arrived in the White Monastery.

Chapter Two

Zachary was in the deep desert, Anthony's desert. He had lost count of the days that had passed since he left Alexandria. In that time he had eaten a dead lizard and the maggot-infested corpse of some small wild creature, too rotten to be identified. He had dug in the cracked mud bottoms of dried-up saline lakes, and drunk the sulphurous, foul-tasting water that slowly welled up at the base of the pit, lying prostrate on the ground and lapping it like an animal. He had thanked God that there was any water there at all, for often he dug until his hands were raw and found nothing.

He had come across a sparse bed of long-dead reeds, and fashioned himself a crude covering from them, otherwise, naked and undernourished as he was, he would surely have died of exposure in the chilly nights. He would have turned back if he had known where 'back' was. But he had quite soon become completely disoriented. His brain, stupefied by hunger and thirst, had totally forgotten that if he kept the sun always on his right hand, he must sooner or later return to the Nile valley. The truth of it was, he no longer expected to get out. He had come here determined to survive in the wilderness or die. Well, if he did not discover a source of water, he would die. No matter. In that case it must be God's will that he die. Die in expiation for the vileness of his sin, his betrayal. That would be a just judgment. Perhaps his present sufferings would be weighed against that sin. Perhaps not.

The irony of it was that for the first few days the demon of lust had continued to torment him with visions of ecstatic pleasure. He fought the visions with every fiber of his will, but it was useless. Over and over again he saw Celia's face, aflame with desire, saw her naked breasts, and the pink opening under its thatch of hair that over and over again, against his will, against his screaming rejection of it, he saw himself touching, licking, thrusting into, until, weeping and shuddering with revulsion, he threw himself headlong in the sand and ground his face into it until the flesh was raw.

In the intervals of these attacks, he tried to pray. But he was unable to focus his mind. If not another of those satanic visions, it was the pangs of thirst that distracted him. or the ache of hunger that he now lived with continually, or the itching of the cracked blisters on his exposed skin. He was driven by a continual restlessness, even asleep, squirming around in the sandy burrows he dug for himself, flinching from the whip of dreams.

The dreams were the worst, less hateful but more scary by far than his visions of lust. Small wonder that he dozed only fitfully. He found himself fleeing through cities of black marble, cities whose buildings soared so high that they blocked out the stars, and these cities were the cities of hell, for they were inhabited only by demons—female demons who pranced and exposed themselves before him, male demons who screeched and jabbered at him in tongues he could not understand, who plucked and tore at him, jeering, laughing, and he knew that they were only playing with him, that they could seize him whenever they chose and inflict on him whatever torments they wished, until the end of time. For his soul had already been judged, and condemned, and placed under their authority, for ever and ever. And yet he kept on running, running, as if in some illusory hope that he could outrun them all, escape...but escape to where?

He was in an underground labyrinth, a labyrinth of narrow tunnels leading in all directions. He knew that it lay far underground, deeper than any mine or cavern, by its absolute darkness, and yet in that darkness he was somehow miraculously able to see. And hear, in the otherwise absolute silence, a slow, constant dripping sound. He must have escaped them, then, for he was alone. More alone than he had ever been among the living, in a place where no living soul but he had ever trodden. And suddenly he was seized with an absolute terror of loneliness, a panic that sent him plunging down one tunnel after another, looking not for a way out (for there was no way out, there would never be a way out) but for another creature, any creature, even one of the demons who had tormented him would be better than this eternal loneliness... And all the time, as he darted this way and that, the sound of dripping continued, getting gradually louder, and louder, and louder, and he knew that whatever those drops were, if one should fall on him, he would immediately undergo some horrifying, irrevocable metamorphosis.

He woke. He must have awoken, for the labyrinth had gone, and in its place was the familiar desert, low rolling dunes in the cool and quiet of the moment before the sun touched them...But a cloud stained the unsullied sky, a cloud of black vapor that spread and spread, and a vile choking smell came with it, a smell of burning flesh and putrefying bodies, and in the distance he heard screaming. Screaming and screaming. It went on and on, the cries of death agony, of men, women and children indistinguishably mixed, and then he saw them. They were ablaze with fire, fire that fell from heaven, great globs of liquid fire that wrapped themselves round their bodies and burned until the blackened flesh curled back and exposed the white of bone, yet they did not die. They could not die. A little child squirmed like a fish on a spear, burning, screaming, and her burning mother crouched over her, rolling on top of her and trying to quench the flames that poured from her, from both of them. He flung himself on them to save them, and then he too was burning, burning, locked in a tarry glutinous mass with the burning child and mother, burning for all eternity...

And after eternity, what?

He was among the stars. After all, he had somehow escaped eternal damnation, or perhaps what Origen had written was really true, that at the end of time all would be pardoned, even the worst of sinners, even Satan himself would be reconciled with the God against whom he had rebelled, and all would be made finally whole. That must be it. He was ascending into the heavens; he would finally look upon the face of God. The stars were passing by him now, passing and receding behind him, he must have penetrated the last of those seven crystalline spheres that enclosed the earth, the one that contained the stars, and any moment now he would perceive the everlasting mansions that housed God and all the saints and angels...But there were only more stars. More and more stars, reaching out into the blackness, passing him and yielding to yet more, more, stretched out before him, glittering, twinkling away blindly, uselessly, to infinity...

And a voice, a vast hollow voice, as vast and as hollow as this universe he had entered (and yet perhaps not a voice at all, nothing that one could have heard with mortal ears) kept repeating, 'No. There is no God. There is nothing...nothing... nothing...'

He came out of it shrieking, covered in sweat. And there around him was the familiar desert, low rolling dunes in the cool and quiet of the moment before the sun touched them...Was he already dead and in hell, was he locked in this cycle of dreams, would it repeat itself for all eternity? He looked for the black and stinking cloud. But the sky was pure, radiant, even as he gazed the high crest of a dune turned golden as the first rays of the rising sun touched it. Still he could not believe he had woken. He pinched himself, rubbed sand on his skin. The sweat of his dream turned chilly in the morning air. he dragged himself from his hollow in the sand and, shivering, teeth chattering, feet slipping and sinking, made his way upwards, slowly and toilsomely upwards, towards the crest, towards where the sun was already warning the desert. He moved mindlessly, like an animal. The lusts of the flesh no longer tormented him. He was past praying, past even thinking. He did not even think about what he had to do to survive. His body thought for him, responding lizardlike to the soft, mellow warmth of the early morning sunlight. His body knew that if he did not find water soon he would die, His body knew that if he gained height he would see further. His body knew that although climbing would quickly exhaust him, the chance of seeing somewhere in this sterile wilderness where water might be found outweighed the moisture and energy he would lose from climbing. His body knew this was its last chance.

The dune stood high. He had to stop for breath, but each time he stopped it was harder to start again. Without a conscious decision he veered away from the summit. His body knew he would never make it. It aimed him now at the ridge below the summit. From the ridge he would see something. Not as much as from the summit, but it would have to do. It might be enough. Who knew? Who cared? If there was anything left that was truly Zachary, it didn't care. That part of him had accepted death. That part of him, to the extent that it was still conscious, wanted simply to lie down and die.

He reached the ridge, and the wilderness rolled out beneath him, sand and stone, hill and hollow, rising and falling away to a remote, desolate horizon.

He blinked, trying to clear his vision. It was essential that his vision not be deluded. More than once he had seen the noonday heat break the line of the horizon into dancing waves, like the waves of the sea, and the waves would reform into groves of palmtrees, and glittering springs, and pools, and he had run towards them, only to see them vanish before his eyes—the delusions of demons sent to taunt and torment him with false hopes. But it was only at the height of noon and thereafter that those demons worked their enchantments. Shading his eyes with his hand, he swept his eyes in a long, slow half-circle over the wilderness.

And stopped, incredulous, paralyzed with a mix of hope and fear.

Rising to his left, perhaps a mile or more away, he saw two straight lines, the shorter one almost vertical, the longer almost horizontal. His gaze had skidded beyond those lines, for the space in the angle between them hardly differed in color from the wastes surrounding it, but he jerked back to them the moment their significance penetrated his sluggish brain.

Two straight lines meeting to form a right angle. Nothing like that was ever to be found in nature. It meant a human artefact of some kind. And an immense one at that, to subtend so broad an angle of view at such a distance. A huge building of some kind, tilted slightly by subsidence, half-buried in the sand.

So humans had lived here, even if they lived here no longer. And where humans had lived, there must have been water. Even if no water remained on the surface, perhaps some trace of it persisted underground—perhaps there were wells, cisterns...Lightheaded with excitement, he plunged down the slope, straight towards that single, high, blank wall. Barely a third of the way down, his feet remained clogged in the sand while head and torso went on flying forwards. He landed heavily on his face, rolled, half-recovered, kept on rolling and sprawled inert at last only when the slope lessened and friction and gravity combined to stop him. He lay there, breathing heavily. The fall had disoriented him. Lifting himself on one elbow, he gazed around him. The wall of the building was no longer to be seen.

His body turned cold with horror, a horror of helplessness such as he had known only in dreams. It would not have mattered if he had not seen the wall. He would have dragged on, his body struggling to live, his soul willing to die, until death arrived, quietly and inexorably, at last. But to be shown a chance at life, so near, so solid, and then have it snatched from him, that was too much. He lay there staring, blinking, praying that the building would miraculously reappear. Of course it did not.

His first conclusion was that it had never been there. It had been yet another trick of the demons, to make him despair, to yield to them in madness before he died and ensure his eternal damnation. But some streak of hope or stubbornness in him told him, no, this was real, other things may have been illusions but this was real. So where had it gone? He had descended from the ridge into a deep bowl, a hollow whose sides now blocked out everything that lay more than a couple of hundred yards away from him. So his goal was hidden behind one of those sides. But which?

Lying there, he cursed himself for his stupidity. If he had stayed on the high ground, worked his way slowly round to his left, he could have kept the building in view. But no, he had had to plunge straight towards it, certain in his mind that he could not fail to reach it, feeling himself already there, seeing the cisterns, tasting the crystalline springs ...Fool! To have been tricked by demons was bad enough, but to have thrown away life through his own sheer folly!

Gradually he got a grip on himself. Recrimination wouldn't help. He had to start thinking, difficult though that might be. He had time. He had yielded once to haste, he must not make that mistake again. He had the day, at least. He could not survive another twenty-four hours without water. But if he could find the building by sundown, now perhaps a bare nine hours away, he would survive. It never occurred to him that he might find the building but there might be no water there.

He looked back. The line of his fall was roughly clear to him from the marks he had left in the sand. If he had not been diverted at any point. So, if he extended that line up the slope that now faced him, he should once more come within sight of the building. Laboriously he pulled himself to his feet.

And in the very instant of rising he crashed to the ground again. Pain shot through his left knee like a bolt of lightning, pain so intense that he thought for a moment he would vomit, empty though his stomach was. He lay there gasping until the pain slowly ebbed. Then, cautiously, he began to feel the knee with his fingers. It was sore and throbbing but he could not find anything that felt like a broken bone. Tentatively he tried to flex the knee, but a warning stab of pain stopped him. Sprain, torn muscle, whatever it was, he could not walk.

Tears of rage and despair rolled down his cheeks. But a stubbornness deep inside him would not let go. If he could not walk, he would crawl. He had nine hours before the light failed. He would crawl.

He threw his weight onto his right side, drew up his right knee, letting the damaged left one trail, thrust out his hands ahead of him, dug in his right foot and straightened the leg, drew up the knee again, thrust out his hands...There was no way he could prevent his injured knee from bumping and dragging on the ground. No matter. The pain stayed within limits he could bear. What he feared most was his own slowness, and his exhaustion. He had very little energy left, and crawling took too much of it, even crawling downhill. After a mere fifty yards or so he had to stop and rest. With a kind of horrified care he marked the progress of the shadow cast by the slope in front of him. How quickly it seemed to move, compared to him! Before he was really ready, he pushed on.

Another fifty yards and he had reached the bottom of the slope. From now on it would be uphill. He meant to rest longer, to try to recover his strength, but he was lying in shadow now, the low sun not clearing the slope ahead of him, and the chill of it drove him on. Yard after yard. He was not sorry to be in shadow, for he had begun to sweat again. He couldn't afford to sweat. Sweat was water. And already his body was as parched as one of the desiccated, mummified corpses that filled the tombs of Egypt. A flash of memory entered his mind—the horror of the Blessed Anthony, when he lay dying, that someone might find and mummify his body, and how he had made his disciple promise to bury him secretly, in the interior desert, where no one could find his grave.

Well, that was no problem for Zachary. He had no one to bury him, but there was no one there to mummify him either. In a day or so his rotting body would bring the kites, the ravens, the vultures, and in a day or so more there would be nothing left but a short, ragged line of bones to bleach in the wind and sun, crumbling to dust in the extremes of heat and cold.

He dragged himself uphill. Thirst raged in him as the

sun climbed the sky, a dry parched burning in his mouth and throat that made his head swim with dizziness. More than once he lost consciousness, but the indomitable force inside him that drove him on pulled him back each time, and after only moments, for the shadows still stood where they had stood before. Yet he sensed he was slowly losing ground. The sun had risen close to its zenith, yet the slope still reared up before him, interminably. He dared not look back to see how far he had come. He dared not, because he feared the distance was so small that once he knew how small it was he would realize he had no hope of reaching his goal before nightfall. That would be too late: he would be mad, or dead, by daybreak.

The summit of the slope appeared before him, or what he believed was the summit, for only blue air appeared beyond it. Once at the summit, he would see his goal, at least he would know whether or not he could reach it. Not knowing this tormented him almost as much as thirst, or as the intolerable weariness he had to fight constantly in order to keep moving. Not knowing kept him in a fever of anxiety, a violent seesawing between extremes of hope and despair. It would be better, he felt, to know for certain that he could not reach it. Then at least he would have an hour or two of peace before the end.

Slowly, infinitely slowly, the stony ridge approached. For two full minutes he lay, just a few feet below it, gathering strength. Then he lurched forwards, striking his injured leg against a stone but hardly noticing it because in a few seconds, right there before him, he would see...

Nothing.

His gaze switched wildly, to the left, to the right and back again. There was nothing. An uneven plateau before him, rising a little at its rim, and then beyond that, barren hills, valleys, a vast expanse of untenanted space without a single sign of human habitation upon it anywhere.

He had been so utterly sure that he would see the building again! He began to sob aloud, tears of frustration and despair rolling down his dusty cheeks, even while he continued to scan the scene incredulously, as if the building had deliberately hidden itself to tease him, and might at any moment reveal itself, like a naughty child caught in a game.

Had it been an illusion after all? He could not believe that. He had stared at it so long and carefully. Even now, in his imagination, he could recreate it in every detail, its precise color, the angle between roof and wall, the proportions of it. But then he had fallen. Could he after all have gotten turned around? Perhaps he had been going in entirely the wrong direction! Perhaps he was further from it now than he had been when he saw it!

It was at this moment, this darkest instant of a despair

beyond despair, that a small, remote voice, somewhere in his head, began to speak to him. 'How can you hope to live through this alone?' the voice said, 'Why should you try to live through this alone? Don't you know that in all this time you have not once called upon God to help you?'

'I am not worthy to receive God's help,' Zachary answered. 'I have sinned grievously. I will pay the price. I am not worthy.'

'It makes no difference whether you are worthy or unworthy,' the voice answered him. 'God's loving grace is free for all who will accept it. Knock, and it shall be opened unto you. Ask, and you shall receive.'

Zachary bowed down his head, and prayed. 'Lord, if it is Thy will, give me strength that I may be delivered from this place of trial. And if it is not Thy will, so be it, for my will shall be Thy will, and into Thy hands, O Lord, I commend my spirit.'

Instantly an immense calm came over him, an oceanic calm, buoyant and boundless. He did not cease to be aware of his thirst, his utter exhaustion, the constant nagging pain in his knee, but these had somehow become no more than incidental points in a softly heaving ocean of awareness, points of no greater significance than a crumbling chunk of reddish stone near his left hand, or the black silhouette of a buzzard, far above him, swung in an arc by the wind. Of no greater significance than the calm reassurance of reason born again, after so many days, in his weary brain: the far edge of the plateau is higher than this, therefore the building could still be hidden by it, so go, keep moving, go in the same direction, don't squander what you have already gained by casting wildly about, but just go.

It was the strangest of feelings. Everything seemed somehow remote from him, and yet he was aware of everything, more keenly aware than he had ever been before: of feathers of cloud near the declining sun, of the movements of lizards, beetles, scorpions under the stones, of the geometry of sandgrains, the grape-blue bloom of lengthening shadows, the fissuring of remote escarpments, and the pale horn of a waning moon, a specter adrift in the serene heaven. Through all of this he moved, as slowly as before, but wholly without anxiety. For this time he had truly surrendered his will. Not as when he first entered the desert, throwing down his soul like a wager before God—'Kill me if you want to, save me if you don't, see if I care!'—the defiant gesture of a spoiled child.

That had been his injured self speaking. His will had remained defiantly itself, an animal beyond control, surviving when his feeble and spurious piety died, clinging to this horrific residue of its existence with the mindless frenzy of a trapped rat. But that was all over now. Since he had truly surrendered his will, neither hope nor fear tormented him any longer. Yet he had not fatalistically accepted his destiny. To accept you must be able to reject, but he had passed beyond acceptance and rejection. He no longer had anything to accept or reject with. He had died to himself. His heart, no longer divided between love of God and love of self, had freed itself at last from all conflicts, doubts, decisions, choices. He existed now in a space of unbounded calm, unbounded peace.

The sun crawled across the sky. Zachary crawled across the desert. As he approached the further rim of the plateau, the sun was already about to drop below the horizon. Behind him, violet shadows consumed the last drops of day; ahead, the light ebbed almost perceptibly from an infinity of dips and ridges. Calmly, with no more than a mild curiosity untouched by hope or fear, he lifted his head and looked out.

And there it was—a vast and ancient temple, its pylons shattered, reduced to a bare rectangle of stone half-sunk in an immense dune that threatened to overwhelm it. The rim of the plateau had blocked it from his sight until he was almost on top of it. Already the shadows were gathering quickly in the hollow valley below the temple, but not quickly enough to conceal the tall palms that grew there, or the dark clumps of fruit-bearing trees, or the still pool that caught in itself a last gleam of light reflected from the sky above it, and then winked out.

It was dark by the time he reached the spring that fed the pool. That didn't matter. Having slid down most of the slope, round and under one corner of the sunken temple, he had been led for the last part of his journey by the soft murmur of the water welling up and then running off over low ledges of rock. He thrust his face into the spring and, lying on his belly, drank—just a little at first, for no frenzy of greed now possessed him, then a little more, as he heard the frogs, no longer fearful of soaring birds above them, beginning their evening chorus. The water was clear, cold, with a faint metallic aftertaste, but more delicious to him then than any wine he had ever tasted. He drank a third time, and then, with his head only inches from the water, passed into a profound and dreamless sleep.

Chapter Three

When the Israelites were enslaved in Egypt, and Moses and Aaron were trying to convince the Pharaoh to set them free, the Lord told Aaron he could impress the Pharaoh by throwing down his stick, which would thereupon turn into a serpent. Aaron did this, but the Pharaoh, unconvinced, called on his magicians Jannes and Jambres, who did the same trick. So Aaron turned all the rivers of Egypt to blood, but again, Jannes and Jambres did likewise, and the Pharaoh remained unconvinced. Then Aaron covered Egypt with frogs, but so did Jannes and Jambres, and it was not until Aaron flooded Egypt with lice that the two magicians, unable to match this one, had to give up.

But they were powerful magicians nonetheless, so powerful that they had gone on to create, far out in the desert somewhere, an exact copy of the original Garden of Eden where Adam dwelt with Eve. Zachary knew this because the Great Macarius had visited that paradise, and the story of his visit had been told to Zachary in Scetis by more than one fellow--hermit.

Macarius had been wandering in the interior desert, without food, for three weeks when he came upon the Garden. It was guarded by demons, of course, but Macarius prayed and went in boldly, to find two holy men already present. The holy men fed him the fruits of paradise and suggested he bring other hermits to spend their lives there. Macarius accordingly set out for home carrying with him fruit from the garden to convince his companions and palm branches that he stuck in the sand to mark the way back. While he slept, the demons pulled out all the branches. But this did not discourage Macarius, who told them, 'If it is God's will, you cannot prevent us from entering the garden.'

But when he arrived in the settled lands and offered around the fruit he had brought with him, the other hermits were not impressed. 'If we were to enjoy this place in our earthly lives,' they explained, 'we would have received on earth all the good things we would otherwise receive in heaven. So what would be left for us? For what sufferings could we be recompensed?' Saddened but convinced, Macarius had never again tried to return to the garden.

Looking around him on that first morning, Zachary thought that the place he had discovered must indeed be Jannes and Jambres' paradise. After all, had not the demons done their best to prevent him from reaching it, causing him to fall down and injure himself, hiding the garden from him even after he had glimpsed it from afar? And was it not his prayer to God, the utter surrender of his own will, that had alone enabled him to breach the invisible barrier of enchantment protecting the garden? And surely even the true paradise above could hardly exceed the beauty of this place, this valley with its softly curving walls that plunged from the desolation around and above it to a rich and almost virulent mass of greenness, of dark, shaggy foliage in which he caught here and there the faint shimmer of orange and gold fruits, this valley through which luminous pools descended, ledge by ledge, joined by links of water that bubbled down over layers of mossy rock.

There were some differences from the story, of course, but these were surely trivial or accidental. The story made no mention of a temple, but since Jannes and Jambres were pagan idolaters, what more likely than that they should have incorporated a temple in their design? The story mentioned three springs, rather than one. Well, perhaps later he would find others, or if he did not, those others could easily have been buried by sand in the more than fifty years that had passed since Macarius's visit. And as for the two holy men...Well, if they were already old when Macarius came, they would be dead by now, and he might find their bones and give them Christian burial, to the best of his ability. If not, they might be here still. He would look for them. But something told him he would not find them. There was no odor of sanctity about this place. For all its beauty, he sensed something strange and frightening—not evil, exactly, but something immensely old and alien, something that had been there long before the birth of the Christian faith. It touched his heart with a sudden, sourceless fear so intense that for a few seconds he was almost of a mind to scale the sides of the valley and throw himself a second time on the mercy of the wilderness.

If he were able to. For he had a funny, sickening feeling that he might not be able to, that the demons who inhabited the valley might be as eager, once he had arrived, to keep him there as they had been to prevent his entrance...

But he did not seek to escape. A few moments of prayer steadied him, and the clarity of the morning, an all-pervasive radiance in which it seemed nothing malevolent could lurk, resolved him to remain. Soon he would begin his survey of the place, and either prove his fears or set them permanently at rest. But first there was something more important to do.

He walked—today it was possible, if still excruciatingly painful, to do so—as far as the nearest clump of palms, picked up two branches that had fallen from them, stripped off their fronds with a sharp flint, bound them together with palm fibers in the rough shape of a cross, and fixed the cross upright, embedding its foot in a small cairn that he built up stone by stone until the cross would stand without tilting too far to one side. Then he fell to his knees and offered up a prayer of thanksgiving for his deliverance from death. For a long time he prayed, while the golden glow of morning spread further and further down the steep slopes of the valley.

All remained silent but for the murmur of the spring and the cry of an occasional bird circling far above. Faint smells of moist vegetation, herbs, and rotting fruit penetrated the thin, dry desert air.

At last he rose and began searching for food. Overripe dates had fallen from some of the tall palms, and he ate of these, being careful to take only small quantities, despite the ravening hunger that gnawed him, for greed was still greed regardless of long famine. Further down the little creek that descended from the spring lay groves of fruit-trees, mostly bare at this season, but there remained a few pomegranates and even some withered oranges that, though dry and tasteless, he could still eat. Not quite the luxury Macarius had found, but one would not starve here. Beyond the groves, a broad hollow in the ground had been filled by the water of the creek (evidently the large pool he had glimpsed briefly the previous evening) and in the soft, muddy sand around its rim he saw the footprints of wild beasts, and of some larger animal, which he knew, although he quickly suppressed that knowledge, was a camel.

He did not want to believe it was a camel. If it was a camel, it meant that this was not after all the secret paradise of

Jannes and Jambres but simply some oasis well-known to the caravans of traders that periodically crossed the desert. Indeed, how could it fail to be known to them, being the only sure source of water for many miles around? But if it was known to traders it must also be known to the feared nomadic tribe of the Mazices, the ruthless barbarians who somehow managed to survive in this wilderness, raiding the caravans and the settled regions and then vanishing into the trackless wastes before justice could catch up with them. For that matter, the valley could be equally well known to the brigands, the bandits, all the riffraff of an unsettled era who, too cruel and greedy to turn hermit, had chosen a life of violence and infamy on the rim of the peaceful world.

He did not want to believe that. He wanted to believe that he had found at last some pure and pristine place, known only, if at all, to a handful of seekers after righteousness such as himself, but best of all, known only to himself—a place where, with no distraction from other humans, he could purge himself of his sins and bring his soul to a state of perfection. He did not wish to have to hobnob with traveling traders, to explain himself or justify his way of life. He did not wish to have to fear for his life from the assaults of bedouins or bandits, to skulk in caves. to be distracted from his prayers by the need for continual vigilance. If any hermit had preceded him here he would gladly accept that hermit as his spiritual master. If he had the place to himself, then God alone would guide him.

He had totally forgotten Cosmas the Flying Syrian.

He continued past the pool. There were more palms, more groves of trees, but these were sparser now as the waters of the creek were gradually absorbed by the sandy soil. Well under a mile downstream the trees had already given way to scattered shrubs, clusters of cacti. The stream itself grew clogged with reeds, shrank to a trickle, expired at last in a series of shallow puddles among the rocks. Beyond, the desert reasserted itself. Either he was alone here, or the others were hiding.

He could not decide between these two alternatives until he had searched the caves which, at intervals, marked the steep sides of the valley. But his throbbing knee had become too painful for any further exertion. For the rest of the day he remained where he was, close to where the stream vanished, alternately praying and dozing, creeping to the stream and drinking, praying and dozing again, munching on the dates he had carried with him. He must have fallen deeply asleep some time in the afternoon, for when he woke the sun had almost set and he lay there, confused, trying to place the strange, ululating cry that had awakened him. It was repeated. Hyenas! He remembered the tracks around the pool, realized that he could be at the mercy of still larger and more savage predators. How had he survived that first night? Surely only God's grace could have preserved him!

Faith was one thing, foolhardiness quite another. He decided not to repeat such a risk. Cursing his almost useless left leg, he began to scale the side of the valley. The sun was already a swollen red ball poised on the horizon, far out beyond the valley mouth, when he finally dragged himself up to the cave's entrance, peered into its dimness—and recoiled, babbling incoherent apologies.

He had been wrong. The valley was inhabited. There just inside the cave a hermit, on his knees, was praying—praying with such fervor that he had not even noticed Zachary's approach. Or had noticed him but chose to ignore him, for the lore of Scetis was full of stories of hermits who had visited famous holy men and been kept waiting for hours, days even, before they were granted an interview. Well, that was understandable. One who had attained such a peak of holiness, where he might at any time find himself in direct communion with God, could hardly be expected to descend from it at the beck and call of any Tom, Dick or Harry who might happen to pass by. That would surely be taking humility too far. Rather it was he, Zachary, who should show humility, waiting until the saint descended of his own will from his peak, and bade him enter, or not, as it pleased him.

So he stepped backwards, out of the unknown hermit's view, and waited on the narrow ledge beneath the cave. The sun was down now and the light ebbing fast. Suppose the man went on praying all night? A surreptitious glance showed him still in the same position, head averted, a wisp or two of white hair on the bald crown. Again Zachary retreated, only this time he cast his eyes nervously about him. There was another cave only a few yards up the slope. Wouldn't it be wisest to take shelter there and return in the morning, when the old man might be more prepared for company?

In the last of the afterglow he scrambled to the second cave, hesitated for a moment outside it (for might it not contain the first hermit's companion?), then plunged in. It was dry and unoccupied. Without bedding of any kind, huddled in his wretched garment of reeds, he twisted and turned, trying to find a hollow that would fit his body. Even when he had settled on a resting place he remained wakeful for a long time, trying to identify the faint sounds—nightbirds, animals, who could tell?—that drifted up from the valley floor. But despite his discomfort he felt a deep sense of satisfaction that he was not, as he had been convinced, alone in the valley. He had been lucky after all. He had discovered, not merely a refuge, but a spiritual guide. For it never occurred to Zachary that a hermit already established in this valley would refuse him that courtesy. In the stories, no matter how long the holy man kept his supplicant waiting, sooner or later he relented, gave him a word of life, allowed him to settle in, if he so wished, as a disciple.

Could he be one of the pair that greeted the Blessed Macarius? Or some later arrival who had been the disciple of these? No matter. From what the poor light had allowed Zachary to see of him, the hermit had been an old and venerable man, somewhat emaciated, as you would expect, but supple and strong enough to maintain the same reverent posture indefinitely. Someone like Poemen the Shepherd, perhaps: someone who could take a soul stained even as Zachary's was and mold it to the way of perfection.

Dreaming of his future in the valley, of the long conferences he would hold with his new advisor, Zachary fell at last into a pure and dreamless sleep, a sleep that lasted until the sun, high in the sky already, cast a trembling beam into the interior of the cave.

Zachary awoke with a deep sense of guilt. This was no way to begin his spiritual life in his new home. His future teacher, still unconscious, perhaps, of Zachary's presence, would have been up and praying for hours, if he had slept at all, for some did not, or so they claimed. Why should such a man waste time on a creature gripped in the vice of sloth?

I will not call on him yet, Zachary thought. I will go to the spring, to the cross I raised, I will pray there and atone for my shameful idleness, and only when I have done that, when I have purified my heart to the best of my ability, will I go again to call on him. So, avoiding the first cave, he made his way down to the valley floor and then up the valley until he came within sight of the spring, and of the temple, whose nearer wall, blank and massive, overhung that end of the valley. But he couldn't see his cross.

For a moment he felt a sense of vertigo. He knew he had erected it here, he couldn't have been mistaken. He felt his reason slipping, scurried this way and that, blindly searching. Then he saw it. It lay flat upon the ground.

Fear seized him. Demons had overthrown it in the night. He was so far from God's love that God had not lifted a finger to prevent them. Then, slowly, his common sense reasserted itself. When he erected the cross he had still been weak from his experiences in the desert. He had not secured it with the necessary care. So he put it back, adding more stones to the cairn, wedging them into place with smaller stones. This done to his satisfaction, he tugged at the cross. It seemed firmly planted. He knelt before it in prayer, pouring out before God his sorrow for his sin, his determination to transcend it, his willingness to dedicate himself to the service of the spiritual counselor whom God, in his infinite wisdom and foresight, had seen fit to put in this remote place so that Zachary might become his disciple.

After that he felt he could present himself to the holy man a second time.

Not before the ninth hour, they had told him in Scetis. Hermits do not like to be disturbed before the ninth hour. I won't insist, Zachary told himself, I'll just show myself briefly outside the cave, let him know I'm here, in case he was so rapt last night he didn't notice me. If he gives no sign, then I'll leave and not come back until the ninth hour. Though, if he had been more honest with himself, Zachary would have realized how much he was driven by his own loneliness, his impatience, his need for wise counseling, and beyond that, for mere human companionship. I won't intrude, he kept telling himself. I really won't. But in his mind he could already hear the hermit's voice saying, 'Come in, my child! Welcome. in the name of the Lord! Come, eat!'

He climbed back to the first cave, and peered inside it. The holy man had not moved! He continued to kneel in exactly the same posture he had taken up the previous evening. Throughout that night and the greater part of the morning, while Zachary drowned in hoggish slumber, he must have been attending to his soul's business, fulfilling literally the words of the gospel that tell us to pray ceaselessly. Zachary marveled. Here indeed and at last was the teacher he had been seeking for, a teacher whose holiness exceeded even that of the greatest hermits of Scetis! He dared not disturb him. Not yet, anyway. But later ...Later, what spiritual comfort he would receive from him! What a reward his sufferings would have earned him!

He backed out of the cave, and in doing so his shoulder caught on a piece of projecting rock, which fell with a loud clatter. He was mortified. 'Oh, I'm so—I mean, Father—I...' His voice trailed off. The hermit had not moved. Not one inch. The bald head remained bowed. A breeze from the cave mouth lightly stirred the few strands of pure white hair that clung to it. A fly circled the head and, as Zachary watched, alighted on it, walked a little way, then raised one of its legs and cleaned it. A nameless horror began to dawn in Zachary's soul.

'Father!' he said urgently, willing the hermit to respond.

He reached out a hand and touched the tunic that covered one shoulder. It crumbled to dust; fine shreds of it floated away, sinking slowly towards the cave floor. He snatched back his hand, and the figure of the hermit lurched sideways and crashed to the ground. He was dead. Had been dead for years—decades, perhaps. Zachary gazed in horror at the withered, toothless, parchment-like face that now seemed to stare up at him from eyeless cavities. The cool dry air of the cave had mummified the hermit as surely as any Egyptian embalmer.

Zachary's first, instinctive impulse was to flee in panic. But quickly he overcame it. This was not some horrific product of pagan ingenuity, this was a true Christian who had lived prayerfully to the end—perhaps the very eyes that had filled those sockets had been granted a glimpse of paradise itself before the spirit left them. Though many years might have passed since that moment, Zachary felt extraordinarily close to it. In the stories, the deathbeds of hermits were always surrounded by eager companions: 'What can you see, Father? Tell us what you can see!' This hermit had had no one to share those last moments—only Zachary, years after the event, to bear witness to its result, to pray for the man's soul, as he now did, though close to certainty that the old saint lay already safe within paradise, after all that he must have endured in his loneliness.

To pray for his soul and give his body burial. That second task laid on Zachary was the harder. He had no tools to dig in the rocky soil. The best he could do was to pull down stones from the roof of the cave—the rock there was loose and friable, as he had proved by accidentally knocking it—and pile them over the pitifully frail and shrunken corpse until it was hidden from view. Then he crossed himself and retreated into the bright day.

But it was as if the spirit of the dead hermit had laid leaden fingers on his soul. At first he thought he was merely disappointed; he had set such store in finding a spiritual father here. But as time passed and he became reconciled to his spiritual loneliness, he still could not shake off morbid thoughts of the hermit and his end. Had the man been one of the two Macarius had met? Had he buried his brother and then waited for death in his turn, knowing that there would be no one to perform that service for him, believing that he would remain forever in that gloomy cave, crumbling slowly to dust as the centuries went by, with none to mourn or even notice his passing? And how exactly had he died? Of old age, sickness. or through the machinations of the demons who, Zachary always felt, were never very far away from one in this valley? Could his end prefigure Zachary's own?

Life fell into a strange rhythm. During the daylight, when the sun ruled, he slept fitfully by the stream, for he felt it safer to sleep then. During the night he kept vigil, praying, reciting the scriptures, pulling his mind back constantly from the darker thoughts that were continually trying to overwhelm him. For at night he felt that there was always someone, or something, creeping around just outside the reach of his senses.

He saw flickers of it, out of the tail of his eye, when his attention was distracted; sensed the tremor of sounds just outside the range of hearing; occasionally smelled it, even—a sour smell like unwashed flesh mingled with rotting meat. Yet whenever he focused his senses, looked, listened, there was never anything there.

On the fourth, or was it the fifth, morning—he had begun to lose all track of time—he saw that his cross had been overthrown a second time. He knew then that he would never have peace in this place unless, like Moses in the youth of his hermithood, he girded his loins and went out to wrestle with the demons in the very place that was surely their stronghold: the wreck of the ancient temple that, like some vast and foundering vessel, loomed over the head of the valley.

Chapter Four

But, first, he had to do something about his cross. He bent down to pick it up, and immediately snapped back upright, startled by a sudden, hissing, chattering sound that came from immediately behind him. He spun round, braced for his first supernatural confrontation, and was relieved and a little ashamed to see two of the small rodents that inhabited the rocky slopes, totally unaware of his presence, fighting one another. He had noticed the rodents on his first day, and forgotten them. He watched them until the vanquished one fled, pursued by the victor, then removed his original pile of stones, dug a small hole with a sharp piece of flint in the ground beneath, forced the base of the upright arm into the hole and laboriously rebuilt his cairn. Then he prayed to God and all his angels that this time they would guard his cross and prevent the demons from harming it, and that they would also give him the necessary strength for the combat that was about to commence. Then, he hitched his battered garment of reeds around him and turned to face the enormous wall of stone.

The demons had done their work well, it seemed. The wall facing him was utterly blank, with no trace of door or window in it anywhere. Since the demons lacked any physical form (save for the illusory shapes they put on to fool the unwary), this wouldn't matter to them. Indeed, it made the place a perfect sanctuary for them, proof against any demon-hunting hermit who might want to expel them from it with holy imprecations.

Zachary stood facing the temple and challenged the demons. In the name of the Savior he commanded them to come forth. If they did not come forth they were cowards and beneath the contempt of any God-fearing hermit. They could throw down his cross by night, while he wasn't looking, but they didn't have the courage to throw it down now, in broad daylight, before his eyes. If they did, then he would make short work of them, or his name wasn't Zachary.

Even as he said these last words he began to feel a little embarrassed. For first, absolutely nothing had happened: the sun went on shining, the valley remained still and untroubled, the spring continued to run. And second, his speech teetered on the brink of vainglory—a sin at any time, but one that bore the added weight of absurdity when no palpable enemy had appeared to refute his claims.

Clearly, he had to do better than this.

There must be some way into it, he thought. How did worshipers get in when it was functioning? Through a door, obviously, somewhere in that part of the building—the greater part of it—that was now buried under sand. How would it have been lit? Possibly, as in the Serapeum, through slits high in the walls or in the roof. But if such slits existed, they too were covered now by the sand that had overwhelmed the roof. In that case, though, the interior of the building would be full of sand, and he did not want to believe that—his mind clung to thoughts of shadowy, cavernous chambers where unspeakable horrors might lurk. Perhaps it had had no windows at all, but had been lit perpetually by torches, whose light could be easily manipulated to create the illusions with which pagan priests deluded their credulous believers...

Illusions! Wasn't it likely then that the temple had a concealed door, through which devices and feigned monstrosities could be smuggled in and out? A door indistinguishable from the wall that surrounded it, but subtly counterpoised, so that the merest touch on the appropriate stone would cause it to swing inwards? He would look for such a door, would examine each inch of the wall for tell-tale cracks in mortar, press against every irregularity in the masonry in case it concealed some secret spring or lever.

He began on the left, at the point where what he supposed to be the side of the temple vanished into the fan-shaped talus slope where sand and stones from above had poured down over it. He worked his way slowly rightwards along the side, pressing, listening, hammering on the wall with a rock to test for hollowness, until he was almost at the end of it, at the corner where the side joined at right angles with what he took to be the rear wall of the building. This wall also vanished, within a few paces, into the slope of the overwhelming dune.

He felt a sudden sense of impending danger. Perhaps, as he thought afterwards, his guardian angel had interceded; perhaps the pressure wave of the falling fragment had impinged on some unconscious sense. Whatever the cause, he hurled himself backwards, just as a massive chunk of masonry, dislodged somehow from the cornice above, came crashing down on the exact place where he had been standing. The thunder of its fall echoed back and forth in the confines of the narrow valley; only gradually did it fade away into the all-embracing silence. Not until the reverberations had ceased could he quiet the trembling in his limbs.

When he had done so, he dragged himself to his feet and went to examine what had fallen. The piece was too heavy for him to lift; if it had struck him it would have killed him instantly. The demons had done a thorough job. But for his angel, they would be rid of him. He looked upwards, hoping that at least the collapse had made some breach in the wall. But as far as he could see from this angle—the piece had fallen from some forty feet or more above him—the wall remained intact.

He was afraid now, and ashamed of his vainglorious boasting. It had put him on a level with the demons, made him vulnerable to them. True virtue lay not in ranting or threatening, it lay in humility, fortitude, perseverance. It lay, above all, in prayer.

Dear Lord, he prayed, if it be Thy will, allow me to find the entrance to this unholy place, that I may purge it of demons and purify it in Thy name. Again, as before, when he had begged God's help in finding the valley, his mind calmed, his fear dissolved. He was, after all, in God's hands, and God was all-powerful. The demons could do only what God allowed them to do. He might allow them to taunt and terrorize His chosen, in order to test their resolve, but He would not allow harm to befall them, and indeed He had not, protecting Zachary who would otherwise have been crushed to a jelly.

Go back to where you started, a quiet interior voice told him. Go up the talus slope. You should look everywhere where the desert connects with the temple. Not just on the original ground level. Only then can you be sure there is no entrance.

Did the voice come from within him, he wondered, or from without? How could you tell? And in any case, what difference did it make, if God was everywhere? He ascended the slope. A little over half-way up, a small tree crouched, twisted, almost leafless, all but dead. Behind its maze of thorny branches he saw what was invisible from below: the wall had crumbled inwards, eaten away perhaps by the same rain-channel that had once allowed the tree to flourish briefly. There was a hole of irregular shape, several feet in diameter; inside it, sand had run down into the temple, forming another slope that descended into absolute blackness.

He paused on the brink of it. Within, all was silent. He could not see to the bottom of the slope. He needed light, a torch of some kind. He had learned painfully under Papnoute's tutelage how to make fire, but he no longer had Papnoute's tools. Now, he struck stone upon stone until blisters formed on his hands, but there was no spark. Either he had the wrong kind of stone or he wasn't doing it right.

He abandoned the task and climbed back to the gap in the wall. Dare he enter without a light? Would any purpose be served by so doing? He dismissed these questions as prompted by cowardice. Perhaps, once inside, his eyes would grow accustomed to the light. He could only try. Slowly, carefully, one step after another, he began to descend the interior slope.

It was true, after a while his eyes did grow more accustomed to the darkness. He was within a chamber of some kind, not the main vault of the temple. The chamber was immensely high (he could not make out its ceiling) but relatively narrow, so that the vague outline of its walls appeared on all four sides of him, dimly visible in the light that filtered through the opening. And the floor of the chamber too was visible—not the original floor, but the rubble that had spread out to cover it. And in one side of the chamber, buried almost to a man's height by the slide, was the upper portion of a doorway. He hesitated, looking back and upward. The opening seemed very small, and perhaps—or was it his imagination?—less bright than before. The greater part of the day must have already passed. If he wasn't careful, he would be trapped in here by the falling of darkness. He felt a shudder of apprehension. He would have to work fast. With his naked hands he scrabbled at the sand and stones that choked the doorway. Gradually he increased the size of the aperture. Soon it was large enough to admit a man. Taking a deep breath, imaging wordlessly a swift prayer, he ducked under the lintel and passed through it.

Immediately, he was in total darkness. He spun round, and it was only with the greatest difficulty that he could make out the doorway through which he had just entered. As for the rest of his surroundings, he could see nothing. He reached out a hand, and touched a clammy stone surface, slick, as if it had been painted over. In the other direction, a similar surface. He was in a passage of some kind. If he kept a hand on one wall, the right-hand wall, the one containing the door, he should be able to make a little progress; he was hoping he might come to some central hallway which, like that of the Serapeum, would be lit from above. But after a few yards, the wall ceased. He groped with his fingers but found nothing. It was impossible to tell whether the space represented merely another doorway, or a corridor joining this one at right angles, or some vast hall in which, if he entered it, he could become hopelessly lost.

All this time, ever since entering the hole by the ruined tree, he had held himself tense, rigid, every sense at full stretch, awaiting the assault of the demons that he felt must inevitably fall on him as he penetrated their sanctuary. But the demons that now assaulted him came from within.

Standing there, with one hand clutching the security of the wall and the other groping in blackest space, he remembered his dream, the dream in which he had run interminably through the bowels of some immense edifice, through halls, down corridors, pursued by some nameless horror perpetually on the brink of revealing itself—*THIS WAS HIS DREAM!* The dream had been prophetic! It was this very temple he had dreamed of, only now when the horror came he would find no escape in waking, it would come, it would reveal itself, rending his body apart, tearing out his soul, dragging that soul down to the fire that burned forever...

In his blind panic he almost let go of the wall. Almost, not quite. Crouching, sobbing, trembling in animal terror, he managed still to keep contact with his fingertips as he stumbled back and saw at last, to his inexpressible relief, the faint lessening of darkness that marked the half-buried door. He squeezed through it, tearing the skin from his back as he did so, and then slipping, kicking, sliding in his blind haste, at last falling on all fours and clambering upwards like an animal, he finally burst into the bright but fading afternoon and did not stop running until he had regained the safety of his cave. There he hurled himself full length on the ground and lay panting, soaked in a sweat that the cooling air turned clammy on his skin.

Gradually the peace of the scene, the soft rays of the declining sun soothed his mind. From the opening of his cave he could look down over the whole valley, the palms, the fruit -trees, to where the stream wound out into the desert and vanished, and beyond, to the endless hills and dunes that receded westwards, an infinite landscape where the only moving object was a single small cloud of dust—one of the duststorms, he told himself, that the wind periodically picked up and quickly dropped again. He was hungry and thirsty—when he had recovered a little more he would go down into the valley, gather fruits for his evening meal, drink from the spring, fill a gourd with water and carry it back to his cave.

And as for the temple...He shuddered even to think of it. What exactly had happened down there? His memories were confused, he could half-believe that demons had really attacked him, although a quieter, saner voice told him he had fled only from the creatures of his own imagination. Not that there were no demons there. They just hadn't confronted him. They hadn't needed to. That was the awkward truth about himself that he had somehow to come to terms with. They didn't think him worth wasting their time on.

But in that case, why had they tried to kill him by throwing down the cornice on him?

He could make no sense of it, and his mind, lulled by the elegiac light, moved into a mindless daze, while his eyes automatically followed the progress of the dust-storm across the landscape. But the cloud wasn't moving the way it should. Indeed, it seemed to have stopped. Stopped moving, that is, across his field of vision. But something else was happening to it, at first gradually, then quite quickly. It was getting bigger. It was headed directly for the valley.

A dust-storm might do that. It wasn't impossible. But a prescient dread overcame him. He could think of only one other cause that produced clouds of dust like that.

Horsemen.

He sprang up, ready to run down into the valley. He had to have food, water, he had to get them before the riders arrived. Of course they might be soldiers: soldiers patrolled the desert to discourage bandits and rebellious tribesmen, or to catch lions for the blood-games in the circus at Rome. If the riders were soldiers, he faced nothing worse than a little coarse mockery (he remembered with shame his cringing before the crude badinage of the Prefect's guards). But they certainly wouldn't be traders—traders didn't move at that speed. And they were unlikely to be bandits, for bandits seldom had horses.

That left just one thing they could be. He started to run down the slope, stopped, turned to gaze at the rapidly approaching cloud. No! There was no time! He would be caught out in the open if he went down. He began to scramble back up the slope. But no! He would be trapped, for how long no one could tell, he must have water. He cursed himself for not building a store of filled gourds in the cave in case of just such an emergency—for yielding to his dream of an inviolate garden, a bogus paradise indeed! He started down again, hesitated, started back, hesitated again, and all of a sudden it was too late, they were there.

They rode small, wild-looking horses, hardly larger than ponies. They wore loose white robes to reflect the sun's heat, and jeweled swords and daggers hung around their waists.

Approaching the point where the stream vanished in the desert, they reined in their horses and proceeded at a walking pace, silently, looking carefully to right and to left, left hands holding the reins loosely and right hands on the hilts of their weapons. They were small, swarthy, wiry men, with expressionless eyes and sharp, cruel features.

Inch by inch, on his belly like a snake, Zachary wormed his way backwards into his cave. Part of him wanted to monitor their progress, part of him felt almost a sense of relief at seeing, for the first time in weeks, other human faces, even ones so unprepossessing as these. But most of him simply felt fear. They were Mazices, savages speaking a tongue no one could understand: men who would torture you for an hour's casual amusement, kill you with less emotion than they would crush a louse. His only hope was that they would water their horses and pass on without suspecting his presence.

They were so close now that in the eternal stillness of the valley he could hear the hooves of the horses passing below him, and human voices exchanging laconic, indecipherable words. Soon the hooves stopped but the words went on. Then there was a period of almost complete silence, during which Zachary tried to tell himself that they had already left. But he knew this was impossible. The valley was a dead end. They would have to pass below him again to leave. They were still there somewhere, and as long as they were there, he could not move.

Then he heard new sounds approaching: a rattle of equipment, the tread of animals heavier than horses, and a cacophony of voices, some male, mostly female. A child cried; he heard a camel's belching cough. Unable to contain his curiosity, he raised his head high enough to peer out from the cave, relying on the dense shadow in back of him to conceal him even from their keen eyes.

The whole clan had arrived: camels laden with gear, more horsemen, women and children who dismounted from the camels and, while others led these to water, began lighting fires and setting up tents of hide. There must have been at least fifty of them, but they were moving about so much that it was impossible to be certain. They were obviously going to camp there for the night—perhaps for several nights. And, a more immediate danger, he saw two men on foot scaling the slope opposite him. Of course—they would be climbing to the rim of the plateau from which he himself had descended, to make sure that there was no one encamped on the heights overlooking the valley.

He withdrew again into the furthest part of the cave. Only then did it occur to him to ask himself, is this what a hermit ought to do? Would Macarius, or Anthony, or any of the hermits of old, have skulked in their caves, terrified of what the barbarians might do to them? It was unthinkable. Surely they would have gone serenely about their business, with an absolute faith that God would protect them? Surely they would have faced down the savagery of the barbarians, perhaps performed a miracle or two—even converted them to the true faith? He had half-risen to his knees, preparatory to standing and revealing himself, when a burst of ferocious laughter from below chilled his blood. It was all very well for the Anthonys of this world—seasoned veterans of the eremitic way, confident in their righteousness, with an absolute faith in God and a perfect willingness to abide by his will, even if that meant the sacrifice of their lives. It was all very well for them, secure in the knowledge that, if martyred, they would soar directly to seats by the Heavenly Throne.

But him, Zachary? With less than a year of striving for perfection, and after that, falling more deeply into sin than he ever did before it? With a faith not strong enough to survive the least reverse, a soul besmirched with unexpiated lust, guaranteeing him an eternity of hellfire if he did not survive long enough to properly repent and do penance for it? No, that was a very different story. How could he trust in God? Why would God want to save him? If he were God, would he consider Zachary worth saving?

No, he would be mad to show himself to them. He had to survive, to survive until by prayer and mortification he had purged his soul. He fell prostrate on the floor of the cave, and poured out from his heart the bitterness of his grief for the loss of his purity, his shame for the cowardice his sins had imposed on him, his longing to become whole and pure again. Outside, the sky slowly turned dark, but he was unaware of this, totally absorbed in his own wretchedness.

Some time later, how long he could not tell, he became aware of a great deal of noise going on below him. He had the feeling that it had been going on for a long time without his really noticing it, but as the fervor of his prayers decreased, the noise gradually took possession of his consciousness. He distinguished voices, singing rhythmically in chorus, while a single voice, high and wild, responded to them. He heard the notes of uncouth musical instruments, drums, some kind of jangling bells, a pipe of sorts, and the rhythmic thumping of feet. Once that noise had filled his consciousness, he could neither pray nor sleep. He crept to the mouth of the cave and peered out.

The whole tribe was dancing. He could see them quite clearly in the light of the immense fire they had built, for which they must have stripped the entire valley of its dead wood. They leaped and bobbed, in lines, the men on one side, the women on the other. They sang as they danced, a wild monotonous dirge, the same phrases repeated over and over, as their feet executed the same monotonous stamps and rushes. Even the musicians hopped and stamped in time with their own music, Only the single voice, wailing and plunging in impossible registers, brought some variety to the dirge. In the flickering firelight, their swarthy, knife-sharp faces appeared, vanished, reappeared. To Zachary's gaze, they seemed like so many evil spirits, rejoicing over the fall of a pure soul.

He could not bear to watch them, but they went on, hour after hour. He did not know when their dance ended. It had blended indistinguishably into his dreams, so that when he woke, and it was still dark, he was surprised by the silence. When he looked out again, the fire had sunk to a huge glowing mound of ashes, and there was no living creature in sight but a few horses and camels, hobbled, sleeping by the stream. A faint greyness to the east indicated that dawn was not far away. The Macizes slept in their tents.

Zachary began to be tormented by thirst. It was not so much the length of time he had gone without water as the knowledge that he could not renew his supply when he wanted to. And for all he knew they might camp there for days on end. But right now, after their night of demonic prancing, they would surely be sleeping deeply and never notice a solitary figure who descended to the stream, filled his gourd and returned before morning had invaded the sky.

He was afraid, but not more than he could handle. After a hasty prayer, for he had not a moment to waste, he picked up an empty gourd and began to descend, slowly and cautiously, fearful not so much of falling as of dislodging a stone that would roll down with a mighty clatter and wake those in the nearest tents, only a few yards beyond the creek. But no stone was dislodged, no one stirred. Step by step, glancing around him carefully after each move, Zachary approached the stream. It was only as he stooped to fill his gourd that he realized he would leave footprints in the sand of the streambed. Too late though to do anything about that now. Perhaps as he retreated he could smooth out the sand behind him so that—

He never saw the watcher who approached him. As he bent over the stream, filling his gourd, all he was aware of was a hand grasping his hair, pulling back his head, and a razor-sharp knifeblade pressed against his throat.

Chapter Five

Zachary's hands were tied tightly behind his back with a rawhide thong. The tip of his captor's knife rested against his neck, just below his right ear; a sluggish worm of blood oozed down from the point where, when he stumbled, the knifeblade had pierced the skin of his throat. In this fashion, he was driven to the center of the barbarian encampment.

Yet the wound, he felt sure, had not been intentional. His captor had not apologized for it, but neither had he abused him, even when Zachary had stumbled and almost fallen. Indeed, neither one of them had uttered a sound throughout the incident. But now his captor, jerking on the rope of a tent, called out in a low voice in their unintelligible language. After only a moment, two men, already robed and armed, scrambled out from under the flap of the tent. In the pre-dawn chill, under a gradually lightening sky, the three stood staring at Zachary as if he were a piece of meat, jabbering at one another. After a while one of them thrust his face up into Zachary's—they were all three shorter than he—and barked out something that Zachary failed to recognize.

He shook his head dumbly to show lack of understanding. The man frowned, slapped Zachary's face and repeated what he had said, more loudly but also more slowly. Zachary suddenly recognized the words as a wretched attempt at Coptic. 'Holy man,' he was trying to say. 'Holy man.'

Zachary's first impulse was to deny the label. But his mouth had scarcely opened when he saw the folly of denial. Sinful he might be, and leagues away from deserving the title, but he had heard that the Macizes held hermits in some kind of superstitious awe, and their belief in his surpassing virtue, or more likely in the supernatural powers thought to go with it, might be all that stood between him and summary execution.

'Holy man,' he repeated, nodding. 'Yes, me holy man!' The man who had been holding the knife at his throat took it away. The one who had not spoken, who looked from the richness of his dress and the elaborately ornamented dagger at his waist to be of higher rank than the others, poured out at him a rapid stream of speech. Zachary shook his head in bewilderment. 'No understand,' he said in baby Coptic. 'Me holy man. No understand.'

His interrogator looked annoyed, as though he thought holy men should at least come equipped with the power of tongues, but instead of hitting Zachary he jabbed him hard in the chest with his index finger, then tilted his head to one side and folded his hands under it, like a pillow, Quickly he repeated these gestures, with a questioning expression, and Zachary understood that he was asking, 'Where do you sleep, where do you live?' Despite his homemade reed garment and his protestations, they were not taking him on trust. The true sign of a hermit was how he lived.

Zachary gestured in the direction of his cave. His interrogator made a circular motion with his hand, embracing the four of them, then gestured at Zachary, then towards the cave. 'Take us there.' Zachary smiled, nodded, and set off. Although they no longer menaced him, they had not cut the thong tying his hands, and they kept close to him, one on either side, the leader directly behind him.

Above, at the cave-mouth, Zachary stood back, motioning with his hand for them to enter. Two did so; his original captor remained on watch. He heard their exclamations of surprise as they looked around it. Indeed, it could leave little doubt in their minds about Zachary's status: it contained nothing but the dried palm-leaves he used as a bed, a second gourd for carrying water, and a few withered dates. The two men came out still making noises of surprise and admiration—even their nomadic life was luxurious, compared to this. The one who seemed the leader drew his bejewelled dagger and gestured to Zachary to turn around. Zachary obeyed, still not entirely sure of the other's intentions, but all he did was cut the bonds tying Zachary's hands. Zachary smiled and thanked him, not that he would understand, but the fragile fellowship that had sprung up between them had to be nurtured in every possible way.

The leader gestured at Zachary to accompany them. Zachary had hoped that, satisfied with his credentials, they would simply leave him there, but he had no choice other than to obey, and together they descended to the camp, under a cloudy sky beginning already to be illumined by the still-hidden sun. Here and there, Mazices were already stirring. Women were lighting fires, fetching water, a baby was crying somewhere, camels coughed and grunted as they roused themselves from sleep. The men exchanged words, and one of them ran off, vanishing among the tents. The leader and the other just stood there, in a kind of clearing in the center of the encampment. They were waiting for something, but what? The supreme leader of the tribe? An interpreter? Zachary thought that if they had been going to kill him, they would have done so by now, but he still felt, not fear exactly, rather a deep unease.

Then he saw approaching them a strange group: an old crone and two younger women, scuffling like agitated hens around a girl of about sixteen, a girl who might have been beautiful but for the raw, weeping rash that disfigured her face. They plucked at her dress, twisted her this way and that; it took a moment for Zachary to realize why. They were maneuvering her through the maze of tent-pegs and guy-ropes that separated them from the open space. And through it all the girl remained completely passive, staring directly ahead, and without any expression at all on her ravaged features.

For one horrifying moment it occurred to Zachary that they were going to offer her to him as a bride. What would he do? What could he do? He had a vision of himself, at spearpoint, being forced to consummate the marriage before a large and appreciative audience, and he almost vomited. Death might be preferable. He had heard dark rumors, from the days of the persecutions, that some sadistic magistrates had tried to force Christians to perform sexual acts upon one another on pain of death. Of course they had refused, or so those stories claimed, and either the magistrates had repented their sin or the victims had gone straight to the Heavenly Throne, depending on whose version you heard. No, he would refuse. That way, undeserving as he was, he would earn a martyr's crown and consequent salvation. Probably the only way, for someone like him.

But the leader was plucking at his arm and gesturing at him; putting a hand over his own eyes, moving his head this way and that, then removing his hand and pointing at the girl, then at Zachary. While Zachary was still wondering what he meant, a dark, thin, sly-looking youth sidled up to him on his left side and spoke to him in what, after a moment, he realized was exceedingly bad Greek. 'Blind,' the youth was saying in a wheedling, insinuating voice, 'She blind woman.'

And Zachary realized that he was right. You could not see anything wrong with the girl's eyes themselves, which would have been large, round and fine had they not been gummed around the edges with mucus. It was their gaze that looked wrong, a fixed, unblinking stare that she directed, not at the person in front of her, but at some point beyond that person's shoulder. The sly youth bobbed up in front of her—his motions seemed more those of a cat or a spider than a human being—and waved his hand rapidly in front of her eyes, which neither blinked nor changed the direction of their gaze. 'I see,' Zachary said. 'She's blind. So?'

The youth looked to the leader, who made some guttural grunts. The youth turned to Zachary.

'He say...You make better.'

Zachary was stunned. He should have foreseen this, though it was with the greatest difficulty that he kept his surprise and shock from becoming visible in his face. But if he had foreseen it, what could he have done? Nothing. Holy men performed miracles; if he was a genuine holy man, he would now perform a genuine miracle. If he failed, he was a fake—a dozen dagger-points would pierce him, and an exsanguinated bag of skin and bone would be all that was left for the hyenas to lunch on, while his soul, not yet purged by repentance, flew to the eternal fires.

And he would fail. He had no doubts on that score. Miracles could only be worked by men who had undergone long years of ascetic discipline. Even then they required that the worker have absolute faith that the miracle could be accomplished. Even both these things together could achieve nothing unless God made available His unfathomable Grace. Three vital ingredients all of which were surely lacking on this occasion.

'Go on,' the sly one was urging, tugging at his arm. 'Make better. Put hands. Make better.'

Zachary gazed wildly around him. There was no hope of escape. A crowd was already assembling, its members chattering excitedly to one another. If he ran he would be cut down in seconds. The most he could do was buy a little time.

'Pray,' he said to the youth. 'First must pray.' The youth translated this. The leader made a magnanimous gesture. Sure, go ahead and pray, the gesture said. You know your own business best. Take your time, do it right.

Sweating with fear, Zachary fell to his knees and turned his eyes heavenwards. O God, he prayed, do something, anything, send a whirlwind, a lightning-stroke, an eclipse of the sun, but save me somehow, give me another chance, you know that weak and wicked as I am, divided as is my heart, I still hunger and thirst after righteousness, I long above everything for purity of soul, and if You let me live I swear that my feet shall never again stray from Your path. from now till the day of my death...

The clouds above parted. The first ray of sun fell, not on him, not on the girl, but on the scrawny living skeleton of a mongrel cur, snuffling around the camp, hoping to steal some scrap of food while everyone's attention was distracted. Zachary's heart sank. That sign could have only one meaning: the dog, beating the hyenas, would get first shot at his bones.
A restlessness began to manifest itself among the spectators: a shuffling of feet, a querulous, questioning tone in their voices. Zachary could postpone the inevitable no longer. Sick at heart, he felt a warm trickle between his thighs. Thanks to his long thirst there was very little of it, but he desperately rubbed his legs together, knowing the least sign of fear might trigger an assault. Holding himself rigid against the tremor in his limbs, he rose slowly to his feet, thrust out his hands before him, laid them, stifling his revulsion, over the girl's eyes and said, in as firm and confident a voice as he could muster:

'In the name of God the Father, Jesus Christ the Son, and the Holy Spirit, I command this sickness to depart from you, and your sight to be restored to you, Amen.'

For the space of three heartbeats an absolute silence held. Then the girl rolled up her eyes and crashed to the ground in a dead faint.

As startled as if struck by the lightning-bolt he had prayed for, Zachary sprang back. What had happened? Had he killed her? How? But no one looked either vengeful or surprised. It was as if they had expected this. The three women who had brought the girl to him crowded round her, fanning her, screaming at her, stroking her, trying to pick her up. At first she remained as rigid as a tree-trunk in their hands, a tree-trunk of unexpected weight, for she seemed somehow to resist their efforts to lift her. Suddenly her body relaxed, she raised her head and stared about her. She cried out something in a loud voice. Answering shouts came from the crowd. Zachary felt himself picked off his feet, hurled forwards. The girl rose to greet him. Unguided, her hand went to his, raised it unerringly to her lips. The sly youth was capering up and down, screaming in his barbarous Greek,

'She see! She see!'

Zachary had performed a miracle.

His soul filled with terror and bewilderment. This could not possibly be God's work. His first time out, a healing like Christ's? Ridiculous! It could only be a trick of Satan, to delude these poor people, make them reverence a false saint. A demon must have entered him somehow; he must be possessed. Who here could exorcize him? No one. To the contrary, these benighted savages would add insult to the injury of his soul by worshiping him.

He had almost rather they had killed him.

Instead, he was dragged into the largest of the tents and forced to squat on the floor. A goatskin bag was thrust into his hands and he was made to drink some atrocious concoction, fermented camel's milk, who could tell what it was, but it went to his head far faster than any of the wine he and Benjamin had drunk in the stews of Alexandria. Dishes of strange meats appeared, swimming in grease. He tried to reject them, saw the expressions on his hosts' faces and desisted—he remembered that to refuse the hospitality of desert dwellers appeared to them, who lived always on the brink of famine, as the worst of insults. Reluctantly he tasted the meat. The peppery sauce that drenched it seemed designed only to hide less palatable flavors, of rot, perhaps. But at every hesitation they prodded him, urging him to eat.

The sly youth had stationed himself by Zachary's side, and, while he ate, poured into his ear a stream of barely intelligible words, uttered in the same whining, wheedling tone. 'You holy man. You make see. She see good now. She prettygirl, ah? You like? Like fucky-fucky?'

Indignantly Zachary denied this.

The youth giggled. 'Good! Cause no can, ah? Get boy already.'

Zachary expressed mild surprise at this.

'No, no! Before get sick. She big person. She...how you say, baby? She baby for that man,' and he pointed to the leader.

'Daughter?'

'Yah, 'a's right, daughter. He no like. Say boy no good. No marry, ah?'

Zachary's guts, shrunk already by long fasting, and unused anyway to this kind of food, felt as if they were going to explode. Sweat poured from his face as he obediently stuffed it. He could hardly focus on what the youth was saying.

'So she get sick. Get blind. First nobody believe. Think she fakey-fakey. Cut hot knife, stuff like that, still say no see. So e'rybody say marry boy. Is all right, now can marry, go.' He giggled. 'But now, boy no want. No like blind girl.' He giggled again. 'Maybe now marry, ah?'

Zachary felt the bile rising in his stomach. He made it to the door of the tent just in time. A torrent of foul-smelling liquid mixed with undigested scraps of food hurled itself from his throat with projectile force, splashing in the sand at his feet. Around him, men dug him in the ribs and roared with laughter.

It was a great joke—maybe even a tribute to his hosts. He was dragged back into the tent, made to take copious swigs at the goatskin which passed from hand to hand. More dishes were brought, piles of beans, fried flour, plucked but otherwise intact birds whose button eyes glared at him reproachfully, nauseously sugared sweetmeats.

After that, things got progressively more confused. He remembered a jangling instrument that a man with bloodshot eyes had played almost in his ear; women who danced before him, and one who made a suggestive gesture to him, only to be dragged away immediately and soundly slapped; a song, made up on the spot, that he believed to be about himself, though he could not understand a word of it; more food, more drink; and finally, seeing it all from a horizontal position, with the Mazices shouting, stamping and swaying all around him, until everything blurred and somehow faded away.

When he woke, it was almost dark. He was lying on a heap of mangy sheepskins. The tent above him had disappeared; the Mazices had disappeared too. The only trace of their presence was the pile of sheepskins, small mounds of horse and camel dung, and the still faintly smoking embers of the immense fire around which they had danced the previous night. Once again he was alone. And still alive.

But barely. His stomach felt as if it had been kicked by

every camel in the barbarians' herd. From the state of his reed garment, he had vomited on it in his sleep. He promptly vomited again, leaning over and retching from the bottom of his gut, although he had almost nothing left to bring up. A pounding, pulsing headache crushed his head in rhythmic spasms. He was running a fever—everything around him seemed weird, distorted.

The suffering of his body dulled his sense of the extraordinary event that had taken place earlier that day. Momentarily, in his delirious state, he could almost accept the miracle of healing as a personal validation. Perhaps after all he was holier than he had believed. Perhaps the miracle signaled his forgiveness, his acceptance into the charmed circle of the elect. His heart swelled with pride at the thought, but only briefly. Reason fought back as with a sickening fall of the heart he knew that he must have been imposed upon, used and abused by the demons who inhabited this place for their own nefarious purposes.

The demons who lurked in the temple.

The demons who he could not reach and defeat in open combat because he lacked...

Fire!

Sick as he was, he had to act now. Tomorrow would be too late. Dragging himself on hands and knees he made for the cooling embers of the great bonfire. The white ashes still felt hot to his hands. He sifted through them until he encountered a chunk of still-glowing charcoal. On this he blew until a fragile flame trembled upwards, died, rose again at his repeated breath. Groping among the embers he found other half-burned bits of wood, which he piled around the first one. By this time, the flame had gone out again. Again he blew, and this time the flame caught and within seconds a merry blaze was going. He cast further afield. There were logs half-burned through, and branches piled in heaps,. ready to burn, that had never been thrown on the fire at all. Enough to keep it burning the whole night, if he tended it carefully.

Although movement of any kind was almost intolerable to him, making his head swim and his bowels contract in fruitless spasms, he forced himself to collect all the burnable timber and stack it close to the fire, yet not so close that a chance spark would ignite it. Then he scraped himself a hollow in the warm mixture of ash and sand next to the fire, lay down in it, and slept fitfully, racked with spasms and fever, tormented by incoherent dreams that were indistinguishable from his waking fantasies, but waking always somehow in time to feed the dying flame—in time to resurrect it, to keep it constantly burning, as the constellations wheeled overhead and the world bore slowly, excruciatingly slowly, towards morning.

Chapter Six

Zachary spent two more days on the valley floor, keeping the Mazices' bonfire going, gathering his strength for the assault on the pagan temple.

Now that he had fire he could penetrate to its darkest corners. He was not afraid of any demon, as long as he could see it. He chose his torch carefully, testing branches to see how quickly or how reliably they would burn. When he had found one that burned slowly and steadily enough, he set out towards the head of the valley.

Even from some distance away he could see that his cross, despite all his efforts to secure it, had been overthrown yet again. Its fall caused him a momentary chill, but that soon passed. If the worst the demons could do to him was tear down his cross while his back was turned, he had little to fear from them. So this time he did not bother to replace the cross. It was only an outward symbol, after all. You kept the True Cross in your heart, if anywhere, where no demons could profane it. Unless, of course, you yourself allowed them in.

He ascended the slope.

The familiar landmarks reappeared—the weathered tree, the cleft in the masonry that the tree partially concealed. Just outside the cleft he paused to blow on the burning tip of his brand and make sure that it was well and truly alight. It flamed and gave off a good deal of tarry smoke; it was far from an ideal torch but it would have to do. It worried him that he had no way of relighting it if it went out. The realization struck him that if he broke a leg in there, he could not hope to escape while the flame lasted. Without light, he would probably never find the way out. He would die there. And his body would never be found—or if found, perhaps centuries hence (a withered mummy like the hermit he had discovered on that first day), no one would realize his motive for being there. He would be taken for some crazed worshiper of ancient gods, one who had died rather than abandon them.

He fought down these fears, they were simply the devil's sly way of deterring him from his purpose. Taking a firm grip on the burning brand, he ducked into the cleft.

There he stopped, amazed. On his previous visit, the light from the cleft had only dimly illuminated the outlines of the chamber within; its walls had appeared to him as grey featureless masses. Now, as he slowly raised the brand above his head, he saw that they were covered with murals—paintings vivid in color, arranged in a series of tiers around the chamber, and so cunningly drawn that, in the jumpy, flickering light of the torch, the people and creatures in them seemed to take on life, to be about to escape from the wall and move freely into the world of living things.

Fascinated, he turned slowly through a complete circle. There were scenes of hunting, of ducks rising from a marsh, of archers in shallow boats shooting arrows at them; there were scenes of feasting where figures in strange headdresses toasted one another from gilded goblets; there were women with elaborate hair and diaphanous gowns from whom he quickly withdrew his eyes; there were monsters, creatures part human and part animal, evil spirits or false gods; there were men and women, women and monsters, men and monsters engaged in acts from which he recoiled in horror, only to feel his eyes drawn back to them, again and again, by a kind of incredulous curiosity.

He forced himself to descend the slope. Again he found the sunken doorway that looked like the only way to reach the rest of the temple. He remembered the corridor beyond, and the fit of panic fear that had driven him to retrace his steps. But with the torch burning brightly in the dry, still air, the corridor no longer held any terrors for him. The point where he had stopped, the space where he had groped in vain for another wall, revealed itself as merely the mouth of another corridor leading off to his right. He ignored it and proceeded straight ahead. The pictures accompanied him on the smoothly plastered masonry, uncomfortably close now, their lifesize figures only inches from him but an illimitable distance away in time, in a world that had died centuries before his birth. The figures in them were human, yet so alien in mood that they might have been painted by another species.

He stopped to blow on his torch, which had begun to smolder smokily, and came face to face with a figure of his own age and sex, matching him exactly in height, who had just hurled his spear into a running boar and whose mouth had started to open in a cry of surprised triumph. So fresh and lifelike was that mouth, frozen for ever in an instant of spontaneity, that for a second Zachary almost expected words to come out of it. It must have been drawn from life, he thought, there must once have been someone who looked exactly like that, who hurled that spear on some sunlit morning in his youth, when death was invisible and his soul felt itself immortal, who cried out in delight at the strength of his arm and the surety of his aim. Someone oblivious to future or past, totally absorbed in the moment. And so he would remain forever now, long after the living body had rotted and crumbled to dust, long after Zachary himself had rotted and crumbled to dust.

He was a pagan, Zachary told himself. An unbeliever. No fault of his, Christ's message hadn't been delivered then. But he would continue to sleep in the earth while Zachary, assuming that all went well with his spiritual life, would be resurrected in the flesh to sing eternal hosannas in the heavenly kingdom. So he told himself. On the surface. Underneath it, he was unable to comprehend, let alone control, the emotions that this underground confrontation had released in him. He forced himself to move on.

At the end of the corridor, another doorway. He lowered his torch as he approached it. He had heard, from somewhere ahead of him, faint sounds, sounds that grew in intensity as he approached the doorway: hisses, whistles, grating creaks, clicks, whirrings...He was approaching it at last, the inner sanctum where the demons had their abode. Now, if ever, they would reveal themselves to him in all their hideous reality, scaly wings, claws, barbed tails. But he would overcome them, he would fight and conquer, immune, impregnable in the faith of the Lord—

He went through the doorway.

And cried out aloud.

It was an involuntary, uncontrollable reaction. The moment his torch cleared the doorway, the sounds quadrupled in intensity, and there swooped down on him a legion of hateful, screeching forms, winged, clawed, leathery, with eyes that flashed evil flame reflected from his torch, forms that flapped and whirred about his head and then rose, chirruping, to hang upside down from the ceiling far above him...

Bats.

It took him the best part of a minute to realize that these were not the demons of which he had many times been warned but simply bats: bats who had found in the abandoned temple a sanctuary where they could roost undisturbed. He felt a fool, and thanked God that there had been no one with him. His moment of cowardice would live on only in his own conscience.

The bats did not settle down completely. They continued to seethe in pullulating heaps on the vaulted ceiling and upper walls, trying to dig beneath one another, to put the bodies of others between themselves and the light. But they seemed gradually to be growing accustomed to that light, and they no longer swooped at Zachary's head as they had at the beginning. He was free to look around him, cautiously, still unsure that the bats were the only peril the temple contained.

He was in the largest space he had yet seen, a hall from the floor of which arose giant statues, several times the height of a man—human figures with inhuman heads, horned, snouted. He walked around them, still half-expecting some diabolic figure to emerge from among them. None did. By the walls, stone sarcophagi crouched, their lids cracked and flung open—tomb-robbers had found this place long before Zachary, and they had left nothing within the tombs, not even dust.

Zachary began to have a sense of the enormous antiquity of this place. Who could tell how long ago it had been built, how many times it had been covered by sand and then revealed and then covered again? And the people who built it believed that they understood the mysteries of life and death, that they could guarantee for themselves an eternity of happiness, in bodies like those they had inhabited on earth, like those they had depicted, as if imagining another life were sufficient to create it, upon these walls.

But there was nothing here. No demons, no mummified pagans, nothing. Only a hollow emptiness that boomed his voice back at him when, greatly daring, he first murmured a few syllables, then repeated them more loudly, then shouted them out at the top of his voice: 'Come on, Satan! Where are you? Are you afraid?'

'Afraid,' the walls echoed back to him. 'Afraid, frayed, raid, aid, ey, ey, eh...'

The torch sputtered. Either it burned more quickly than he had reckoned or the time spent in the temple had been much longer than he supposed. Demons or no demons, he realized he would not care to be caught in this place in darkness, surrounded by those shadowy two-dimensional figures that still somehow seemed to be hovering on the very brink of life. With a profound sense of anticlimax he made his way back through the great hall. The bats still seethed above him, but no other sound or movement disturbed the sepulchral silence and stillness of the place. The dust of millennia on the stone floor muffled the fall of his feet.

Why had no demons appeared to him? Everyone knew that pagan temples provided them with their favorite resting places. Countless were the stories of holy men who had spent the night in temples and been tormented by demonic apparitions, even beaten black, blue and senseless by them. If none had appeared to him here, that could only mean one of two things. Either the demons regarded him as so weak, trivial and inconsequential a person that they need not bother with him...

Or they possessed him and knew that he already belonged to them!

At that thought, a dizzy sickness came over him, so violent that he had to catch and steady himself against the wall, almost dropping his torch as he did so. Was he possessed by the Devil? Was it possible he could be possessed and not realize it? To whom could he turn, from whom could he learn the truth?

No one. He had come here alone, by his own free choice. Against all of the training he had received, he had put himself, pathetic novice that he was, beyond the reach of spiritual guidance. He could have returned to Scetis, could have confessed, could have done penance and eventually expiated his sin. They would not have judged him. Alone among men they had renounced judgment. But he in his rank pride and folly had refused to humble himself before men. No, for him that wasn't good enough, he could only humble himself before God. Alone in the desert, just he and God alone.

Only God wasn't with him. Why should God be with him? What had he done to deserve God's presence? Sinned, willfully and recklessly, then hurled himself into the desert in a suicidal challenge to God's grace and mercy. And God, patient as ever. had spared him, given him one more chance, let him reach the valley alive. How had he taken that chance? By mooning around, stuffing himself with dates, dreaming romantic dreams of one-on-one combat with the Calumniator himself, skulking from the Mazices and then posing as a holy man and joining with them in their swinish feasts, when he should have been purifying his heart with fasts and vigils! No wonder he had performed a 'miracle'! He knew that now for what it was—a subterfuge of the devil to flatter his conceit, to convince him he was ascending the one true path whereas in reality he was falling head over heels into damnation!

He could not escape from this place quickly enough. Panting, stumbling over his own feet, dropping the torch, then snatching it up before it could extinguish itself, he ran back down the corridor, past the shouting face that so strangely mirrored his own, past the tiers of murals on the outer chamber walls, up the slope, out through the rift in the wall, out into the light of day.

Of late afternoon.

He passed a hand over his brow and sat down abruptly. It had been morning when he entered the temple. It seemed to him that no more than an hour could have passed. What had happened to him there? Had he fallen under some enchantment? Had his body lain unconscious while his soul was carried off, who could tell where? No, surely not, for in that case his torch would have gone out.

Unless it had been kept alight by demonic powers!

He had thought to find relief on leaving the temple, but the whole valley seemed to crowd in on him, imprisoning him. You will never get out of here, the shapes of the encircling hills seemed to be saying. Your body will never get out of here alive. And your soul will never escape from here to paradise.

He had seen no demons. Small wonder. They were too smart to stand out in the open, flourishing tails and tridents, grimacing, snickering obscene laughter. Instead, with their unfathomable cunning, they had crept into his defenseless heart.

Chapter Seven

That night, he dreamed a strange and terrible dream.

It began with a deceptive innocence. He was a child again, or rather, though he did not feel like a child, he had again the nurse who looked after him when he was five or six years old. She was supposed to be a Christian but she could not have been a very good one, for she was always telling him tales of divination and sorcery, witches, ghosts and omens, horoscopes, predictions. Prediction fascinated her; to know the future, even though, for a fat middle-aged Egyptian widow from the poorest classes, the future could hardly have held anything very exciting. Once, he remembered, she had told him of an oracle at Oxyrhynchus where they speeded up the process by giving you a numbered list of all the questions you could ask: 79, Shall I receive the money? 82, Is my property to be confiscated? 90, Shall I be divorced from my wife? 91, Have I been poisoned? All you had to do was give the oracle the appropriate number:

84? Yes, you will pull off what you have in mind (whatever it was).

For some reason, all this had amused him enormously, and he had gone around shouting out numbers until his parents, cross-questioning him, uncovered the tale. The nurse, an employee not a slave, had promptly been fired as a bad influence, something she surely never predicted, and he had felt awful guilt over it for a long time afterwards. But now in his dream she hadn't been dismissed, she was still with them, and she was telling him how the night before she had gone to the temple of Helios the Sun-God to dream her own future.

Having abstained from wine for three days and fasted for twenty-four hours as instructed by the priests, she had lain down on the floor of the temple to sleep and sure enough the Sun-God had appeared to her, showering her with coins. And this, as his own dream transmuted, Zachary not merely heard about but saw: blobs of gold being showered down on a fat woman asleep among curtained statues by a figure of more than mortal height, blobs that even as he watched transformed themselves into a flight of arrows crossing a sky of deep, flawless blue.

The arrows, golden in the sunlight, soared and then fell towards a tract of brilliant green marshland, cut by deep channels that reflected the blue of the sky. A flight of waterbirds rose from the marshland and dispersed, screeching. A few, struck by arrows, fell, and following the descent of one of them, Zachary found himself suddenly chest-deep in the reeds. Never at any moment of his life had he felt as fully conscious of the physical world as he did at that moment. He could feel the squishy, spongy vegetation between his toes, the cool buffeting of a brisk breeze on his face. He could smell the rich rot of decomposing plants, touched with a whiff of salt, hinting that the sea could not be far. He could hear beneath the screaming of the birds the stiff rustle of each reed against its neighbor. He could see the maze of insects in the air, the bugs, the mosquitoes, the dragonflies with their jeweled wings, skimming the glittering chop of the breeze-blown water.

Then, without any warning, he found himself face-to-face with the young man whose picture had so disturbed him when he saw it on the wall of the temple corridor.

Just as in the picture, the man's mouth was half-open in the beginning of a shout, but the spear had not yet left his hand, and the face looked somehow different. With a shock of horror, Zachary recognized it as his own, and knew instantly that his soul had passed from him and entered the body of the other, while the other's soul had entered his body. 'Don't! Don't kill me!' Zachary's soul cried out through its alien mouth, but the creature in Zachary's body, baring its teeth—his teeth!—raised the spear and struck, and Zachary felt a searing pain in the side of the body he now inhabited, a pain that blinded him, obliterating the world in a white sea of blazing fire.

When it cleared, he stood alone in the valley before the temple. But slowly, between him and the temple, there coalesced out of the air a figure double the height of a man—human yet more than human, the figure of a man in the prime of life, yet radiating such a brilliance of light that Zachary could not look at it directly. Zachary, listen, the figure seemed to be saying, yet not in any mortal voice, rather the words somehow formed themselves in Zachary's mind. Zachary, listen to me. I am all there is. I am Life. Enjoy life, for beyond me there is nothing. No god, no devil. No heaven, no hell. Nothing. Only life, with no beginning. And no end. And no meaning.

And the figure—Zachary had to shade his eyes with his hands to see it—smiled at him. Smiled calmly, indulgently, a little mockingly, perhaps. And Zachary saw that it was naked, with an enormous penis, fully erect, sprouting from its loins. As Zachary watched, paralyzed, unable to tear his eyes from the obscene spectacle, the figure took that penis in its right hand and, still smiling the same mocking smile, gave it a couple of leisurely strokes. Immediately, an enormous jet of liquid spouted from it, spurting upwards like a fountain, pulsing across the sky and falling on Zachary's own naked flesh, falling in drops that burned as they landed upon him. And as each drop landed, it spread. In incredulous horror, unable to move or cry out, he watched the drops falling and spreading, watched his flesh and the bone beneath it dissolving, dripping to the ground like wax from a burning candle.

He awoke, trembling like a dog, gibbering with fear. He could not believe that he was awake. He could not believe that what had happened to him in the dream had not happened, was not still happening. In the grey light of dawn that was already seeping into the cave where he lay, he gazed at his own flesh, pinched and pulled at it, unable to believe that his body remained intact, that it could in any way have survived that shower of flesh-devouring semen. Not that its survival made much difference. He felt unclean to the very depths of his soul, with an uncleanness that nothing could ever purify. For he knew now the meaning of the dream. He knew that he was damned.

He should have realized it when he decided not to replace his cross. Justifying his decision with some fancy nonsense about the True Cross living on in his heart! In what kind of heart, for God's sake? No, he had surrendered then to the demons, if he'd only realized. Allowed them to destroy his cross, acquiesced in their victory. And then gone on, unclean in spirit, to enter the temple, under the pretext of challenging evil, but really out of a mixture of vainglory and idle curiosity. Well, his curiosity had been satisfied with a vengeance! Through those devilish pictures, those idols, the demons had entered his soul and taken possession of it.

But a small core within him had not yet yielded. He could strike back. He would strike back. He would never admit defeat. And suddenly, miraculously the way was made plain to him. They had attacked him first through his cross. Well, there was an answer to that. He would give them something that they could not throw down. He would become his own True Cross.

He took with him neither water nor food. He walked down the slope to the stream, along it until he reached the point where the cross had stood, and faced the temple. Standing erect, his feet together, his arms stretched out horizontally from his shoulders, he looked north-eastwards, towards the Holy Land, towards the place where Christ Himself had been crucified. Motionless he stood there, as the sun hauled itself wearily, red-eyed, over the bluff at the head of the valley, Motionless he continued to stand as it rose slowly into the sky on his right hand.

Spring was coming. A hot wind from the south had started to blow. Before the third hour had passed, sweat was pouring from his forehead. He did not move. Passages from the Scriptures repeated themselves constantly in his mind. By the sixth hour, they had become confused, a passage from Galatians slipping into the Gospel of Matthew, lines from the Gospel cropping up amidst the Psalms. Blinking the sweat from his eyes, for he would not withdraw his hand from its set posture to wipe his brow, he saw two suns dancing around one another in the whitish sky. His arms trembled with weariness. He longed to relax them, if only for a moment, reach and stretch and bend them before reassuming his pose, but he would not. While the sun crossed the sky, until it had fallen below the further horizon, he would not move.

What a trivial sacrifice it was, after all! He was standing on solid ground, Our Savior was propped on a nail driven through his ankles. His hands were intact; Our Savior's hands, nailed to the transverse bar, took all the weight of his sagging torso. His side was unpierced, save by the spear of the other Zachary in his dream; Our Savior's side dripped blood and lymph from the callous spear-thrust of the Roman guard. He had come to his ordeal fresh from slumber, terrible though that slumber had been; Our Savior had spent his last night being arrested, tried, scourged, abused, had had the last remnants of His strength exhausted by the weight of the cross He had been forced to carry. Zachary's sufferings were nothing, nothing compared to these, and Zachary himself a mere sinful mortal, while He who had suffered far worse was the Son of God! He, Zachary, deserved to suffer twice as much, ten times as much!

The sun burned his flesh through gaps and rents in the reed garment he had woven for himself. It dried the liquids from his body, parching his throat; the murmur of the spring flowing quietly and sweetly only a few paces to his right was a constant torment to him. How he longed to break away, to plunge his head and shoulders in those cooling waters, if only for a moment! But Christ had said to take up your cross and follow Him, and Zachary was his own cross and could not let it go.

By the ninth hour his arms and shoulders ached so from the strain of holding them up that only by a constant effort of will could he maintain his posture. His head throbbed, his whole body flamed with fire, but his will remained unbroken, He no longer recited scriptures in his mind. His mind had shrunk to a small kernel of determination, a passionate, wholly unreflective desire to keep on, to endure to the end. And as the sun sank towards the horizon, a small breeze sprang up, as if sent by God as a sign. He felt it stir his hair, felt the coolness of it, saw the shadows cast by the sides of the valleys acquire a purplish tinge, saw them spread and soften, saw the sky gradually lose its white cast and take on the blue of evening. He had survived! He had triumphed!

But only for a day. That was only the beginning. The next day he would return, and the next, and the next after that. Continually, until he received a sign, an unmistakable sign of God's forgiveness. Not a mere breeze sent to alleviate his penance, but a sign in the sky, a dove bearing bread, an angelic vision, something that would unambiguously inform him that he was pardoned, that he might dare to hope once more for the salvation of his soul. Until then, he must continue to endure.

Once the sun was down, he drank sparingly from the spring. He had resolved to eat only every second day. If his strength permitted, only every third day. And he would do something about his sleep, the profound hoggish slumber into which he had allowed himself to fall, or into which he had been lulled by the demonic influence of the place, so many times since he arrived there. He would keep awake for as long as he could, but even when he could no longer do so he would refrain from lying down on his reed mat. Instead, he would prop himself up in a sitting position, so as to doze only fitfully, for an hour or two at most. Then he would wake again and watch and pray till the morning.

So, at any rate, he planned. But when he woke, after a night of terrifying dreams—none of which, God be thanked, he could remember with any clarity—he knew that something was seriously amiss. His head shook with a pounding headache, all his limbs ached, the slightest movement seemed to require an enormous effort. His skin was red raw wherever the sun had touched it. Somehow he dragged himself to the slope beside the spring before the sun rose. He would have preferred to face his ordeal without drinking but knew he could never last through the day, so he crouched at the spring, cupping his hands, drank long and deeply, and splashed water over his burning flesh—not that that really did anything for his pain.

Suddenly his guts contracted in a spasm of nausea, and he vomited, spraying out a mix of water and foul-tasting bile. He had nothing in his belly to throw up, but the fit of vomiting racked him for several minutes. When it finally passed, he lay helplessly by the spring. Already the mouth of the valley was filled with light; within minutes, the sun would appear over the eastern bluff. Somehow he dragged himself to his place and extended his arras as before. He knew in his heart that he was very sick, but his mind refused to admit this. He insisted to himself that it was nothing, it would pass, and that once it had passed the second day would go more easily than the first. See, he told himself as the first rays of the sun touched him, see, it doesn't hurt, it's not really hot at all.

He tried to recite scripture, but his mind hopped feverishly about, he could not concentrate, he repeated phrases he thought he had not said and mixed up or omitted others. Spells of dizziness surged over him as irresistibly as waves of the sea. The reddened welts on his skin had begun to swell and blister. His head felt as if it were being crushed, as if some torturer had wrapped a ring of molten metal around his temples and was now slowly but inexorably tightening the ring.

About the fourth or fifth hour he fainted. When he regained consciousness he found himself sprawled on the ground, with a new ache on the back of his head where he must have hit it in falling. He had no idea how much time had passed, but it was still broad day. He tried to rise, and could not. Resting for a few moments he tried again, tried repeatedly until somehow, staggering, he managed to balance himself.

He did not remember the second fall, nor how long had elapsed before it took place, since his mind had become a feverish blur that recorded nothing. He only knew that when he came round a second time, the sun had set and it was almost completely dark.

His shame that he had not achieved his promised goal gave way almost immediately to a more violent emotion: fear. From the first day he had known that hyenas frequented the valley by night. He had seen their footprints by the stream, heard their howls during the hours of darkness. But they had remained on the valley floor, they had never attempted to scale the slope that led to his cave. Now he was at their mercy, unless he could return to the cave in time.

On that nightmare journey he could not distinguish reality from dream. Did their hateful blotched muzzles really loom over him, as he lay helpless between spells of staggering, drunken walking, or were they specters of his imagination, fever-fueled? Had he seen the light of a moon bright enough to read by reflected from their encircling eyes? Had there been a moon at all that night? He would never know. He must somehow have regained the cave, for he found himself there when the fever finally left him. He did not know how many hours or days had passed, although some covert sense told him several days: an eternity of torment while he endured it, a timeless nothingness once it had passed. He felt weak, weak to the verge of death, but there was a lightness and clarity in his head that had not been there since the first day of his self-imposed crucifixion.

He examined his body. It had shrunk to no more than a skeleton with a little flesh and skin stretched tightly over it. He realized that he must have come very close to death. Indeed, if he were still alive, it could only be because God in His unsearchable wisdom had determined that it was not time for him to die. There had to be some purpose for which he was being preserved.

He felt a profound sense of relief. He could not be irretrievably damned, as he had feared. Had he been damned, God would surely not have spared him—would have flung him, body and soul, into the fires of hell. But by preserving him, God had given him a sign, not that his penance was enough, but that he should continue it and could still, if only he persevered, hope to continue the struggle for perfection.

He saw his body differently now. Not as a gambler's last coin, to be flung down recklessly on the table in a last desperate attempt to recoup the losses his sins had brought him. No, if God valued it enough to have preserved it, it was worth more than that, it should be nourished, cared for, protected. Not as if his body had any value in itself, something to be pampered or indulged for its own sake. Just a means to an end, but an indispensable means, at that. He would treat it as such, humoring it when he had to, disciplining it as much as it would accept before rebelling.

He had no water in the cave. But despite his thirst he let the afternoon pass into early evening before he trusted himself again in the sun. He walked like an old man, painfully slowly, with shuffling steps, pausing often. When he arrived at the stream he drank, but only a little, then went in search of dates. He ate only a small handful, knowing that to burden his stomach would only bring on more vomiting. and they stayed down. Having picked another handful and filled a hollow gourd with water, he made for the cave immediately, since the uphill journey took so long that dark had fallen before he reached it. Once there he stretched himself out full length—no nonsense about sleeping upright this time! Despite his weakness, he felt curiously light, purified and refreshed. He floated quietly into a tranquil sleep.

The next day, he worked out a discipline. He would stand by the spring again, if only for a few minutes the first time, making his cross. The moment he felt tired or dizzy, he would stop. But each day he would stand there a little longer. In time he would achieve his goal of enduring from sunrise to sunset, not just for one day, but for however many days it took to obtain a token of forgiveness.

When was Easter this year? It could not be far away. He might be facing Jerusalem, in the posture of Our Crucified Lord, on the very day, the three hundred and something anniversary, of the Savior's Passion. Perhaps, on that day, a sign would be given him. Perhaps a whole year would pass before that sign came. What matter? It all lay in God's hands. There was, after all, nothing more important he could be doing with his life. He had all the time God chose to give him.

The days passed. After a week or two he achieved his target. Now he could stand from dawn to dusk, a human cross, without stirring or flinching.

The days lengthened. No matter. The extra minutes were no burden to him. His darkened skin resisted the sun. His desiccated body held thirst at bay. He stood as if hammered out of stone. Seen by no one.

For no one came to disturb him. The Mazices did not come back, and if any Libyan caravan paused to refresh itself, it did so in the pools at the mouth of the valley, and had passed on before he returned to his cave in the late evening.

The monotony of his days was only twice interrupted. Twice, as he stood facing the temple, fragments of its wall detached themselves and fell to the ground beneath. He was not sure how to interpret this. Had the force of his prayer, his endurance, somehow served to undermine those unholy walls? Was he gradually destroying the temple through his increasing virtuousness? He hesitated to think such thoughts, which smacked of vainglory. Somehow he knew this was not quite the sign he was seeking.

Once or twice, usually on the edge of falling asleep or waking, memories of his dream returned to him. He pushed them quickly out of his conscious thoughts. But somewhere, far below the surface, beyond the deepest level even of subliminal awareness, somewhere there continued to reverberate those words of ultimate horror: No god, no devil. No heaven, no hell. No beginning. And no end. And no meaning.

Chapter Eight

The sky darkened. A wind began to blow, gustily, fitfully. The temperature rose, despite the absence of the sun. A sense of brooding oppression lay heavily over barren desert and fertile riverbank alike. In Scetis and Nitria, those hermits who grew herbs and vegetables hurried to cover them with straw mats, then retired to their cells, closed the shutters and stuffed the gaps with reeds. They knew what was coming. On the river, boat-captains sought for secure moorings, moored with unusual care, battened down the hatches. In the fields, peasants gathered their tools and headed for shelter. Far out in the desert, the Mazices, more sensitive than others to the vagaries of desert weather, had long since moved into a narrow draw, riddled with caves, where they tethered their beasts rump first to the approaching storm and then hunkered down to wait it out.

Only a small army patrol, a half-dozen cavalrymen and a couple of dozen disgruntled infantry, kept on going. They had been sent out to hunt lions for the Roman arena. The leather-faced centurion who was in charge of the infantry approached the mounted officer, saluted just on the right side of sloppiness and said, 'Sir! begging your pardon sir, you don't think we ought to be looking for cover?'

'Cover?' The officer was fair-skinned, well-born, younger son of a family of senatorial rank, the kind who were letting the Empire fall to bits in their hands, the centurion thought bitterly.

'Cover, sir.' The centurion was not in a mood to be any more helpful than he had to be.

Nor was the officer, Decius Capillus. He had just lost two lions, through his own total stupidity, although he would never admit that. They had caught them the previous evening, and the infantrymen had been taking turns carrying them, slung upside-down from long poles with their feet securely tied, a process that had not improved the tempers either of the lions or the soldiers. Heading back across the desert towards the Nile, they had stumbled into a gang of bandits fleeing a successful robbery on the fringe of the settled lands – or at least, so one of the bandits informed them, just before he was executed. When the bandits ran, Decius should by rights have ordered the cavalry to pursue them and catch them in the strong nets they used to catch lions with. The bandits were on foot. There was no way they could have escaped. Even if they had resisted, they would quickly have been disarmed. No one would have been hurt.

What Decius actually did was let loose the lions on them. It seemed like fun when he first thought of it. He was bored to tears after months of duty on the backside of nowhere, far from the hippodromes and arenas, the taverns and brothels of the great cities. It did not occur to him until too late that he would be putting his own men at risk, for a hungry and irritable lion could hardly distinguish soldiers from civilians.

As things turned out, his troops were skillful enough with their shields and the flats of their broadswords to turn the lions in the right direction at no cost beyond a few scratches. But from then on, things went downhill fast. The lions succeeded in cornering four bandits, but another couple took off, and the troops were too preoccupied with the impromptu beast-fight to intercept them. Nor did the four do what they were supposed to—run, trip, struggle helplessly with the beasts, get themselves disemboweled and die screaming for mercy. No, the impudent rogues formed square, all four of them back to back, drew their daggers and prepared to sell their lives dearly.

The lions hurled themselves at the bandits. For a few moments there was a confused melee of men and animals, roars, cries of defiance, swinging hands and claws. One man was dead, another staggering, but the lions, snarling, had already backed off, dripping blood from their wounds. The second time they went in more cautiously. The wounded bandit, on his knees, was trying with both hands to keep his guts from falling out, but the two who remained on their feet were crouching, teeth bared, daggers at the ready, and this time it was a lion that went sprawling, its throat ripped open by a lucky thrust. It picked itself up immediately but it was finished. It limped off leaving a thick trail of blood and lay down quietly to die while its companion circled the bandits, snarling, impotent. The bandits laughed and jeered at it, ignoring their partner, who slowly keeled over on his side and lay still.

Livid with fury, Decius yelled out, 'Take them down!' An infantryman threw his javelin, then another. The light throwing-spears whistled as they cut the air. Hit between his shoulderblades as he squared off against the surviving lion, one of the pair crashed to the ground face down, without a cry. The other, glancing quickly from left to right and seeing no hope anywhere, threw up his hands in surrender. No one took any notice. Missiles continued to fly in steady succession as he ducked, weaved, tried to dodge them, gesticulating, shouting incoherently. Finally a javelin through his thigh brought him down. The soldiers closed in.

Decius's first concern was his lions. But one was dead when he reached it, the other too badly wounded to live long. He ordered the centurion to put it out of its misery, then had his men chop the heads off three of the bandits and briefly interrogated the fourth, the one with the javelin through his thigh, before having him too dispatched. Then he remembered the money.

The sacks were lying where the bandits had dropped them. One of them had split open and gold coins were lying strewn around in the sand. Some of the soldiers had already taken advantage of the confusion. Decius was on the point of ordering them to open their knapsacks when a sudden thought struck him.

If he returned the loot to its rightful owners, as law and morality obliged him to do, he would also be obliged to explain how he had obtained it. Whatever story he concocted as his official report, his illegitimate use of the lions might eventually be revealed. And that was no laughing matter. Lions captured for the games in Rome were Imperial property. Negligence in their care, let alone outright abuse of them, was therefore a serious offence. Perhaps his family connections would save him from anything worse than a severe reprimand. Perhaps not.

But far more than any punishment Decius dreaded the scorn and contempt of his fellow-officers, most of whom cordially detested him. If he went back lionless and his criminal negligence became known, he would never hear the end of it. The story would follow him from posting to posting and even if he died a full general in battle, in Germany or on the Persian front, they would still be guffawing over it in the camps. Or at least, so he feared.

'Lads,' he called out.

His use of this term was so uncharacteristic, he could have sworn one or two of the men actually sniggered. He ignored them. Now was not the time to be a stickler for minor points of discipline. 'Lads, you've done well. You deserve a reward. Centurion, you will divide this money equally among the troops. And, needless to say, none of you need mention anything to anyone about this little incident. We will do what we can to replace the lions, but if we can't...' He shrugged. Some of the men raised a ragged cheer. The money took quite a long time to count out. While it was being counted, Decius remembered the two bandits who had escaped. Too late to do anything about them now. They would be miles away.

The centurion approached him with a jingling sack.

'Your share, sir.'

He stared at the centurion. 'What do you mean, my share?'

'Well, sir, you said share it out equally.'

'Yes, but I...' He really hadn't meant to include himself. But the centurion said insistently, 'Go on, sir, take it, sir,' with a kind of wheedling threat in his voice, and Decius suddenly saw the point of it: if he stayed pure, he could always denounce *them* for corruption at some later date, and as an officer he would be believed. But if he too accepted a share, he himself was equally implicated. He hesitated only for a moment: it was a long way back to the Nile, and if he refused the offer, the centurion could always say later, 'Well, it was like this, Colonel. We're chasing this bunch of barbarians, and Lieutenant Decius is out front, like—you know how brave the poor fellow was—and one of them turns and lets go an arrow, and whoops, that was it! Straight through the heart, sir. Died instantly. Buried him out there, yes of course, sir, no way he'd have lasted, carrying him back, not with the heat and all. Put up a stone, of course. Not sure I could find it again, sir, but it's out there.' Wouldn't be the first officer that had happened to. And if all the others told the same story...

He took the sack. But he remained in a vile temper, so that when the centurion started talking about cover, he fixed the man with a contemptuous gaze and said, 'Cover against what?'

'Against the weather, sir.'

'Against the *weather*?'

It flashed through the centurion's mind that if his officer repeated one more thing he said, he would draw his sword and cut the fool down. He wouldn't, of course—it wasn't worth torture and crucifixion, but the thought made him feel better. 'Yes, sir. Very bad sandstorm coming.'

Decius had been in Egypt less than a year; he had never seen a sandstorm, bad or otherwise. 'Centurion, do I understand you correctly? Are you asking me to take Roman troops, *Roman troops* into cover because of *bad weather*?'

'Begging your pardon, sir, but...Well, I've had experience, and— '

It was the worst thing he could have said. Decius's eyes flashed. 'You're suggesting that I'm inexperienced!'

'No, sir. Certainly not, sir. Just that...Well, if you haven't actually been through one of—'

He was abruptly cut off. 'When I want the benefit of your extensive experience, Centurion, I'll ask for it. That will be all for now. We have work to do.'

'Sir!' The centurion gave a salute that this time fell on the insolent side of sloppiness, and went back to his men. The officer's knuckles whitened on the reins, but he thought better of it. He knew now that his folly had put him in their power. They could do anything they liked short of outright mutiny, and he would be powerless to prevent them—he had lost his moral authority.

The patrol kept moving. The sky continued to darken,

and if you had very good hearing and kept an ear close to the ground, you might fancy you heard, far off, at the lower limit of audibility, a strange, dull, booming sound.

Darion the bandit heard it, a mile or two to the west of them. 'It's coming,' he said to Copros, his companion.

'Shit! And we've got no water.'

'There a well or a hole or anything round here?'

'The fuck should I know!' Copros was an improvement on Ater, Darion would admit that, but not much. 'Dunghill', his name meant, because that was where his mother had left him. Not out of contempt—out of kindness, actually. So that the warmth might keep him alive long enough for some kind stranger to find him and adopt him, as must have happened, of course, or he wouldn't be here.

'Thought you said you knew these parts,' Darion complained.

'I did. But that was years back. Things change.' Too bad it had to be you made the break, Darion was thinking. Any one of those other poor bastards would have been better. He'd seen the Romans turn the lions loose on them, but hadn't waited for the result. They would have given the lions a hard time, that bunch, but one way or another they'd all be dead by now, poor sods.

'Not much point going on, then,' he said, looking around

him. Out on the flats below them, beyond the maze of spiky, spiny rocks and thorny scrub through which they had been scrambling for what seemed like hours, he could make out the dry, cracked bottom of a mud lake. That's fed by something, he thought. When it rains, must be a watercourse that takes the stuff from up here to down there. Which way would it lie? While Copros stared round him like a dumb ox, Darion tried to read the terrain, figure out the likeliest direction to head in. Down and to the left, he decided. But the first and most important thing was to find protection from the storm.

'Try that way,' Darion said.

They picked up the sacks of money they had dropped when they paused to reconnoiter. Good job we split the loot first, Darion thought, or those Roman bastards would have had it all. Then immediately it occurred to him that if two of them went into shelter and only one came out, that one would get a double share, He himself wouldn't kill a comrade for money, but what about Copros? He hardly knew the man. He would have to watch his back. Maybe Copros was thinking the same about him. Should he bring it out in the open? No, might put ideas in his head—plenty of room for that! He grinned at the thought.

'What's the joke?' Copros asked.

'Oh...nothing.'

'Always grinning to yourself about something,' Copros grumbled. 'Might at least share the joke.'

I must be more careful, Darion thought. He's bigger than me. Can't afford to antagonize him.

The way they had taken wound down into a cleft in the rocks. To their right they saw a broad overhang, looked at one another, nodded. Not as good as a cave, but almost. They squeezed under it, squatted there, cross-legged, and waited. The air grew darker. The dull booming sound grew gradually louder, amplified by the walls of the cleft.

To Zachary, standing with arms outstretched in his valley, the storm seemed at first to come from within himself. Like the Roman officer Decius he had had no personal experience of such things. He had merely noted, that morning, a certain unwillingness to move, a sluggish lethargy that pervaded his entire body. I must be falling sick again, he thought miserably. But he had taken up his station, as always, as he had done for an uncounted number of days. At least I don't have the sun to contend with, he thought.

He stood there like a ragged scarecrow. His homemade garment of reeds was disintegrating. Beneath it, the skin on his emaciated body, burned dark by the sun, hung from his bones. His ribcage was clearly visible, his shoulderblades stood out like incipient wings, as if his body, like his soul, was struggling to resemble the angels. But his eyes still held a light of fanatical determination. He would conquer and tame this base remnant of flesh. Already he had all but overcome the demon of lust. The demon of gluttony had been harder to subdue. But finally he had broken through into a state that had all the pleasures of intoxication with none of its brain-fuddling effects.

His body had—at least until this morning—felt light, elated, as if the burning-up of its own flesh gave it a fuel somehow richer than normal food. Even the sensation of hunger had become almost pleasurable to him, like a constantly rising barometer that assured him of growing control over his physical self. His sense of time too had become distorted. Days sometimes seemed to pass in a flash, yet at other times a moment could stretch eternally. His eyes had grown so sensitive to the light that he kept them closed the greater part of the day. But that was a small price to pay for the certainty that he was approaching his goal, surpassing the mundane achievements of other hermits, inexorably moving towards the purity of spirit that would alone ensure his salvation.

But today he no longer felt elated. He strove desperately to regain that feeling, concentrating on the most powerful images of his faith: the virgin mother and her child; the agony in the garden; the empty tomb. His own favorite image came from the Gospel of John—it was of the Risen Savior standing by the charcoal fire he had made, on the shores of Lake Tiberias, just as the sun rose, and speaking to Simon Peter and the others, offshore in their boat after a fruitless night's fishing. He could see the charcoal reddening, its ghostly flames shortening and lengthening in the fitful dawn breeze—could see the sun's first pale, hesitant light peering through a bank of horizon cloud, and hear Christ's voice, not raised at all, though the boat was a hundred yards out over the glassy water, but clearly audible, resonant in the dawn calm, saying, 'Cast the net on the right side of the boat...'

The vision came, but he could not fix it, could not focus his mind. Peripherally he was aware of something strange in the atmosphere, a thunderous tension building up, a darkening and a concentration of vapors in the eastern sky that looked less like a cloud than an enormous bruise. He ignored it. What went on in the physical world seemed unreal now, compared to what went on in his mind.

A sudden spiral of wind picked up dust and debris, even small stones, whirled them around and then collapsed, hurling them outwards. A flying chip of rock struck his cheekbone. Demons, his fevered mind told him. At last they're attacking me head-on! This testament to his growing virtue filled him with satisfaction. He felt a trickle of blood down his cheek, but he overcame his impulse to touch the wound, let the blood trickle down to his mouth and licked it away with his tongue.

Another whirlwind came, but this time it passed by him towards the mouth of the valley. The sky, darker, seething, seemed to be hanging lower and lower over his head. The passage of the second whirlwind was followed by a period of breathless calm.

Something was pending, surely, some great manifestation, whether divine or diabolic he could not yet tell. He braced himself to meet it.

The wind began quite suddenly, a roaring wall of air that came cascading over the bluff in front of him. For a moment he thought he was being assailed by a swarm of locusts. Then he realized it was sand, sand driven by the wind with terrifying velocity and force. He reeled and almost fell, his hands going up instinctively to cover his face and eyes. Staggering, he pulled himself upright as the wind slackened for a few moments. Then it came at him again, with redoubled force.

This time it lifted him clear off his feet and flung him headlong, several feet away from where he had been standing. Crushed, winded by the fall, he struggled to rise, but the force of that torrent of air kept him pinned to the ground. The roar of it had now risen to something approaching a shriek. Prone as he was, he felt it beginning to push him along the valley. He had a. frightening visual image of it lifting his weak body as lightly as a leaf and sweeping him off to some unknown destination. Now all his efforts were concentrated on trying to maintain his position, clutching at the uneven ground with his fingertips, groping for a hold with his toes, trying to flatten his body still further to the rocks like a climber on a vertical face.

He had no way of measuring time. He clung there, not thinking, not even praying, his whole mind concentrated on resisting the wind. Then above the demonic screeching of the wind he heard a sound like thunder. But what kind of thunder shakes the ground?

For a brief instant he dared the flying particles and looked up, and what he saw filled him with bewilderment and horror.

A huge chunk of the temple wall had fallen. And the rest of the wall seemed to be leaning out towards him. What could it mean? In a sudden flash of lucidity, he knew.

The mass of the half-buried temple had served as a dam for an enormous mass of sand that had built up behind it. Decayed by the passage of time, it had already been on the verge of collapse, as evidenced by the fragments he had seen falling from it. Now new masses of sand, driven by the wind from the desert above, had piled up behind that enfeebled dam and finally overwhelmed it. Within minutes, seconds even, the dam would break.

In a fit of blind panic he let the wind take him. It picked him up, rolled him over, carried him sprawling head over heels down the valley. Then with a sound louder than a clap of thunder directly overhead, the ancient walls finally gave way.

An immense avalanche of sand and stone came surging down into the valley, pouring like floodwater along the valley floor. Moving faster than Zachary was being moved by the wind, it flowed over him and beyond, slowing as its energy spent itself, falling silent and still at last as the wind continued to whip sand from its surface and send it on downstream to where pools of water from the spring finally merged into the desert sands.

Zachary was buried alive. He could not breathe; any attempt to breathe drew sandgrains up his nostrils and down into his lungs. He flailed his limbs frantically, or rather he ordered them to flail, but it was as if he were bound hand and foot. Lights flashed behind his eyelids; within seconds, he knew, he would lose consciousness. He forced his body into a final effort. He felt the sand shifting under him, settling into the hollows of the ground. Again he flailed his limbs, and suddenly his head was clear and he sucked in a great gulp of air—air laden with sand-grains, for sure, but still breathable. Then he must have lost consciousness, for when he became aware once more of his surroundings, the wind had died down, and although the sky remained the dull purplish color of a bruise, the ominous sense of menace in the atmosphere had passed.

He pulled himself out of the sand and gazed around him at the ruin of the valley.

A few palm-trees had been left standing, but their tops had been snapped off. and the lower parts of their trunks lay submerged in the sand. The few remaining trees that were visible had been stripped of their leaves, their smaller branches smashed to matchwood. All that remained of them were splintered skeletons.

But worst of all was what had happened to the spring.

Where the spring had been now lay under tens of feet of sand and rubble; the whole course of the stream that the spring once fed had vanished beneath the landslide, even the pools at the end of the stream had shrunk to mere patches of mud, choked with debris stripped from the trees. The paradise of Jannes and Jambres, if indeed that was what it was, existed no more.

For a long time, Zachary could not believe his eyes. He found it impossible to believe that this place where he had lived so long and suffered so much could have vanished for ever in a matter of moments. He kept imagining himself the victim of some enchantment—soon, surely, the spell would dissipate, the valley would reassume the features he knew so well. He wandered aimlessly through its ruins, awaiting the event. But nothing happened. Daylight began to fade. A bird of prey, its feathers awry, landed on a bare branch and stared at him through its yellowish eyes. Except for himself, it was the only living thing in the entire landscape. When it rose and soared eastwards, he realized he too would have to leave. Without water, he could not hope to survive there. Whatever happened to him now, his life in the interior desert was over.

What did it mean? Throughout the rest of the night that followed, Zachary lay awake and tried to make sense of what had happened. It never occurred to him that this disaster could have resulted from pure chance. He had been taught to believe in a world driven by purpose. Not a sparrow could fall if God had not meant it to fall. Of course some things might come about through the machinations of the Evil One, but even Satan held no powers that were specifically his own, only those that God in His unsearchable wisdom allowed him to have, to test the man of righteousness or to punish the sinner.

Was he being told to return to the world, that his period of penance had been completed? It seemed unlikely that God would have used so drastic a means to convey his message, when a simple visit from an angel would have sufficed. He grew more and more certain that a far different message was intended. After his visit to the temple, he had believed himself irretrievably damned, but he had forced himself into one last desperate effort to achieve redemption, and for a while he had fooled himself into thinking that he was succeeding in this. But now he became convinced that God was telling him, Stop! It's no use! Nothing you could ever do can bring about your redemption! Stop your blasphemy, your posturing, your obscene imitation of my Son's agony! You are anathema! And there is no sea wide enough nor desert deep enough to come between you and My wrath!

He had planned to leave, in the morning, to head eastwards across the desert, to hope that he could reach the settled lands before thirst overcame him. Now that all seemed pointless. He felt very weak, weary to the point of death. What purpose would be served by prolonging the struggle? He might as well accept the inevitable.

As morning came, he lay down on the ledge outside his cave and prepared to die.

Chapter Nine

'Which way now?' Darion asked.

Copros scratched his head. 'There's an oasis round here somewhere,'

'Yeah, you keep saying that.' Darion was beginning to lose his temper. He wouldn't mind if Copros admitted that he was hopelessly lost. Then he himself could take over, as he had done the previous evening when they searched for water. They'd found some, too, in the end, after digging a hole in the bottom of the dried watercourse that Darion had predicted would be there. Or, to be more precise, they dug a hole with their daggers to a depth of almost four feet, to the accompaniment of Copros moaning that they were wasting their time, they'd never find anything, why didn't they move on and look for a proper well or spring or something. Then they sat there, Copros still muttering, while slowly, incredibly slowly, the bottom of the hole filled with a few inches of muddy, foul-smelling water. With this, over Copros's objections, Darion insisted that they fill their goatskin waterbottles. And a good job he had, because, vile as the stuff undoubtedly, was, it looked like it was all they were going to get for the foreseeable future.

'There was a big temple,' Copros was saying. 'From the old days. A spring. Palm trees. Nobody would live there, though, except a couple of crazy monks. Something funny about the place. Guy told me once. Can't quite remember what he—'

Darion interrupted him. 'What's that?'

'Where?'

'There. Over there by that whitish rock. See it?'

'Yeah... Something metal, huh?'

'Right. Looks like a helmet.'

'Well I'll be...' Darion and Copros exchanged glances.

'The Romans,' Copros said.

'They don't leave their helmets lying around.' Darion grinned. 'Not if they're still alive, they don't.'

Copros looked apprehensive. 'Could be a trap, though, couldn't it?'

Really, Copros, Darion thought. If they'd known how you'd turn out, they'd have left you on the dunghill. 'Sure,' he said cheerfully. 'It's full of birdlime. On the end of a rope, see. Put your hand in it, it sticks, they just reel you in.'

'You're putting me on,' Copros said reproachfully.

'As if I'd do that...Want to check it out?'

Copros looked at Darion., looked back at the helmet, shrugged, nodded. 'Uh-huh. I guess. If you say so.' They approached it cautiously. When they were within a few yards of it Darion, who had taken the lead, stopped suddenly and whistled.

'Holy shit! His head's still in it.'

'And there's the rest of him,' Copros said, pointing to a huddled heap half-hidden among the boulders. 'Well,' he said a moment later, turning a little pale, 'there's most of him.'

'Missing his privates?'

'Uh-huh.'

'Fuck!' Darion slapped his right fist into his left palm. 'That's all we need! The Mazices!'

Copros looked startled. 'They won't bother us, will they?'

'Want to take a bet?'

The two men gazed around them nervously. For as far as they could see, the barren landscape was empty. But that didn't mean a thing. There were countless cliffs, dunes, gullies, from beneath or behind or within which armed barbarians could emerge at any second.

'It's the Romans they don't like. The Romans probably went for them first.' Copros was only too obviously trying to convince himself.

Darion shrugged. 'Who knows? They're crazy. They don't know themselves why they do stuff.'

'So what should *we* do?'

Copros was looking baffled. At last, Darion thought, he's actually asking for advice. He would have to choose the one time I don't have any. 'What can we do?' he admitted. 'Nothing. Just keep going. Hope we find this oasis of yours before the Mazices...oh-oh.'

He stopped abruptly.

'What's the matter?' Copros asked.

'If there is an oasis, that's probably where they are.' Darion turned and sat down on a rock. 'Let's think before we do anything,' he said. 'We've got about enough water to last till tonight. What are our chances of getting some anywhere else?'

Copros looked glum. 'Not much.'

'Really?'

'I don't know of anywhere. Not within a day and a half's walk of here. Or more,' he added after a moment.

'That's it then. We'll take a chance on it, or...' Darion blew a kiss into the air. 'Goodbye, Egypt.'

He got to his feet, slung the bag of coins that was his share of the loot over his shoulder. Well over three hundred gold pieces, by his count. His biggest score ever from robbing live people, his third biggest even if you counted tombs. For all the good it did him, might as well have been three hundred donkey-turds. At least with donkey-turds you could make a fire if they were dry enough. And they wouldn't spell an automatic death-sentence if you were caught with them.

They had gone about a quarter of a mile when they saw the horse. It wasn't dead—not yet. It was making feeble efforts to rise, but as they came nearer they saw one of its legs was smashed so badly that the splintered white bone stuck out through the flesh. They looked at each other. 'Can you do it?' Darion asked. 'I'll do it if you can't, but I'd rather you did it.' In the village where he was raised, there was a big farm where the owner, a rich man, kept horses, not to work with, just for sport, so they were the best, the fastest. He and a couple of other kids used to steal rides on them when no one was looking, but the stewards caught them at it and Darion got the beating of his life. He didn't blame it on the horses, though. They just wanted to be free like he did.

Copros took out his dagger. 'I'll do it. But why didn't he do it?'

'Who?'

'Guy was riding it.'

Darion jerked a thumb over his shoulder. 'Why don't you ask him?'

'Oh-oh.' Copros paused, dagger in hand. 'Is he... you know...like the other one?'

'Let me check,' Darion said. It saved him from having to watch the horse die. He heard it though, whinnying in fear as it saw what was going to happen to it, scrabbling with its uninjured legs, and then the whistling, bubbling sound as blood and air forced themselves through the gash Copros had made in its throat. He tried to concentrate instead on the dead cavalryman, in one piece this time except for the bits that were missing. Poor bastard, he thought, Roman or no Roman. Just some poor sod following orders, a slave to that blond lunatic with the lions. Never had a chance. May whatever gods there are, if there are any, protect his soul, if he had one.

An idea occurred to him, and he lifted one of the man's arms and let it drop. Copros, behind him, asked, 'What do you think happened?'

'Stiff as a board,' Darion said. 'Dead since last night, probably.'

'So where's the vultures?'

'Don't worry. They're coming.' And sure enough, to the westward, far away against the blue, two dark birds were circling slowly, coasting on currents of air. 'Guess they got blown away by the storm' Darion went on. 'No, you know what I think? The dumb shits didn't take cover. If you've ever been in a real sandstorm, you know what it's like. Can't breathe, can't see your hand in front of you. They would have gotten scattered. Then I guess the Mazices must have come out and taken them one after the other.'

'And you think that was yesterday not today.' Copros was looking a little brighter.

'Last night, probably.'

'So they could be long gone.'

Darion laughed. 'Don't bet on it.'

'And we don't have to worry about the Romans any more.'

Darion nodded. 'Right. If there'd been any left alive they wouldn't have left their buddies out like this.'

'What about... ?' Copros squatted down and slid his hands under the man's body. 'D'you think...'

'Money? Nah. They only left him his tunic.'

'You're right. Took his sword, too.'

Darion had already begun to walk on. He wondered how long he would hold onto the money-bag. As the day heated up, it got heavier . A time would come when he might have to choose between that and survival. Survival, he thought, any time. What good did money do you anyway, more than the little you needed for the necessities of life? He would have dropped the bag already except he was pretty sure that, if he did, Copros would pick it up. And that would create problems.

'Look, tell me the truth,' he said to Copros as the other caught up with him. 'Do you have the faintest idea where we are?'

Copros smirked, 'I know exactly where we are.'

Darion laughed skeptically. 'Since when?'

'No need to get like that with me...See that hill? I recognized it. While I was killing the horse. Just below that. That's where the temple is.'

Darion shaded his eyes. 'I don't see any temple.'

'You can't see it from here. It's in a valley. The hill's just the marker. You can't mistake the shape of it.'

'And you say there's a spring there?' Darion asked, beginning to hope.

Copros made a kissing face. 'The best. Just you wait.' He took the waterbottle from his shoulder and removed the cap that was attached to it by a string.

'Steady!' Darion said. 'We're not there yet,'

'Think I was going to drink it?' Copros made a gesture of contempt. 'Screw that. I'm not drinking any more of that catpiss.' And he began to pour the water onto the ground.

Darion snatched the waterbottle from him. Copros grabbed it back. Before Darion got possession of it, most of the water had spilled. 'Dumb fuck!' Darion said, putting the cap back on. 'What'd you do that for?'

'Why not? Fill it again at the spring.'

'How do you know the spring's still running?'

'It's been running since Pharaoh times,' Copros said complacently. 'Why would it stop now?'

Darion grunted. He didn't have a ready answer but he knew there were two places, the ocean and the desert, where you couldn't afford to make even one mistake. He wanted to take a drink himself but he wasn't going to. Not until he absolutely had to. He kept on going.

'Hey!' Copros shouted. 'Hey! That's my waterbottle!' Darion ignored him.

'Hey! Give it back to me!'

'So you can pour it in the dirt?' Darion asked.

'It's mine! Give it to me!'

Darion stopped and faced him, his right hand near enough to go for his dagger if he had to. This is ridiculous, he thought, two grown men in the middle of nowhere, acting like little kids. Why should I feel responsible? Do as he says. But instead he said, 'Promise me you won't empty it.'

Copros cursed obscenely. 'Why should I? I can do what I like with it.'

'All right,' Darion said, with an appearance of reasonableness. 'I'll give it back if you let me drink it first. I mean, someone might as well get the benefit.'

He ducked and sprang aside as Copros went for him, then flung the bottle at him—crazy to shed blood over a thing like that. Copros caught the bottle, unfastened it. 'It's mine. I'll do what it like with it.' Defiantly he tipped it up and let the last drops run out. Darion watched them as they were absorbed by the sandy soil. He did not say anything. After a few moments they walked on in silence,

Half an hour later they were approaching the head of the valley. Darion, in the lead, signaled to Copros to drop to the ground, Upright, they would be clearly visible on the horizon to anyone who happened to be in the valley below. They moved for the last few yards on their stomachs, wriggling like lizards across the hot rocks. Darion raised his head a few inches and peered over the edge. 'Where's your temple?' he asked.

Copros eased in beside him. 'Should be over on the...Hey, wait a minute! What the....Holy Serapis, what happened to it?'

'More to the point, where's your spring?'

Copros' face was a picture. Shock, incredulity, outrage chased one another across it—then finally, anger. 'You think I was shitting you, don't you?'

'I never said that.' Darion spoke in a placatory tone. No point in getting mad about it. There'd been water there once, obviously, because the trunks of decapitated palms and the skeletal tops of fruit-trees still rose above the great wash of sand and rubble that now completely filled the floor of the valley. But there was none now. They just had to accept that.

'You don't have to say it,' Copros fumed on. 'I know you. That sly look of yours. I know what you're thinking.'

'Ah, shut up, Copros,' Darion said. 'I believe you. There was a temple there, I can see that.' He pointed to the ragged chunks of masonry, half-submerged in the sand. 'It just collapsed. And the spring got choked up. Tough, but there you go. How far did you say it was to the next water?'

Copros got a grip on himself. 'A day...maybe. Like, by noon tomorrow. If we're lucky...Give me half your water.'

Darion was so startled he didn't hear properly, or didn't believe what he heard.

'Give me half your water, shithead.'

Darion gazed at him in total incredulity. 'After you threw yours away? What the fuck...Are you out of your mind?'

Copros ploughed on stubbornly. 'We're partners, right? Partners share everything, right? So you got to give me half. I'm talking about survival now, get it? If one of us doesn't have, one of us doesn't survive.'

Darion saw the reason as well as the injustice of it. Trouble was, he had always been able to see both sides of things. He did a quick calculation, a very rough one, because he simply didn't know exactly how little water one could survive on in the desert in late spring for twenty-four hours or maybe thirty-six or however long it took. It seemed to him that with what he had, one person could almost certainly survive, and two could very possibly not.

'All right,' he said. 'I'll share with you. But I get to keep the bottle. And to say when we drink and how much.'

'No,' Copros said. 'That's not good enough.'

'Got to be.'

'Says who?'

'Says this.' Calmly and without anger, Darion drew his dagger. 'I just made you a very generous offer, Copros. I didn't have to. You fucked up, not me. You threw your water away. I did my best to stop you, but no, you knew best. Now, are you prepared to kill me for it? Or die for it? Because I swear to you, Copros, if you go for me, if you try and get it, I'll kill you. And you won't be my first, as you may have heard.'

'You bastard,' Copros said. 'You cold-blooded bastard.'

Darion laughed. 'Look, spare the abuse. I made you a fair offer.'

'And you can blow it out your ass, fuckhead.'

'Your choice.'

'And my choice whether you find the next waterhole or not,' Copros cried triumphantly. 'Had you thought of that?

No, you hadn't thought of that, had you, smartass?'

And he took off down the slope. Halfway down he paused, turned, and shouted back: 'You think I don't know where I'm going? , Well, I'm telling you, buddy, you don't know where you're going! So I don't want your stinking water. You can keep your stinking water! Make the most of it! It's all you'll ever get.'

And, turning, he ran down to the valley floor, thumbed his nose at Darion, crossed the bottom and headed up the farther side.

Darion made no attempt to follow him. Copros's words didn't worry him very much. On his showing so far, Copros had no better chance of finding water than he, Darion, did. And at worst he was rid of the aggravation, of worrying about having to kill or be killed, for gold, for water, whatever. He felt a sense of lightness, of relief. He had not realized he would feel so pleased to find himself alone.

Which way to go now? Pointless to descend into the valley, as Copros had done. Better to walk around the rim until he reached the head of it, then strike due east for the settled land. If he could keep going through the night or part of it he might still make the Nile valley before his water ran out. Better that than wander all over the desert looking for waterholes that might not be there. But as he stood up and turned to go, something caught his eye. Halfway down the slope, on a narrow ledge, lay the huddled shape of something. What, he could not tell without going lower. The hell with it, he told himself, it can't be anything that would be any use to you. But it did no good. All his life he had been both observant and curious, facets of his personality that had gotten him into trouble many times, but given him good things, too.

He just had to look, to make sure. It will take only a moment. he told himself, then I'll be on my way. Here goes nothing. The stones skittered under his feet as he made his way down. Copros must have passed within feet of it, he thought, and never even gave it a look. Could be a dead goat or hyena or anything...

But no. It was a man.

A man, though, who looked hardly human. With wild hair and beard almost entirely covering the shrunken face. Blackened by the sun, limbs like a mummy's, with the flesh caved in and the skin stretched like parchment over the bones. Three dead men so far today, Darion thought. Is that an omen? But this one was no soldier, and his body had not been mutilated. The only clothes the body had on were the tattered remains of some strange garment that seemed to be made out of reeds. What had Copros said about hermits in the valley? This must be one of them.

Well, that's the end of his story, Darion thought. May the weird god those folks have, the one who can't stand other gods, look after his own in whatever other world he's entered, if any. Clumsily, he tried to make the sign of the cross as he had seen Christians do, only he did it backwards. Then he turned, unsure whether it would be easier now to climb back up the slope or take the route Copros had taken—

The body shuddered.

Darion blinked. Surely his eyes were playing him tricks? He knew that if you went short of food and water, and he hadn't eaten for nearly two days, your mind could do strange things. No, he must have imagined it. For the body had not actually moved at, it was lying in exactly the same position as when he had first seen it. You can't afford to lose your grip, he told himself, out here, almost waterless, alone. He took a couple of determined steps towards the valley floor. Then he stopped.

He had to know. He had to know absolutely for sure that the man was dead. Otherwise he would have no peace on his journey. All the time he would be thinking, well, suppose the guy was alive after all. Suppose as you were going down the hill he woke and saw you and tried to wave to you but your back was turned and you never noticed him. How would the guy feel? How would Darion feel if that happened to him?

Pretty bad. So he might as well set his mind at rest. Wouldn't take a second. Just to confirm what he really knew already.

He put his hand round the hermit's wrist.

It was like putting your fingers round a bird's claw. Thin, bony, with that feel of awful fragility to it. He could break that wrist between finger and thumb. And it was completely lifeless, wasn't it?...Wasn't it?

To his astonishment and consternation, he felt under his fingertips a faint, abnormally slow pulse.

You're imagining things, he told himself. Try his mouth. Bet you there's nothing there. He drew his dagger, polished the blade on the hem of his shirt until it shone like a mirror, then held it an inch from the hermit's lips. A faint, scarcely visible mist formed on it. Dropping the dagger, he reached over and with his thumb flipped back the man's left eyelid. For a second the eye's pupil fixated on him; then slowly it rolled over, exposing the white. Darion let the eyelid fall back. Squatting on his haunches, he let out a long string of obscenities, mostly Coptic, some Greek, and a couple he knew in Syriac. You dumb shit, he said, why couldn't you have just stayed decently dead?

He would have to leave the poor bastard there to die. What else was he to do? With half a waterbottle of all but undrinkable water, he could see no other option. It was quite possible that he himself would not come out of this alive, even with no additional burden. With a helpless hermit on his hands, he was doomed. Two would die instead of one, and that one was almost certain to die anyway. Best thing he could do would be cut the guy's throat. Put him out of his misery. Just like the horse.

He laughed to himself. Good job Copros didn't get to you, he said. He wouldn't have had too many second thoughts. But there was no way Darion could do that to a helpless stranger. Sorry, he said to the unconscious man, and he meant it sincerely. Sorry, I would help you if I could, but I can't. Hope you go quick and don't linger. Best of luck, if that's the right expression.

He plunged downhill, having reckoned that this would now be the easier route. He went without a backward glance, for he feared that if he looked back, some mysterious link might be forged between him and the stranger, he might be drawn back, as if by some enchantment, against his will. He crossed the floor of the valley and began to ascend the opposite slope.

As he did so, suddenly his mind flashed back to the jail in Terenuthis and the big black hermit who had set him free. Moses. The ex-bandit. Probably not your typical hermit. Probably only did it out of fellow-feeling for someone in his old profession. Still, it was one of the very few occasions in Darion's life where someone had done something for him without expecting anything in return. For that reason, it had impressed him deeply. And now, a small voice deep inside him seemed to be saying, you have a chance to pay back the favor, if not to Moses himself, at least to one of Moses' own kind.

That's ridiculous, he told himself. Must have been crazy, trying to live out here. Serve him right, he asked for it. Brothers, they call themselves. Well, *I'm* not his brother. And in any case I've gone too far to turn back now, not enough time, enough water, enough strength, enough anything...

Enough heart? the voice asked. Enough courage?

'Shut up, fuck you!' Darion cried out loud, and he began to curse again, with a fury born of desperation.

When he had finally exhausted his vocabulary, he stopped, and remained there, without moving, for the best part of a minute. Darion, he told himself, you are the biggest, most stupid fool that was ever born in Egypt. Then abruptly he turned on his heel and began to retrace his steps.

Chapter Ten

As Darion walked back towards the dying hermit, he tried to make some sense out of what he was doing. It was beginning to occur to him that he might after all not have chosen the most sensible course by heading off across the desert in the heat of midday. There was shade and shelter in the caves of the valley—mightn't it be better to wait there until dark and then try to travel by night, thus reducing the need for water? For that matter, why had both he and Copros despaired so quickly of finding water in the valley? If it had held, until recently, so plenteous a supply, there should still be something there, under the surface.

Instead of ascending to the hermit's ledge, he turned right at the foot of the slope and walked towards the valley mouth. The further he went, the moister the sand and mud under his feet became. He stopped and began to dig, and this time he had only gone down a few inches when water began to ooze into the hole. Water that looked a lot cleaner, too, than what he had found the previous evening. He capped his hands, raised them to his lips. It had a sharp mineral taste, but it was clear and relatively pure. He emptied his bottle, refilled it from the hole, and walked slowly back up the valley.

He was hoping the hermit had died. Then he would have no further responsibility, he could go on, tonight or tomorrow, as he pleased, with a clear conscience. He would have done all he needed to do, all he could do.

But the hermit had not died. He had not moved, either, but his breath still blurred the shine of Darion's dagger, his eye still rolled up when Darion thumbed back the lid. His flesh felt hot to the touch. Got a fever, poor bastard, Darion thought. Doesn't have the faintest idea there's anyone with him. I could go now, he'd never know the difference. Perhaps his spirit has already passed into another world. Nothing left here but a lump of flesh. So why bother?

Gently he lifted the hermit's head with one hand, took the waterbottle in the other and brought it to the hermit's lips. The hermit did not open his mouth, and water ran all over his face. Darion pushed the mouth of the bottle between his lips, forcing them apart, and tipped the bottle up, very carefully, so as not to choke him. This time some of the water ran into his mouth, but when his head slid to one side, it ran out again. This is a losing battle, Darion said to himself, taking the bottle away. But no sooner had he done so than the hermit's lips opened slightly, the tip of a tongue appeared and drew in a drop of moisture from the lips.

To his own surprise, Darion felt a flush of pleasure. He had done something for somebody, and it had worked. He put the bottle back to the hermit's lips and tilted it, ever so gently, until a trickle ran out of it. Equally gently, with his free hand, he parted the hermit's lips. No sooner had a few drops run into the hermit's mouth than he tipped the bottle back—no need to choke the guy. And this time the hermit swallowed. The motion of his throat muscles was hardly perceptible, but it was there, and when Darion repeated the procedure it came again. He repeated it five or six times, then stopped. He did not know why he had stopped, but he knew it was right to do so. So intense was his concentration that some invisible bond had formed between him and the hermit, some link of empathy that made him aware beyond any overt consciousness of what the hermit was feeling. And by this same instinctive bond he somehow knew when to start giving the water again.

You idiot, he told himself. If he lives, what can you do with him? You won't be able to leave him here. You'll have to carry him out. Then you're both dead.

It didn't do any good. He was experiencing the same feeling he had had when he rescued that girl, what was her name, she had never told him her name, the one Ater had tried to rape. It was a strange and inexplicable and, in the light of rational self-interest, totally absurd feeling, yet the satisfaction he derived from it could not be denied.

When Darion felt that the hermit had drunk enough, he carried him into the cave. Here he found the rough bed of palm-fronds the hermit had made there, and laid him down on it, arranging his limp body as comfortably as he could. The hermit stirred restlessly now and made a hoarse sound in his throat that Darion thought at first was the death-rattle, but it passed and moments later the hermit's eyes opened briefly. But his gaze gave no sign that he was seeing anything, and the eyes soon closed again. Now Darion could hear his breathing; it was faint, but regular.

Darion took his waterbottle and a hollow gourd he found in the cave, carried them down the valley, filled them and returned to the cave. He scraped a hollow in the ground a few feet away from the hermit and went to sleep. When he awoke, the light in the cave had almost vanished, it was evening already. He went outside. The western sky was a wash of luminous green in which the evening star burned with a white incandescence. Other, weaker stars were appearing across the heavens. Funny, you never actually see them appear, he thought. You look and there's nothing and then you look away and when you look back, there they are. What were they? Were they lamps that someone lit every night or did they burn all the time but disappear in daylight, overwhelmed by the stronger radiance, as the light of a lamp left burning in a room all night is swallowed by the dawn?

Foolish to ask. Such questions would never be answered. He felt content to savor the growing cool of the night air, the sense of infinite peace that came over the desert at this hour. Impossible at such moments to believe its hostility, the knife- edge of insecurity on which life was lived there, the violence and cruelty it provoked in men! He had seen more than enough of that, in the last couple of days. But things need not be that way, the evening calm seemed to be saying. Men don't need to kill and mutilate one another. There is another way, if only the greed and pride and anger in our hearts could be driven out. After all, what difference does it make? None. Men spend their furious little lives and in moments they are gone—what did they gain from all that futile scurrying? But we remain the same, evening and desert and sky. We were here before you came, and long after you've gone. we will remain; the same stars will wheel across the heavens, the same night wind will cool the sands..

A shiver passed through him. Such thoughts were strange to him, and frightening, and he thrust them from him, he had business to attend to. Check the hermit first. He touched the man's cheek. and was surprised to feel that it was cool and moist with sweat. His fever's broken, he thought. He may still live. This time his lips closed around the mouth of the waterbottle and he seemed to be sucking at it, like a baby, but he never recovered consciousness. Darion refilled the bottle from the gourd, drank what was left in it and threw it away, because he could not carry the hermit and the gourd too without spilling its contents.

Next he groped his way into the back of the cave, felt around until he discovered a cleft in the rocks and put his moneybag into it, having first taken out some coins which he concealed in the hollowed-out interiors of the heels of his sandals. No way he could carry all that money as well as a man. Indeed, he would be safer without it, for if any Romans had escaped massacre by the Mazices they would have reported that two bandits and their loot were loose in the desert somewhere and anyone who saw him would immediately suspect him. He covered the cleft with stones, working entirely by touch, and hoped the result would go unnoticed in the unlikely event that anyone entered the cave. Indeed, he himself might not find it again, but he had to take that chance.

By the time he finished these tasks, darkness had fallen. He looked out of the cave. No moon, but the stars shone brilliantly. He turned, slung his waterbottle over one arm, picked up the hermit and with a single swift movement swung him across his shoulders. He didn't weigh much—maybe half the weight of a normal man, and Darion's body, though not big, had a wiry strength. It's not now you'll feel it, he told himself, it's around noon tomorrow you'll get some idea what he really weighs. Holding a leg and an arm, he twisted his shoulders until the hermit was balanced on them exactly, with legs hanging on Darion's left side, arms on his right. Then he took a foot in one hand and a wrist in the other to keep the hermit in place, and set off down the slope.

He walked for two hours. The hermit's mouth was only inches away from his right ear, and Darion could hear him breathing. A couple of times, when Darion stumbled and almost fell, he mumbled a little, quite incoherently, still without regaining consciousness. Even if his fever had passed, he was so weak that the least shock might finish him. And Darion no longer hoped for the hermit's demise. On the contrary, he now desperately wanted him to live. He had invested a great deal of time and energy in saving the hermit—he would feel almost resentful if, after all his efforts, the hermit ungratefully went and died on him.

So after two hours he stopped to rest, laying the hermit gently on the ground, giving him water as before, drinking sparingly himself, then dozing for an hour or so. When he awoke there was a reddish smear on the eastern horizon, and within minutes the moon had risen, red and swollen, three-quarters full. He could now see more clearly and travel with greater confidence. So the night slowly passed, with alternating spells of rest and travel, until the moon, now well over towards the west, began to pale, black faded to grey above, then to a faint greyish-blue, streaked with cirrus clouds, and at last the rim of the earth turned golden before him.

As he walked, tiring now, feeling the pressure of the hermit on his aching shoulders, Darion gazed around him in disappointment. An oasis had been too much to hope for, but at least there might have been a cave, a cliff, a tall rock that cast some shade, if only for an hour or so. There was nothing. The flat, stony landscape, with a few patches of thorny scrub here and there stretched away on all sides for as far as he could see. No shade anywhere. Nothing to do but keep going. He had started to feel thirst already but couldn't be sure how much came from a genuine need for water and how much from fear of having none. He resolved not to drink until the feeling had become really intolerable. And then only the merest mouthful. The worst thing was not knowing how long the little water he had would have to last.

I've carried him all night, he thought, isn't that enough? How long must I go on? Until I drop from exhaustion? Then it'll be too late for me. If I leave him, I have a chance.

You can't do that, another voice inside him said. It's a sacred trust. You took it on voluntarily; you can't let it go now.

I'll give him another two hours, he told himself. If there's water then, or shade, or people who will help us, fine. If not, that's it. Finish. I shall walk away and not look back. You can only do so much.

You can do whatever you choose to do, the voice assured him.

Shut up! he said. I don't need this. I'm doing what I can. I'm a fucking saint to have done this much. aren't I? Who else would? Who else in our bunch, eh, answer me that! Not one of them and you know it, And what about his brothers? The other hermits? How many of them would have done this much? They'd have folded his hands on his chest, said a couple of prayers and dumped him.

Not Moses, the voice said.

Well, maybe not Moses, but so what? Guy like that could carry one under each arm and not notice it. Besides, he's supposed to do stuff like that. He's a holy man. I'm not. I'm a robber, a brigand, if there's a hell like those folks say there is, that's where I'm going so why am I wasting my time doing this kind of shit? Should have dumped him hours ago. Should have left the dumb bastard back there where I found him. Why did he have to go there, anyway? Dumb prick!

However, he kept on walking, and he did not put the hermit down. An hour passed. Two. Remorselessly, the desert heated up. He could feel the sweat oozing out of his forehead. Water that he must replace or die. But more than half the contents of the bottle had gone already, and there was no refuge anywhere, no shade, nothing. The same flat emptiness stretching out on every side. To the south, to the north, low undulations that looked like, if you got into them deep enough, they might become hills. But he dared not go south or north. He had to go east, because that was the only place where he could be sure of water. And to the east of him, the stone-strewn wilderness stretched out as far as the eye could reach, an endless monotony of flat and featureless space.

When almost three hours had passed and nothing had appeared on the horizon, he stopped, laid the hermit on the ground, sipped at his diminishing supply, hesitated a moment, decided it would be a waste to give the hermit any and began to walk again. That's it, he assured himself. That's enough. You've all but reached the end of your strength and nobody could blame you. You did everything possible. Now walk. Just walk, don't look back. You look back, you're finished. He can't complain. Just bad luck. Things could have gone differently but they didn't. Shit happens to all of us, more to some than to others.

He looked back.

He tried not to but he couldn't help it. He looked back and there on the bare baked ashen-colored ground lay a small brownish heap, the sun-darkened body in its pathetic tatters of reed. Frail as a bird's body, bones sticking through the skin. No hope now. Doomed. Doomed by you. You're not dead yet, are you, Darion? You'll go on and you'll live and one day you'll be drinking in a tavern somewhere with the sun shining outside and the thought will come upon you, he died. He died because you let him. All these years you've been enjoying your life and all this time he's been dead and had nothing. Your choice. Because you were weak and afraid. Because your heart wasn't big enough for anyone but yourself.

Darion hopped from foot to foot, cursing, but unable to move forward. All right then, fuck you, he cried out—turned, and walked back. Standing over the hermit, he called him every unspeakable name that his memory could call to mind. When he could think of nothing more to say, he picked up the hermit, less carefully than the last time, threw him across his shoulders, and started once more to walk eastwards.

Another hour passed. His legs were beginning to sag. Each time they bent, at each step, he had to make an effort to straighten them again. How much longer could he go on like this? He had slowed down already. At this pace he could never hope to get there, wherever there was. Already he was beginning to feel lightheaded. Soon, delusions would set in. After that, he wouldn't last long. This was his last chance to abandon the hermit. Within minutes, perhaps, it would be too late.

He kept on going. He knew now that their fates, his and the hermit's, were indissolubly bound. They would live or die together. He couldn't abandon him now. He had passed up too many chances.

Then, on the horizon, came a sudden flicker of movement.

He stopped, let go the hermit's arm, which swung down limply, so as to shade his eyes against the late morning glare. It was a moving cloud of dust with a small black dot at the head of it. As he watched, the dot resolved itself into a man on horseback, riding fast. He was coming nearer, but at an oblique angle; Darion calculated that, if he maintained his present course, he would pass within half a mile of them. The thought that came instantly to mind—signal to him, somehow!—was succeeded instantaneously by another: don't!. No one but a barbarian or a Roman would be riding a horse in the desert. Few Egyptians rode horses and those that did would have no business here.

But which would be better, a quick death from a swordstroke or a long and lingering death from thirst? Darion was still hesitating when the horseman saw him. Immediately he tightened his reins and swung the horse into a new direction. And as he did so, his left hand went to the sheath at his belt and drew out a long, wickedly-curving scimitar.

A rush of adrenalin poured into Darion's bloodstream. Seconds before he had been on the verge of collapse from exhaustion. Now his brain was racing, while a surge of energy from some source he never knew he possessed coursed through his system, waking every cell in his body, releasing urgent messages that sped from brain to extremities, from extremities to brain. Here, facing a death that was less than a minute away, he had never been more alive, more aware. In a matter of seconds, he had worked out his only chance of survival.

He swung the hermit off his back and dumped him, without even looking, on the ground behind him. He drew his dagger, gripped it with his thumb along the hilt, the sharper edge of the blade uppermost. The rider was left-handed. He was going to pass a yard or so to Darion's left and would probably try to take off his head in a single stroke. For whatever reason. Maybe to see if he could. Maybe he'd just had the blade sharpened and wanted to test it. Maybe it was a new weapon and he wanted to first-blood it. Darion had heard of people like that.

At the last possible instant, Darion would throw his left arm up and forward, at an oblique angle. He would lose the arm, of course. He was prepared for that. When he was little more than a kid he had learned how to fight from an old bandit, a knife-fighter with a scary reputation. If you're in a fight and you don't have a shield of any kind, the old man had told him, use your hand. Go for the knife. But you might lose the hand, Darion had objected. True, said the old man, who still had both hands, although they were both fearfully scarred. But which would you rather lose—your hand or your life? He'd never forgotten that. This time it would be a whole arm, but the argument still held. He wouldn't be good for much, afterwards, except begging. Actually he might do better at begging, without an arm. At least he would still be alive.

As his left arm absorbed the stroke of the scimitar, he would strike upwards. Since the horse was a small one, hardly more than a pony, the blade of the dagger should enter the horseman's groin and his very speed, without effort on Darion's part, should drive it in up to the hilt. As it went in, Darion would rip it upwards, letting his wrist turn over with the pressure. At best, this would tear his opponent's guts out;

in any case, it would give him a wound that would probably make him fall from his horse, and before he could recover...

How Darion would then catch the horse and mount it, with only one arm, and what he would then do about the hermit, were things he could safely leave until afterwards, if he was still there to worry about them. All of these thoughts raced through his mind in the couple of dozen seconds it took from the drawing of the horseman's scimitar to the moment when, only a few feet away, he raised it to strike.

In those seconds, Darion had seen something that might have struck terror in the heart of a less reckless man. A round object hanging from the barbarian's belt, tied to it by its own hair, had resolved itself from a vague thing the size and shape of a coconut to Copros' head, its mouth gaping wide, its glassy eyes round and open, fixed in an expression of unspeakable horror and dread.

Now! Now was the moment!

Darion flung up his left arm and hurled himself up and forward, thrusting with his right—

He leapt into vacancy.

He could not understand what had happened. One instant, the horseman was there in front of him, scimitar raised, barreling down at full speed, his face a frozen mask of ferocity. Then, off balance, out of control, Darion was plunging face foremost towards the sand, fighting in vain to recover himself while the thunder of flying hooves circled round him. Then he hit the ground, the air forced from his lungs by the force of impact, helpless, vulnerable, his neck exposed to the rider's fury.

He lay there, waiting for the stroke that would finish him.

Chapter Eleven

The barbarian horseman had swerved at the last instant. He had fully intended to kill Darion, for the same reason that he and his companions had killed Copros. Both men were obviously bandits, and while the Mazices had no principled objection to armed robbery as such, since they frequently practiced it themselves, they had a particular objection in this case. For if Egyptian bandits took to hiding out in the area, then Roman troops might come in after them, and if Roman troops were constantly patrolling there, life would become that much more difficult for the Mazices.

But even as his arm rose to strike, the rider saw behind the bandit. lying in the sand, what he had hitherto assumed to be the carcass of a sheep or goat, but now saw was a man. A man, moreover, that he thought he recognized. Or at least he knew the man's profession, what he stood for. He kept his scimitar raised, swung his horse's head round and the beast's hooves missed the unconscious hermit by inches. Then he slowed the horse to a walk and brought it back in a slow circle.

Darion was scrambling to his feet. He could not believe that he was still alive, actually unhurt. Bewildered, he saw the horse walking slowly towards him, the rider sheathing his scimitar. He realized his own dagger was still in his hand, and quickly put it back in its sheath. The rider stopped a couple of paces away and said in bad Coptic, 'Greetings, traveler.'

Darion stared as if mesmerized at the head of his former companion that still hung from the rider's belt, just above eye level, thinking, he cuts my buddy's head off and then greets me as an equal, what's happening here? It cost him a physical effort to pull himself together enough to answer, 'Greetings to you, and peace be with you.'

The rider nodded acknowledgment, and pointed to the unconscious hermit. 'Holy man?'

Darion nodded furiously. 'Yes, yes, holy man,' he repeated.

The rider pointed at Darion, made a gesture as if hoisting something onto his shoulder. 'You? Carry?'

'Yes,' Darion agreed. 'I was carrying him.'

The rider sought for a word, failed to find it, and then, pointing at the hermit, began to breathe in an exaggerated fashion. Darion thought at first the man was having some kind of fit—the Mazices were known for such things, trances, possession, all manner of psychic weirdness. Then he realized the rider was asking, 'Is the holy man still alive?'

'Yes! Alive, alive,' Darion said eagerly, thinking, by the gods he'd better be, hope I didn't snap his neck, dropping him like that, because if he's dead, I'm gone too.

The rider walked his horse forward until it was almost on top of the hermit, then made a lifting gesture. He was asking Darion to lift the hermit onto the horse. Obediently Darion did so, putting his cheek close to the hermit's face as he lifted him, and feeling, to his inexpressible relief, a faint current of air from the man's breath. The body brushed against Copros's dangling head as the rider took it from him, but the rider seemed to notice nothing incongruous in this. He carefully arranged the body across the horse's back, directly in front of him, face-down, like a half-folded jackknife, with trunk, head and arms dangling one side, thighs and legs the other.

What now, Darion wondered. With luck, he leaves me; without, he cuts me down. He braced himself, ready to spring to one side. But the horseman took neither course. Instead, he tapped his ankle, then gestured at Darion's hand. He had to repeat the gestures before Darion grasped his meaning.

Incredulous, Darion pointed to himself, then made as if to grasp the rider's ankle. The rider nodded impatiently. Darion held on and the rider clapped his heels into the horse's flanks. Instantly it took off, not galloping this time, but at a brisk trot.

Darion's heart alternately soared with elation and plunged in sheer panic. For some inscrutable reason, perhaps because he thought Darion too was a holy man—who but a brother would carry a brother?—or perhaps through some irrational whim such as the Mazices were famed for, the rider had apparently decided to save him too. But the horse was moving slightly faster than Darion could have run, even in peak condition. Exhausted as he was, the journey was a nightmare. He knew that if he let go the rider's ankle the rider would never bother to turn back for him. So he moved in a series of irregular bounds, periodically losing his footing, being jerked forwards while his feet, kicking in midair, fought frantically to grip the speeding ground. He knew that whenever this happened the rider must suffer discomfort or even pain and he expected momentarily that the scimitar would come swishing down and he would be left standing there with the stump of an arm spouting blood. But the rider endured it all stoically; one does not survive in deserts by letting minor discomforts disturb one.

Soon Darion's fear of the rider's displeasure gave place to a more realistic fear, that he would cease to be able to hang on. His hand felt weak and sore, as if his wristbones might at any moment be torn from their sockets. He gasped for breath, his head spun dizzily, he could hardly see. But the horse kept up its steady pace, and he dared not ask its rider to slow down. Nor could he cease to be aware of Copros's head, almost on a level with his own and a mere couple of feet away from it, bobbing up and down rhythmically in time with the horse's motions, but without any change in its stare of frozen horror.

Darion was barely conscious when they finally came within sight of their destination. For some time they had been descending into a gradual fold in the ground, to the north of the route Darion had been traveling, and quite invisible from it. Then the fold opened out and in a shallow valley they saw sparse vegetation, a cluster of tents. Horses and camels were tethered close to a stone parapet where men were hauling up buckets of water and emptying them into a long stone trough, while others were bringing beasts to the trough to drink.

The horseman dismounted at the well, and Darion, dizzy and staggering once he had let go the man's ankle, collapsed in a heap. He no longer cared whether they killed him or not. But after a while a tribesman with a leather bottle came across from the well and offered it to him. He drank greedily. Over the tribesman's shoulder he saw that the horseman had removed Copros's head from his belt and a group of boys were using it as a football. Three or four other Mazices were carrying the limp body of the hermit into the encampment. 'Where are they taking him?' he asked, but the man simply shrugged his shoulders. Then the horseman and two others came towards him and gestured for him to accompany them.

Darion walked, with one either side of him and a third close behind him, to a tent in the center of the encampment that looked more ornate than its neighbors. On the floor of the tent was a rug that had been woven into the form of a picture, a triumphal procession of some sort, but Darion's attention was immediately drawn to the figure seated cross-legged at the far end of the rug, an older man with a hawk's beak of a nose and darkly glittering eyes that fixed on Darion with an unblinking stare. The elder motioned to Darion to sit down—a slight, almost unnoticeable gesture. but the man exuded an air of absolute confidence that his least gesture would be unquestioningly obeyed.

Darion sat down, and the three men accompanying him sat too, in the same formation—one each side, one behind—so that he knew that, no matter what politenesses were exchanged, he was effectively a prisoner. The elder withdrew his gaze from Darion and addressed the men in their own language. Darion didn't understand a word of it but he could infer a good deal from the quick, incisive questions and the more rambling, painfully respectful answers. Then the elder looked back at him and greeted him in passable Coptic. He responded suitably. He was asked his name, and gave it. The elder said, 'You're a bandit, aren't you?'

Darion hesitated only a second. Futile to lie to a man like that, and probably fatal, too. 'I am,' he admitted.

'Why were you carrying the holy man?'

'He's sick. I was trying to take him to the settled lands.'

The elder laughed. It was not an unfriendly laugh, but it held complacent overtones of superior knowledge. 'You would never have made it.'

Darion shrugged.

'Where did you find him?'

'There's...I mean there was an oasis back there,' Darion gestured towards the west, 'a day's march or so, with an old temple that— '

The elder pounced. 'What do you mean, was?'

'It collapsed. In the storm, maybe. There's sand everywhere now. 'The spring's gone.'

The elder stared at him in amazement, then he and the others spoke rapidly, overlapping one another, in their language. But they did not sound as if they disbelieved him.

Then the elder said, 'We know this holy man. He lived by that temple. He cured one of our people. A woman. She was blind. He is a good man.'

Darion said nothing.

'Did you know him, before?'

Darion shook his head.

'Then why did you help him?'

'I don't know,' Darion said.

'You knew you were risking your own life.'

'Yes, I knew that.'

The elder shook his head as if in puzzlement and there was another exchange in the barbarous language. Then the elder said, 'Our women are cleansing him now. They will do what they can for him. But we cannot keep him. We are a nomadic people. We cannot care for the helpless.'

Again, no reply seemed expected, and Darion kept silent.

'If we take you both to the settled lands can you find people to look after him?'

'Yes, of course,' Darion said, without even thinking whether he could or not.

'If we had found you alone, we would have killed you. This is our territory. We don't want bandits, escaped slaves or fugitives from justice here. If you come again, we will kill you on sight. Do you understand that?'

'Yes, I understand.'

The curt flip of the elder's hand indicated that the interview was at an end. As Darion and the three tribesmen stood up, the elder said, 'I will lend you two horsemen for the journey. You cannot reach there today. You will start at dawn tomorrow. You will have food and shelter here until then. No one will harm you.'

Darion bowed his head. 'I thank you, sir. You are very generous.'

The elder made a dismissive gesture. 'Don't thank me. Thank the holy man. Look after him well. We care nothing for you. Our hospitality to you is merely part of our debt to him.'

The three men escorted Darion out of the tent. He was only just beginning to realize the full significance of the day's events. He had believed he was putting his own life at risk by helping the hermit. In fact helping the hermit was the one thing that had saved him. He remembered how many times he had been on the point of abandoning the man, and how rational and irrefutable the arguments for doing so had seemed. But the instinct for self-preservation did not always choose the best way to preserve the self. And virtue, at least sometimes, could be more than its own reward.

Yet things could have easily turned out differently. If the horseman hadn't intercepted him, if he had walked on past the limits of his endurance, the same actions would have spelled death. How were such things decided? Was it pure chance? Or was there a destiny that guided men's paths?

He spent much time pondering such questions during the next twenty-four hours. Not that he had ever felt philosophic inclinations, indeed he had never before concerned himself with such things. But he had nothing better to do now. Although the Mazices treated him civilly, it seemed that hardly any of them spoke anything but their own barbarous tongue, and then most of the next day he spent with his nose in a tribesman's smelly hair and his arms locked round the man's waist, bouncing up and down on the bony buttocks of a horse being ridden at full speed eastwards, with the hermit draped across a companion's horse at his side—circumstances hardly conducive to conversation.

He had learned, at least, that their path would bring them to the Nile valley somewhere between Oxyrhynchus and Arsinoe. In a village called Tebtynis, to the south of Arsinoe, he had family, a cousin with a small farm and his wife, who had accepted Christianity and who was working hard to get her husband to follow her. The cousin quite liked him, the wife didn't, but between blood ties, religious affinities and the gold coins he had secreted in his sandal, Darion thought he should be able to swing something.

The two horsemen stopped a mile or more short of the settled lands. 'No further?' Darion asked. Whether they understood or not, they shook their heads, and he realized that Mazices in the settled lands would have an even shorter life expectancy than bandits in Mazices territory. So he dismounted, and the hermit was handed down to him. The riders saluted coldly, turned, and galloped off.

Darion walked about four miles, with the hermit across his shoulders, until he reached a hamlet. There he succeeded in renting a donkey and a small cart. He had by now become quite attached to the hermit. He spoke to him often, although the hermit, now wrapped in a clean robe, but still apparently in a profound coma, never once answered him. He led the donkey most of the time, riding in the cart with the hermit only occasionally, so as to spare the donkey. Either side of the road they followed, men and women were hard at work in the fields, gathering in the grain harvest before the Nile rose and flooded the land. They were too busy to do more than stare, occasionally wave and shout something at the passing cart, for which Darion was grateful. He waved back and they passed by, without questions.

In the afternoon of the next day they came to Tebtynis. The cousin's farm lay to the south of the village, so they did not need to enter it. As Darion had expected, cousin and wife too were out working in the fields. He explained his mission to them. The cousin was incredulous at first, then amused. The wife was skeptical. Who was this fellow? How did they know he was a hermit? How did they know he wasn't a member of Darion's gang, and Darion was just using them, getting a hideout for him? What would they say if the police came? Darion showed one of his gold coins, and at this the cousin, who had been growing visibly more impatient, said, 'Shut up, woman,' and Darion felt he would probably have hit her if he and a couple of neighbors helping with the crop had not been present. They adjourned to the cousin's house, a low, dark cottage of mud brick, where the only light came from the outer doorway or from narrow, open niches left in the walls; chickens ran in and out freely, and roosted on the roof-beams. For an agreed sum, the couple would look after the hermit until he recovered and could earn his own living.

'What if it's not enough?' the wife asked. Darion told her that she could recoup the balance from the hermit's wages. 'What if he's never fit enough to earn anything?' she objected. 'What if he's paralyzed?'

'Then I'll make it up to you,' Darion said, mentally vowing never to go there again. 'Next time I come.'

'A likely story,' the wife sniffed.

But the cousin had had enough. 'You're always on to me about Christian charity,' he grumbled. 'Well, now you've got a Christian of your own to look after. So go look after him, woman. Make up a bed for him in the back room, and make sure you tie the donkey so it can't kick him.'

And thus the matter was settled. When the bed was made up, if you could dignify by that term the throwing of a couple of moldy blankets over a heap of straw, Darion and his cousin carried the hermit from the donkey-cart into the house. On being lifted, he twisted spasmodically and Darion thought his eyes were going to open, but they did not. As they laid him down, Darion surreptitiously squeezed his hand. So long, old buddy, he murmured to himself. Like the girl that time, you don't even know my name. Just as well, really. Bad for my reputation if stuff like that gets around.

He refused his cousin's offer of a night's lodging, pleading urgent business, and rattled off in his donkey-cart. His plea did not derive entirely from a distaste for his cousin's wife's company. Mazices or no Mazices, he was going to rent a fast horse and go back for those three hundred gold pieces while he could still remember the way there. It was one thing to do a charitable deed, quite another to let oneself lose money by it.

Chapter Twelve

In the White Monastery, Leila was working out her three-month novitiate. She was lodged in the gatehouse, under the watchful eye of the Master of Novices. It had surprised her at first to find a man in charge of a group of virgins, especially in an institution where, she had heard, men and women were treated equally. But the Master was not the only male authority figure. Although the women's monastery was supposed to be ruled by the Elder Mother, aided by her Second, the Elder Mother could decide nothing without the consent of the Elder Brother who also lived within the women's monastery. Only gradually, as the months passed, did she come to understand the reason for this.

Shenoute controlled the White Monastery absolutely. Nothing happened within it that he did not hear about. Nothing that happened without his consent went unpunished. The Elder Brother reported directly to Shenoute, telling him everything, no matter how trivial, that went on among the women. He passed on Shenoute's instructions to the Elder Mother, and checked to see if those instructions were carried out. He had more sinister functions too, but some months passed before Leila realized what these were.

For the time being, she slept in the dormitory of the gatehouse. If they admitted her to the women's monastery proper, one of the other novices told her, she would share a cell with another virgin.

'Not like at Tabbenesi,' a second novice chimed in.

They were not supposed to be talking. They were supposed to be silent while they worked, in the communal living quarters, sewing tunics for the monks. But the Mother of Novices was meeting with the Elder Mother and her Second, while the Master of Novices had gone off somewhere, no one would presume to ask him where.

'What about Tabennesi?' the first novice asked.

'At Tabennesi you get a cell to yourself.'

'But you don't get a bed in it,' a third novice aid.

'That's not true!' the second novice protested.

'It is too!'

The other novices hushed them urgently. Who could tell when the Mother of Novices might return?

'I know because I have a brother who went to Tabennesi,' the third novice went on in a hoarse whisper. 'And he said they all sleep on chairs.'

'That's just the men,' the second novice insisted. 'The women get beds.'

'They do not!' The third novice was adamant. 'That's the Pachomian Rule. Same for everybody. And they have to get up and pray half the night, too.'

'That's why they only have chairs,' said a voice from the back of the room, and several of the novices giggled.

'Well, that's more holy, I think,' the second novice said.

'What, sleeping in chairs?' More giggles.

'No, keeping vigil.'

'Our holy father Shenoute thinks it's bad for us,' the first novice said proudly. 'Our holy father Shenoute thinks we should rest our bodies so we can work better.'

'And how do you know what Father Shenoute thinks?' the second novice asked.

'Because the Mother of—'

The first novice broke off abruptly. The Master of Novices, treading noiselessly, had appeared in the room before anyone had noticed his approach. He was a lean, bald man in late middle age, who moved with a look of intent preoccupation, as if wholly absorbed in his interior world. However, as the novices had soon learned, this abstracted manner served only disguise a beady-eyed vigilance that missed nothing. Now he stood in silence as the women bent over their needles, eyes downcast, a picture of industrious virtue.

'Thaesis,' he said after the better part of a minute had passed.

'Yes, Father?' A somewhat older, heavy-featured novice with a faint mustache on her upper lip answered him.

'Thaesis. Who was talking just now?'

'Sansno, Isidora, Tanouris and Leila, Father.'

'I was not speaking!' Leila cried out instinctively. Then she bit her tongue.

'Did I address you, Leila?' the Master asked.

'No, Father.'

'What is the rule for novices in this institution?'

Leila flushed crimson. 'A novice does not speak unless a superior addresses her, Father,' she mumbled.

'Exactly. As you are our most recent entrant I shall overlook this occasion. But make sure you don't do it again.' He turned back to Thaesis. 'Did Leila speak?'

Thaesis hesitated. 'Well...Tanouris was speaking to her. But I didn't actually hear her answer.'

'So it was just Tanouris, Sansno, and Isidora.'

'And somebody else said something, but I couldn't see who it was.'

The Master of Novices clasped his hands behind his back and rocked gently backwards and forwards on the balls of his feet. The faint creak of his sandals alone disturbed the silence.

'What were they talking about?' he asked at last.

'Tabennesi, Father.'

'*Tabennesi!*' The Master pronounced the name of the rival monastery in tones of theatrical surprise and horror. 'And what were they saying about Tabennesi, my child?'

'Isidora was saying it's nicer than here,' Thaesis said smugly.

'Nicer than here, hm?'

'More holy, Father.'

The Master brooded, pulling on his lower lip. 'And the others?'

'The others were saying it wasn't.'

'I see.' The Master turned, as if to stalk out, then stopped and said, 'Well in that case, perhaps I might turn a blind eye to Sansno and Tanouris...This time.'

Utter silence followed his departure. Leila longed to ask, what will happen to Isidora now? But she dared not. Soon the Mother of Novices returned from her meeting, and she must have been briefed by the Master, for she did not let them out of her sight for the rest of the day. Isidora tried to assume an air of blithe indifference whenever her gaze met anyone else's.

Neither the Mother no any of the superior sisters said anything to her, and she was still there when they went to bed. But when Leila awoke next morning, Isidora was gone.

Thereafter, it was as if she had ceased to exist. Nobody mentioned her, and when Leila started to ask any of the other novices, they ignored her or hushed her into silence. Like it was some secret too dreadful to be talked about. But none of them were supposed to have secrets. The Mother of Novices was most strict about that. They were supposed to confess to the Mother any secret thoughts they might have. Thoughts of lust or pride or avarice, anything at all that they wouldn't like other people to know about. And they were also expected to report immediately any sin they had committed, or any sin anyone else had committed. Was a novice hoarding personal possessions, even anything so trivial as a needle? Had a novice gossiped about another, or called her names? Was anyone eating too little (vainglory) or too much (gluttony)?

Leila found it vaguely disturbing that there were secrets and secrets—one rule for the novices, another for their superior—but she told herself that this was as it should be. You had to have strict rules for novices if they were going to be become seasoned sisters. It wasn't for her to question authority.

So she remained quiet, and attentive, and obedient. Obedience, she had divined, was the highest-rated virtue in the

White Monastery. Once a day at the ninth hour she filed into the gatehouse refectory with the other novices, and ate in silence the meager meal of bread, water and vegetables brought in daily from the women's monastery. Several times a day she filed meekly with the other novices into the gatehouse chapel, where the Master of Novices conducted the service and the Mother of Novices watched like a lynx for whispered exchanges, lack of due reverence, inappropriately loud psalm-singing and the like.

Unlike some of the other novices, Leila found nothing irksome in this enforced decorum. Naturally modest and pliable, she felt no impulse to gossip about her companions, to hoard food, to show off her superior holiness or do any of the other things that might prevent her acceptance into the women's monastery. That part of the discipline at least she thoroughly understood and sympathized with. And she would surely find life less restrictive once she had graduated from the gatehouse. Then, surely, the occasional meanness and pettiness of spirit she had encountered, perhaps deliberately designed to test the patience and forbearance of the novices, would disappear. She would find herself then in the company of sisters far more advanced than herself in the paths of righteousness—sisters she could admire and imitate, and hope one day to equal in the selfless service of Our Lord.

One morning, the Mother of Novices came to wake her, before all the others. For the first time in three months, she left the confines of the gatehouse, crossed a broad cobbled courtyard in the grey light of dawn, and entered the women's monastery for the first time. Along a corridor, through an arched cloister, into the main chapel. Beside the altar stood the Elder Mother, her Second, the Elder Brother, the Master of Novices—the whole hierarchy, save for Shenoute himself.

'Kneel,' the Mother of Novices whispered in her ear. Leila knelt before the altar. Her heart was filled with joy. A joy at least as profound as any bride might feel on her wedding day. For this was indeed a wedding, as many learned writers had pointed out. She was a Bride of Christ. The loyalty and devotion other women gave to a mere human like themselves, she would give to Him Who was both human and more than human, Who partook of two Natures (although he remained one Person). But this marriage would not be soiled by the selfish vileness of lust nor by the anguish of childbirth that lust brought in its train. It would endure eternally, if she herself did not betray it.

The Elder Brother stepped forward. 'Do you, Leila, renounce all worldly possessions, whatsoever their nature, and promise that you will surrender to the White Monastery any possessions that you may, through any gift, transaction or inheritance, receive in the future?'

'I do, Father,' Leila answered.

'Then sign this,' the Elder Brother said, presenting her with a sheet of papyrus. 'You know how to write?'

'I can write my name, Father.'

'Good.' He waited while she scratched awkwardly.

'Now before you can be admitted to the monastery, you must take a solemn oath, before this altar, and hence before the Almighty God Whom this altar represents, that you will abide by the Rule of this monastery, under pain of eternal punishment. Do you understand the solemn and binding nature of such an oath?'

'I do, Father.'

'Good. Then repeat after me, I vow in the presence of God...'

'I vow in the presence of God...'

'In this holy place...'

'In this holy place...'

When she had finished, the Elder Brother handed her another piece of papyrus. 'You know how to read?'

'If there aren't too many long words, Father,'

The Elder Brother permitted himself a smile. 'Then read this carefully before you sign it. It's what you just swore to. If there's anything you don't understand, you may ask me.'

Leila took the sheet and read, 'I vow in the presence of God in this holy place, the words which I utter with my mouth bearing witness, that I will not pollute my body in any way, I will not steal, I will not bear false witness, I will not lie, I will not practice any kind of deceit in secret. If I break this vow, may I behold the Kingdom of Heaven but not enter therein. May God in whose presence I have sworn this oath destroy my body and soul in the fires of Hell.'

She signed.

'And I should warn you that there will be punishment in this world as well as the next if you violate any article of this covenant,' the Elder Brother said sternly.

Leila bowed her head,

'You may rise,' the Elder Mother said, speaking for the first time. 'You are now a sister in the White Monastery. That is a high honor. See to it that you deserve it.' She signaled to her Second. 'Mother Tachom, will you show the new sister to her cell?'

In the wake of the lean harsh-faced woman who did not even look at her, but who turned and walked ahead of her in perfect certainty that she would follow, Leila left the chapel to begin her new life.

Chapter Thirteen

It was some days before Zachary recovered consciousness. They had called in the village doctor, or what passed as such, a discharged legionary who had been an orderly in the medical corps of the Roman army. But since his experience did not extend much beyond setting simple fractures and administering purges, he could do little to help. The hermit would either live, or he would not, he assured them. 'I could have told you as much,' Darion's cousin Didymos said testily, 'without charging five drachmas for it.' At which the ex-legionary, in a huff, washed his hands of the case. And Didymos's wife, being a Christian, would allow no traditional healers, since that would involve sorcery and other pagan practices. So, there the matter rested.

After a couple of days the wife, who had been born Thenapychnis but preferred to be known as Sophia, because it had more class, noticed that the hermit's eyes were open. She passed her hand in front of them, and the eyes blinked. She gave a small shriek and ran to tell her husband. 'Can he speak?' Didymos asked. She admitted she had not thought to check that. 'Then go back and see,' said Didymos, who was playing dice with a friend, since he had sent all his grain to the threshing-floor and would have nothing to do now until the Nile flood had come and gone. He had just thrown Venus twice running, and didn't want to break his luck.

Sophia hurried into the room Zachary shared with the donkey. 'Are you awake...sir?' She wasn't sure how the hermit should be addressed. Despite his sickness she could see he had been handsome, with a delicacy of feature you didn't often see in country villages. She had heard tales of the sons of great families, from Alexandria, Rome even, who had given up everything to go off into the desert. If he was one of these, his family might give a large reward to know where he was. 'Sir...can you hear me, sir?' she asked.

Zachary's lips moved but no sound came out.

'Can I get you something? Something to eat?'

Zachary tried to speak, but the effort was too much for him and his eyes closed, his head rolled over on the old sack stuffed with straw that served as his pillow. Though he seemed unconscious, his mind was working again for the first time.

Where was he? The last thing he could remember clearly was the collapse of the temple, the great avalanche of sand and stone crashing down into the valley, burying the spring. After that, only confused, nightmarish fragments—whether these reflected reality or dreams, who could tell? He had not expected to live, he remembered that. He had assumed, when he first recovered consciousness, that he must already have arrived in the next world. But his surroundings, what little he could see of them, did not fit any description of the hereafter known to him. Rather they resembled the interior of an Egyptian peasants' hut, and the female figure that had just confronted him resembled nothing more than an Egyptian peasant's wife. He must therefore have moved somehow from the interior desert to the settled lands. But how? And who were his hosts, and why?

Too many questions, each could wait. And while they waited, his interest flagged. What did it matter, anyway? He felt his whole being submerged in a profound apathy. And when he thought of the weeks that had preceded the fall of the temple, when he remembered the desperation of his prayers, it was as though he were watching another person entirely. Someone who had nothing to do with the Zachary that was lying here, who shared with him only a name, who might as well have died back there in the desert, for of that other person there was left only a half-incredulous memory.

He repeated the words that had held such power for that other Zachary. God. Christ. Holiness. Salvation. They had no resonance for him anymore. They fell through his mind like stones into a waterless well, a well so deep that if they struck bottom anywhere, the sound of it was too far for him to hear. It was as if what had happened to him in the desert had burned out of him every feeling he had ever known.

Idly his mind wandered over his past life. The figures who inhabited it looked tiny, remote, filling him with a sense of indifference. Papnoute, a fanatical martinet. John Colobos, Johnny Bobtail, a scatterbrained old fairy, ducking into his desert hole. Celia, the Prefect of Egypt's whore—much good that would do her when he got a new posting. His mother, a bustling fool, bowing and scraping to bishops. His father, a figure of glacial remoteness, strained correctness. What did they all mean to him? Nothing. What did anything mean? He was alive. He existed. Did that matter to anyone? No. Did it matter even to him? No.

He had expected death out there, but his body had not died. Only his soul had died. And the passions of his body had died with it. He no longer felt hunger, thirst, sexual desire. When the peasant woman, Sophia, as she incongruously called herself, brought him gruel or bread soaked in goat's milk, he ate it, but without desire, without pleasure.

It was ironic, really. Or rather, the irony of it might have amused him, if anything amused him. The hermit's avowed aim was to die to the world, to slay the passions. He had achieved both these goals. But the whole purpose of achieving them was to become alive in the spirit, and his spirit had died too.

As the days passed, he told them as little about himself as would curtail their curiosity. Yes, he had been alone in the desert. And before that, in Scetis. And he was born and raised in Alexandria—his accent made it futile to deny that. But for anything else, he feigned memory loss.

'And won't your family be wondering what's happened to you?' Sophia kept asking. 'Won't they want to know where you are? We can send them a message, you know.'

No, he told her, his family wouldn't care. He hinted that they had disowned him, without saying so in as many words. As for his own curiosity, that had vanished too. He did not ask who had brought him here or why. Whoever they were, he felt towards them neither gratitude nor resentment. And the people now looking after him? He gathered from what he heard that they had been paid to do this. He seemed as unwilling to ask who had given them the money as they were to tell him, so by tacit agreement the subject was never discussed. Meanwhile they treated him almost as one of the family, and he accepted their treatment without question. And the future? He did not even think of that. It did not interest him. His mind did not want to look beyond the next few hours, the next plate of gruel. It cost too much effort.

Many more days passed before he was strong enough to leave his room, even for a few moments. Then, supported on Didymos's arm, he hobbled to the door and looked out over the flat countryside towards the river. And an extraordinary sight met his eyes.

The Nile was in full flood. Didymos's house stood at the edge of the village, and the red-brown, muddy water lapped almost to the foot of its walls. Far to the east, low barren hills rose out of the flood; here and there to the south, isolated hamlets stood out as islands, completely surrounded by water. In the farthest distance, the flood took on the color of the sky, and flashed golden gleams from its ripples. A half-mile or so away, a man in a punt made out of bundles of papyrus stalks slowly poled his way across the flooded fields, while his companion fished with a handline. Much nearer, a drowned rat, bloated with gas, drifted by with minnows nibbling at its belly.

Zachary knew, of course, that the Nile flooded every year, due to the fact that on his feast-day, the Archangel Michael would deposit in the river a drop of a special liquid that made it ferment. But since his experience had been limited to the city, the coast and the desert, he had never seen the Nile in flood. So he tried to show the wonder, the delight, the appreciation that Didymos seemed to expect. In reality all he felt was, oh yes, the Nile has flooded, how interesting, how soon can I go back and lie down? The odor of feces and urine from the donkey no longer upset him, if it ever had.

As he grew stronger, these ventures into the outdoors became a daily occurrence. And it as not long before Sophia was saying, 'I'm sure you'll want to go to church, as soon as you're able to. Of course we don't have a proper church here. Not yet. There's not enough of us yet,' with a reproachful glance at Didymos, who was sitting there with his jar of beer and whistling defiantly. 'But we do have a priest now, whom I'm sure you'll want to meet.' Zachary expressed no enthusiasm about meeting the priest. Indeed, he said nothing at all, but Sophia continued, unabashed, 'Yes, I'm afraid we still have to meet in a private house, a charming Greek family, you'll love them, they're so well-bred. Oh, and you'll never believe who came here just two months ago.'

Zachary, sharing the jar of beer with Didymos, expressed neither interest in the charming Greek family nor curiosity about the visitor. 'It was the blessed Archbishop Theophilus himself! Can you imagine? Coming to a tiny little place like this? And do you know what he told us? If we can raise half the money for a church, he'll match it! He has a special fund, you see, just for building churches. Mostly in the big cities, naturally, but he doesn't forget the little villages!

Such a wonderful man! Did you ever meet him?' she asked Zachary.

Zachary did not particularly wish to recall the occasions on which his path and that of Theophilus had crossed. So he remained silent, and Didymos refilled their pot from a large earthenware jar under the table, which he could have hardly afforded without his cousin's money.

'Now we are trying to raise our share,' Sophia went on. 'Everybody contributes what they can,' and she stared malevolently at her husband, 'Of course, there are always those who would rather spend their money on their own selfish pleasures—'

'We hardly make enough to feed ourselves,' Didymos objected, 'without putting money into some newfangled—'

'It's not newfangled! It's four centuries old!'

And they were off into one of their regular arguments. Zachary tuned them out. He had the capacity, nowadays, just to sit there through an argument or any conversation that bored him without hearing a word of it. He seemed preoccupied with his own thoughts. In fact, he had no thoughts. He existed in a vegetative haze, a not unpleasant stupor that he could endure indefinitely, without boredom.

Then came a Sunday on which Sophia said, 'I'm off to church now,' in a threatening tone that said quite clearly, and what about you, you infidels?

'That's nice, dear,' Didymos said absently, whittling at a digging-stick that he would need for the fall sowing.

'Zachary, are you coming?' she demanded.

Zachary shook his head.

'I don't understand you. You were supposed to be a Christian. You were a hermit. In the desert. Or so we were led to believe. Me, I don't believe it for one moment. If you were a Christian, let alone a hermit, you'd want to go, you'd want to worship Our Lord with your fellow—'

'Shut up,' Didymos said without looking at her.

'I don't see why I should shut up, it's perfectly true what I'm saying, if you ask me your precious guest here is sailing under false colors, and I for one would like to know—'

'Shut up, woman!'

Sophia hesitated only a moment. She was into it now, all she'd been longing to say for weeks. Her nostrils flared, she banged on the rickety table, and the chickens roosting under it, alarmed, fled the house with an outraged cackling. 'I will not shut up! It's high time we got this straight, we might as well have it out here and now.' She glared at Zachary. 'Just who and what are you?'

Didymos finally looked at her and asked, 'Why don't you do what this fancy religion of yours tells you to do?'

'What do you mean? What are you talking about?'

'You told me,' Didymos said, reasonably and calmly, 'that this Jesus fellow of yours told you to love your neighbor.'

She drew herself to her full height. 'Yes. So what?'

'So love him and stop yelling at him!'

'You don't understand—' she flared out contemptuously.

'No, I never do, do I?'

'—that it's because I love him that I'm trying to get him to come with me. Because I care about his immortal soul, because—'

'And yelling at him is loving him,' Didymos said thoughtfully, as if he was really trying to understand.

'If it's for his own good! Of course it is!'

Didymos put aside the stick he was whittling and stood up. 'And just exactly what gives you the right to decide what's good for someone? Show me! Show me in that book you're always lugging around, even though you can hardly read a word of it. Just show me where it says you can yell at people and bully them if you think it's for their own good.'

Sophia faced him defiantly. 'It says you have to preach the Word—'

'Don't dodge the issue! Show me where it tells you what I just said.'

'*You* couldn't read it if I did!' she crowed triumphantly.

'All right, show him,' Didymos jerked his head at Zachary. 'Let him read it. Just show him where it says that.'

She stamped, and flounced towards the door. 'I don't have to show you anything—'

'You can't, that's why!

'—and I've had enough of this stupid argument—'

'Because it's not there, is it?'

'—so I'm off! I'm late already! Do whatever you want to do!' And she was gone, in a whirl of righteous indignation.

Didymos sat down again, and the two men remained silent for several minutes. Then, Didymos took a jar from a niche in the wall, filled it with beer and placed it on the table between them. 'The water's going down already,' he said. Zachary made no reply.

'Soon as it's down, we start the wine harvest.' Again Zachary did not speak, He drank reflectively from the jar, which Didymos had pushed over to him, then passed it wordlessly back to his host.

'I don't have any grapes, myself,' Didymos said. 'I hire out to those that have. Care to come along with me?'

After a long moment of consideration, Zachary said, 'Yes. Yes, I think I'd like that.'

'Good,' Didymos said, and the two men drank alternately from the jar, in silent companionship.

Chapter Fourteen

'Is it him?'

'Yes...Yes, I do believe it is. Anyway, I recognize the donkey. '

'Amazing.' Dioscorus, newly-appointed Bishop of Hermopolis, and his fellow Tall Brother Ammonias were leaning over the balcony of the episcopal residence, gazing down into the busy marketplace beneath. Above them, huge thunderheads soared, driven by the clash between a cool northerly wind and the late summer's receding heat. Ammonias absently fingered the scar left by his missing, ear, which tended to itch during changeable weather. 'Two things he never does: leave Scetis and answer a bishop's summons,' he said. 'You should be flattered.'

'Maybe he hasn't come to see me,' Dioscuros said. 'Maybe he's just come to sell his baskets.'

Ammonias shook his head. 'Not Poemen. He doesn't believe in gadding about. He'd think it wasteful to travel for only one purpose.'

'Well, I wonder which will get precedence.' They watched as Poemen tethered his donkey, called to a couple of ragged urchins who were kicking a stone around and pointed to the baskets. They were amused to see him squat down, bringing his head to the boys' level so as not to overawe them; the urchins were grinning at him as if he had just cracked a joke. 'He's coming here first,' Ammonias said..

'How can you tell?'

'He's getting them to watch the baskets for him. On credit. too. Never has any money. Hates the stuff.'

Ammonias was right. Waving to the boys, who puffed out their cheeks self-importantly and gave him a parody of a military salute, Poemen turned and vanished into the doorway beneath the Tall Brothers' feet, without having seen them. 'I'll leave you to it,' Ammonias said. 'I've been here too long already. I only came for your inauguration.'

'I wish you'd stay,' Dioscorus said almost plaintively

'Find him intimidating?' Ammonias's long, sardonic face curled into a smile.

'No, no, it's not that...It's just...Well, I think what I have to say to him may not go down too well.'

'You'd like some backup?'

'Frankly, yes.'

'From ME?' There was nothing feigned about Ammonias' amazement. 'I'm just about the last person to tell someone he should be ordained.'

Dioscorus smiled ruefully. "Since you mention it, yes, I suppose it is a bit odd. But I would still really value—' He broke off abruptly. Poemen, who must have somehow charmed his way through the screen of acolytes and secretaries below, had already appeared, unannounced, on the balcony. Dioscorus cut short with a firm gesture the obeisance Poemen had been about to make.

'May I congratulate your Grace on your appointment,' Poemen said.

Dioscorus listened intently for any shade of irony, but found none. Poemen's tone was sincerely respectful. 'Enough of this "Your Grace" nonsense,' the Bishop said roughly. I haven't forgotten where I came from. We're still simply brothers—I hope.'

'Of course.'

'And it was good of you to come, at such short notice.' The two men clasped hands briefly. As they did so, thunder spoke from the passing clouds, and a few heavy drops of rain fell on the balcony. 'I think we had better go indoors,' Dioscorus said. 'And at least I can now offer you something decent in the way of refreshment. You take wine. don't you? My predecessor may have been heretical, but he kept a very impressive cellar.'

Poemen said nothing. One reason he never left Scetis was because everyone came to him. They came for a word of righteousness, but in exchange they left other kinds of word: gossip, rumor, even sometimes genuine news. Not much went on in Egypt that he didn't hear about.. And he had heard that the last Bishop of Hermopolis's heresy had been somewhat exaggerated—if not actually fabricated, with the help of a couple of forged homilies.

Inside, they seated themselves at a round table, and Dioscorus, looking awkward and hesitant, rang a bell, first almost inaudibly, then louder. A black-clad servant appeared and received his instructions. Turning rather shyly to the others, the Bishop said, 'I don't know that I'm really cut out for this sort of thing. I suppose one gets used to it.'

'Many people were surprised you accepted 'it,' Poemen said, in a carefully neutral tone.

'Yes, I expect they were.'

'Some even feared you'd been coerced.'

Dioscorus laughed. 'Oh, come on! Surely not! Coerced how? Are you suggesting our good Archbishop has some hold over me? A secret sin, perhaps?'

Poemen shook his head, smiling, 'I never believed that for a moment.. But I did wonder...'

'I know. I was reluctant, of course. And not everyone agreed it was the right choice.' With a jerk of his head, Dioscorus indicated Ammonias. who smiled ruefully and said to Poemen, 'Don't blame me; I did what I could.'

'Don't think for a minute' Poemen said, 'that I'm not glad you did accept. I am. I think you were an excellent choice.'

Better than one could have expected from Theophilus, he was tempted to say, but quickly suppressed the words, even the thought, for that was judgment.

'And don't think he's flattering you, ' Ammonias said to the Bishop. 'I know him. He'd never have come all this way if he hadn't believed that.'

They were silent while the servant silently placed between them an elaborate decanter and three silver goblets. Poemen sat looking relaxed, attentive, as he always did, but this time his appearance deceived. He could never feel at ease in the presence of power differentials. If we were all equal in Christ, what was the point of them? What authority had they? Not that he resented those differentials in any personal sense. It bothered him not in the slightest that Dioscorus should be above him, he was only too willing to believe that the Bishop was his moral superior in every way. No, it was the sense of an imbalance in human relationships, symbolized by the elaborate drinking equipment, the overly obsequious servant who even backed away from them, his body bent in a half-bow, when his office was completed. How could a bishop keep his humility in such an atmosphere? How could anyone reconcile power with virtue?

Dioscorus, perhaps sharing his feeling, said as he rotated the goblet in his hand, 'I think I shall have to get rid of these. Pity—they're nice pieces. But a family could live for a year on what they'd fetch.'

He turned to Poemen and went on, 'As God is my witness, Poemen, I didn't accept this for any personal motive. But I had become deeply disturbed by...' He broke off and stared fixedly at Poemen. 'May I ask you a serious questions?'

Poemen, a little surprised, said, 'Of course.'

'How do you, personally, conceive of God?'

Poemen gave this a long moment of thought. 'I don't know.'

Dioscoros and Ammonias exchanged looks. This seemed not quite what they had expected. 'You must have some kind of concept,' Dioscorus said.

Poemen reflected, shook his head.

'None at all? The flicker of an all but unthinkable suspicion lit up Ammonias's eyes. 'You don't...disbelieve in God...do you?'

'Of course not.

'Then...'

'I think what we have to consider here, Arnmonias,' the Bishop said swiftly and diplomatically, 'is Father Poemen's humility, for which he is justly famous throughout Egypt. He would consider it a sign of spiritual pride on his part even to assume that he is worthy enough to know God's true nature.'

Poemen said nothing, but looked suitably modest. Actually things went a lot further than that. He didn't believe any human could know God's true nature. He regarded it as the height of blasphemous arrogance that people calling themselves Christians should dare to debate whether God was Three Persons with one Nature or One Person with Three Natures, whether Christ and God were of the same or merely a similar substance, as they had been doing for more than a century now. But he had the sense to keep his mouth shut. In an age of heresy hunting, the notion that there was no such thing as heresy would have itself been damned as heretical.

'At any rate,' Dioscorus went on, 'I take it that you don't regard God as in any sense...corporeal.'

'As you might if you took Genesis 1.27 literally, ' Ammonias put in.

Poemen hesitated only half a beat, then assented. If he didn't know God's nature, his assent was, of course, true in a literal sense. And he felt no moral obligation to add that he didn't think God was the Logos, the Divine Wisdom of Greek philosophers, either.

The two Tall Brothers smiled, relaxed. 'You're familiar

with the thinking of Evagrius Ponticus, I take it.' Again, Poemen nodded. Origen's disciple, he thought. Another of those who have to trim God's edges and nail Him firmly into place before they can even start to think about doing His will. 'I had always assumed,' Dioscorus went on, 'that God was a spirit. What else could he be? So that what Evagrius wrote, that made sense to me. From the beginning. Imagine my horror, ' he said, leaning forward towards Poemen across the table, and speaking slowly and with great emphasis. 'Imagine my shock and disbelief when I discovered that, far from sharing this view, many—maybe most—of the hermits of Nitria violently opposed it. Insisted on the literal meaning of Genesis. That God was a corporeal entity with an appearance much like yours or mine. And denounced the true interpretation as outright heresy.'

O God, Poemen prayed silently, know that I love You, in whatever form You may take, or not take, as the case may be. But please, do not put me to the test. Do not let them try to make me take sides in this.

'Obviously,' Dioscorus went on, 'such a situation could not be allowed to continue. And when it came to the attention of the Archbishop, I must say he was extremely supportive of our position. In fact, the thing I invited you here to talk about is connected to that. In a way. Don't worry; I'll get to it in a moment.' He paused to sip from his goblet. 'What do you think?'

'Of the Archbishop?'

'Of the wine.'

'Oh. Excellent, excellent,' Poemen said automatically. He neither knew nor cared anything about the quality of wine. In moderation it warmed the heart; in excess, it maddened the brain. What else did you need to know? 'So,' he said, 'that was what led you to accept Hermopolis?'

'Exactly. The Archbishop was most explicit about what he expected from me. "Get rid of the images," he told me. "See that they worship a pure God, without attributes. Otherwise, they're no better than pagan idolaters." I must confess I haven't always seen eye to eye with him in the past. That Serapeum business, for instance. Very ill-advised, if you ask me. We should have converted them peacefully. But then, he has this thing about images.'

'I hope you're not going to make image-worshiping the latest heresy,' Poemen said.

Dioscorus hesitated a second, but Ammonias, stepping in quickly, said 'Certainly not—we just want to make sure they don't make heretics out of *us*.'

'In other words, you took Hermopolis so an Anthropomorphite wouldn't get it.'

Dioscorus did not look too pleased at this bluntness. 'You can put it that way if you want to. I would rather think in terms of...well, of educating them. Convincing them that Holy Writ must sometimes be taken in an allegorical sense.'

Poemen sipped his wine in silence.

'But that's by the way,' Dioscorus went on. 'The real reason I asked you to come here is that Scetis is soon going to need a new priest. It hasn't been announced yet. I'd prefer not to announce it until we have a successor in place. But the Archbishop has chosen Isidore as his personal emissary. He will be traveling to Palestine to act as peacemaker in some theological disputes that have broken out there.'

'Over the teachings of Origen, ' Poemen said matter-of-factly. Dioscorus gave him a long, keen look. 'You don't miss much, do you, out there in that cell of yours...So, Isidore must be replaced.'

He remained silent for some moments, until Poemen said, 'And you want my advice.'

'I don't want your advice,' Dioscorus said. 'I don't need your advice. I just need you.'

Now it was Poemen's turn to keep silence. Finally, he said, 'No.'

'Why?'

'I'm not worthy.'

'Spare us that, Poemen,' Dioscorus said, almost angrily. 'You don't have to prove your humility to us. If we hadn't known about it already, we wouldn't have chosen you.'

Poemen spread his hands, 'Father, believe me, I'm not putting on an act. You can't see into my soul. So you'd better believe what I tell you.'

'Well, look at it this way,' Ammonias cut in. 'We all of us know we're sinners, so none of us is worthy. But somebody has to do the job. What do you want to do, deprive your brothers of the Eucharist? If you want to show some true humility, just accept the will of your Bishop.'

Poemen tipped back his chair and fixed him with a level gaze. '*You* are telling *me* that?'

'I warned you!' Ammonias turned on Dioscorus, flushed with anger. 'I told you it would just mess things up if I was here.' Quickly he gained control of himself. 'I'm sorry, Father. It's my own fault. I could have just left. I won't say another word.' And he sank back into his chair, twisting his empty goblet between his fingers. .

'Ammonias,' Poemen said, 'I think it's I who owe you an apology. I had no business bringing up your past like that. And I am not being willfully disobedient to you, Father,' he went on, turning to Dioscorus. 'Haven't you wondered why I never took a disciple?'

'Mm...No. Not really. I suppose it is...unusual. For anyone of your standing.'

'Well I'll tell you. Alone, I can be of service. People come to me, ask my advice . I'm not personally responsible for them so I can look at their problems objectively, not bent this way or that by their interests nor, I hope, by my own. I quiet my own voice and try to let the Holy Spirit speak through me. Not always successfully, as I know only too well. But some tell me I've helped them. If I have any gift at all, that is it. And that is all it is.'

He paused and drained his goblet. 'Thanks, Father, I will take a second. For the road. Because I shan't let you waste any more of your valuable time trying to persuade me. You see, I have this defect. Whatever discernment I may have simply falls apart if I become personally responsible for anyone. If I have any sort of authority over them, however slight. Then I worry about what I can or can't tell them to do, how they'll react to what I do, how I'll react to what they do, how they'll react to one another if there's more than one of them...' He laughed. 'No, this is not some quaint quirk of personality of which I'm secretly proud. Like I said, it's a defect, a limitation. I wish I didn't have it. I respect those that don't have it. Choose one of them. Don't try to turn a half-way passable hermit into an incompetent priest.'

This plea left behind it the longest and most lugubrious silence of all. The Bishop refilled his own goblet and Ammonias's. But his hand stopped halfway to his mouth and he sat staring moodily at the dark red liquid, as if an answer to his problem might suddenly emerge from it. It was Ammonias who spoke first.

'There's nothing that would change your mind on that?'

'Oh yes,' Poemen said. 'Two things.'

'Whatever you—' the Tall Brothers both began simultaneously, then broke off and stared at one another. Dioscorus frowned, Ammonias grinned.

'One,' Poemen said . 'If I were elected unanimously by the entire congregation, of Scetis. Two, if you put all the old men in a circle, spun a bottle, and the neck pointed at me.'

'How do you justify that?' Dioscorus was still frowning.

'If the bottle pointed at me, then that would be God's will, wouldn't it?' Poemen said innocently. 'And if I was everyone's first choice, how could I refuse?'

'Are you saying the congregation has power, or mere chance, yet the Bishop doesn't have the power to—' Ammonias began.

'Oh, the Bishop has the power to ordain me, ' Poemen said. 'I don't doubt that. The right, too, I'm sure—I don't know much about administrative matters. But much as I respect and admire you personally, Dioscorus, I believe you've chosen the wrong man . And because of the things I admire you for, I don't think you'll try to force me against my conscience.'

The two Tall Brothers exchanged looks. Dioscorus conjured up a wan smile, 'I was afraid you might take that tack,' he said wistfully. 'All right, then. Give us the benefit of your discernment. Who should we ask?'

Poemen did not hesitate. 'Moses,' he said.

Dioscorus stiffened. 'The black man? The one they call the Robber?'

'Right.'

'Why Moses?'

'Because he does God's will-.'

'You think it was God's will that he should be rude to Archbishop Theophilus?'

Poemen laughed. 'Oh, you heard about that, then? Well, you heard it wrong. He wasn't rude. He simply avoided contact, as I did myself albeit in a more cowardly way—simply in the interests of keeping the peace. Because Theophilus was off on his idol-bashing adventure, which you yourself didn't approve of, you said just now, and if Moses had stayed to hear him preach on it, there would have been a head-on confrontation.'

'We're all doing our best to do God's will,' Ammonias

grumbled. 'Tell us what's so special about Moses.'

'Sorry. I wasn't explicit enough.' Poemen spoke slowly, choosing his words carefully. 'Moses does God's will automatically. He doesn't care what other people think. He doesn't care what *he* thinks. He doesn't think, "Is it risky? Dare I? Might I offend someone powerful? Am I absolutely sure it is God 's will?" He doesn't think, period . He just somehow knows what it is and does it. Someone like that couldn't be spoiled by ordainment, like I would. He'd take it in stride.'

'And respect authority.'

'God's authority. Certainly.'

'A priest's place is to respect the authority of the Church,' Dioscorus insisted. 'The Church is God's authority on earth. It can't be a committee of anarchists.'

Poemen threw up his hands . 'Look, we're not talking about some upper-class suburb of Alexandria. We're talking about Scetis. Just about everyone there is there because they can't take authority. Moses they can accept because they know he could knock all their heads together if he chose to, but he won't. And he won't get into any conflict with you because he knows better than anyone the damage that pride and anger can do to the soul. Believe me, I know him. We go back a long way.'

Again the Tall Brothers exchanged meaningful looks.

'Shall we tell him?' Dioscorus asked.

'Why not?'

'We were just testing you. Moses was our second choice.'

Poemon spluttered. 'Why, you really had me fooled that time, didn't you?'

'Bishops aren't all as bad as Moses thinks they are,' Ammonias said. 'Maybe you'd better pass that on to him.'

'But we still have a problem,' Dioscorus said.

'Right,' Ammonias said. 'You wouldn't accept. Will he?'

'Good point, ' Poemen agreed. 'What do you think?'

'If you asked him flat out, he'd say no.'

'I told you so, ' Ammonias said to Dioscorus.

'There's got to be a way,' the Bishop answered.

'Could I help?'

The Tall Brothers turned together. 'Would you?'

'If I can,' Poemen said. 'Like I said, we go back a long way. And I think I might just be able to do something.'

Chapter Fifteen

It felt good be walking back alone across the desert, the donkey ambling patiently at his side, relieved now of its burden of baskets. Throughout his childhood and youth as a shepherd in the Thebaid and his long sojourn in the desert, Poemen had seen little of towns and wanted to see less. How could anyone stay virtuous in a town? The noise, and the stink of greed and angry competition penned within too little space. He felt, as he always did, even in an insignificant place like Hermopolis, that any secular man or woman living a decent life in such surroundings must have greater strength and virtue than any hermit. We boast about being God's athletes, he told himself, but really it's our weakness that drives us to a life of solitude. It's only there, freed from all the pressures that urbanites live with daily, that we can even hope to attain singleness of heart.

It was near noon on the day following his meeting with the Bishop, He was beginning to feel qualms about his forthcoming interview with Moses. It was one thing to make promises, with an eye to leaving fast on a good note, but quite another to accomplish them. Should he plan his strategy carefully? Or just pray and trust that God would put the right words in his mouth? Your faith has been weakened, he told himself sternly. You shouldn't even be asking that question. Just a few hours in a busy marketplace and a whiff of episcopal ambience has proved too much for you. Shame on you!

He began to empty his mind, closing it down section by section, sealing up its fears and uncertainties, silencing the chirpy, gossiping voices that bounced around in his brain, that told and retold all the scraps of senseless experience he had encountered in the town: a beggar's toothless smile, a decapitated pagan statue, a drunken laugh in the dark, Ammonias's scar, the Bishop's silver. When all was still, focused, centered, like a room emptied, swept, scrubbed clean, prepared for a new tenant, he composed himself to wait in patience, fixing the still point to which his mind had shrunk upon the thought of God. Not on an image of God, not Jehovah, not an old man in the sky, not the Three-in-One or the One-in-Three, not the Logos, but on whoever or whatever it was that frail human intelligence struggled to capture in these images of the inconceivable Ground of All Being.

For that target, so seemingly inaccessible to the restless brain, was in fact everywhere…here, there, near, far...The Kingdom of God is within you, he repeated to himself, and then the verse he loved most from the Gospel of Thomas: an apocryphal book, scorned by official Christians, tampered with by gnostics, but at its best as true a guide as any. 'Cut the wood and you will find me, turn the stone and I am there.' Every stone in the desert that surrounded him, every grain of sand was infused with that Being. And if the stones, how much more the human heart!

Only the heart, Poemen believed, could know God. Not the precarious, fragile reach of human understanding, blown about every which way by fear, desire, prejudice. Not that illusory intelligence on which the great ones of the earth so prided themselves. Only by the heart directing its love towards God, pouring it out into the darkness, not in fear, not in desire for heavenly benefits, but in pure selfless worship of that which was so inestimably greater than the petty human self. Even if there were no hell to fear and no heaven to hope for, would his heart still reach out in love? Oh yes! He knew that as surely as he knew his own existence, but took no pride in it, for it was a hunger and a yearning within him that drove him as imperiously as the hunger and thirst of mere flesh.

He did not seek spiritual benefits. If divine Grace provided them, good. If not, good also. The seeking of God was enough. Seek and ye shall find, the scripture promised. How could that be? Because the seeking was the finding! Knowing God was not like receiving a prize at the end of a children's game. It wasn't a result you got by working out a sum correctly. It was a process that never finished, certainly not in this life. It could show growth, but no terminal goal. Not for nothing was it called the Way, the Path. Once your feet were on it, they were on it, even if only on the merest beginning of a Path that could never end.

When he entered this meditation, the immense circle of desert around him had been empty of any living form, save his own. When he left it, and became once more aware of his surroundings, several hours must have passed, for the light had changed and the shadows cast by the low hills now filled the hollows between them with purplish dusk. But the desert was still unpeopled...or was it?

Far ahead of him, he made out a tiny human figure, going in the same direction. Led by his wise donkey even in his altered state, he realized he had cut into the main trail that led south from Nitria to Scetis. In all probability, then, the figure would be that of a fellow-hermit traveling between the two centers. For a moment, he felt disappointment at not having the visible world entirely to himself, but he quickly crushed the feeling. The command to love one's neighbor equaled the command to love God. If God had seen fit to place another pilgrim in his path, he must hasten forward to overtake the brother, to see if he could offer him assistance, or at least companionship in his journey. He walked more quickly, his feet, hardened by the years, impervious to the roughness of the ground. Gradually, as the light faded, he began to overtake the other, who had not turned in all this time and thus had not seen him. The stranger's figure increased gradually in size. Clad in the familiar black tunic, swinging the familiar staff, carrying a battered leather satchel with a few poor possessions, it was clearly that of a hermit, except that...

Except that there was something unusual in the way it was walking.

For a while, Poemen tried to figure out what was odd about that walk. it was not that the man was limping exactly, just something in the way the feet were put down, or was it a subtle difference in the rhythm of it?

Then it hit him. That was the way a woman walked. Tales of hermits tempted by demons disguised as woman flashed into his mind. He smiled to himself. Without wishing to denigrate Satan's capacities, he tended not to take such stories too seriously. Out here, in this isolation, a restless mind could conjure up anything, convince itself of anything. Indeed, it was inside one's head, rather than before one's eyes, that the Calumniator did his most successful work.

No, in all probability the person he was following was a creature of flesh and blood. The fact that it was a woman did not deter him, as it might have done some hermits. He did not believe himself to be wholly free from temptation. Indeed, anyone who believed that ran the gravest risk of falling. But he himself, when asked by another hermit for a word, had said, 'Just as a king's bodyguard stands always on guard at his side, so the soul should always be on guard against fornication.' Interior vigilance, that was what counted. And remembering that the person before you was a sister in Christ, worthy of your fullest respect.

When he was within about twenty yards of her, the donkey brayed, something it hardly ever did. The blessed animal, he thought, it's got more sense than I have, at least it warned her somebody was approaching, The figure turned, and even in the failing light Poemen could see that it was indeed a woman. Well, said the mischievous imp of humor that all his ascetic practices had never quite managed to destroy. Not likely you'll have much to fear from that quarter, is it?

It wasn't that she was actually ugly. Indeed, stretching a point or two, you might even have used the word 'handsome', for her features were regular, albeit somewhat larger than normal. No, it was the brusque. no-nonsense air she projected that struck Poemen most forcibly, that made her more manlike than her appearance alone suggested. 'Good evening, Father,' she said, in a tone that, though in no sense hostile, managed to convey both a challenge and a warning.

'Good evening...' He had been about to say, 'sister', but the term seemed somehow too flimsy for a person of this bulk. '...Mother,' he substituted. As she said nothing further, he added, 'My name's Poemen, of Scetis. Sometimes called the Shepherd.' He was relieved to see that she did not, apparently, recognize the name. Thank God my humility is not really famous throughout Egypt, he thought; so much for a Bishop's attempt at flattery.

'I'm Theodora,' she said. 'So, you're on your way home.'

'Correct.'

'I too am going there.'

'To consult someone?'

She laughed. Her laughter was deep, rich, confident. 'No. I'm going to live there.'

'You're what?' The words were out before Poemen could stop them. But he had been shocked, Scetis was, after all, a place for men . No woman had ever dwelt there. Or, to be more precise, and bearing in mind Paesia/Theron, no one had ever dwelt there as a woman.

'I'm going to live there,' she repeated. 'Is that a problem for you?'

'For me personally, no,' Poemen said. 'But I can think of some for whom it might be.' Papnoute for one, he thought. He's sworn he'd leave Scetis immediately if a woman ever settled there. We'll see how serious he is about that. 'Nothing like this has happened there before,' he added.

'About time it did, then.'

Her tone discouraged further inquiry, but Poemen persisted. 'Do you have any...prior experience of this kind of life?'

'If you're worried about, can I stand up to it,' Theodora said, 'forget it. I've had six years in a cell on the edge of the Delta. Five years before that in a convent in Pelusium. I know what I'm doing.'

'I don't doubt it,' Poemen said sincerely. 'How do you handle accidie, by the way?'

'Is that a trick question, or do you really want to know?'

'I suffer from it myself.' It wasn't a flat-out lie; it had been true, years ago, and it mattered more to put others at their ease by pleading one's own weakness than to stick to the exact letter of the truth. 'So I do want to know.'

She made a snorting noise of contempt. 'I should know about that! Creeps up on you. Around mid-day, usually. Gives you itchy feet. You can't pray, work, settle to anything. Always up and down, peering out the window, fabricating excuses to quit your cell. Then, if you don't get on top of it, it gets worse. Your knees go weak on you. You start running a low fever. You despair of salvation, yet at the same time you think of killing yourself. You won't take it to an elder because you feel shame, and even if you didn't, you just wouldn't have the energy.'

'And how should one deal with that?'

'Directly.' Her eyes flashed. 'Nip it in the bud. Do violence to your nature. If you can't pray, say to yourself. "Look, I'm dying. If I don't pray now, that's it. It'll be too late." Force yourself. The only way.'

Poemen disagreed. He and John Colobos had always taught that if you suffered from accidie you should pamper it, relax your controls, eat and drink what you felt like when you felt like it, work a little whenever you could and ease yourself out of it that way. But who could tell? What she said might work for some people. Discernment lay in realizing that not every cure fit every person, in fitting the word of salvation to the individual case.

In any case, common courtesy forbade that he should get into an argument with her. 'Thank you, Mother,' he said. 'That helped. I'm greatly edified.'

'Good,' she said with a chuckle. 'I should make it clear though that I'm not coming to Scetis to hand out advice. Unless I'm asked, of course. On the contrary. I've come to learn.'

'Really.'

'Yes, Scetis still has a great reputation.' It was at this

precise moment that Poemen realized he liked her, as a person. He had been a little intimidated by her at first, but that passed, And his change of heart certainly had nothing to do with what she was saying, for he would have disagreed with her equally about Scetis—it should have been obvious to anyone that the place had lost the pristine glory it had enjoyed in the days when Macarius abandoned the nitre-hauling trade and settled there with a bunch of starry-eyed visionaries who dreamed of recreating the purity of Adam and Eve upon earth. No, it was a kind of jolly confidence she exuded, a joy in being what she was and doing what she did, that spoke to Poemen not of the kind of righteousness that comes from hard work, endless fasting and prayer, but the kind that springs spontaneously in some fortunate souls, without much tending, unmistakable when you meet it. He knew that he would disagree with her on almost everything, and that this would make no difference to how he felt about her.

'Where do you plan on living?' he asked her.

'Oh, I'll build my own cell.' Then, seeing Poemen's expression, she said, 'What's the matter? Think a woman can't lay a stone wall?'

'I don't doubt that you could,' Poemen said, smiling.

'Should hope not. I did it in the Delta. Had to haul the stones myself. In a barrow. Miles!'

'I'll give you a hand,' Poemen offered.

'You don't have to.'

'I know. But it helps.'

Charity was not his only reason for offering. If from the beginning she was publicly assisted by one of the oldest hands in Scetis, this should help to ease her passage into a community that would not, to put it mildly, be prejudiced in her favor.

'Suit yourself,' she said in an off-hand tone. 'I shan't refuse. It's hard on the hands.'

They walked in silence for a while, then Poemen asked, 'Are you tired?'

'No, are you?'

'I was going to say, you can ride the donkey for a while. He can be ridden. I don't, as a rule, but there's no reason why you shouldn't.'

'Thanks,' Theodora said. 'I'll stick to the means of locomotion that God gave me...I fell off one, once.'

'You fell off a donkey?'

She laughed. 'Sounds stupid, doesn't it? I was trying to ride it sidesaddle. For modesty's sake. Do you know the Hundred-and-Third Psalm?' Poemen lost a few seconds trying to figure out what, if anything, the Hundred-and-Third Psalm had to do with donkeys.

'It's a favorite of mine,' he said finally.

'Let's sing it then. Journeys go quicker if you sing a psalm or two.'

So they went on their way, singing: 'As for man, his days are as grass; as a flower of the field, so he flourisheth...' She has a good strong voice, Poemen thought. It will make people sit up, the first time she comes to synaxis.

The last light faded, the stars began to come out. 'Have you eaten yet?' he asked.

She had not. They stopped; Poemen unslung a bag of oats from the donkey's back and hung it by its cord round the donkey's neck so the donkey could get his muzzle into it. Only then did he unwrap a package containing bread and dried figs and, sitting, shared them with his companion. After a while the donkey, bored with oats, pulled his head from the bag and thrust it over Poemen's shoulder. 'No,' he said, pushing the donkey's muzzle gently away, 'you know figs disagree with you. I'll begin to think you're as bad as us, wanting all the things we'd be far better off without.'

Theodora snorted her agreement—at last Poemen had said something she could thoroughly support. They finished their frugal meal in silence, then headed southwards again. As the miles passed and no sign of human habitation appeared, Theodora began to stare around her suspiciously.

'Are you sure this is the right way?'

'Of course. I have an excellent sense of direction.' But the remark reminded him of a story. 'Ever hear of a hermit called John Colobos?'

'Isn't he the one they call the Dwarf?'

She'd heard of John but not of him! Poemen stamped quickly on a brief, involuntary flicker of resentment. That was envy, and vanity! Instead of rejoicing that your friend's virtues were so renowned. How hard the passions die! 'That's right,' he said. 'Did you hear about the time he got lost on this trip?'

'No.'

'It was a night darker than this. Several brothers along with him, they even had a guide. So-called. Turned out he had no idea of the way. Eventually they realized they were lost. "I'm going to complain to him," says one of them. "No way," says John. "You'll make him feel bad."'

Theodora snorted. 'That wouldn't have bothered me. Serves him right.'

Poemen ignored the interruption. '"What shall we do, then?" the brother asks. "Simple," says John. "I'll pretend to be sick and say I can't walk any further. So we'll all stop here until it gets light, then we'll know where we are." So that's what they did. And they never said a word to the guide, so he never knew he'd gone wrong.'

'And the next time out he could mislead the next lot of

brothers.'

'Possibly,' Poemen admitted. 'Possibly not. Who knows?'

'They should have told him. '

'No, ' Poemen said. 'John was absolutely right. Refrain from doing harm whenever it's in your power to do so. Don't do that harm in the hope that it might prevent some future harm,. Because you don't know. And it's arrogance to suppose you do. If everyone took the same thought for their neighbor's feelings as John did...'

He did not finish his sentence, so Theodora did it for him. 'It would be paradise on earth, is that what you're saying?'

'Something of the sort.'

'People have to learn that acts have consequences.'

'No. People have to learn to obey the Commandment.'

Poemen had spoken with unwonted vehemence. Am I coming on too strong, he wondered. He had not wanted this to degenerate into an argument. In fact, he knew only too well how the good hermit should behave. If anyone started arguing, the good hermit would just say, "Well, that's your opinion," and shut up. Was it perhaps because she was a woman, and he wanted to assert his masculine authority over her? That would be unworthy.

'I doubt if I could have kept quiet, ' Theodora said in no uncertain fashion.

'Oh, me too.' Poemen lied. 'It's hard. Nobody denies it's hard.'

'But you've got to be practical, too. The world's a mess, and it gets worse every day.' She sighed heavily. 'I sometimes wonder why God's delaying Judgment. Maybe He expects us to get it into some sort of order first. I'm afraid if we don't keep on top of things it'll go to pieces entirely.'

Poemen remained silent. If he had spoken he would have said, well, since Adam we've had thousands of years of people being practical, not giving way to wild-eyed idealism, getting on top of things, trying to put things in order. and look where it's gotten us! In fact it's the practical man who's the impractical fool. Only if we truly followed the Commandment might we break the endless cycle of wrong and right and wrong, injustice and justice and injustice...But he said none of this, for he knew he could not convince her, and would only cause her to feel anger at him.

'How about another Psalm?' he said at last.

At that instant there came, from far away, a piercing, sobbing shriek, that wavered interminably in the air and then stopped, abruptly. But the cry was of the kind that reverberates in the imagination: a cry of unspeakable anguish, a death-cry.

It came as a shocking reminder of their loneliness., their vulnerability in the desert night. Theodora shuddered.

'Demons, d'you think?'

Poemen shook his head. 'More likely the hyenas got hold of some poor creature.'

'Well, our singing should keep either of them away.' She laughed. 'Your turn to choose.'

'Twenty-three.'

'So be it.'

And they began, 'The Lord is my shepherd, I shall not want...' When they came to the part about walking through the valley of the shadow of death, Poemen could not resist interpolating, 'Appropriate, huh?', without losing the rhythm.

She laughed, nodded, and they went on, two small, lonely figures in that dark immensity, with the innocent donkey making a third at their side, their side, forming around themselves a fragile bubble of protection against whatever raw evil might lurk in the encompassing night.

Chapter Sixteen

Brother Ibison, Papnoute's disciple, had been sent by Papnoute to Father Serapion with a basket of grapes that had been given to Papnoute by another hermit. This had originated as a gift to the Blessed Macarius from a rich secular who had visited Scetis for advice. Macarius, in one of his more lucid moments, had thanked the secular, told him how grateful he was, how thoughtful of the secular to bring such a delicacy to one for whom age and infirmity had made the regular diet unpalatable, how much he, Macarius, was going to enjoy the grapes, and so on and so forth. When the secular left, Macarius said to his disciples. 'I really can't accept this.'

'But Father, you need it, it will do wonders for your health.'

'Why should I worry about my health?' Macarius objected logically. 'I'll be dead pretty soon whether I eat the grapes or not. Why shouldn't somebody else have the benefit? I'm sure there's lots of people who need them more than I do.'

And he suggested a couple of names. So, one of his disciples delivered the grapes to another hermit, who thanked him profoundly and, as soon as he had gone, sent them on to somebody else. Eventually they came round to Papnoute, who reacted as everyone else had, and sent Ibison off with them.

They had begun to look, the brother thought as he squinted at them, somewhat the worse for wear, going brown around the stems, squishy, one or two of them split and furred with a greyish-white mold. Who'd know if I took a couple, he said to himself, and furtively did so.

Feeling bad about that, he assured himself that it didn't matter, he'd taken only bad ones—if I hadn't eaten them, they'd only have been wasted. He glanced quickly round to make sure no one had observed him, for if word of it got back to Papnoute, he could imagine the consequences. 'What? You picked up something you hadn't put down? You stole from Father Serapion? Because that's what it was, no matter what excuses you may make!' Papnoute wouldn't actually strike him, as some old men had been known to do with their disciples, but somehow Papnoute's contempt could hurt you worse than any blow.

He stopped dead in his tracks.

They hadn't seen him, but he had seen them. And what he saw filled him with such shocked disbelief that he blinked, rubbed his hand across his eyes, and looked again. Was this some diabolical illusion? No, it could hardly be that, for the two figures betrayed not the slightest awareness of his presence, and went on about their business, unloading stones from panniers slung on the sides of a donkey and laying them carefully on top of a wall that had already been raised to the height of a man's waist. Ibison started to walk, then broke into a run, and did not stop until he came within sight of Father Serapion's cell.

He slowed down to regain his breath and his composure, for he did not want to babble like a fool in front of Isaac, Father Serapion's disciple, whom he despised. Isaac was in the outer chamber, as he had expected, and said, as he had expected, 'I'll take it. The Father doesn't want to be disturbed.'

'Father Papnoute sent it because he knows Father Serapion has a bad stomach and this should help,' Ibison said loyally, without mentioning the prior history of the basket. He saw Isaac looking suspiciously at its contents and wished he'd had the forethought to rearrange the grapes so the best ones were on top.

But, at least Isaac had the discretion not to comment. 'Please thank Father Papnoute,' he said. 'Tell him Father Serapion will greatly appreciate them.' And he took the basket in a way that suggested the interview was over.

'You'll never believe,' Ibison said quickly, 'what I saw just now.'

Isaac stopped and waited expectantly.

'A woman.'

'A secular?'

'No, a woman hermit! Building herself a cell, too!'

'Hm,' Isaac said reflectively. 'A hallucination, d'you think?'

'No!' And Ibison just managed to restrain the, 'Damn you!' that was on the tip of his tongue. 'A real live woman!'

'Did you touch her?'

Ibison was outraged. 'Touch her? What do you think I am?'

'Well, if you didn't touch her, you can't be sure, can you?' Isaac said in an infuriatingly reasonable tone. 'So she could have been a demonic illusion.'

'I'm as sure as I'm seeing you!'

'Doesn't make sense,' Isaac said. "There aren't any female hermits in Scetis.'

'There are now! One, anyway. Go look for yourself if you don't believe me.' And Ibison turned on his heel and took off. He could not wait to tell his news to his Father.

On the way back, he passed them again, They were still working on the wall, the unknown female and the hermit who he now recognized as Father Poemen, laying the big stones carefully, filling the gaps with smaller ones, far too engrossed in their work to notice anyone, even an indignant brother who stood glaring at them from fifty yards away for several minutes before he left at a dog-trot and vanished behind a low dune.

Today, Ibison had no qualms about violating Papnoute's privacy. He banged on the cell door, shouting, 'Father, Father!'

'Stop...that!' came a low, intense hiss from within the cell. Then he heard the bolt being drawn, and Father Papnoute appeared with a look of loathing on his austere features. 'If it's the Day of Judgment, I'll hear the trumpet,' he said icily. 'If it's anything less than that, you have your instructions. Who told you to disobey them?'

'Nobody, Father,' Ibison said humbly 'But—'

'I don't want to hear "but",' Papnoute said, his hand on the bolt, already taking a pace backwards.

'But there's a woman come to Scetis, Father.'

Papnoute paused, still holding the bolt. 'A visitor.'

'No, no! Come to stay!'

Papnoute went white. 'Are you certain? How do you know?'

'She's building a cell! And Father Poemen's helping her!'

Papnoute looked left, looked right, stepped to one side and held the door open. 'Quick! Come in!' He closed the door and bolted it behind Ibison as if by so doing he could keep this ghastly secret between the two of them, stop the other hermits from ever finding out how their sanctuary had been desecrated. 'Sit down.'

Ibison obediently seated himself on one of the low papyrus stools, and Papnoute perched on the other, his face only inches away from Ibison's.. 'Now, tell me exactly what happened,. right from the beginning.'

Ibison did so. 'And Brother Isaac wouldn't believe me,' he complained.

'What did she look like?' Papnoute asked.

'Like...well, like a woman.'

'How old, idiot? Young? Middle-aged? Tall? Short? Was she ugly? Good-looking? Describe her!'

Ibison had been so struck by her mere presence that details had not registered , but he dredged his memory.

'Sort of...well. about your age. I guess. Big. A big woman.'

'Attractive?'

Ibison blinked. He had been trained not to think of women in such terms.

'I'm not asking because I want to fornicate with her, you nitwit,' Papnoute said, squelching a notion that hadn't even occurred to Ibison yet. 'I'm asking because I have to know how much of a temptation she poses to the brothers.'

'Well...she looks a bit like my grandmother looked.'

Papnoute sighed. 'It could be worse, I suppose. But it's quite bad enough. You said Father Poemen was with her? Are you sure?'

'Quite sure, Father.'

Papnoute shook his head gravely. 'An old man like that! He ought to know better. But I always harbored my doubts about the good Father.' He turned to Ibison. 'Well, one thing I swore, and you know it, if ever a woman came to Scetis, I'd be out of here. Go tell the rest of the brothers to start packing.'

'Sir?'

'You heard me! Tell them to start right away.'

Ibison was stunned. Had he realized this would happen, he might have thought twice about telling his tale. 'But...but where are we going, Father?'

'None of your business,' said Papnoute, who had not yet even thought about possible destinations. 'You'll find out soon enough! I swore the sun would not set on me here once a woman came! Now don't waste any more time, go!'

Alone, however, he did not immediately begin his own packing. He paced nervously back and forth for the few steps the narrow confines of the cell allowed him, cracking his hairy knuckles and frowning intently. It had occurred to him that he had perhaps acted too hastily. Not in his determination to leave, that was set in marble, but in the readiness with which he had accepted Ibison's tale. Suppose the boy had made a mistake? Shouldn't he go out and look for himself before doing anything irrevocable? To leave one's cell was a serious matter, not because of the effort it cost—their few possessions could be quickly disposed of—but because of its moral implications, on which Scetis held two sharply divided schools of thought.

But to countermand his order or even delay the move, having spoken so imperiously, would look like weakness, and a Father could not afford to show weakness before his disciples, or what would happen to their respect? Had he time to run over there before they finished packing? Possibly, but he did not wish to give an impression of unseemly haste, of dashing to and fro in pursuit of rumors, either. What should he do? He chewed his fingernails in indecision. Well, at least he could quickly pack up his own things, so as to be ready, then he might just have enough time left to check the story...

He was halfway through his packing when a fist hammered on his door. 'Ibison!' he shouted, wrapping his spare tunic around an amphora that he had had for years and did not want to break. 'How many times do I have to tell you—'

'It's not Ibison,' a voice thundered.

Goose-pimples broke out on Papnoute's neck. Although the best part of two years had gone by since he first heard that voice he knew he could not be mistaken. Quickly he knelt, as if in prayer, in a corner of his cell. 'Come in,' he called meekly.

'I can't come in,' the angel said. 'Your door's bolted.'

Surely if you were a proper angel, Papnoute thought, that wouldn't bother you, you'd come in anyway. But he dared not give voice to this thought, and once the door was open, the radiance that, as before, seemed to pour out from the figure before him left little room for doubt. But why in heaven's name had the angel chosen this day of all days to visit him?

'Leaving, I see,' the angel noted, casting his eye around the cell, and Papnoute kicked himself for his childish attempt at deception—he should have known it wouldn't fool an angel.

'Well, er...'

'Not so good, that. Loses you merit.'

There was the one school of thought that believed a hermit should leave his cell at the first and faintest whiff of anything evil, anything that might disturb the compass of a holy life. There was the other school that believed a hermit, once he had chosen his abode, should stay there, through thick and thin, slugging it out with the forces of Satan, because those who abandoned their cells merely showed themselves up as fickle, frivolous folk, never satisfied, fooled by the false hope that they could change their inner lives simply by changing their environment. Now it began to look as if the second school had the right of it.

'Unless there's a very good reason, of course,' the angel added.

'But there is! There's a woman—' Papnoute began, then he remembered his doubts. The angel could settle them, if anyone could. 'I mean, is it true a woman's come to live here?'

The angel looked mildly surprised, but consulted his roll of papyrus anyway. 'Hm, yes...Does look like it. Name of Theodora. Arrived yesterday.'

'That's the end of Scetis!' Papnoute cried out.

The angel consulted his scroll. 'Wrong, I'm afraid,' he said, 'The end isn't scheduled for several years yet. Well, *an* end. Even an end is always a beginning, they say.'

'You don't understand,' Papnoute persisted, missing what under more favorable circumstances he would have quickly seized on as a prophecy. 'Scetis can never again be what it was. An abode of men, dedicated to righteousness. Women are snares of Satan, vessels of fornication, foul pits of corrup—'

'Here, steady on!' said the angel. so sharply that Papnoute stopped in mid-career. There was a moment's embarrassed silence, 'I thought you wanted to know your merit, ' the angel said, a little reproachfully.

Papnoute had totally forgotten. He had been praying

that he might learn exactly that at the very moment when Ibison had so rudely interrupted him. But the horror of his disciple's news had driven it completely out of his mind.

'My merit,' he stammered. Yes...Yes of course. Can you—er, tell me?'

'Of course,' the angel said. 'Why else would I be here'?'

He consulted his scroll again. 'Yes, it says here your merit is now equal to that of some of the better citizens of Terenuthis.

Papnoute's face turned ashen. 'Is that...all?'

'It's progress. Last time, as I recall, you were only equal to an average citizen of Terenuthis.'

'But...but...' Papnoute didn't know where to begin. 'Since last time I've fasted twice as long, prayed twice as hard, done good deeds... Just this afternoon I sent some lovely grapes round to Father Serapion, didn't touch one of them, though I was tempted. How can I only—'

'Not for me to say,' the angel responded brusquely. 'As I told you last time, all we do is deliver messages. But,' and his voice dropped confidentially, 'though I'm not really supposed to, I can give you one word of advice.'

Papnoute bent forward eagerly. 'And that is...'

'Think a bit longer before you move. They don't care for flightiness, Up There. And They might get the idea you're afraid of temptation. You could easily lose a couple or three grades, that way.'

'But...but surely for cause.,.'

'They might not see eye to eye with you even on that.' Papnoute's eyes glazed with shock. He blinked, and somehow in that blink the cell had become vacant once more. What had happened? Had he dreamed the visit? No. Faint but unmistakable, a heavenly odor hung in the air, an elusive fragrance that for a few moments overcame the sour reek of the palm-branches steeping in buckets of stale water that was the habitual smell of Papnoute's abode. But if the angel had not been able to get in, how had he got out?

Then in a flash Papnoute realized. Of course the angel could have got in—if he had wanted to. But he didn't want to. He wanted Papnoute to let him in. He wanted to draw Papnoute's attention to the fact that the door was bolted. Barring access from outside, fencing him off from his neighbor, making even an angel feel unwelcome. Papnoute suddenly remembered something Poemen had once said. after synaxis, when a brother asked him for a word. 'We were not taught to bar the door of our cell, but to bar the door of our tongue.' In other words, let your neighbor come and go freely, but watch your mouth, make sure you say nothing that might be hurtful to him or to others.

He can do more than bring messages, Papnoute thought. He can teach, even if only by what he does. Can it be that there are still things I have to learn?

Time enough to think about that later. There was more urgent business to be done. He unbolted his door, called his disciples together. When they were all assembled, he arose, rolled his eyes heavenwards and began, 'My children, I have been vouchsafed a vision. Just now, in this very cell, an angel appeared to me...'

Chapter Seventeen

While all this was happening in Scetis, the fat camel-driver arrived in the hope of collecting baskets. After making the rounds of several cells, he arrived at the hole in the ground that gave access to John Colobos's cavern. Sticking his head in the hole, he shouted, 'Got anything for me?'

At first, no one answered. The driver was about to leave, but thought he'd give it one more try. Cupping his hands around his mouth, he squatted over the hole and bellowed, 'Got anything?'

John had been so deep in meditation that it took the second shout to penetrate his consciousness. 'What was that?' he called back.

'Got any baskets?'

'I can't hear you down here. Hold on a second.'

John took his wooden ladder, which he had moved to prevent interruptions, and put it in place. Scrambling up it, he peered out of the hole and saw a camel half-loaded with baskets and its swarthy driver standing with arms folded beside it. 'Oh, it's you,' he said, recognizing the man. 'Sorry, my hearing's not what it was, I'm afraid. You want baskets?'

The driver assented with an expression of grim patience.

'Well, yes, I do have some.'

'I can pay you up front.'

'How much?'

The driver named a figure so low that even John balked a little. On the other hand, it would cover his immediate needs and save him or someone a journey to the World.

'All right, let me get them.' John descended the ladder, trying to pick up the thread of the meditation in which he had been engaged when the driver interrupted it. Something about the Blessed Virgin...some quality of the Virgin....No, that wasn't it exactly. Something to do with the Virgin and Jesus. Motherhood. Looking on from a distance while her Son was raised up on the Cross. What had She felt? What had He felt? Honor thy father and thy mother, Deuteronomy 5.16. I came to set sons against fathers, and daughters against mothers, Matthew 10.35. Somehow he had managed to reconcile those two texts, but how exactly... ?

His eye fell on the half-completed basket that he had been making before his mind became involved in this problem. Baskets! Yes, that word had been in his mind too somewhere. He must have been reminding himself not to get so lost in speculation that he neglected his work. It will come back to me, he thought, seating himself and beginning to weave again.

Work will settle my mind, any thought I had that was worth keeping will come back in God's own good time if I simply stop searching for it, concentrate my mind on the task...

'Hey! Down there!'

A rude shout pierced his ears. He dropped his work and hurried back up the ladder to see what ill-mannered ruffian was disturbing him. A swarthy figure confronted him. All too familiar-looking.

'Look, I don't have all day,' the driver complained.

John clapped his hand to his forehead. 'Oh! Oh dear! D'you know, I'd completely forgotten! So sorry! I'll get them for you right away.'

'Oh, and by the way,' the driver said as John's head and torso were about to disappear, 'I meant to ask you—have you gone bisexual over here?'

John stopped, 'Wh-a-t ... ?'

'You got women here now. Didn't you know?'

John's immediate thought was, it's Paesia! Someone's exposed her. And that means they've exposed me, too, as a liar and a cheat. He panicked. 'Where? How? What's happened?'

'Some old battleax, 'bout a mile from here,' the driver said resentfully. 'Asked her if she'd got any work for me, she gave me the wrong side of her tongue. Thought for a moment she'd start throwing stuff.'

John's heart rose in relief. Not Paesia/Theron, then, for sure. 'Perhaps she misunderstood you,' he said. 'Well, that is remarkable. A woman in Scetis! Thanks for the information.' And he continued down the ladder, amazed and bewildered by the news. Disturbed, too, as he considered possible consequences. A real woman, only a mile away! How long before she met Paesia? How long after that before she suspected? Seconds, probably. You could fool men with a thing like that, but another woman? And if the camel-driver's description had any validity, not the kind of woman who would put up with pretenses. She'd demand that Paesia show her true colors. He'd be exposed after all. His mind in a whirl, he sat down and began his weaving a second time.

This time, the driver didn't bother shouting. The first thing John became aware of was the thump of feet on his ladder, and he looked up to see a pair of worn boots descending through the hole. He gazed at them a moment in consternation, then cried out, 'Oh, no!'

'I thought we had a deal,' the driver said, stepping off the ladder.

'You're not going to believe this,' John began. 'I totally forgot you were there. Totally and completely. What is happening to me?'

'Dunno,' the driver said. 'Happens to some people. I

had an aunt went like that. Forgot her own name, in the finish.'

'It gets worse?'

''fraid so.'

'Oh, my!' I'll have to do something about it, John thought. I've always been forgetful, but nothing like this, making myself look like a complete idiot. There must be something I can do to cure it. Or at least delay its onset. I'll go to Poemen about it, he thought, soon as it's past the ninth hour. If anyone knows what to do about it, he will.

That afternoon he cut short the words with his disciples that usually followed their meal. The sun was declining, the day's heat sinking to a comfortable warmth when he set off. Although it added considerably to his walk, he could not resist making a detour in the direction that the camel-driver, before leaving, had pointed out to him. Sure enough, there was a cell there that hadn't been present the last time he passed this way.

He approached it cautiously. The door, a pair of battered planks nailed to a crosspiece, looked as if it had been salvaged from some ruin. It stood open, and as he moved round the cell in a wide arc, John tried to see into the interior. But the cell appeared to be vacant, and as yet unfurnished. He continued on his way, feeling vaguely disappointed.

Poemen was out picking herbs in his garden. 'Have you eaten yet?' he hailed John. John explained that he had, and

Poemen said, 'Well, my meal will keep for a while. Did you want to ask me about anything in particular?'

John racked his brains. He could remember that he had some urgent matter requiring Poemen's attention. He could even recall that he had had that matter clearly in mind as he set out. But try as he would he could not recall what it was. All he could think of was the female hermit.

Poemen nodded when he mentioned her and said, 'Come inside. No, leave the door, let the place cool off a bit...As a matter of fact, I was the first from Scetis to see her. And I gave her a hand building the cell you were looking at just now.'

John blinked rapidly several times. 'Did I say I went by her cell?'

'No.'

'So how did you know?'

Poemen smiled and shrugged.

'It's not on the way here!'

'I know. I just guessed. Was she home?' John, a little miffed, shook his head. 'I guess she was out trying to borrow a few furnishings. Mats and stuff. No, I knew you wouldn't be able to resist taking a look. She's caused quite a stir.'

'And is there much—' John rephrased his question. 'How are people taking it?'

'Surprisingly well. I was afraid they might give her a

hard time. That was why I stuck around for a couple of days. But even Papnoute—' He broke off and said with a perfectly straight face, 'I'm sorry, John, I'm forgetting how strict you are about gossip. Please forgive me. I should have known better.'

Torn between curiosity and his own preaching, John felt glad the interior of the cell was dark enough to hide his expression. 'Yes, you're right. Of course. Nobody guards their tongue any more, I used to think Benjamin was the exception but he seems typical of the kind of person we're attracting nowadays...but then, there's gossip, and... well... news.'

Poemen sighed enviously. 'Ah, to tell the difference,' he said. 'That must take a lot of discernment.'

John squinted at Poemen suspiciously, but the other's face remained perfectly serious. 'Oh, I wouldn't claim that.'

'But it must. I'm always telling other people to guard their tongues, yet I still have problems with my own...Well, at least I managed to control it this time, thanks to your edifying presence, John.'

'Yes, but...' John hesitated. 'I think perhaps...in this case...I mean this is a momentous event. A first. One needs to know, ahm, the general mood...the reactions of...of different people. Don't you think?'

'You mean this is news, not gossip?'

'Ah...Yes. Yes, definitely.'

'I bow to your superior discretion.'

'You're teasing me!' John exploded. 'I know you, Poemen! You're just making fun of me!'

'Wouldn't dream of it!' Poemen spread his hands and smiled at John affectionately. 'Now I know I can tell you everything with a clear conscience. What a relief. Where was I? Ah, Papnoute. As you know, Papnoute has sworn he'd leave here if ever a woman showed up. But he hasn't. Seems he had a vision—an angelic visitor. Who told him to stay right where he was.'

'Must have been genuine, then,' John said thoughtfully.

'Right. Real angels always tell us what we least want to hear, otherwise why would they bother to come?'

'And if Papnoute stays-..'

'Those who would have quit with him will probably stay too,' Poemen finished his sentence for him. 'There's been a good deal of grumbling, mostly directed at me, for aiding and abetting. But...'

'But nobody's actually trying to get rid of her.'

'Not yet. Maybe never. In cases like this, the best time to act is yesterday. Once somebody's settled in, it gets harder with each day that passes.' And Poemen settled down, relaxed, with the air of a job well-done. He did, indeed, feel reasonably pleased with himself, that is, as pleased with himself as a good hermit can let himself feel, which is not very. He had somehow remained free of the misogyny that affected so many male Christians, something he regarded as no more than a convenient cop-out for sinners—Lord, the woman made me do it! Yet God had made woman as companion for man, Genesis 2.18, one who was bone of his bones and flesh of his flesh, Genesis 2.23. So if Eve sinned, did that condemn all women? Certainly not, if the way Jesus had treated Martha, Mary Magdalene, the woman taken in adultery and all the rest of them was anything to go by. Obviously He hadn't felt this pervasive, corrosive distrust and repugnance.

In the silence that followed Poemen's last pronouncement, the real reason for his visit suddenly popped into John's head. And John began to tell him what had happened earlier that day with the camel-driver. He told it slowly, haltingly, overcome with embarrassment, because it was something of which he felt ashamed and believed he ought to be able to control. But Poemen only nodded sympathetically.

'You know, a weakness is often the other face of a strength.'

'How do you make that out?'

'Concentration. You're very good on concentrating on whatever you're doing,' (or saying, he almost added), 'to the exclusion of everything else. It's a great gift. You can use it to focus on God or any holy thing. Without it, meditation is hard—'

'Why are you flattering me?'

'I'm not.' Poemen was perfectly sincere; he simply knew that if you don't focus first on someone's strengths, then no matter how skilled your solution to their weakness, they will never get the strength to put that solution into practice. 'You see, part of your problem is, by focusing only on your immediate thought, you block out what led up to it. But thoughts don't just pop up out of nowhere, they're like burrs on a sheep's fleece, they have to find some snag of wool to hook onto. So train yourself. Several times a day, when a thought comes to you, just stop, retrace your steps, see what there was that went before it, what that thought got attached to. With practice, you'll learn to go back two steps, even three. You'll become aware of whole chains of thought as they form in your mind...But that takes time. For now, there's a simple exercise that'll help you in situations like this morning's. Just repeat, over and over to yourself, a couple or three words that'll remind you what you're supposed to be doing. Like 'baskets—driver.' Repeat them and repeat them until you've actually done what you have to. Don't let yourself think of anything else.'

'Thanks,' John said sincerely. 'I'll try that. I'm sure it'll help.'

'I hope so.'

But once John had left, Poemen's mind returned to a weakness of his own that was far worse than forgetfulness.

Forgetfulness did not involve an act of the will: procrastination did. More than half a week had passed since his interview with Dioscuros, and he still hadn't talked to Moses about being ordained. He didn't want to, because he was afraid he would fail. And that's pride, he told himself. Pride and cowardice. You simply can't put it off any longer.

The next day was the Sabbath. He would see the Robber at synaxis, he could no longer use his work with Theodora as an excuse.

Chapter Eighteen

Seldom in Scetis had there been a bigger turnout for the agape. Hermits who occasionally missed a week, so plunged in meditation that they lost track of the date, and even some who seldom came anyway, sarabites, as Moses called them, who considered themselves too holy to be led or guided by or even to mix with others—even these had shown up. The long rickety tables of the refectory began to fill at a much earlier hour than usual, hermits hustling to make sure they got a place, and Moses, whose turn it was to take charge of food distribution, began to worry that he might not have enough.

But the person who was most anxiously expected still had not arrived. The last stragglers were coming in, and Isidore sat with his spoon poised, ready to beat on the table for silence, for the buzz of voices had risen to a new level of intensity as hermits speculated on whether their newest and most controversial recruit would dare to show herself. The odds were running that she would not, and Isidore was clearing his throat preparatory for the grace, when there appeared in the distance four figures: first Isaac, Father Serapion's disciple, leading the way, followed by Serapion and Poemen, one either side of Mother Theodora.

If they were aware of being the center of attention, they gave no sign of it. They continued to talk to one another, quietly, seriously, as they approached the refectory. The buzz of conversation around the tables gradually died down into a tense and ominous silence. Every eye followed them as they moved to the serving table. Would the servers serve a woman? Poemen stepped forward, caught Moses' eye, glanced at Theodora and back again. Moses gave a fractional nod. 'Don't leave,' Poemen said, 'after synaxis. There's something very important I have to talk to you about.'

'Don't worry; I won't.'

Poemen fell in behind Serapion and Theodora. He had felt close to Serapion ever since learning of his embarrassing problem, had visited him often and brought him delicacies from his herb-garden which, Isaac gratefully assured him, had much improved the atmosphere of their cell. Now these kindnesses had paid off, he thought, somewhat guiltily, because that was not why one did kindnesses. Still, he consoled himself, at the time he did them he had no advantage in mind. And he had not even suggested to Serapion that the latter might owe him a favor. He knew, though, all too well that without all those kindnesses and favors, Serapion would have been highly unlikely to act as co-sponsor of Theodora's social debut.

For Serapion was known as one of the oldest and most conservative of the hermits of Scetis. If you had told him, cold, 'A woman is trying to join us', he would have reacted more violently even than Papnoute had done at first. But Poemen had not gone that route. Poemen, to the contrary, had come around with a bunch of herbs and stayed on to talk about a new arrival in Scetis. And he quoted that new arrival's opinions, using actual words Theodora had spoken to him while they worked on her cell, words that he knew would go straight to Father Serapion's heart, and which indeed the latter had eagerly agreed with, leaning forward on his papyrus stool, smiling out of his virtually toothless mouth and nodding so hard Poemen feared his old head might drop off. Yes, yes, he had said, what discernment, I must meet this holy father and learn his wisdom, and Poemen had said, fine, that can be arranged, why don't we all walk to the agape together (he had already talked with Isaac and extracted a promise that all news of Theodora would be carefully kept from his mentor).

Poemen wished some artist could have been present when Serapion first set eyes on Theodora, for his expression of shock, consternation, total amazement, coupled with Theodora's cheery refusal to notice the least thing amiss, surely deserved to be kept for posterity. But here again his judgment had been vindicated. Had Serapion really been your hard-nosed, fanatically-conservative hermit, all Poemen's careful conditioning would have gone out the window, Serapion would have flounced off in high dudgeon and held it against Poemen for the rest of his life. But Serapion was a very gentle, rather naive old man, not given to displays of outraged virtue, who held conservative views because that was the way he had been brought up and he hadn't heard of any other kind. Given a real-life situation, he could be relied on to react to it as a human being, rather than a dogmatic engine, and in no time he and Theodora were deep in animated talk about the passions and how best to control them, with Poemen content to watch and listen and put in an occasional word here and there.

Now as the three of them, bunched together, holding their plates, followed Isaac who, running ahead, sought for them a place on the crowded benches, a voice suddenly came from their right:

'Father Poemen!'

It was Isidore the priest. If Poemen had not long since cured himself of the habit of swearing, he would have sworn now.

'Father, I need to talk to you after synaxis.'

'Of course, Father.' How could he had been so thoughtless, so discourteous? He should have known that as soon as he returned from Hermopolis he ought to have told

Isidore the result of his interview with the Bishop. Isidore had no say in the choice of his successor but it would have been only polite to keep him informed of the process. Poemen once more confronted his weakness: anything remotely official, that smacked of protocol or formal procedure, glided smoothly out of a mind quick to concern itself with more intimate matters: Theodora's adjustment, John's forgetfulness, Serapion's flatulence. Pure self-indulgence. He would have to work on that, as soon as more pressing matters had been taken care of.

Isaac was coming back, his expression lugubrious, his hands spread apart. No room left, it seemed. And Poemen saw that the eyes that had all been fixed on them when they first appeared were now looking everywhere and anywhere but at them—studiously avoiding them, treating them as if they did not exist. Poemen took the bull by the horns. 'Elias, if you move down to the next table,' he said in a low, clear, friendly voice, 'and you, Amoun, squish over to your right a bit, we can just squeeze in on the end here. And there's room for Isaac over the other side, isn't there? Yes. Good. I thought so.' They moved, reluctantly at first, then as Poemen continued to smile confidently at them, with an awkward, slightly excessive politeness. Even one or two of them smiled back and joked a little as they squeezed against one another to give the newcomers more space. Hardly were they seated when the spoon rapped, silence fell once more and Isidore began the grace.

Poemen breathed a sigh of relief. He had been right in surmising that people could accept the most startling innovations provided those who introduced them presented them as ordinary everyday occurrences. When the grace finished, he attacked his bowl of lentil stew gratefully, quite unaware that, two tables away, he had support from an unexpected quarter.

'I can see we'll have to redesign the church,' a voice heavy with sarcasm said to Isidore's right.

'How so?' Isidore asked.

'We'll have to put in a women's section.'

'Really?' Isidore laid down his spoon and turned to face the speaker. 'Why is that?'

'Because a woman has seen fit to join herself to us, contrary to all decency and modesty.'

'I had noticed that,' Isidore said in a voice that discouraged further comment.

Unimpressed, his neighbor pushed on. 'Well then. Is it your plan to divide up the church?'

I don't have a plan, Isidore felt like saying, because in a couple of weeks it won't be my responsibility, somebody else will have this problem dropped in his lap. But he was sworn to secrecy until a successor was chosen, so he simply said, 'Why should I?'

His neighbor seemed upset by this answer. 'Why? Well, because... because that's how it's done, isn't it? Alexandria, Constantinople, everywhere where they have women in churches, they put them in a separate section...I mean, don't they?'

'Why?' Isidore asked.

'Well...I mean...that's just how they do it, isn't it?'

'Yes, but why?' Isidore persisted. 'I mean, they must have some logical reason...Or don't they?'

'Well, I suppose it's because...because otherwise the women might flirt with the men.'

'Or the men with them.'

'I suppose so.'

'Seculars.'

'Well...yes.'

Isidore frowned. 'And you're afraid you might do that?'

'No! No! Certainly not!'

'So you must be accusing your fellow hermits of a weakness in that direction.'

The neighbor became agitated. 'Father, you're putting words into my mouth. I never for one moment suggested—'

'I'm not putting anything in your mouth,' Isidore said,

very severely, 'that you didn't already put there yourself. By implication, if not overtly. So the only other thing you could mean,' he added, with an irony unwonted in him, inspired perhaps by a sense of newfound freedom—in a few weeks he would be off, out of here, in Palestine, Syria, maybe even Constantinople itself—'is that Mother Theodora would start making eyes at you if the two of you didn't have a nice solid partition to separate you from one another.'

'No, no, I never said that,' the neighbor protested.

'Do you know who you're talking about?'

'I... No. I don't follow you.'

'Did you know that Mother Theodora has the confidence of the Patriarch?'

Startled by this unexpected turn, the neighbor stammered, 'No...has she really? I never knew that. If I'd known that...'

'You would not have said what you did, I'm sure. Oh yes, they have consulted one another several times, on spiritual matters. Archbishop Theophilus has the highest respect for her discernment, I understand. He has spoken highly of her to me on more than one occasion.'

'Did you know she was coming?' the person on Isidore's left asked.

'No, as a matter of fact I did not. I personally have not

yet had the privilege of meeting her. If she had approached me, I would have made sure that she had some kind of formal welcome. She avoided that. That is her humility. To come here as if she were just some ordinary hermit. Well, it's her choice, and I hope everyone respects it.' And, with an air of finality that stopped the conversation, Isidore returned to his stew.

Afterwards, in church, Theodora remained with Poemen and Serapion, not in splendid isolation, but at least, in deference to the feelings of many, well towards the back of the building. There was no mistaking her presence, however; as Poemen had expected, her voice soared out above the others, not in any desire to show off or assert herself, but in a contagious exuberance of spirit. Throughout the seemingly endless succession of prayers, psalms and scriptural readings, she remained alert, her large, somewhat protuberant eyes lively and glinting in the lamplight, their gaze focused on reader or priest, never wandering to feed curiously on her fellow-worshipers. Others blinked, dozed, peered about them from time to time; more than one sneaked a glance at her when they thought no one was looking. But Theodora remained serene, unassailable.

When dawn came and synaxis was over, Poemen made a beeline for Moses. 'Look, something came up that I ought to have done, days ago. Please don't wait. I'll come to your cell later.'

'That's all right,' Moses said. 'I'll meditate in the graveyard until you're through.'

'You don't have to.'

'I need to. High time I thought more about my last hour.'

'Whatever. I'll try not to keep you.'

To Poemen's surprise, Isidore and Theodora were standing deep in conversation in the doorway of the church. They were talking about Theophilus; what a strong character, what a great force for truth he was, how implacable an enemy of heresy, paganism, laxness among the flock... Poemen stood by them, patient, attentive, until Isidore excused himself, saying how much he hoped they could continue their conversation soon, and turned to Poemen.

'Let's walk a little way.' They did so, until they were out of earshot of the other hermits. Then Poemen apologized profusely for not having talked to Isidore sooner.

'You know how it is. Things kept cropping up...But I really don't have any excuse. Well, Dioscorus asked me to take your place, I suppose you knew he would?'

Isidore nodded.

'I refused.'

'I was afraid you would,' Isidore said. 'I suppose it's no use my—'

'None,' Poemen said quickly. 'I couldn't do your job, I'd be a fool to try. Luckily we hit on a much better candidate.'

'Who is...'

'Moses.'

Isidore drew a sharp breath. 'Whose idea? Yours?'

'No. Both of us thought of him, independently.'

Isidore remained silent for some moments. Poemen said, 'You're troubled.'

'Frankly, yes...As a hermit, what Moses does is his own business. As a priest, it's the church's. A priest must be obedient to his bishop. Here, we're talking about a man who was grossly disrespectful to Archbishop Theophilus, the last time—'

'Theophilus isn't his bishop.'

Isidore blinked. 'I beg your pardon?'

'Dioscorus is his bishop. I guarantee you that he will be perfectly obedient to Dioscorus—'

'Don't split hairs, Poemen,' Isidore burst out. 'A priest can't pick and choose which bishop he'll obey and which he won't! That would make a travesty of the whole system of church administration.' Not such a bad idea, at that, the mischievous imp said from a corner of Poemen's brain.

Instead, he smiled and said diplomatically, 'I think you'll find Moses as hermit and Moses as priest are two quite different things. You're forgetting the salutary influence of his former career.'

'As a bandit?' Isidore exclaimed, incredulous.

'As a bandit leader. How do you suppose he handled insubordination?' Isidore looked baffled. Poemen drew his index finger across his throat. 'Like that, is my guess. I think you'll find that Moses understands what a hierarchical organization means much better than most hermits do. And that once he's part of one, he'll honor it. But when I talk to him—I still haven't, you know—I'll reassure myself on that point before I commit us to anything, I promise you that.'

Isidore came as near to a grin as he ever allowed himself. 'I don't envy you your job.'

'I'm not looking forward to it myself.'

And indeed, as he climbed the low hill on which the graveyard stood, Poemen felt himself sharply conscious of the absurdity of his task. He was trying to get Moses to accept a position that he would not accept himself. Every argument against taking it that he had made to Dioscorus, Moses could equally well make to him. And probably would.

Moses was seated at the top of the low hill, on a stone that had slipped loose from the cairn supporting the cross, morosely regarding the headstones on the slope beneath him. 'You wonder, don't you, in a place like this,' he said, 'just how your account will stand, when you're called.'

Poemen, nodding, eased onto the stone beside him.

'Do you really think,' Moses went on, 'that anyone like me can ever balance the sins he committed in his youth?'

'I think you already have.'

'Ah, but you don't know what sins they were!' Moses turned, his dark features set with an unwonted grimness. 'I tell you, Poemen, my blood runs cold, even today, when I think of some of the things I did, without even thinking.'

'Without even thinking,' Poemen repeated.

'Exactly.'

'Exactly what?'

'Sins you committed before you entered the life.'

'Still sins,' Moses insisted.

'True. But when you entered the life, you repented them—didn't you?'

'And how many times since!'

'You did penance for them.'

'I did.'

'Then what's the matter with you?' Poemen asked. 'Don't you believe in forgiveness?'

'In principle, yes,' Moses said gloomily, shifting his haunches awkwardly, as if in physical as well as moral discomfort. 'But how do I know if I, personally, am forgiven?

I mean, if it was automatic, if it happened to everyone, it wouldn't count for much, wouldn't be real forgiveness, would it?'

'I suppose not,' Poemen admitted.

'So how can you know? Unless you get a sign. Me, I never yet got a sign. Nothing. Ever.'

Poemen was on the point of saying, we have been told that if we forgive others, God will forgive us, Mark 11.25-26, and since you even made us forgive Benjamin, even when most people didn't want to, what do you have to worry about? But something went click in his brain, and he almost snapped his fingers. Yes, that was what he needed. But it required care, it was like fishing. If you jerked the line too soon, you lost the catch.

'What kind of sign?' he asked. 'An angel, like with Papnoute the other day? Lights in the sky? What would convince you?'

'Oh, it wouldn't have to be anything spectacular.'

'I should hope not!'

'Something...anything. I'd know it, if it came.'

Poemen allowed this last thought to linger on the air. The sun had already grown uncomfortably hot, but he did not want to move, to break the progress of the conversation. 'You know Isidore's leaving us,' he said.

Moses sat upright. 'No! I never knew that. Why?'

'Keep it to yourself,' Poemen said confidentially. 'Nobody's supposed to know yet. He's off on some kind of mission for Theophilus.'

Moses absently picked up a pebble from the ground and tossed it from one hand to the other, back and forth. His brow was deeply furrowed. I love Moses, Poemen thought, anyone can tell when he's thinking, not like me, devious as I am, the picture of innocence. 'We'll need a replacement, then,' Moses said.

'Oh, I don't know.'

Moses made no effort to hide his shock. 'What do you mean, you don't know?'

'Well, back in the old days we didn't have a priest here. Someone would come over from Nitria, or if they didn't, we'd just take turns conducting the synaxis ourselves.'

'But the Holy Sacrament,' Moses complained. 'How can anyone administer that if they're not ordained?'

Poemen shrugged.

'No, they'll appoint someone,' Moses said. 'Dioscorus will insist.'

'Suppose there's nobody worthy?'

Moses shook his head decisively. 'Somebody has to do it. And even if they weren't worthy, at the beginning, then with

God's grace they might...' He groped for the right word.

'Grow into the office?'

'Something like that.'

'But in your case that wouldn't be necessary.'

Moses' brain, although reliable, didn't work as fast as Poemen's, and the latter had the added advantage that he knew where their talk was headed. Moses blinked twice, then said, 'What do you mean—my case?'

'Because when I talked with Bishop Dioscorus a few days ago, he said he wanted you as Isidore's successor.'

Moses stared at Poemen, stupefied. 'Me? A priest!'

Poemen smiled. 'Who better?'

'You're insane!'

'Who—me or the Bishop?'

'Both of you.' He half rose to his feet.

'Sit down, Moses.'

'All right, as long as you'll admit that this is some sort of a joke or something—although if it is, I must say it's in pretty poor taste,' Moses grumbled, seating himself again.

'You said something just now,' Poemen said. 'About a sign.'

'I did, but what's that got to do with—'

'Hear me out. You said, it didn't have to be from angels. It could be from men. Right?'

'Yes, but—'

Poemen stopped him with a warning hand. 'No buts, Moses. This is your sign. No,' he said, as Moses' mouth started to open again, 'please listen, then say whatever you want to say. It wasn't a question of, oh well, let's see who there is; now we can't have so-and-so for this reason, or such-and-such for that one, so let's settle for Father Moses as the least objectionable candidate. Nothing like that at all. Dioscorus had picked you out, all by himself. So had the other Tall Brothers. So did I-- just like with them, you were my first choice. They didn't tell me that. They waited to see what I'd say.' God forgive me for lying by omission, he thought, but I'm only omitting myself, and in a good cause, too. 'How many hermits are there in Scetis?'

'Nowadays? Oh, I don't know. Hundreds.'

'At a conservative estimate. So what are the odds against each of us choosing the same one?'

'Are you suggesting it was—'

'Divine guidance? What do you think?'

Humility alone would have kept Moses from agreeing, but Poemen could see that the argument had impressed him. 'You were praying just now for a sign,' he pressed on. 'A sign of forgiveness. Well, ask and you shall receive. God gave it to you, right away, just like that, Or,' he added, allowing a faint tinge of sarcasm to creep into his voice, 'does the great Father Moses require the Archangel Michael to appear in person, waving banners and blowing trumpets, before he'll consent to believe in God's mercy?'

Moses winced, shuddered. 'Don't say that. Not even as a joke.'

'I'm sorry,' Poemen was all contrition. 'Forgive me, Moses, that was unfair. Quite uncalled-for. I know your humility. Which is now telling you you're not worthy. Am I right?'

'Right.'

'So I'll quote your own words back at you. "Somebody has to do it ...And if he's not worthy, with God's grace he'll grow into the office." Isn't that what you said?'

Moses nodded glumly.

'You see, you can look at this humility thing two ways. You can say, oh, I'm humble; I'm not worthy. But other people don't agree. Isn't it just pride, spiritual pride, if you set your judgement up against theirs? Wouldn't true humility lie in just accepting what I and your Bishop and lots of other people feel you should do?'

'Poemen,' Moses asked, 'can your donkey still walk?'

It was Poemen's turn to be puzzled.

'Don't you know the old Egyptian saying—he can talk

the hind leg off a donkey?'

Poemen threw back his head and laughed unrestrainedly, clapping Moses on the shoulder, and the old robber grinned back, albeit rather wanly. 'I deserved that! But it's all perfectly true, what I'm saying. Deny it if you can.'

'No, really I can't.'

'Give me one good reason.'

'I'm black.'

Poemen started as if a snake had bitten him. This was something he had never anticipated. 'You're what?'

'Black.'

'So what?'

'I can't be a priest.'

Poemen came as near to anger as he done for a long time. 'What difference does that make? What do you think they do in Nubia, Abyssinia? They've got Christians there, you know. What do you think they do, dip them in a bucket of whitewash before they ordain them?'

'That's there,' Moses said reasonably. 'This is here. I can't be a priest over white people.'

'Just because there are folk here who are prejudiced? Well listen to this,' Poemen said, speaking fast and vehemently, 'it'll be the best thing that ever happened to them, you know why? I told you that choosing you was divinely guided, but

I'm doubly sure of that now, just from what you said, because God meant for those—' He just managed to avoid using a word that hadn't passed his lips since his shepherding days. '—those so-called hermits to get a lesson in charity and humility that they really, seriously need, and if you want to frustrate His purposes...' Poemen spread his hands in mock despair. 'Well, I give up. I'll tell you one thing, though. I for one will be bitterly disappointed if you don't accept, because I know that we'll have lost the best priest Scetis ever could have had.'

Moses stared at him. Poemen thought for a moment the old bandit might burst into tears, he seemed so deeply moved. 'Do you really mean that?'

'As God is my witness, with all my heart.'

Moses forced a wry smile. 'Yes would have been enough.'

'Right! I'm ashamed of myself! Swearing oaths at my time of life! You see, Moses, how you surpass me in virtue?'

'No I don't.'

'Yes you do, but let's not get into one of those. Will you accept ordination?'

Moses sighed. 'I can't refuse it,' he said sadly.

Poemen smiled and clasped Moses' hand. 'It's not a punishment, you know. Just another way of serving God. Let me find someone who's going to Hermopolis and get a message off to the Bishop as soon as possible—in case you should change your mind,' he added impishly.

'As if I'd do that!' Moses cried indignantly.

Clinched it, Poemen thought. But I broke my promise to Isidore to make Moses swear priestly obedience...Oh dear, what a manipulator I am! Is that a sin, I wonder, even if it's done from pure motives? That's the excuse of godly sinners the world over! But if it's a sin, what sin is it exactly? Not lechery, gluttony, avarice...Vainglory, I suppose. Liking to see myself as more ingenious than the next man. I should be more like Father Serapion, a simple soul, with never a thought of scheming, content to worship God humbly, regarding myself as nothing—a soul as innocent as the birds of the air...

'Poemen!'

He turned. It was John Colobos. 'Poemen, you remember I came to you, a couple of days ago, about a problem I had?'

'About forgetfulness?'

John's face twitched, his eyes would not fix on Poemen's, he shuffled his feet. 'Yes...And you told me what to do about it...Oh, I feel such an idiot!'

'What's the matter?' Poemen asked. 'Didn't it work?'

'I don't know. By the time I got home, I'd forgotten what you told me!'

Chapter Nineteen

Shenoute's servant knocked timidly on the door of Shenoute's study. Shenoute, reading the latest report from the Elder Mother of the White Monastery, took no notice. After a pause, the servant knocked again, a little louder. Again, no response. The servant turned and came out from the cool gloom of the cloisters into the glare of the monastery's central courtyard. The strategos, the district magistrate, was standing there impatiently in the sun, his polished bronze chain of office around his neck, flanked by his two assistants. The servant bowed low and said, 'The holy father the blessed Abbot Shenoute is in the company of our Lord and Savior Jesus Christ and regrets that he cannot see you at the moment.'

'I'm surprised,' the magistrate said. 'In fact, I'll go further than that. I'm incredulous.'

The servant bowed, as much to hide his expression of hatred as anything, but did not speak.

The magistrate picked up a straw from the cobblestones of the courtyard and stepped over to the big stone sundial that stood in its center. 'You have as long as it takes for the shadow to get to...here,' he said, placing the straw on the dial only a finger's breadth from where the shadow now fell. 'If you do not bring him out within that time, I will have you flogged.'

The servant bowed again, said 'Yes, sir!' and disappeared.

The magistrate and his assistants exchanged looks. The magistrate was a Christian, or at any rate he attended church regularly and made substantial contributions to church funds. But he was first and foremost the upholder of Roman law and order in the *nome* of Akhmin, one of the thirty-odd administrative districts into which, even in Pharaonic times, Egypt had been divided, and within which the White Monastery was located. By keeping him standing in the hot sun, Shenoute was offending not merely a government official but the whole awesome political system that the official represented.

The three men stood alone in the deserted courtyard, but they did not feel alone. Each of them was conscious of the pressure of eyes, eyes of monks watching them with unconcealed hostility from the cloisters that surrounded the courtyard on three sides. They tried to stare back, gave up on that and fixed their eyes on the sundial. You could not actually see the shadow moving, it went too slowly, but the gap between straw and shadow gradually narrowed. The shadow was almost touching the straw when a heavy wooden door, flung upon so violently that it smashed against the wall to one side of it, sent thunderous echoes reverberating through the cloisters. As the echoes died, Shenoute stepped ponderously into the courtyard.

Though his dress was plain and a good deal the worse for wear, he made an impressive figure. He stood more than six feet tall, his body built like a crude slab of rock, his head another block of it, with a protruding jaw that seemed to tilt the block back at a slight angle. His pale eyes looked almost white. His coarse black hair, trimmed close to the scalp, grew in irregular tufts and clumps. His weatherworn skin was ridged and wrinkled like a crocodile's hide. He was missing a couple of front teeth where a pagan had landed a lucky punch before being pounded into submission. His face set in a scowl.

'Who are you and what do you want?' he asked in something between a growl and a roar.

'I am Ptolemaios Damarion, *strategos* of Akhmin,' the magistrate said.

'I am Shenoute, Archimandrite of the White Monastery of Atripe. State your business.'

The magistrate was minded to reprove Shenoute for his peremptory manner, but decided that this would be beneath his dignity. 'I am here in answer to complaints that you have physically assaulted a monk of this monastery, to wit one Seras, son of Heraklion, causing him severe bodily injuries such that he has lost the use of his right arm and right leg and is forced to beg for alms to obtain a living. Further, that when Christian tenant farmers from the river island of Paneheou complained to you of extortionate contracts forced on them by their pagan landlords, you did willfully trespass upon vineyards of the latter and destroy by uprooting two and two-thirds *arouras* of mature grapevines, property of Hermias son of Tothes, Hierax son of Hierax—.'

The pale eyes glared bleakly. 'What are you? Are you a man or a devil?'

Taken aback, the magistrate could only repeat, 'I have told you once, I will not tell you again, I am Ptolemaios Damarion, *strategos*—'

'And I rule this monastery under God! I am responsible only to God!' Shenoute took a pace forward and laid one knotty, hairy-knuckled hand on the magistrate's chain of office. 'If you are a spirit or an angel who comes from God, know that I too am His servant. But if you have ceased to serve him, well, I have not ceased.'

'Take your hands off my chain. Respect my office,' the magistrate said, his voice sounding tinnier and more high-pitched than he had hoped, as a tremor of physical fear struck cold into his soul. He knew Shenoute's reputation—it had simply never occurred to him that Shenoute might dare to lay hands on so high-ranking a representative of the state.

But, he had gravely underestimated his man. 'This is what I think of your office,' Shenoute roared, and taking the chain in both hands he twisted it, pulled it so that it tightened around the magistrate's throat, and jerked it violently. The magistrate stumbled forward, flinging his hands in the air. His mouth flew open but his cry was stifled by the chain that was strangling him. As the magistrate started to fall, Shenoute dropped the angled block of his head and butted the magistrate in the face, breaking his nose. Then he wrenched at the bronze chain, which snapped in half, and the magistrate, dizzy, semi-conscious, blood pouring from his nose, was hurled to the ground.

His two assistants, who had been paralyzed by the suddenness and fury of Shenoute's attack, now sprang towards him. But Shenoute threw back his head and bawled, 'Brothers! Seize them!'

The monks who had been watching from the cloisters came swarming out into the courtyard. The assistants looked at the monks, looked at one another, and took off without a word, running at full speed through the gate of the courtyard, which luckily for them had been left ajar, and across the field outside, from which more monks, who had been sowing seed for next year's harvest, reared up like so many dark specters and joined in the pursuit. Shenoute, bellowing in fury, leapt on top of the prostrate magistrate and trampled on him, the bare but leathery, calloused soles of his feet striking the fallen body with sickening force. When his fury had spent itself, he brought down a final foot on the man's skull and kept it there, pinning his head to the ground, standing with his own head thrown back proudly, like a hunter who has just slain a wild beast and now stands, in an attitude of triumph, for the admiration of his followers.

'Here,' he called to the few monks who remained in the courtyard. 'Take this diabolical excrement and throw it outside.'

'I hope you haven't overreached yourself this time, Father,' a voice came from behind him.

Shenoute swung round. It was the Elder Brother.

'I didn't kill him, if that's what you're worried about.'

'He'll come back.'

Shenoute snorted. 'With what? A few village policemen? How many monks have we here, as of the last count?'

'Over twenty-one hundred, Father.'

'Well, let's see him fight them!'

The Elder Brother looked sour and dubious, although

little more so than usual. 'He can go to the *epistrategos*. He can go to the military commander and get troops.'

Shenoute grinned wolfishly. 'And what happened last time the military commander was here, the year the floods were late?'

'You prayed to God to let the floods come, and they came.'

'And then what?'

'He asked you for one of your leather girdles. You blessed it.'

'And what happened when he forgot to wear it?'

'The barbarians beat him.'

'And when he wore it?'

'He beat the barbarians and slaughtered them unsparingly.'

Shenoute gave a deep sigh of satisfaction. 'I don't think we need worry about the military commander, do you? And if the commander's ours, forget the *epistrategos*. He's helpless without the army. That fool Denarius or whatever his name is knows that perfectly well. Know what I think he'll do?' The Elder Brother shrugged his shoulders, frowning.

'Nothing! Pretend it never happened. The man's a coward as well as a disloyal Christian. The impertinence of it! Coming here to threaten me, the Archimandrite, can you believe it? I put the fear of God into him! He'll know now that if anyone's overreached himself, it's him.' He took the Elder Brother's arm and steered him back out of the sunlight; as far as he was concerned, the incident was over. 'Come to my study, I have some disciplinary measures I'd like to discuss with you...'

News of the event spread quickly through the White Monastery. By the time it reached the women, the unfortunate magistrate had been converted into no less than his Satanic majesty himself, accompanied by a cloud of demons, who had descended on the monastery determined to root out once and for all their deadliest adversary in all Egypt. But Shenoute, unbeatable, had subdued the Arch-Enemy in single combat and trampled him in the dust, whereupon the attendant demons, terrified, had dematerialized in a puff of smoke.

Leila, rounding her eyes in astonishment, looked shocked, then delighted, at the appropriate moments, just as the others did. She had learned, over the months since she took her vow, that if you wanted a quiet life in the White Monastery, you did as the others did. If you did not, if you were tagged as strange, different in any way, look out! You would find enemies, enemies would spread gossip, slowly a wall would form about you, with everyone else on the other side of it, glaring across disapprovingly at you, and it was then only a matter of time before you were found guilty of something, heresy, disobedience, crimes so vague they could be pinned upon anyone, but of course they were not, only on those who had been singled out from the beginning.

She had hoped that such things were confined to the novitiate, for it seemed natural enough, if deplorable, that women competing with one another for entrance to the monastery should intrigue, tell tales, curry favor, go behind backs and carry out all the detestable stratagems that people do who become rivals for a goal. She had believed that once she left the gatehouse and entered the monastery proper, all that would disappear—the bad apples would have been sifted out during their novitiate, while the good ones who were left, feeling themselves secure now in a career that not even death need terminate (for the faithful would continue to sing God's praises, albeit in another world), would have no further motive for conniving. Gradually, unwillingly, she had learned better. The unspeakable Thaesis, who spied on everyone and masked her duplicity with an oleaginous parade of virtue, had been admitted, and not merely admitted—the older sisters obviously favored her. She would rise in the hierarchy, they confidently predicted. Sansno and Tanouris, who after the incident with the Master of Novices had taken good care to behave with absolute decorum whenever there was a chance that their superiors might see them, had been admitted too, even though, when no one was looking, they relapsed into the same lazy, gossipy behavior as before. And those who had passed through the novitiate before them were not, as Leila had hoped, some better, higher breed. Indeed, so far as she could tell, they differed not in the slightest from her own cohort.

She had been placed in a cell with Demetria, a girl who, though she had been in the monastery longer than Leila, was in fact a year or two younger. She liked Demetria, a modest, pretty girl with a skin so light it looked almost translucent, who insisted on apologizing every time she had to explain to Leila some rule or traditional practice of the monastery. 'You needn't apologize,' Leila would tell her, 'I'm the beginner, not you.' But Demetria would just blush and avoid Leila's gaze, and next time it happened she would apologize again.

She had two brothers, both older than her, in the men's monastery, and she would tell Leila endless stories about the most trivial things they had done when they had all been children together. Leila had been irritated at first, then she realized that if you nodded from time to time and said, 'Oh!' and 'Really?' and 'Imagine that!' at what seemed appropriate intervals, you didn't have to listen, you could relax and let the placid stream of Demetria's voice flow over you, for these tales were really soliloquies that Demetria spoke merely to remind herself of a time when she had been free and happy.

It took Leila a good while to realize that Demetria was deeply unhappy. In all probability she did not realize it herself, or did not admit it. For a long time Leila saw her as the perfect sister, meek, obedient, her will surrendered, if not to God, at least to the Elder Mother. They shared a tiny cell that contained nothing but two hard, narrow wooden cots and some pegs to hang their few clothes on, but Demetria never breathed a word of complaint, even when they were hurrying to dress for the pre-dawn prayer at the chilly end of night and kept bumping into one another in the darkness because there wasn't enough space. On days when fasting was decreed she remained as cheerful as one could without deteriorating into unseemly levity, never grumbling nor growing ill-tempered as some of the others did. On other days she ate just enough of the plain fare, often no more than bread and water, to absolve her of the charge of spiritual pride.

In the intervals between prayers and the few hours of sleep allowed them, they were engaged in the manufacture of linen, spinning flax and then weaving it on ponderous hand-looms. The rooms where they performed these tasks were policed by vigilant Elder Sisters, who quickly stopped frivolous conversations and, in some cases, refused to allow a sister to use the toilet until the previous user had returned. But since the toilet was shared by the workers in more than one room, and because a few Elder Sisters were lax in enforcing this rule, it was sometimes possible to enjoy a few moments of talk in the barren little shed with its odoriferous trench. Otherwise, one could talk only for brief moments in the confused intervals that immediately preceded and followed the single daily meal, or, with one's cell-mate only, during the hours of darkness.

It was on these latter occasions that Demetria told the tales of her youth, and often Leila had ridden into the forests of sleep on the soothingly cadenced flow of Demetria's tongue. Then one night she woke to the sound of Demetria's anguished sobbing. So alien to her image of Demetria did this sound seem that for several moments Leila believed what she was hearing was simply the continuation of a dream. When she realized her mistake, her first impulse was to leap up, take Demetria in her arms and try to comfort her. She did not yield to this impulse, in part because she was not yet fully awake, in part because of repeated admonitions never to touch another sister, least of all when the two of you were alone together. Even when one had to touch someone, a sick person, for instance, who had to be oiled or bathed, several other sisters and even the Elder Mother herself were required to be present.

So Leila had hesitated, and while she hesitated, a still stronger reason for refraining occurred to her. She knew by a sudden intuition that Demetria would be deeply upset to know that Leila had overheard her. Their whole life together, Leila now saw, was based on a fragile eggshell of mutual pretense—-crack that shell, and the life might well deteriorate until it became intolerable. So she lay there, acutely uncomfortable, but unable to lose herself again in sleep until the sobs had subsided and Demetria herself dozed off.

Often in the days that followed Leila had longed to reach out and comfort the lost child who dwelt somewhere within the outwardly patient and submissive woman. Before she came to the White Monastery, she would have surrendered to such feelings without the least thought that they could be misinterpreted. Indeed, when the Master of Novices had warned them, in suitably veiled language, against the sin of obtaining pleasure from one another's bodies, Leila had not even understood what he was talking about. Sex she knew, from her father's barnyard, from the gossip of farm girls and the lewd overtures of farm youths, from her traumatic experience with the bandits. But sex was, by definition—at least by her definition—something that happened between men and women. How could two women even do it? They didn't have the right bits and pieces.

She had asked Sansno to explain to her what the Master of Novices had meant, so innocent was she, and Sansno laughingly had said, 'Well, you came to the right person!' and then proceeded to give her a quick but thorough course of instruction in the mechanics of lesbian relationships. Of course, since both were then still novices and also strangers, unsure of one another, this information had come accompanied by repeated insistences that 'Naturally, I've never actually seen anyone do that,' or, 'I'm just repeating what other girls have told me.' Even then, these insistences had not impressed Leila very much—anyone as well-versed in the subject as Sansno seemed to be had surely done more than garner a few scraps of hearsay, and she caught, too, a note of enthusiasm in Sansno's tone that did not exactly smack of the detached observer.

It was not until after she had taken her vow that Leila became aware of the extent to which forbidden practices flourished in the White Monastery. Not among all the sisters, of course, nor even among a majority. But once you became attuned to them, you would have had to be blind and deaf (Leila thought) to ignore the exchanges of doting looks, the covert whispers, even the occasional scuffling and groping in dark corners from which she always, on principle, hastily averted her gaze. And she had noted, too, how Sansno looked at Demetria. Even in the chapel, at night, even in prayer she had seen by the fitful illumination of lamps the looks of yearning hunger that Sansno fixed on her quite unconscious room-mate. On these occasions, she thanked God that He had seen fit to make her ordinary-looking, though even she had begun to suspect guarded overtures in some of the remarks addressed to her by older sisters. Youth, it seemed, constituted a currency only slightly less valued than beauty.

If the rhythm of life were not so unchanging, she thought, or if we were not so constantly crushed together, or if 'it'—she resolutely refused even to give those hateful practices a name—were not kept continually before our minds by repeated condemnations, surely there wouldn't be so much of 'it' going around. But none of those three conditions was ever relieved, except for the monotony. And, given the way in which that was relieved, she would have found its persistence preferable.

Little more than a month past the end of her novitiate, the square metal plate that hung from a post in the main courtyard of the women's monastery had been beaten furiously. Nothing odd in that: it was beaten regularly to signal the hours of prayer and eating. But this time the summons fell in the middle of a work period, something hitherto unknown in Leila's experience. She noticed a kind of unhealthy excitement on some of the faces as they made their way to the courtyard, of fear or at best unease on a few others. Hurrying down a long corridor, she whispered to her neighbor, 'What is it?'

'Punishment time,' the other responded, tight-lipped.

They formed up in a rough circle, several deep, around the sides of the courtyard. In the center stood the Elder Mother, her Second, the Elder Brother, and a dozen or so of the Elder Sisters. The Elder Brother had obviously taken charge of the proceedings: he had a look on his gaunt features as if someone had just made a bad smell, and in his left hand he held a roll of papyrus. But Leila did not look at his left hand. She looked at his right, which held a supple tamarind rod twice the length of his arm and the breadth of two fingers in diameter. This he held lightly, making one or two short, preparatory swishes with its tip as the last of the sisters shuffled into place and a deathly quiet fell on the courtyard.

'Sarah, sister of Brother Apollo, step forward,' the Elder Brother said, reading the name from the scroll in his left hand. Leila peered over the shoulders of those in front of her. Opposite where she was standing, she saw a woman hitherto unknown to her, dark-haired, pallid, her face blurry with tears, ejected suddenly into the open circle by her neighbors. She glanced nervously around her, hung her head and shuffled forwards.

'Sarah, for giving instruction when not entitled to do so, forty strokes,' the Elder Brother intoned.

The Elder Sisters fell upon Sarah, dragging her to the ground, pinning her arms. The Elder Mother seized one ankle, her Second the other, and the two women pulled on Sarah's legs, raising her naked feet high in the air, while one of the Elder Sisters threw a pair of arms around her legs, pinning her dress in place about her thighs and thus preventing the exposure of any parts that ought not to be exposed.

She did not cry out, or perhaps one of the Elder Sisters was gagging her, Leila could no longer see her face in the huddle of struggling women. The Elder Brother stared for a moment at her naked soles, held out to him like two plates by the two senior women of the establishment. Then, standing a little to one side so that his stroke would impact both soles at once, he lined up the tamarind rod on her feet, like an archer taking aim, whipped it up behind his head and brought it down with all his strength. The flat crack of rod on flesh re-echoed across the courtyard, and in its train, almost simultaneously, came the woman's scream: gagged or not, she had succeeded in making herself heard. One of the Elder Sisters quickly stuffed a cloth in her mouth. Leila felt the bile of nausea rise in her throat.

A voice in her head somewhere said quite clearly, This can't be right.

Of course it's right, Leila told her disobedient voice. This woman deserves her punishment. The authorities have ordered it, and they know what is best for us. If they didn't, they wouldn't be in authority, now would they?

The Elder Brother, taking his time, without rage, without rancor, struck again. This time the sound of the stroke was followed only by a muffled grunting, a noise such as a pig might make with its snout in a bucket of swill. The legs flexed violently, rocking the two women that held them. The Second almost lost her balance, but she recovered and they got the legs under control and into position for the third stroke.

Three down, thirty-seven to go, the disobedient voice said. This can't be right. You know it can't be right.

She deserves it, Leila insisted stubbornly, loyally. The teaching of doctrine can only come from those in authority. To usurp that role shows pride. Pride is a sin. Sin sends us to hell for eternity. Those who save us from sin are doing us a kindness no matter how they do it. Better to suffer a brief pain in this world than everlasting agony in the next.

The disobedient voice quieted down. But the nausea did not go away. As the blows continued to fall, she felt the sourness swelling irresistibly into her mouth; she clapped both hands across her lips, pushed her way back and out through the assembled throng, raced to the foul-smelling shed that housed the communal privy and added her part to the mix of fetid matter in the pit.

Retching, gasping, she pulled back her head to see an Elder Sister regarding her disapprovingly from the doorway. 'I'm sorry, Mother,' she felt obliged to say. 'I don't know what came over me.'

'Your first Punishment?' the Elder Sister asked.

Leila assented.

'Make sure you learn from it, then. And don't hang about, if you've finished, get back there.'

Silently she obeyed and regained her place. The Elder Brother was by now more than halfway through the forty strokes. Sarah lay limp and no longer struggled; the soles of her feet were crisscrossed with livid welts, some of which had burst, sending trickles of blood down her ankles. There was blood on the hands of the two women holding them. But not, of course, on the hands of the Elder Brother.

When it was done, two of the Elder Sisters picked the woman up, still limp and motionless, with eyes closed and face drained of all color. Between them they carried her off to the infirmary; it would be days, perhaps weeks, before she could walk again. The Elder Brother, his face still expressionless, save for its permanent look of someone exploring a blocked drain, glanced down at his scroll and read, 'Thais, the sister of the younger Tanouris, step forward...Thais, of whom you inform us that she sought out Syncletica in carnal desire, fifteen strokes...'

There were ten or a dozen women punished, all told, for various offences, for theft, for lying, for disobedience, for insulting their superiors, or just for unspecified failings in judgement or understanding. Only the number of strokes varied. At the end of it, the Elder Brother's arm remained as firm and vigorous as it had been at the beginning. When all was done, an Elder Sister pulled him up a bucket of water and he washed the rod clean with it. Later he would rub oil into it to keep it supple. When he was through with the bucket, the Elder Mother and her Second used it to wash their hands in. Slowly the rest of the assembly broke up and, suitably chastened, returned to their various tasks.

Somehow Leila managed to get through it all, in part by not looking, although she knew that her not looking would have been noted and remembered as a black mark against her by the Elder Sisters who moved among the spectators, watching for reactions, for the least gesture or whispered word that might convey the spirit of disobedience. Somehow she managed to convince herself that it was all for the best, part of the steep and flinty path to righteousness that she had vowed to follow to its end.

After all, what else could she do? She was there for life.

Chapter Twenty

Zachary and Didymos hired out for the grape harvest. The vines were raised on trellises of flimsy stakes to keep the grapes safe in years when the Nile rose by more than twenty-five feet (if it rose as much as thirty-six feet, as it occasionally did, there was nothing much you could do about it). That meant you didn't need to stoop in order to pick, but it was still hard work, filling the big wicker basket, then hoisting it onto your back, heading across the vineyard to the shallow stone trough, and tipping the grapes out among the feet of the treaders.

Hard, but not as monotonous as the work of the treaders, who stamped back and forth, back and forth, all day long, their legs stained up over the ankles with purplish juice, while a flautist, hired specially for the occasion, sat under a crude roof of palm leaves and played to them to alleviate their boredom. At least when you had tipped out one load of grapes you could loiter back to the picking ground with the empty basket slung over your shoulder, mindlessly relaxed, so long as you didn't do it too obviously and rouse the ire of the weasel-eyed foreman who scurried constantly from one end of the vineyard to the other, trying to spot anyone who was shirking. You were paid by the day, not by the basket, but they could still dock you a half-day's wages for idleness.

Zachary didn't mind the work. His life in the desert had inured him to hardship, and after the first few days he took it in stride. It was varied enough to hold his attention, yet not exacting enough to require any kind of mental effort. His days passed in a dream of sun and sweat, the smooth play of muscle and the delicious languor of relaxation when the work was finally done. They drank wine in the evenings with the other workers; they avoided Sophia as much as they reasonably could. The other workers had tried to tease him at first but had quickly given up, between Didymos's threats and Zachary's total lack of any kind of reaction. Now he was accepted, passively, as an oddity, and mostly ignored, which pleased him.

What was so wonderful about this new life was that you didn't have to make any effort. Ever since childhood, Zachary had had goals to meet. Somewhat different goals had been set by each of his parents. Both had wanted him to be a model of decorum, but there the similarity ended. His father wanted him as the Young Executive, worldly, shrewd, sophisticated, driven by the profit motive, eager to succeed, to help expand his father's business. His mother had wanted him as a paragon of the virtues, dedicated to expanding his Heavenly Father's business, but without taking things to the extremes of monkhood or hermithood, vocations she accepted as praiseworthy in the abstract but too lower-class for any son of hers. Being an idealist, with little interest in material things, he had found his mother's goals more acceptable than his father's, yet his enthusiasm had been tempered with a sense of unease he had never quite understood until he came to Scetis and saw real holiness.

Then, even when he had taken over his own life, nothing had really changed. Goals were still there, goals so high now as to be all but unreachable, and all of life had become a constant struggle, against the flesh, against the passions, against the constant fretting of his own mind—a continual process of striving and falling short, always and inevitably falling short. And finally, even going alone into the deepest desert had not changed anything either. His goals were no longer set by his mother, or by his fellow-hermits. But still they remained, set now only by himself, with no one else to guide or restrain his headlong rush towards an unattainable perfection, so that like a spring that is wound ever tighter and tighter, the time had finally come when he simply...

Snapped.

Snapped just like that, without warning, but completely

and irrevocably. As a spring, once broken, can never be wound tight again. What did all his old ideals matter to him now? All that mattered was the warmth of the sun on his back, the satisfaction of another emptied basket, the deliciousness of the grapes he ate while picking (for the foreman did not grudge them the odd handful) – grapes that were warm, soft, ripe, that burst on the tongue in a juicy jellied sweetness. That was reality. Not the dreams, the fears, the insatiable longings of his former life, things that had dissolved like the phantoms that they were.

One day a traveling prostitute came touring the vineyards. She knew or pretended to know the flute-player, and sat curled up under his palm-branch shelter while he played, ogling the workers with her hennaed eyes. Maybe he was her pimp. After nightfall, someone made a bed of straw in an abandoned shed and the workers formed a line outside it, cracking jokes and one or two of them occasionally pinching or slapping at someone's erection, then playfully dodging the real or feigned rage of the offended party, while the others guffawed.

'Care to come along?' Didymos asked, heading for the end of the line.

Zachary shook his head. Out of habit, perhaps, but beyond habit, out of an immense indifference. Physical desire seemed to have gone as dead in him as any other emotion, or perhaps it was no more than fastidiousness, a reluctance to put any part of himself into an unwashed vagina along with the seed of a couple dozen Egyptian peasants.

'Wait for me, then,' Didymos called over his shoulder, and Zachary took a lazy turn or two among the stripped vines, watching the slender horn of a young moon that had just emerged over the eastern horizon. His meanderings took him within earshot of the open shed, and he heard the animal grunts of the current customer and the woman's faked squeals. They caused him neither excitement nor disgust. They merely reminded him that he, too, had once linked himself in that same act with another. He tried to remember it, to see if he could stir in himself some faint ember of lust. Nothing. It was as if the two participants his memory conjured up were complete strangers to him, beings from another world. They did so-and-so, and such-and-such. Well, what about that, then!

He had to laugh to himself. One great goal of the ascetic life was complete indifference to any human emotion. It was not an end in itself, of course. Merely a pre-requisite for the divine union, a purging of the things of earth so one could lay oneself open to the things of heaven. But he, having ceased to seek it, had somehow achieved it, and found beyond it...nothing. Nothing at all. And he could not even bring himself to feel disappointment.

Finally Didymos emerged from the shed and they walked back towards the village. 'Aren't you going to ask what she was like?' Didymos asked.

'No. You don't need to lie to me.'

Didymos, who had a good sense of humor, laughed and said, 'Well, not so hot, to be honest. Mind you,' he added reasonably, 'who would be, after taking on that lot. Still, makes a change. Did you, ever, before you, er...'

'Yes,' Zachary said sharply, cutting off the conversation with his tone. They walked on in silence.

'I guess we'll be through with the grapes, in a week or so,' Didymos said after a while.

'So what's next?' Zachary really didn't care, but felt his friend expected the question.

'The water's down. That means I can sow my own land. After that there's the olive crop. Always something.'

What he liked most about Didymos, Zachary decided, was the man's utter lack of curiosity. Most other men would have questioned anyone like Zachary about his past, or what he intended to do in the future. Didymos never did either. His horizons were his land, his work, his village friends, his uneasy relationship with his wife—a choice Zachary suspected he regretted, but he never complained, except perhaps very obliquely ('makes a change...'), and seemed to accept it as he accepted all the other inescapable conditions of his life. To Zachary, after a lifetime of mixing solely with strivers, overachievers, this common fatalism seemed an exotic bloom, infinitely relaxing to his soul.

So he was glad to work with Didymos on the few *arouras* of land that the latter termed his own, although in fact they were leased on a five-year contract from a rich businessman in Oxyrhynchus. Following Didymos, his mule and plough, he scattered barley seed (borrowed at fifty per cent interest, one and a half *artabas* of grain to be repaid for every *artaba* of seed) over the rich, dark, furrowed land, still moist and clinging stickily to the feet after its yearly inundation. 'Think, this will all be beer, one day,' Didymos encouraged him, although they would never get to make it themselves: some would go as rent, payable in kind, the rest direct to a commercial brewery in the village so they could live for the year, and for any beer they drank they would pay, just like everyone else.

Didymos did not offer to pay him for his work. Zachary vaguely knew that someone had given Didymos money to look after him, and knew for a certainty that if he had not been working, Didymos would have had either to hire someone or do all the work himself, taking time away from the olive-harvest and thus forfeiting the cash that this would have brought him. In other words, Didymos was profiting financially from Zachary in two quite distinct ways. Yet Zachary could not bring himself to feel that he was being exploited. After all, Didymos gave him board and lodging, and used his extra money to keep them both constantly supplied with wine and beer. And what would Zachary spend more money on, if he had it? His wages from the wine harvest remained virtually untouched. There was little to be bought in Tebtynis, and still less that he wanted.

He was relieved that Sophia seemed to have given up on him. She no longer tried to introduce him to nice Greek families or persuade him to attend the local church. Her attitude towards him reeked of disapproval, as if he had entered her house under false pretenses. Plates of food were slapped down defiantly in front of him, removed in chilly silence almost before his jaws had stopped moving.

Didymos ignored this, maintaining his good humor throughout their meals, save for the occasional remark like, 'I see you're in good voice this evening, dear.' But more than once Zachary was kept awake by their arguing, and once heard the sound of blows, and her screaming. Her face was bruised the next morning. He ignored it. It was no concern of his.

So the year turned. The sowing was quickly followed by hoeing, for in the deeply moistened ground, still warmed by the autumn sun, weeds grew as quickly and vigorously as did the barley. Then came the olive harvest, and the two men hired out again. Afterwards there were dates to gather, and winter figs, the darkest and sweetest, although time had to be taken off from these tasks to keep the growing barley crop free of weeds.

During all this time, Zachary had vaguely believed, insofar as he had bothered to believe anything, that life in the countryside was at least as anarchic as life in Alexandria, and that his presence in Didymos's household was not only a matter of no concern to the authorities, but would go entirely unnoticed by them. What he had not realized was that only in the city, with its vast, constantly shifting population, or in the desert, where none went but those, whether bandit or hermit, who chose to live outside of civilization, could a man even hope to exist without exposing himself to official scrutiny. Things moved slowly in rural Egypt, but they did move with the torpid relentlessness of a country that had been governed and over-governed for millennia.

One evening the village clerk appeared at their door.

'Hear you have somebody else living here,' he said to Didymos.

Since Zachary sat there as visibly as anyone well could, given the low quality of the oil the household burned, there seemed little point in denying it.

'Who is he?' the clerk asked, still not addressing Zachary directly.

'Oh, just a fellow who works with me.'

'Was he registered in the last census?' Didymos looked blank and shrugged, so finally the clerk was obliged to acknowledge Zachary. 'Were you registered in the last census?'

Zachary was about to say 'No' when he remembered that failure to register was an offence that could get him arrested, so he said, 'Yes.'

'Where? Here?' The clerk raised incredulous eyebrows.

'Alexandria.'

'I've heard of people leaving here for Alexandria,' the clerk said skeptically, 'but this is the first time I've heard of anyone leaving Alexandria for here.'

'He was a hermit in the desert,' Didymos explained.

'Really? Are you a hermit?'

Zachary thought that over. He could not recall any time at which he had decided he was not a hermit any more. But to claim that he was one now would be absurd, as well as inaccurate.

'Then what are you, exactly?' the clerk asked, getting impatient.

'I told you,' Didymos said. 'He works with me.'

'I didn't ask you. I asked him.'

Zachary spread his hands.

'This is most unsatisfactory,' the clerk said. 'I'm going to have to refer this to the *strategos*, let him decide what to do about it.'

Didymos knew the village clerk all too well. This last remark constituted an open invitation for Didymos to offer him a bribe. It did not need to be a large bribe. Nothing that Didymos, with the extra cash Zachary brought in, could not easily afford. But Didymos did not want to bribe the village clerk. For one thing, he didn't like him, and for another, he didn't see why he should waste his money if he could find another way round it. 'I suppose what you really came about was the liturgy,' he said.

Zachary blinked. To him this term referred only to the forms and procedures of divine worship. And indeed the clerk, equally puzzled, said, 'What's that got to do with it?'

'Well, now you've got an extra live body to dispose of.'

The clerk said nothing for a moment. His eyes calculated. Then he said, 'You know I had you down for this year, Didymos.'

'Sure I know. My turn, isn't it?'

'But what you're saying is...'

'He can come too.'

'Is that right?' the clerk asked Zachary.

'Yes, yes, of course,' Zachary said, not having the faintest idea what he was committing himself to.

'Hm...Well in that case, just for this once I might overlook...Mind you, you'd better make sure you stay out of trouble, you—what's your name, anyway?'

'Zachary.'

'Zachary. Keep your nose clean, or else.' And the clerk took his leave.

'What was all that about?' Zachary asked.

Didymos explained. In rural Egypt, the term 'liturgy'—-whose literal meaning was, 'work for the people'—meant precisely that: compulsory, unpaid labor on behalf of the state. 'People are always trying to get out of it,' Didymos went on, 'on one excuse or another. And some of them offer him bribes. Now, if somebody offers him a bribe, and from the look on his face I'd say someone already has, and a nice fat one too, very likely, he can take the bribe, let the person off, and put you in his place. The numbers still match, who's to know? Who's to care, long as the work gets done?'

'And that bit about your turn?'

'Well, they're only supposed to take one per household. If they take me, they couldn't take you too. Not legally, anyway. Unless of course you volunteer. Which you did. So now everyone's happy.'

'And the work?'

'Cleaning irrigation ditches. Shoring up dykes. Shoveling shit of every conceivable kind.' Didymos could not help grinning. 'Oh, you'll love every minute of it!'

Chapter Twenty-One

When Archbishop Theophilus of Alexandria heard who Bishop Dioscorus of Hermopolis Parva had selected as the new priest of Scetis, his first reaction was to explode with rage. Etched in his mind was the still-vivid picture of a slatternly black giant leading a donkey through the desert and speaking to him through a large mouthful of bread and cheese. He could hear that deep, contemptuous voice as clearly as if it spoke in that very room: 'Moses?...Why would you want to see him?...You're as big a fool as he is if you do...' Even the donkey had defecated on cue.

He threw the Bishop's letter to the floor, trampled on it, then seized the nearest available object, which happened unfortunately to be an exquisite crystal bowl presented to him by a pious widow for his Ecclesiastical Building Fund, and hurled it blindly. It hit the wall, bursting noisily into a thousand pieces that rained down in a clattering cascade on the tiled floor. Then he seized the silver handbell from his desk and rang it furiously.

A head peered cautiously round the door. The servant had heard the crash and did not want to become the target for the Archbishop's next missile. Normally Theophilus would have taken exception to such cautious behavior and given the servant a tongue-lashing, but right now he had only one thing on his mind. 'Send the Archdeacon in,' he roared. 'Immediately!'

In the five seconds that was the closest to immediacy Timothy could manage, Theophilus had stooped, scooped up the Bishop's letter and was now smoothing it so that it could at least be read. He caught fire fast and cooled fast, but for form's sake, or out of habit, his tone still carried the rage he no longer felt so sharply. 'Have you heard about this?' he demanded, thrusting the letter into Timothy's face.

'Sir ... what—?'

'Read it!' He paced, tense with unreleased energy, while Timothy quickly ran his eyes down the letter. 'See what your advice has done!'

'My advice...I'm sorry, your Reverence, I don't quite—'

'Your advice to appoint Dioscorus, oaf!' Theophilus hurled himself into a high-backed chair with lions carved on its arms, but did not offer Timothy a seat. 'You were there, you saw how that...that black creature insulted me! Go and write to Dioscorus at once and tell him that on no account, on no account whatsoever is he to—What's the matter with you, man?'

For Timothy was gazing at him with a drooping lower lip and an expression of unwanted obstinacy on his face.

'Go on! Spit it out!'

'I think that would be extremely unwise, sir.'

'Oh, you do, do you?' Theophilus had leaned forward, elbow on the desk in front of him, hand cupping his jaw. His ice-cold brain, blinded for a moment by rage, had clicked in and reasserted itself. 'Well, go on.'

Timothy hesitated. 'Well...the appointment of Dioscorus was part of a much larger program—'

'To ensure that we had the full support of the anchorites, yes, that's correct.'

'—and what anchorites value most is their independence—'

Theophilus did not need to have it spelled out for him. 'I see what you mean—if I start telling them what they can or can't do, it'll put their backs up, we'll lose them.'

Timothy nodded.

'And of course they all hang together, all the Nitrians, the Tall Brothers, Evagrius Ponticus and the rest of that crowd.'

'Exactly, sir. Scetis, too. Moses wouldn't have been chosen without the approval of a majority in Scetis.'

His dark eyes hooded, abstracted, the Archbishop weighed his personal pique against his larger designs. No contest. His own feelings must take second place.

And then, as an idea hit him, he smiled. His smile spread and broadened as Timothy looked on uncomprehendingly. He slapped the desk with the flat of his hand. 'All right, Timothy,' he said. 'Write to the Bishop anyway. But you'll say as follows: Dearly beloved brother in Christ, Bishop Dioscorus, etcetera. I was delighted by your choice of Father Moses as Father Isidore's successor. So delighted that I would like to make the following suggestion. I myself will shortly be ordaining a group of young priests here in Alexandria. If it proved possible to ordain Father Moses in the course of the same ceremony, he would serve for these youngsters as an invaluable exemplar of the triumphs and glories of the ascetic life. May I say also that nothing would give me greater pleasure than to be allowed to ordain Father Moses personally. I hasten to add that this request in no way reflects on your right or capacity to conduct the ceremony yourself, should you wish to do so, and is in no sense an order, rather a personal favor I ask of you, which you may feel perfectly free to refuse, should you so desire, entirely without prejudice. Needless to say you yourself would be more than welcome at the ordainment, in whatever capacity...With sincerest greetings and all the usual formulae, right?'

Pen poised, the Archdeacon fixed Theophilus with a

look.

'Are you sure you know what you're doing, sir?'

He expected another explosion, but none came. Theophilus grinned, cracked his knuckles, and said, 'Yes, Timothy, I'm absolutely sure.'

Chapter Twenty-Two

'Leila! Just a second, please!'

A hand tugging her sleeve, a body squeezing in beside hers as the women poured down the narrow corridor that led from the linen looms to the refectory. It was Sansno, formerly Leila's fellow-novice.

'I hardly ever get to talk to you any more,' Sansno complained.

Leila murmured some sort of agreement, although she was less enthusiastic about their reunion than Sansno seemed to be. Sansno had never shown that much interest in her when they were novices, and still less afterwards, so this sudden effusion could only mean that Sansno wanted something from her.

'Have you heard we may be getting a new Elder Mother?' Sansno asked, lowering her voice to a conspiratorial whisper.

Leila hadn't. 'She's resigning?'

'No. Far worse than that. It's the most awful scandal, really.'

'Tell me,' Leila said, curious despite the inner voice that told her, what is it to you who's Elder Mother or what she did?

Just greed for useless knowledge, that's all it is. Look to your own sins, not those of others.

'I'd love to ... But I can't now—if we don't eat in our proper places the Elder Sister gets into an awful tizzy...I'll meet you...oh...' It was impossible, at short notice, to think of any time and place in their minutely-regulated lives that they could meet without attracting attention.

'Somewhere,' Sansno said, pulling away from her as they entered the refectory. 'Don't worry. I'll think of something.' And she was gone.

For a few moments, Leila wondered about the Elder Mother Probably just some rumor, some gossip Sansno picked up, nothing to it at all, she decided. Within minutes, she had forgotten the incident altogether, and did not remember it even when, several days later, the Elder Sister in charge of her weaving room called her name. She hurried to the front of the room. Obedience was taken for granted; it was speed in obedience that counted for points.

'Leila, you're needed for kitchen fatigue.'

Leila was puzzled. Normally there was a roster for cleaning out the kitchen refuse, and her next turn wasn't due for weeks yet, But she knew better than to express either surprise and resentment. Bowing to the Elder Sister, she headed towards the kitchen, and it was only when she saw Sansno there that she made the connection.

'Take this,' Sansno said, thrusting a palm-leaf broom into her hand, 'and get cracking. I've been all on my own, my partner went sick on me this morning.'

There were other kitchen staff around and her eyes quickly told Leila, just shut up for now, we'll get a chance to talk later. So for the next half hour they swept assorted vegetable detritus into piles, scooped it up and dumped it into big two-handled wicker baskets. Then when the floor was clean to the cook's satisfaction. they took a handle each of the first basket and headed out towards the compost-heap that lay alongside the herb garden. It was only then, when they were in the open air and out of earshot of anyone else, that Leila asked, 'How did you manage that?'

'Manage what?'

'Getting them to pick me as your partner. When someone doesn't show, they take whoever's next on the roster.'

Sansno smiled slyly. 'Oh, that was easy. I bribed the Sister in charge.'

'How could you bribe anyone,' Leila, all innocence, persisted, 'when none of us are allowed to have any money?'

It was as if Sansno simply hadn't heard her. 'You remember what I was telling you? About the Elder Mother? Well, it's definite. She's out. End of this week.'

'What did she do?'

'The worst thing anyone can do. Went up against the Holy Father and Prophet Abbot Shenoute.' Sansno lowered her side of the basket. 'Put the thing down for a minute, why don't you? They can't expect us to carry it all this way without a rest. Our wombs would drop out.'

Leila, who was not without wit, said, 'Would that matter?'

Sansno laughed. 'Come to think of it, no. Strictly speaking. But it might be painful.' Leila put down her side of the basket and Sansno looked at her with a more genuine warmth than before. 'What happened was, it seems she got sick of the system of discipline here.'

I don't wonder at that, was Leila's first thought. But in a moment she learned that the cause for the Elder Mother's dissatisfaction differed widely from hers.

'You know how she has to report everything that happens to the Abbot, and then the Abbot has to decide what the punishment will be? Well, she got sick of that. She figured that if she was in charge of the women's monastery, then she should decide who got punished and—Pick it up!'

'I beg your pardon?'

'Pick it up, walk, someone's coming.' They got started just in time, gave a polite 'Good morning, Mother!' to the Elder

Sister who cut obliquely across their path, and kept going. 'They can overlook this part from the Accounts Office,' Sansno warned. The literate women who tallied the monastery's sales of linen and other goods, subtracting therefrom its minimal outlay on raw materials and supplies and thereby determining its immense profit margin (labor costs forming no factor in the operation) were notoriously pro-establishment and guaranteed to report any lower-echelon workers seen lollygagging about and thus reducing those profits.

'Don't worry, we can walk and talk,' Sansno went on. 'No, she wanted to say who and how much, and she told the Abbot, you know, men and women are supposed to be equal here.'

This came as a surprise to Leila, and she must have showed it, because Sansno said, 'Well treated equally, I mean like we take the same vow as the men, follow the same Rule, eat the same food—that kind of stuff.' They had arrived at the compost-heap. 'Just drop the front end and turn it over. Easy does it...Tha-a-at's right. Anyway, instead of her regular report she writes the Abbot a letter and puts in all of this. Can you imagine?'

Sansno's eyebrows, naturally arched, raised still higher, while her mouth curled into a shocked circle. 'He hit the roof! It was all the Elder Brother could do to keep him from coming over here and chastising her in person. Finally he—Recite a psalm!'

'What?'

'Recite a psalm, quick, out loud!'

'Which psalm?'

'What does it matter, stupid? Hear my voice, Oh God, in my prayer, preserve my life from fear of the enemy, hide me from the secret counsel of the wicked, from the insurrection of the workers of iniquity...'

Without further argument, Leila followed Sansno in the Sixty-Fourth Psalm. The tall, gaunt Elder Sister swept past them without a word and entered the Accounts Office.

'What was that about?' Leila asked.

'Her. Didn't you see her? I don't know her name, but she's a cow. She saw our lips moving.'

'So?'

'So if she hadn't heard us saying a psalm, she'd have stopped us and demanded to know what we were talking about. I've been warned about her. She's famous for it...Now where was I?'

'You were just going to tell me what the Abbot did.'

'Right! He wrote back to her, he used the most awful language, called her an imbecile and a barbarian and a destroyer of all monastic order and I don't know what else.

Gave her a week to come to her senses and apologize. That was last week. But she won't, so that's the end of her.'

'How do you know all this?' Leila asked, still not sure whether to believe or not.

'Oh, one has friends,' Sansno said airily, 'and the friends have friends, stuff gets around real quick here...Talking of friends, how are you getting on with Demetria?'

Innocent Leila might be, but at the mention of her cell-mate a warning bell rang in her brain. She remembered the looks of longing she had seen Sansno cast in Demetria's direction, and thought, couldn't she have at least been a little less obvious? But she answered plainly enough, 'Oh, we get on well, I'm really fond of her.'

'Fond of her,' Sansno repeated thoughtfully. 'You don't mean...'

'No, no, nothing like that! We're good friends, that's all.'

'You know, she reminds me of someone...' Sansno began, then broke off as they approached the door of the kitchen. 'Tell you in a moment. We'll just grab the second basket and get out of there.'

They did so, without interruption. Once outside again, Sansno said, 'You know, I'm convinced we know each other, from somewhere. Maybe when we were little kids. There's something about her...Oh, I don't know. I'd really like to talk to her, get to know her.'

'So why don't you?' Leila asked. Sansno laughed, a forced laugh, false and stagey. 'Why don't I? You've got to be kidding! You've seen what it's been like this morning. We've hardly managed to say a word to one another, even after going to all that trouble. And it's not like we don't know each other already, I mean, as novices and all, so that bit's not difficult. But I've never had chance even to say hi to her. And she's shy. You don't have to know her, you can tell that just by looking at her.'

Leila did not dispute this. But what kind of fool does Sansno take me for, she couldn't help thinking, does she think I'm blind, not even to notice the way she keeps looking at Demetria? 'I'll ask her,' she said blandly. 'If she remembers you.'

Sansno shook her head decisively. 'That wouldn't work. If she remembered me she'd have shown it somehow. I'd have to really talk to her, remind her of stuff, like the names of kids we used to play with—'

'If indeed you did.'

'Yes, of course, but you know how it is, when you're a kid, you forget stuff unless something triggers it off. Happened to me before now. People saying, hey, I used to know you, and here's me thinking I don't know them from Adam, then they'd say something and I'm like, yeah, right, now I remember you!' And Sansno, round-eyed with sincerity, stared full into the doubting eyes of Leila.

'So I figured out a way I could get to talk to her,' Sansno went on. 'At least, if you'll help.'

'How?' Leila asked reluctantly.

'Oh—just swap beds for the night.'

Before Leila, stunned, could think of any adequate response, they were back at the compost-heap, and the emptying of the basket kept Sansno's gaze from her confusion. So that's what she wanted, Leila thought, that's what all this sudden pretense of friendship was really about. As they turned to go back to the kitchen, she asked, more collected now, 'What was that you just said?'

'I said you could swap beds with me and that would give me a chance to talk to her,' Sansno said casually, as if it were the most natural and trivial thing in the world. 'It's just for one night.'

'No,' Leila said. 'I can't do that.'

'Why not?' Sansno pleaded. 'You won't get into trouble. All you have to do is slip into my cell after evening prayers, instead of your own. My cell-mate won't mind, she does what I tell her to. They never check to see who's where, long as you don't go wandering around in the middle of the night, they don't care. And if by any chance they do catch us, I'll tell them it was all my fault. Honest. That's a promise.'

'It's not that I'm scared,' Leila said. 'It's because you're not being honest with me. I know what you really want.'

'Oh, you do, do you?'

'You want to...to...' Leila still couldn't think of a word for it. 'To *do things* with Demetria, don't, you?'

'No I do not!'

Sansno made a good show of looking sincerely shocked, but Leila remained unconvinced. 'Why else would you need so much time with her? All night, indeed! And what's she going to think, if I don't show up, and you do? I've got to protect her.'

'*You've* got to protect *her*?' Sansno laughed harshly. 'What for? She's been in the life longer than you have! She should protect you...Well then, if you feel that way about it, you can ask her. Ask her whether she minds.'

'I won't ask her,' Leila said stubbornly.

'You know, Leila,' Sansno said, letting a look of weary sadness come over her face. 'I was mistaken about you. I thought you were a decent type. I didn't think you were one of those lickspittle, kiss-your-backside, prissy little do-gooders this place is full of. I thought you were a real person. Oh well, more fool me.'

Leila remained unmoved. 'I'm sorry, Sansno. I just can't

do it. Whether Demetria would want it or not, and I'm pretty certain she wouldn't, I mean, I live with her, I know her, believe me. But even if she did want it...No, I couldn't. I mean be an accessory to her sin. No. No way.'

'Well, if that's how you see it...'

'It is, I'm afraid.-

'You bitch,' Sansno spat out. 'You sanctimonious little bitch. Now I suppose the next thing we'll hear about will be you running off to one of the Elder Sisters and telling her the whole sordid story. That you've made up out of your own evil-thinking soul.'

Leila shook her head. 'I won't tell on you, Sansno.'

'You'd better not!'

'You don't need to threaten me.'

'You'd better not, Leila, you'd better look out, I've got lots of friends here, like I told you, and they don't like lickspittle tell-tales any better than I do, you hear?'

And Sansno did not say another word to her. They went back into the kitchen and finished their chores in a brooding silence, punctuated only by the venomous looks that Sansno kept sending her and that she studiously ignored.

The incident left Leila feeling deeply depressed. If only she had someone to whom she could talk, with whom she could discuss what had happened, and determine how she should act! But she could hardly ask advice of Demetria, for Demetria was even less experienced in such things, and she had yet to find one of the Elder Sisters whom she could really trust. Not one of them, she felt, would fail to report everything she heard, confidential or otherwise, to the Elder Mother.

Time and again, though, in the days that followed she hesitated on the brink of telling Demetria everything that had happened, everything she suspected about Sansno's intentions. Surely she should at least warn Demetria? But something always held her back at the last minute. Judge not, the gospel said. And wouldn't it be judgment to accuse Sansno of evil intentions? After all, Sansno herself had denied them. And feeling certain about something wasn't the same as knowing it for a fact. Suppose she created enmity between Sansno and Demetria, and it turned out after all that she had made a mistake! And so she waited, and prevaricated, until the end of the week came round, and with it the synaxis.

Leila knew right away that at least one thing Sansno told her had proved correct. For as the service began, Mother Tachom, the Elder Mother's Second, stepped into the Elder Mother's place, without a word of explanation. That was how things happened in the White Monastery; that was how Isidora had disappeared during the novitiate. If you were going to stay, you would be punished, your sins exposed, your person subjected to public obloquy. But if they decided they were through with you—nothing. You ceased to exist. You became a non-person, never again to be mentioned, even as a warning to others.

The service proceeded as it always did, with no indication that anything had changed. Mother Tachom spoke all the Elder Mother's lines, performed all the Elder Mother's liturgical functions. She might have been merely filling in for her former superior, for all the congregation knew, but Leila knew that the next week and the next after that, Mother Tachom would still be filling her shoes, with never an official announcement, while more and more inaccurate versions of the Elder Mother's disappearance shuttled to and fro in the great whispering gallery of rumor that was the women's monastery.

The service ended, the women waited for the order of their dismissal. It did not come. Instead, Mother Tachom strode to the lectern and said, 'I have an announcement to make.'

I was wrong, Leila thought, they are going to tell us.

Mother Tachom let the silence of anticipation build up, savoring her new power. 'There is a book missing from my study,' she said. 'A book entitled, "On First Principles", by Origen. If anyone present has taken this book inadvertently, or merely intended to borrow it, she may return it now, and nothing further will be said.' A profound silence followed her words. No hand was raised, no one came forward. 'Then I must assume that the book has been deliberately stolen. Which makes it, I'm afraid, a very serious case. For this book is considered nowadays by many of our most reliable theologians to contain doctrines that are frankly heretical.'

Then what are you doing with a copy, Leila thought. As if Mother Tachom had been clairvoyant, her query was answered immediately. 'It is permissible for me, as your superior, to possess such books, in the first place because I have the experience to recognize and reject their false teachings, and in the second because I must familiarize myself with such doctrines in order to combat them successfully. Neither of these considerations applies to any of you. As I see it, the only motive that would lead anyone to take this book—unless they intended to sell it for profit, which I consider extremely unlikely—would be the desire to learn and propagate the false doctrines it contains.' She paused, to let the full significance of this sink in, then delivered her punch-line. 'In other words, whoever took this book is guilty, not of one grave sin, but two: theft, and heretical teaching.'

This time, Mother Tachom allowed an even longer silence to elapse before continuing, 'This offence will be reported to our blessed superior the holy Abbot Shenoute, who will determine the appropriate punishment. That punishment may be lightened if the offender now makes a free and voluntary confession.' She paused. No one responded. Her lips set in a grim line.

'You will all return to your cells. You will, however, not enter those cells, under pain of immediate expulsion, until I and my Second have inspected them.' With a jerk of her head she indicated her new Second, and Leila, to her disappointment if not her surprise, recognized the Elder Sister against whom Sansno had warned her, the one who asked people with moving lips what they were talking about.

'Until then,' Mother Tachom went on, 'you will remain standing in the corridors outside your cells, and you will not speak to one another until your cells have been searched.' An Elder Sister approached the lectern and whispered a word in Mother Tachom's ear. The whispering went back and forth while the congregation waited. Then Mother Tachom said, 'Since you have been here for so long, you may visit the latrines before you return to your cells. You will not be permitted to visit them again until the inspection is completed. If any of you have the book in your immediate possession, do not think you will be able to dispose of it in this way, for I have designated Elder Sisters to watch each latrine carefully and ensure that no objects are disposed of.'

In absolute silence, the chapel emptied. In absolute silence, long lines formed at the latrines, shrank gradually under the eagle eyes of the Elder Sisters, and reformed in the corridors. Time passed. Occasional whisperers were quickly hushed into silence. Although Leila had relieved herself, it wasn't long before she wanted to go again: knowing it wouldn't be permitted always had this effect on her. She wondered how many others had the same problem. Shifting from foot to foot, looking at Demetria, she wondered if her cell-mate had the same problem. Probably not; she looked perfectly composed, as always, humble, demure, accepting whatever was given her. Who could tell what was going on in her heart?

At last they heard voices at the end of their corridor, and the new Elder Mother and her Second appeared, vanished into a cell, reappeared, moments later, empty-handed, and vanished into a second cell. Six cells to go, Leila counted, before it was their turn. Lucky the cells had so little in them, searching them could hardly take long. In a few minutes she would be free to go. But others would have to wait, whoever stole the wretched book could hardly have thought what it would lead to, putting all of them to this unmerited penance. Who could it be? She couldn't think anyone would be so stupid, anyone with a brain could see they were bound to get caught.

The two superiors had reached her and Demetria's cell.

Without acknowledging its occupants' presence, ignoring them as if they had been furniture, they entered it. Leila, acutely uncomfortable by now, began to count the seconds—in a matter of moments it would be over, they would move on to the next cell, she could go. She caught Demetria's eye and smiled at her, and Demetria smiled back, and then suddenly from behind them they heard Mother Tachom's voice.

'Leila! Demetria!'

They turned, not frightened yet, surprised, puzzled, wondering what item of monastic etiquette they might have overlooked—were their beds improperly made up, were their clothes untidy?

Then they saw the small, elegantly-bound volume in the Elder Mother's hand.

'Come to my study, immediately,' Mother Tachom said.

Chapter Twenty-Three

The delegation from Hermopolis was late. Did Moses suspect what was in store for him, Theophilus wondered, had he refused to come? The Archbishop was awaiting him in the forecourt of the Caesarium on a bright morning with a brisk north wind that flurried the vestments of the assembled priests, ordinands, deacons and acolytes, standing in an irregular crescent, ready to process into the nave as soon as the delegation arrived. Spring is here, thought Theophilus, another year and Nectarius still hangs on in Constantinople.

He stood a little apart from the throng, talking to Photinus, a neat young visiting deacon from Cappadocia. A small fish compared to the Patriarch of Alexandria, but small fish could grow to be big fish, especially if they were intelligent and well-informed, as Photinus appeared to be. And even if he remained a small fish, a few courteous words from the Patriarch, delivered when the latter had nothing better to do, could turn that fish into a partisan, a sure vote, a potential spy — one more cog in the immense machine of influence that Theophilus was patiently building, all around the eastern Mediterranean, ready for the moment when he would impose his will on Constantinople and wield power greater than the Pope's.

A year or two previously, the execution of that program had seemed simplicity itself. Wait for the senile Nectarius to die, field a plausible but appropriately docile candidate for the consequent vacancy, ensure the election of that candidate by skillful maneuvering and calling in all the favors owed him that Theophilus had accumulated over the years—then it would be as good as being Archbishop of Constantinople himself. Better, because he would still be Archbishop of Alexandria, still in absolute control of the political machine he had crafted so carefully over the years, leaving his surrogate, under guidance, to build an equally powerful machine in the capital.

And then Epiphanius, Bishop of Salamis, had, quite inadvertently, put his whole scheme into jeopardy.

Epiphanius had ordained a priest in Palestine. Bishop John of Jerusalem had objected, as he had every right to do, since one bishop had no business ordaining priests in another bishop's diocese. Left at that, it would have been a simple turf war between the two of them, which Epiphanius, in the wrong, would probably have lost. But Epiphanius didn't like losing. So he had raised the stakes by accusing Bishop John of heresy.

Everyone did that nowadays. Theophilus himself would probably have done it, in Epiphanius's shoes. It was too easy. A century ago, in persecution times, you could afford to disagree about many points of doctrine. If scripture didn't tell it clearly, you could hold to different versions of the faith and nobody would complain. Now there were people who spent their whole lives working out to the last trivial detail what a Christian might or might not believe. So specific had things gotten, so narrowed down and hidebound that no matter who you examined, however saintly their lives might be, you could find somewhere, in their speech or their writings, some idea that was heretical. So, if you were in a power struggle, or envied someone his position, or simply had a grudge against him, you now had a quick and easy way to get even. Denounce him as a heretic—but make sure you did it before he denounced you.

Looking for a way to discredit John of Jerusalem, Epiphanius had settled on the teachings of Origen, the great third-century theologian some of whose more radical speculations, alas, conflicted with the new orthodoxy. That choice was predictable but deplorable. Predictable because Epiphanius had had a bee in his bonnet about Origen for the past twenty years, and John was a staunch Origenist. Deplorable because as many people still supported Origen as opposed him. That meant the fight could no longer involve just the two bishops. It was spreading already, it could easily spread right through the Church, splitting it into two warring factions. If the Church was split, Theophilus would be forced to take sides. If he took sides, the other side would resist him and if he picked the wrong side, goodbye to his Grand Design of controlling the Church.

That was why he had sent Isidore to Palestine: to try to reconcile the two sides and thus ensure the maintenance of a united Church. And (neatly killing two birds with one stone), Isidore would get on-the-job training in high-level negotiations and make contacts that would stand him in good stead when Theophilus ran him as his chosen candidate for Nectarius's post. Now with luck he could get a progress report on Isidore from Photinus, a presumably unbiased observer. 'When you came through Jerusalem,' he asked, 'you didn't happen to run into my emissary, Father Isidore, by any chance?'

Photinus had. No surprise, really: the Christians in Jerusalem, islanded among Jews and pagans, formed a small, intense, inbred, and morbidly self-scrutinizing community.

'How is he doing, d'you think?'

Photinus prevaricated. 'Early days, yet, too early to tell. An able man, I'm sure. But he'll have his work cut out, I'm afraid.'

Theophilus was afraid so too, and probably knew, through his spy system, far more about what was happening in

Jerusalem than Photinus did. But he encouraged Photinus to talk, for in talking Photinus would reveal much about himself. Too, there was always the chance that in talking he might let drop, without realizing its significance, some small nugget of information that, fitted with those already in the Archbishop's possession, would turn a messy jigsaw into a meaningful picture. And finally, a feigned eagerness for news would allow Photinus to shine as the source of it, thus making Photinus feel good about himself, and grateful to Theophilus in consequence. Years later, perhaps, fond memories of their meeting would surface in Photinus's mind when the missive from Alexandria arrived, requesting him to say this, do that, report the other.

'Too many people are coming out against Origen—Jerome, for instance,' the innocent Photinus began, referring to a Roman hermit-turned-theologian now domiciled in Jerusalem and already making a name for himself as a polemicist with a vitriolic pen. 'That's a bad sign, because I don't think it comes from conviction. He's smart, he knows which way the wind's blowing.'

'Really.'

'I don't see what else it can be. I mean most of his own early stuff is just full of Origen's ideas. Take his commentary on Ephesians. He mentions that there will be no gender in the life to come, that human souls are fallen angels being punished for sin, that resurrected Christians will not have physical bodies, that all sinners, even the Devil himself, will eventually be saved. All ideas that started with Origen. I grant you he doesn't endorse them in so many words—but he doesn't denounce them, either.' Photinus leaned forward confidentially. 'You know what I think? I think Jerome's convinced the next Council will anathematize Origen as a heretic, and he's scared he'll get condemned too.'

'Sort of a pre-emptive strike,' Theophilus hazarded.

'Exactly. Why else would he attack Rufinus? I mean he and Rufinus were like—they go back thirty years, they were students in Rome together, now all of a sudden Jerome starts calling him all manner of names, just because Rufinus translated Origen's stuff from Greek into Latin, and since they used to be so close, nobody can accuse him of doing it out of personal spite...No, Jerome chose his target carefully. He wants to distance himself while there's still time. And then over the years he's developed some close links with Epiphanius.'

Theophilus grunted. His current nemesis again, the frustrator of his Grand Design. 'The ex-Phibianite,' he said sourly.

'I beg your pardon?'

'Our holy Bishop Epiphanius started his career as a Phibianite. Or at least, too close to Phibianites for comfort.'

'What's a Phibianite?' Photinus asked.

'You don't know?' Theophilus asked, genuinely surprised. 'They're a heretical sect, originating I'm ashamed to say right here in Alexandria, and they had the most...well, to be quite frank with you, I'd prefer not to describe their version of divine service.'

'Really bad doctrine, huh?'

'That's not the half of it,' Theophilus said. 'They celebrated the Eucharist with...disgusting practices, that's the only word for them—so disgusting I don't think I could bring myself to even tell you what they were.'

Photinus looked shocked. 'And Epiphanius—I agree with you entirely, his theology's pernicious, but...Was he really one of those, er, what-do-you-call—'

'I can't prove it,' Theophilus admitted. 'But he described the whole filthy business in one of his books, how he could stand to even write about it I don't know. If he wasn't in it himself, how could he have he known all the details? I mean they didn't do it in the street, can you imagine, it was like a mystery cult, you had to be initiated, sworn to secrecy. Either he was one himself or he got someone to break their oath for him...What do you feel yourself about Origen, if you don't mind my asking?'

'No, I don't mind.' Photinus thought seriously for a

moment, then smiled nervously. 'He covered so much ground, it's hard to—Well, some of his ideas were a bit...off the wall? You know. But all in all, a deep thinker, a really deep thinker. And spiritual. Oh, very spiritual, very down on all those literalistic readings of the scriptures that were obviously never intended to be taken that way.'

Theophilus nodded. 'Pretty close to my own opinions. We have too much of that in Egypt—literalism, I mean. Folk who think God is a dignified old gentleman with a long white beard. No better than pagans. Can't worship unless they've got some kind of image in front of them. We don't let them make graven images of God, but what good does that do, they've got the image right there in their heads. The Bishop you'll meet today, Dioscorus, he's very much against that too, I'm trying to promote people like him, trying to stamp out all this neo-pagan nonsense...'

'God is a spirit, ' Photinus opined solemnly.

'What else could He be?'

A gust of wind blew the stole from the Archbishop's neck; Photinus fielded it neatly. To their left, the nervous young priests-to-be stood in a group, forcing out bright and pious chatter. Clouds scudded southwards across the sky, driven by a wind that blew from Jerusalem; the puffy white clouds resembled Origen's wilder ideas, Theophilus thought, stable enough in calm weather, but let a breeze of contention arise and they shredded, disintegrated, their lack of substance pitilessly revealed. Such a shame! Such reckless misuse of a genius that was pure and true at its core! But what could you expect but rash and self-opinionated words from a man who'd go so far as to castrate himself?

'Is that them?' Photinus asked, pointing past him.

Theophilus turned. A small procession was approaching from the Street of the Soma, banners snapping in the breeze. He quickly made out the dark figure of Moses, towering above the others. Theophilus smiled wolfishly. His deacons had their instructions for the aftermath to the ceremony. I'll get my own back, he thought, for that mouthful of bread and cheese.

Bishop Dioscorus greeted his Archbishop, bowing low, as if threatening to prostrate himself, before Theophilus restrained him. Theophilus introduced the visitor from Cappadocia. After a few whispered words between Archbishop and Bishop, the latter turned and indicated to Moses that he should join the little knot of ordinands. He did so, and the priests-to-be stilled their chatter, peering at him in wonder, awe and mystification. Moses ignored their stares, neither flattered nor irritated—a model of composure, a true son of Scetis. Up ahead, Theophilus's own acolytes unfurled the banners they had kept prudently rolled during the wait, and the whole procession lumbered into motion, heading through the huge double wooden doors, studded with iron bolts, into the interior of St. Michael's.

The ceremony took a long time. Each ordinand had in turn to be presented to the Archbishop, interrogated as to his faith and way of life, adjured as to his future conduct, consecrated in his office, and fitted out with the appropriate raiment. Moses' turn came last. Dioscorus stepped forward and said, 'Theophilus, Archbishop of God's holy Church in Alexandria, Patriarch of all Egypt, on behalf of the clergy and people of the diocese of Hermopolis Parva, we present to you Moses of Scetis to be ordained a priest of the orthodox Christian Church.'

Theophilus asked the ritual questions of Dioscorus: had Moses been selected according to the canons, did his way of life make him suitable for the ministry? Dioscorus agreed to everything, while Moses knelt humbly at his side. The strained, muted light within the church was kind to the old robber, erasing the deep lines cut in his face by the decades-long struggle to turn monster into saint, giving his downcast features a look of childlike innocence. Looking at that face, Theophilus saw no sign of recognition, not the slightest awareness of their previous encounter.

'Will you be loyal to the doctrines and disciplines of the Church?' he asked him.

'I will.'

And the big question: 'Will you obey your bishop and other ministers who may have authority over you?'

'I will.'

Moses' responses rang with the melancholy certainty of a deep bell in the still, mote-laden air of the church. They continued to do so, as he was led through an interminable succession of questions, punctuated by occasional prayers, readings, and homilies by Theophilus on the duties and responsibilities of a priest. At last the Archbishop turned to face the congregation that had suffered patiently an hour-long wait for the Hermopolis contingent and all the hours that followed. It was a congregation ranked in order of virtue: virgins and unremarried widows nearest the sanctuary, separated from the rest by a low marble balustrade; regular church members behind them, divided by sex; catechumens and sinners at the back, along with non-Christian relatives of the ordinands, ready to be whisked out by the subdeacons before the celebration of the Eucharist began. Addressing the congregation, Theophilus asked them, 'Dear friends in Christ, if any of you know of any offence against God or man by reason of which we should not proceed with the election of Moses to

God's holy ministry, will that person come forward and make that offence known before all.'

In one of his wilder moments, Theophilus had toyed with the idea of paying someone to run in at this point and shout out, 'Yes, what about x number of murders, I don't know how many rapes and goods to the value of thousands of gold coins stolen?' Of course, he couldn't do that—or rather, he could do it easily, but it wouldn't be worth the fall-out. And no one from the congregation responded. There were some, doubtless, who knew of Moses' past, but all of them knew his present. He knelt there as living proof of God's mercy, a physical assurance that, no matter how broad or how deep the ocean of sin into which a man might sink, by the Divine Grace he could be raised out of it.

Theophilus turned again and an acolyte rang a bell for absolute silence. After some moments of mute prayer, the bell rang again and the Archbishop began the consecration, first reciting the appropriate prayers, then laying his hands upon Moses' bowed head (feeling with some repugnance the cap of wiry wool that covered it) and saying 'Oh heavenly Father, through the ministry of Your Son Jesus Christ, let Your Holy Spirit fill Your servant Moses of Scetis with righteousness and humility, and render him worthy to serve You as a minister of holy Church, now and hereafter, Amen.'

Dioscorus now came forward holding the ephod, the white robe of an ordained priest, which he handed to Theophilus. Theophilus took the garment and, bending forward over the kneeling Moses, draped it about his shoulders. As he did so he whispered in Moses' ear, 'Now, Father Moses, finally you're white all over, just like me.' He felt the giant body go tense, stiffen under his hands—the purely instinctive reflex, impossible to control, of a once-proud man who knows himself to have been coldly and deliberately insulted. Theophilus took a quick step backwards, reflexive too, for had Moses lost control he could have snapped the Archbishop's neck like dry kindling. The move gave him the opportunity to see Moses' face. Too late, though—already, in that fraction of a second, Moses had recollected himself, composed his features in a faint, sad smile.

'That may be true of our outsides, Father,' Moses said, in a voice as soft as it had previously been loud. 'But what about Him who can see the darkness inside our souls?'

Theophilus blanched. Who would have thought the old rogue had the wit to make a comeback like that, and one you could not even hold against him, for it could be taken either way—as a humble admission of his own sinful nature, or as a shrewd hit at the sins of the Archbishop. Never mind, my beauty, he told himself. We're not through with you yet.

He handed Moses his bound copy of the Bible, uttered the rest of the formulae appropriate to the occasion and—how reluctantly!—pressed his lips against the black skin in the Kiss of Peace. Immediately the subdeacons swung into action, herding out of the church all but those who had undergone confirmation and were currently free of major sins. As soon as this was done, the deacons began to prepare the Lord's Table and Theophilus, followed by Dioscorus, entered the sanctuary to administer the Holy Eucharist. Behind them, their presbyters fell into line and began to shuffle forwards, and behind them, the newly-ordained priests. Moses took the last place in the line. But as he came to the rail that divided sanctuary from nave, the rail beyond which none but officials of the Church could pass, deacons rushed out and barred his path.

'Get out, black man!'

'We don't want black demons in here!'

'Go on, outside!'

'Where people like you belong!'

Moses turned without a word and walked out of the church, watched in puzzlement by members of the congregation, too far away to hear clearly what had been said, as they lined up ready to communicate when all the clergy were done.

Dioscorus, bending down to administer the Body of Christ, was alerted by the sudden sound of voices, and looked up just in time to catch the tail-end of the incident—the last urgent imprecations, Moses turning wordlessly away.

'What is this?' He hissed out of the side of his mouth to Theophilus, close behind him with the Blood.

'I've no idea!'

'You must stop it—stop it at once!'

Dioscorus paused to press a fragment of bread into the open hands of the kneeling ordinand next in line, who could see nothing of what had happened, and who was gaping, at him goggle-eyed.

'Don't you dare disrupt my service,' Theophilus hissed back.

'I dare and I will, if you—May the Body of our Lord Jesus Christ keep you in everlasting life,' Dioscorus remembered to say. '—if you don't do something about it.'

'What am I—May the Blood of our Lord Jesus Christ keep you in everlasting life—supposed to do?'

'Something. Anything.'

They came to the end of the line, and, stepping back, handed the sacred vessels to the senior presbyters, who in turn stepped forward to give the sacraments to the assembled laity. 'I'm serious,' Dioscorus said. 'Your deacons, for reasons best known to themselves, have insulted my priest, and through him have insulted me, his bishop. All of which is trivial alongside the fact that they have also insulted Almighty God by denying communion to one of his duly anointed servants. So what exactly do you propose to do about it?'

Theophilus stared at Dioscorus, taking his measure. I made a mistake, he thought, I was treating him like a bishop, I forgot that he will always be a Tall Brother. 'I shall see to it,' he said curtly, and signaled his archdeacon with a glance.

The ratlike little Timothy, always alert for Theophilus's summons, eased his way to the Archbishop's side. 'Go after Moses,' Theophilus said out of the corner of his mouth, his lips barely moving, 'tell him that it is my order that he return immediately and take the sacraments, and that if anyone tries to stop him, may God have mercy on him because I won't.' He turned to Dioscorus. 'Now I'll see what my deacons have to say for themselves. '

Timothy scurried out of the church. In the forecourt, Moses stood patiently, his back to the Caesarium, his hands folded behind his back, staring northwards at the twin obelisks and the top of the Pharos peering over the huddle of roofs at the wharfside. 'Father Moses,' he called urgently.

Moses turned to face him with large, sad eyes.

'The Archbishop insists that you return immediately.'

Moses shook his head. 'How can that be?'

'He sent me specially. He's terribly upset; he absolutely insists. That's an order. And,' Timothy thought fast, 'you just swore to obey all ministers who have authority over you.'

'Well, I'm sure his deacons have authority over me,' Moses objected patiently. 'And they just told me to get out, so I obeyed them. And,' he went on, keeping a straight face, 'it all seemed perfectly reasonable to me. I mean, they were absolutely right to act as they did.' He lifted a massive forearm. 'Take a look at this. Black as ashes! I'm not a man; I must be some kind of demon. So why should I be allowed to mix with proper men?'

Timothy was dancing from one foot to another. 'Please!' he said. 'If you don't come, I'm in terrible trouble.'

He had pressed the right button. 'We can't have that,' Moses said. 'But just to save you, mind. Don't think for a moment I'm claiming that I deserve it.'

'Go up front,' Timothy urged him, ushering him back into the church. 'Go right to the head of the line. Don't mind the seculars.'

'I can't do that!'

'You must! The Archbishop insisted!'

'Sorry! I can't put myself in front of others.'

Meanwhile, Theophilus was whispering to Dioscorus:

'I've spoken to them. They were just testing him, that's all. Testing his humility. They'd heard all these stories about the great Father Moses and how humble he is, they wanted to see for themselves if it was really true.'

'I'd like to know,' Discourse whispered back, 'why they chose to test him and none of the other ordinands.'

'Why?' Theophilus smiled blandly. 'Because none of the others had any reputation for humility, that's why. Mind you, I agree absolutely, they showed a shocking lack of discernment about the time and place for it. I reproved them very strongly, you may be sure of that. I don't think they'll do it again.'

Dioscorus shrugged. He would have to be content with that. His eyes moved to the rear of the church, where Moses still stood with Timothy while the last of the communicants trickled forward to the rail, received the bread and wine, remained for a moment in prayer and retired to their places.

Not until the last of them had left did Moses come forward. In solitary state, in an immense silence, he walked the length of the aisle and knelt at the rail. Theophilus made frantic gestures for him to enter the sanctuary, but either he did not see them, kneeling as he was with bowed head, or he ignored them deliberately, waiting at the rail like any secular, too humble to claim what was now his by right. The officiating presbyters, uncertain how to proceed, glanced from Moses to the

Archbishop and back again. Finally, as the silence stretched interminably, and neither side yielded, the presbyters gave way, administering the sacraments to Moses right where he was.

Theophilus stepped forward and proceeded to give the blessing and the dismissal. Never had he been more relieved to end a service.

Afterwards, there was a reception and a communal meal in the Caesarium for the new priests and their colleagues. Theophilus presided. He would have liked to excuse himself, pleading pressure of work, but knew by doing so he would be admitting defeat. So he put the best face he could on it, spoke animatedly to everyone, even Moses—in short, performed as well as ever his favorite trick of seeming to place himself on his companions' level without ever letting them lose sight of the power he commanded. But the strain this put him under was perceptible to others in the sharp vertical lines that creased his forehead just above the eyes, and to himself in the pounding headache that grew and grew until, a half-hour earlier than he had intended, he was obliged to bring the proceedings to a close.

Throughout, not a word was spoken by anyone about what had happened in the church. It was not until the Hermopolis contingent was ready to leave that Dioscorus locked long and steadily at Moses. 'I see now,' he said, 'that humility can be a terrible weapon. In the right hands...I'll have to watch out for you, Father Moses, priest of Scetis.'

Moses bowed his head and kept silence, like a true hermit.

Chapter Twenty-Four

Leila's first reaction, when she saw the volume of Origen in the Elder Mother's hands, was one of shocked disbelief. This couldn't be happening! This must be some nightmare from which within moments she would wake sweating, profoundly glad that it had been no more than a dream.

'Which of you two took it?' Mother Tachom demanded.

Never for one moment did Leila believe that Demetria had taken the book. And she knew that she herself had not. So there was no answer she could make, and she made none. Demetria too remained mute, ashen-faced.

'Come on, answer me! Or was it both of you?' Both remained silent, for neither had anything to say. Leila's mind was in a whirl. How could it have happened, how could it have happened, she kept repeating futilely to herself. It wasn't possible! Or could she have walked in her sleep, stolen in her sleep? No explanation seemed too bizarre to be dismissed entirely.

'All right!' Mother Tachom snapped, clamping her lips in a thin line. 'Follow me, both of you.' And she led them down the corridor and across the courtyard to her own office, her

Second bringing up the rear as if to ensure that the prisoners did not escape. As if there was anywhere to escape to!

'I'll take you first,' Mother Tachom said to Demetria. 'And you,' she said to Leila, 'wait!' The heavy door of the office closed behind them, and Leila was left standing in an anteroom, with the Second staring at her malevolently. Leila still could not rid of herself of the feeling that none of this was really happening, that it was all an illusion that some beneficent agency must soon dispel. But that feeling got harder and harder to cling on to as time passed, as the Second continued to glare at her, and as she heard, through the ill-fitting door of the study, Demetria's passionate sobbing. Afterwards, Leila would try in vain to remember whether it was then or later that the thought first occurred to her:

We've been framed!

If it did occur to her then, though, it was in some chaotic and indefinite form, huddled indistinguishably in a crowd of other, equally confused thoughts, with none of the burning clarity that it would later attain. The next thing she became clearly aware of was the door of the office opening and Demetria coming out, looking oddly shrunken, with head bowed, evading Leila's passionate gaze of interrogation. They were given no chance to speak to one another. Holding the door open, Mother Tachom signaled to Leila to enter, returned and sat behind her desk. Leila stood in front of it.

'You're lucky,' Mother Tachom opened

This was not quite the adjective Leila would have chosen to qualify her position. She remained silent.

'Your cell-mate has confessed,' Mother Tachom said with an air of profound satisfaction.

Leila was thunderstruck. Totally incredulous. 'Confessed...to what?' she stammered.

'To stealing the book, you idiot! Don't try and come the dewy-eyed innocent with me. I wasn't born yesterday. I know all your tricks, so you might just as well save both of us some time and tell me everything you know, right now.'

'But I don't know anything, Mother,' Leila protested. Mother Tachom leaned forward, an ugly expression on her face. 'Of...course...you...knew,' she grated, drawing the words out, planting them precisely. 'You were in the same cell with her, how could you not know? Especially since her motive for stealing it could only have been to spread the pernicious doctrines it contains. Come on now, admit it—she's been trying to teach you out of it, hasn't she?'

In the midst of her confusion, Leila still kept the wit to latch on to the words, 'could only have been'. Those words meant that Demetria, even if she had confessed the theft, had refused to admit any motive, or at least that particular motive, a motive that would have proven her guilty both of an intent to teach—in itself a grave offence, since none but the superiors could teach—and an intent to teach false doctrine, heretical doctrine, graver still.

'No,' Leila said, 'she taught me nothing.'

'Nothing?' Mother Tachom pounced. 'You only just completed your novitiate. She has been here two or three years. Are you trying to tell me that she never taught you anything?'

Leila fought against the deliberate effort to fluster and confuse her. 'Of course she taught me things, Mother. About the monastery. How the work was divided. How we are supposed to behave. But doctrine...No, she never tried to teach me doctrine.'

'Not about where souls come from? Or everyone being saved?'

'Nothing like that, Mother.'

'I don't believe you,' Mother Tachom said flatly.

'It's the truth.' Leila's voice was desperate. 'What else can I say?'

'You can say nothing!' Mother Tachom shouted, growing red in the face. 'You can say nothing until you are asked a question! What is the discipline of this place coming to? I can see my predecessor really let things slip. But I'll bring them back to order, you can be sure of that.'

She sank back into her chair, bringing herself under control. 'Well, this will all be reported to the holy Father Shenoute, it'll be up to him to decide what to do about it. You're dismissed for now.'

Leila turned towards the door.

'What was that you said?'

'I didn't say anything.'

'Exactly. What were You supposed to say? Or didn't Demetria teach you that?'

Leila hung her head. 'Thank you, Mother,' she said indistinctly.

'Louder!'

'Thank you, Mother!'

'And you'd better watch out. I think you're a liar, and if I can prove it, I will. Remember that. I'll be keeping my eye on you, that's one thing you can be certain of.'

Leila returned to her cell. Demetria was stretched out on her bed, face down. She did not stir when Leila entered.

'You confessed,' Leila said in a tone of bewilderment.

Demetria made no reply.

'Why did you confess? You didn't do it, did you?'

A faint noise, like a stifled sob, rose from the bed, but Demetria neither moved nor spoke.

'I know you didn't,' Leila said. 'So don't try and pretend

you did. I know you and I know it just isn't in your nature. Besides, if you'd taken it, I'd have known. You'd never have been able to hide something like that. I'd have known from your manner, even if you didn't tell me, even if I never saw anything.'

Now it was clear that Demetria was sobbing in earnest. Forgetting all about the ban on physical contact, Leila bent down and put her arm around Demetria's narrow, trembling shoulders. 'Tell me,' she said, 'I'm your friend. You can tell me anything Demetria thrust her arm away, and sat up, pale but determined. 'I did it to protect you,' she said.

'You what?'

'I confessed. So you wouldn't be punished.'

'You're mad! What do you mean?'

'I didn't want you to be punished,' Demetria persisted doggedly. 'I've been here longer than you, I should have kept you from doing anything like that. But I didn't. That means I'm responsible. And I should take the punishment.'

It was not until that moment that Leila realized, incredulously: she thinks I'm guilty! She thinks it's *me* that took the wretched book!

'I didn't take it,' she said flatly.

'Well, you can go on believing that, if you, want,' Demetria said. 'Now I've confessed, it makes no difference. I mean, as regards the punishment. But God sees you, He knows, so you can only damage your own soul if you go on denying it.'

Demetria's voice was sad, resigned, but absolutely convinced. Leila felt again as if she were trapped in some illogical nightmare in which reality had somehow been turned inside out. How to convince her? 'Demetria, I swear to you, as God is my witness, it wasn't me.'

'How can you add blasphemy to all your other sins?' Demetria asked, turning her head away.

'How can you say I did it, if you never saw me, if you have no evidence?' Leila demanded, feeling a sense of injustice rising within her, telling herself, do not give way to it, for this way lies anger.

Demetria turned her head back to look at Leila in genuine surprise. 'But it must be you! I know I didn't do it, and the book was found in our cell, wasn't it?'

Leila's heart shrank. What could you do with anyone so naive? And it hurt, too, that Demetria had not held as firm a faith in her innocence as she had in Demetria's. 'Did it never occur to you,' she asked, 'that the book could have gotten into our cell by some other means? I mean, our cells aren't locked. They don't even have doors. Anyone could come and leave a book here.'

Demetria shook her head. 'I can't believe that anyone would be so wicked.'

'No, but you can believe I'm wicked enough to steal the book and then lie about it,' Leila said, feeling the anger surging up, almost out of control now. 'Demetria, we've been together for months, I thought we really knew one another, that you'd know it couldn't have been me, just like I knew it couldn't be you. I mean I never believed it was you even when I knew you'd confessed, and I still wouldn't, even if someone swore they'd seen you doing it. How could you believe that about me?'

Demetria burst into tears. 'I don't know,' she said. 'I didn't know what else to believe.'

For a while there was silence, broken only by Demetria's sobs. Then Leila said, 'I think I know who did it.' And she told Demetria, for the first time, all that had passed between herself and Sansno, from Sansno's description of how women made love to women, through what she had surmised from the way Sansno looked at Demetria, to Sansno's most recent attempts to gain Leila's confidence, culminating in Sansno's extraordinary proposition and her own response to that.

'But I don't see,' Demetria said, brushing a tear from her eyes, 'for the life of me. I don't see what this has to do with it.'

'She wanted to get even with us,' Leila explained. 'With

me because I wouldn't go along with her proposal, with you because you wouldn't take any notice of her. It's the only thing that makes any sense. Nobody else could have a grudge against us. It must be that.'

'How could anyone be so wicked?' Demetria wailed.

'I'm sorry. There are people like that.' Leila remembered Sansno's boasts. I've got lots of friends here. My cell-mate does what I tell her to. I bribed the Sister. Sansno sought power over others and used ruthlessly any power she could get for her own ends. Leila wished now that she had reported Sansno's proposal to someone in authority. If she had done so, they would be more likely now to believe her story. Told after the event, it would sound like something she had invented so that her cell-mate could escape punishment.

'But I'm going to tell them anyway,' she said.

Demetria became distressed. 'Tell them what? What are you talking about?'

'Everything I just told you, of course.'

'You can't do that!'

'Whyever not?'

'Because we're supposed to accuse ourselves of sin, not others!' Demetria fell to hear knees in front of her cell-mate. 'Promise me, please. Promise me you won't!'

'You know what'll happen to you if I don't.' Or maybe

even if I do, her doubts told her, but she quickly silenced them. Surely, if the truth came out, surely it must prevail.

'Yes, I know.'

'You want that? To be beaten, tortured, humiliated like that for something you didn't do? And have you stopped to figure out how many strokes they might give you?' Leila knelt too, so that her eyes were on a level with Demetria's and could look directly into them. 'It's not just one thing, you know. It's three! Theft for sure, and they'll probably decide you're guilty of teaching, and heresy too. You could be crippled for life!'

Demetria composed herself. 'God wouldn't let that happen,' she said complacently.

'Oh no?'

'No. He's a God of Justice and Mercy. How could He let that happen?'

'Suppose they expel you, would He let that happen?'

'If He lets them,' Demetria said resignedly, 'then it must he His will that they expel me, and I must accept that.'

Leila gave up. Some people you just couldn't talk to, and she might have been tempted to abandon Demetria to her self--inflicted fate, but for two things. Guilt was one. Leila could not escape the sense that she herself was still somehow responsible—if she had told someone about Sansno, if she had even warned Demetria, all of this might have been avoided.

The other was a sense of justice. She could not stand to think that someone so vilely devious as Sansno should get off scot-free while someone as harmless and innocent as Demetria received the punishment owed to Sansno. Demetria did not want her to appeal to authority, but what difference did that make? She had not wanted Demetria to confess, but confess she had. Everyone did what they had to do, by their own lights.

That night, she dreamed she was at home again with her family. But as so often happens in dreams, the times were all mixed up—although she was at least as old in the dream as now in reality, she found herself closer to her parents than she had ever been since she revealed to her father her desire to live as a virgin. And yet the bandit was in her dream too, and he came from a later time. Only he and her family now seemed to know one another, to be on good terms, even. And she wanted, in the dream, to have him make love to her. Even within the dream, she felt terrible guilt at this desire, yet she still reached out her arms to him, tense with longing. But he rejected her. I cannot, he said, I am to be a hermit. You told me to. But don't worry, you'll marry someone even more handsome than I am.

So real was the dream to her that for several moments after waking she remained under its influence, half-believing that the state of things portrayed in it really reflected the reality of her life. Then with sickening force the realization hit her: the stolen book, Demetria's punishment, her own involvement. For a few moments more she fought against that realization, tried to replay all that had happened and somehow make it come out differently. Futile. And anyway, though it was still pitch-dark, it was already time for the first prayers of the day.

At the first opportunity, and without telling Demetria of her intentions, she made her way to the Elder Mother's door.

A harsh voice answered her knock. Mother Tachom clearly showed her displeasure at being summoned from her own business to attend to the needs of a new entry still damp behind the ears. 'What is it? Have you come to confess your part in it?'

Leila shook her head. 'I think someone else put the book in our cell, Mother.'

Mother Tachom rose to her full height, a not inconsiderable height at that, and said, 'That is an outrageous suggestion. If you are inventing this, so your friend can escape punishment, it is a vicious crime, and one for which you will pay dearly. Do you still wish to go on?'

'Yes, Mother.'

'Who do you accuse?'

'Sansno. Or someone Sansno told to do it.'

'Sansno, eh?' A mean smile curled the Elder Mother's lips. 'You haven't made a very plausible choice of scapegoat, have you? I have received excellent reports of her progress, excellent...And what are your grounds for making this accusation?'

Leila told her. She fidgeted impatiently while she listened, and Leila's heart sank. But if only she could confront Sansno, face to face, she felt sure that Sansno would somehow or other, either through fear or overconfidence, betray the truth.

When she had finished, Mother Tachom said, 'These are grave accusations.'

'I know, Mother.'

'Why did you not report to me before?'

'Because I don't like carrying tales about anyone.'

'It is your duty, ' Mother Tachom said sternly, 'your absolute duty as a member of this establishment to report to me, immediately, any breach of monastic discipline whatsoever. No excuses. Neglect of a duty is an offence like any other. It will be reported to the holy Abbot Shenoute in due course.' It took Leila a moment to realize that she too was now liable for punishment. 'But...but what about Sansno?' she stammered.

'We will see about that. So far I have only your word that she is guilty – guilty of an offence that another person has already confessed to, in case you have forgotten.' Mother Tachom opened the door of her office and shouted, 'Martha!

Fetch Sansno to me immediately.'

The two women waited in silence until Sansno appeared. She shot a single malevolent glance at Leila, then folded her hand and composed her features in a look of angelic innocence.

'Sansno, Leila says that you are consumed with lust for her cell-mate Demetria.'

Sansno's expression changed to one of utter horror and disbelief. 'That's not true, Mother!'

'She says that you asked her to spend the night in your cell so that you could spend the night with Demetria.'

'She's lying! I never said that!'

'Is it true that you were on duty with her in the kitchen about a week or so ago?'

Sansno nodded. 'Yes, that's true, but—'

'And was that a regular occurrence?'

'No. It was just that once.'

'Why?'

Here it comes, thought Leila. My vindication.

Sansno did a dumb-show of consulting her memory: slight frown, eyes abstracted inwards. 'I think it was...That's right, the one who's normally on with me was sick.'

'And why did Leila happen to take her place?' Sansno's frown changed to a look of puzzlement. 'I don't know ... I suppose because her name was next on the roster.'

'It wasn't,' Leila cried triumphantly. 'I know it wasn't. Sansno fixed it. You know you did, Sansno, you—'

'Quiet!' Mother Tachom thundered. 'I am conducting this investigation, not you. You will remain silent unless I ask you a direct question, understand? I will not repeat that ...Martha!'

Chapter Twenty-Five

Martha was sent in search of the Elder Sister in charge of the kitchen roster, and again silence reigned, with Sansno rolling up her eyes in pious reproach and refusing to meet Leila's gaze. Finally the Elder Sister came in, and the Elder Mother began, without preamble: 'You remember when Sansno and Leila were on duty together?' The woman nodded. 'Why was Leila chosen that day?'

'Because her name was next on the roster,' the Elder Sister said, in a flat mechanical voice, as if she had been rehearsed.

Leila's stomach sank. 'But that's…' she began, and then broke off, despairing. It was useless. She'd only earn more punishment.

'I can bring you the roster, if you want to see it,' the Elder Sister said.

I bet she can, Leila thought. If Sansno's evil enough to bribe her–and by now Leila could guess the probable currency of that bribe, sexual favors from Sansno–then she's careful and cunning enough to have had the roster re-written.

'No need for that,' the Elder Mother said. 'That will be all, Sister. And you may go too, Sansno.' Sansno left, saying 'Thank you, Mother,' shooting back, once she was safely at the door and out of the Elder Mother's line of sight, a final vitriolic glare at Leila. The Elder Mother let Leila stand there until the silence grew painful, then said, 'So you see how much is left of your allegations.'

Leila hung her head and said nothing.

'Are you not ashamed of yourself?' Ashamed of making a fool of myself, she thought. Ashamed of dreaming I would get justice here.

'I'm not surprised you have nothing to say,' the Elder Mother said smugly. 'There's nothing you can say, is there? Well, you will be reported to the holy Abbot Shenoute for the offence of calumny. The punishment is for him to determine. Now go, get out of my sight.'

Leila went back to her work. She said nothing to Demetria about her disastrous attempt to help her, and luckily Demetria did not tempt her to lie by asking questions. The days passed. And slowly, inevitably, the day of punishment rolled around again.

Once again, the Elder Sisters herded everyone into the main courtyard. Once again, the Elder Brother tested the strength and suppleness of his rod. But this time there was a difference. The massive figure of Abbot Shenoute, with his raw slab of face and piercing eyes, flanked the Elder Mother—as if, after the brief rebellion of her predecessor he intended to make it perfectly clear to the women where the real power in the monastery lay. This time it was he, not the Elder Brother, who held the list of offenders and their punishments, and he too, it seemed, who would inflict those punishments, for at an almost imperceptible signal the Elder Brother handed over to him the tamarind rod.

'Demetria, sister of Kronion and Cheos, of whom the Elder Mother informs me that she stole a book and did not confess immediately even when the book was found in her possession, but only after interrogation by the Elder Mother: fifty strokes.'

Fifty strokes! Leila's head swam; she all but fainted. That was the heaviest punishment she had heard of. More than anyone had received merely for theft. Only the suspicion of heresy could have prompted anything so severe. They couldn't prove it, they wouldn't even state it in the accusation, but the message to the women was clear: don't steal, but if you must, don't steal heretical books.

Demetria was brought out, white-faced, tight-lipped but outwardly calm, composed, ready for the voluntary martyrdom undertaken to protect her companion. Without resistance, she let herself be pulled down and held by the Elder Sisters while the Eider Mother and her Second grasped her ankles and presented her naked feet to her Abbot.

Perhaps it was the sight of those feet that made Leila react as she did. All through the days that preceded this moment she had agonized about what she would do when it came. Should she protest? What good would that do? Should she remain silent? How could she? It was an unbearable situation, one that could not be amended no matter what she did. And then she saw the slender, innocent feet held up for sacrifice, and just as before, when she saw the bandit who had fought for her on the brink of death, something inside her snapped.

She was already moving when the first blow fell. She did not hear it fall. She had made no conscious decision—her conscious mind, as shocked as anyone else's by what she was doing, labored in vain to catch up with her imperious body. As the rod was raised for the second stroke she burst through the front rank of watching women and headed straight for Shenoute. Shenoute saw her coming, there was time for that; she had several yards of cobbles to cross. His eyes registered her approach but his mind refused to accept the evidence of his eyes. The only tangible effect of her emergence was that, at the furthest withdrawal of his arm, he delayed for a fraction of a second its forward motion, so that when he began the stroke she was able to catch the rod in both hands, wrest it from him—his body had not yet prepared for this possibility—swing it through a short arc and lash it, with all her strength, across his face,

For a second after Leila struck, the whole scene remained frozen. Shenoute, too stunned even to clutch reflexively at his damaged face. Leila, paralyzed as the significance of what she had done penetrated her consciousness. The watching crowd, unable to believe what had just taken place before them. Then the silence was shattered by Shenoute's roar of pain and fury as he raised himself on his toes and prepared to hurl himself at Leila.

Only her sex saved her. Had she been a man, Shenoute would have inflicted mayhem on her, and the result, as on at least one previous occasion, could have been fatal. But in the last instant before his body committed itself to the assault, something in his brain reminded him of the possible consequence to his reputation if he, a man of giant size, beat to death a rather small woman. He swayed a moment, off balance, then recovered, planted his feet firmly, stared down at her with obsidian eyes, while from the lower edge of the livid wheal on his left cheek a little blood oozed and ran down his chin.

'You are Leila, aren't you?' he said.

She nodded mutely, conscience-stricken now, letting the rod slip from her fingers and fall to the ground.

'You too were to be punished. For calumny.'

'Father, forgive me, Demetria is innocent, I'd never—

'BE SILENT, WOMAN!' Shenoute roared, looking for a moment as if after all he might physically assault her. When he had brought his anger under control, he went on, 'Well, you have shown yourself in your true colors, haven't you? I think you can guess what your punishment will be.'

She did not respond. 'We chastise those for whom there is some hope,' he went on. 'We chastise them because there is hope, hope that through suffering they will learn the error of their ways and return to the path of true righteousness. In your case that does not apply. You have proven yourself incorrigible.'

He turned from her to the assembled company. 'I hereby expel Leila from the White Monastery, permanently and irrevocably.'

Chapter Twenty-Six

Martha was sent in search of the Elder Sister in charge of the kitchen roster, and again silence reigned, with Sansno rolling up her eyes in pious reproach and refusing to meet Leila's gaze. Finally the Elder Sister came in, and the Elder Mother began, without preamble: 'You remember when Sansno and Leila were on duty together?' The woman nodded. 'Why was Leila chosen that day?'

'Because her name was next on the roster,' the Elder Sister said, in a flat mechanical voice, as if she had been rehearsed.

Leila's stomach sank. 'But that's–' she began, and then broke off, despairing. It was useless. She'd only earn more punishment.

'I can bring you the roster, if you want to see it,' the Elder Sister said.

I bet she can, Leila thought. If Sansno's evil enough to bribe her–and by now Leila could guess the probable currency of that bribe, sexual favors from Sansno–then she's careful and cunning enough to have had the roster re-written.

'No need for that,' the Elder Mother said. 'That will be all, Sister. And you may go too, Sansno.' Sansno left, saying 'Thank you, Mother,' shooting back, once she was safely at the door and out of the Elder Mother's line of sight, a final vitriolic glare at Leila. The Elder Mother let Leila stand there until the silence grew painful, then said, 'So you see how much is left of your allegations.'

Leila hung her head and said nothing.

'Are you not ashamed of yourself?' Ashamed of making a fool of myself, she thought. Ashamed of dreaming I would get justice here.

'I'm not surprised you have nothing to say,' the Elder Mother said smugly. 'There's nothing you can say, is there? Well, you will be reported to the holy Abbot Shenoute for the offence of calumny. The punishment is for him to determine. Now go, get out of my sight.'

Leila went back to her work. She said nothing to Demetria about her disastrous attempt to help her, and luckily Demetria did not tempt her to lie by asking questions. The days passed. And slowly, inevitably, the day of punishment rolled around again.

Once again, the Elder Sisters herded everyone into the main courtyard. Once again, the Elder Brother tested the strength and suppleness of his rod. But this time there was a difference. The massive figure of Abbot Shenoute, with his raw slab of face and piercing eyes, flanked the Elder Mother—as if, after the brief rebellion of her predecessor. he intended to make it perfectly clear to the women where the real power in the monastery lay. This time it was he, not the Elder Brother, who held the list of offenders and their punishments, and he too, it seemed, who would inflict those punishments, for at an almost imperceptible signal the Elder Brother handed over to him the tamarind rod.

'Demetria, sister of Kronion and Cheos, of whom the Elder Mother informs me that she stole a book and did not confess immediately even when the book was found in her possession, but only after interrogation by the Elder Mother: fifty strokes.'

Fifty strokes! Leila's head swam; she all but fainted. That was the heaviest punishment she had heard of. More than anyone had received merely for theft. Only the suspicion of heresy could have prompted anything so severe. They couldn't prove it, they wouldn't even state it in the accusation, but the message to the women was clear: don't steal, but if you must, don't steal heretical books.

Demetria was brought out, white-faced, tight-lipped but outwardly calm, composed, ready for the voluntary martyrdom undertaken to protect her companion. Without resistance, she let herself be pulled down and held by the Elder Sisters while the Eider Mother and her Second grasped her ankles and presented her naked feet to her Abbot.

Perhaps it was the sight of those feet that made Leila react as she did. All through the days that preceded this moment she had agonized about what she would do when it came. Should she protest? What good would that do? Should she remain silent? How could she? It was an unbearable situation, one that could not be amended no matter what she did. And then she saw the slender, innocent feet held up for sacrifice, and just as before, when she saw the bandit who had fought for her on the brink of death, something inside her snapped.

She was already moving when the first blow fell. She did not hear it fall. She had made no conscious decision—her conscious mind, as shocked as anyone else's by what she was doing, labored in vain to catch up with her imperious body. As the rod was raised for the second stroke she burst through the front rank of watching women and headed straight for Shenoute. Shenoute saw her coming, there was time for that; she had several yards of cobbles to cross. His eyes registered her approach but his mind refused to accept the evidence of his eyes. The only tangible effect of her emergence was that, at the furthest withdrawal of his arm, he delayed for a fraction of a second its forward motion, so that when he began the stroke she was able to catch the rod in both hands, wrest it from him—his body had not yet prepared for this possibility—swing it through a short arc and lash it, with all her strength, across his face,

For a second after Leila struck, the whole scene remained frozen. Shenoute, too stunned even to clutch reflexively at his damaged face. Leila, paralyzed as the significance of what she had done penetrated her consciousness. The watching crowd, unable to believe what had just taken place before them. Then the silence was shattered by Shenoute's roar of pain and fury as he raised himself on his toes and prepared to hurl himself at Leila.

Only her sex saved her. Had she been a man, Shenoute would have inflicted mayhem on her, and the result, as on at least one previous occasion, could have been fatal. But in the last instant before his body committed itself to the assault, something in his brain reminded him of the possible consequence to his reputation if he, a man of giant size, beat to death a rather small woman. He swayed a moment, off balance, then recovered, planted his feet firmly, stared down at her with obsidian eyes, while from the lower edge of the livid wheal on his left cheek a little blood oozed and ran down his chin.

'You are Leila, aren't you?' he said.

She nodded mutely, conscience-stricken now, letting the rod slip from her fingers and fall to the ground.

'You too were to be punished. For calumny.'

'Father, forgive me, Demetria is innocent, I'd never…'

'BE SILENT, WOMAN!' Shenoute roared, looking for a moment as if after all he might physically assault her. When he had brought his anger under control, he went on, 'Well, you have shown yourself in your true colors, haven't you? I think you can guess what your punishment will be.'

She did not respond. 'We chastise those for whom there is some hope,' he went on. 'We chastise them because there is hope, hope that through suffering they will learn the error of their ways and return to the path of true righteousness. In your case that does not apply. You have proven yourself incorrigible.'

He turned from her to the assembled company. 'I hereby expel Leila from the White Monastery, permanently and irrevocably.'

Chapter Twenty-Seven

Leila was ejected bodily from the White Monastery, the place that she had entered with such high hopes scarcely a year previously.

She fell face foremost on the bare earth just outside the gatehouse, hearing behind her the thumping closure of the massive wooden door, the screech as the rusty bolts were shot into place. As she struggled to her feet, her first reaction was a helpless bitterness at the fate that had overtaken her. She had not merited this. Well, perhaps to assault the Abbott did call for some kind of penance, but even the possibility of performing such an act would not have occurred to her even in her dreams until Sansno's treachery, and even then she would never have consciously planned any such thing.

She had asked for nothing but to play her modest role in the life of the monastery, to work, to pray, to learn, to benefit from the wisdom of her elders and try to perfect herself. She had not sought special treatment, or influence over others, and still less had she wished to indulge her pride, her lust, her envy, as some—only a few, perhaps, but certainly too many—sought to do. All she needed had been to be left alone to pursue those goals, without interference. But even that modest requirement had not been granted her.

Bitterness soon gave way to fear. What was she to do? She had planned her whole life around her virginity, her monastic vocation. Now that that life had been so cruelly disrupted, she did not know what to do. In the extremity of the moment it never even occurred to her that she might seek admittance at some other monastery, and that in another establishment she might find a Rule less vindictive and hypocritical than that of Shenoute—that she might retain the goals and ambitions she had chosen and still, despite this setback, even achieve them. To the contrary, what had happened seemed a final blow to her whole scheme of life.

In any case, she had a more pressing problem. On entering the monastery she had surrendered what few possessions she had, including the little money that was left after her journey upriver. Now she was totally destitute, for of course nothing had been returned to her. She would have to beg merely in order to eat. But where could she go, whom could she beg from? Atripe, where the White Monastery was located, was a ghost town, or ghost hamlet, rather. Once, under the Pharaohs, a thriving provincial center, it had fallen into ruin and most of what buildings still stood had been taken over by Shenoute to form the core of the White Monastery. She could see nothing outside the monastery walls, in any direction, save a few scattered and makeshift hovels that could belong only to people almost as impoverished as herself.

She had hoped, rather selfishly, that Demetria would be expelled with her.Not that she wished Demetria too to end her monastic career, but no-one could deny that it was only through trying to defend and protect her cell-mate that Leila had brought her own career to an end. She had not realized how fond she had become of Demetria; she missed her now, perhaps, as much as the life she had left. Moreover, Demetria had family in the area, and they might have helped her, since she had helped their daughter, or at least allowed her to work as a servant for them to earn her bread. But although she waited for what seemed a long time, the door did not re-open.

She began to walk away from the monastery. At the moment she had no plans, none whatsoever. Even if she had money, she could hardly return home—that would be too humiliating, after she had won that desperate conflict of wills with her father simply so that she could escape from there. She had vague thoughts about returning downriver, not because home lay in that direction, but because she didn't like southerners very much and wanted to be among people whose ways resembled hers. So if for no other reason she headed in a northerly direction, moving instinctively towards the bank of the river, for the nearer she came to it, the greater the likelihood that she would encounter movement and life of some kind, and perhaps prevail upon some passing stranger to help her.

At no time did it occur to her that she might be in danger, that the world of the monastery, harsh as its discipline might seem, did at least have discipline, and to that extent might be preferable to the lawless world outside its walls. She had largely forgotten that world, having thought to put it behind her for ever, and accordingly the only danger she conceived of was that of starving.

By the time she reached the river and the rough road that ran along its bank, night was approaching. Where could she sleep? She had never spent a night alone out of doors; she was terrified of demons. She realized suddenlythat in her anger, bitterness and fear, in all the hours that had passed since she had been thrown out of the monastery, she had not once prayed, had not once asked God for help. She felt like a fool, as well as unrighteous. Her very first act should have been to appeal to the Lord for help. Had she done so, help might have arrived by now. She had left things awfully late. Within minutes, darkness would have fallen. She believed herself a deserving person, whom God would surely want to help after the injustice she had suffered, but He would have to move fast, she could hardly expect Him to move so fast.

But within minutes she thought her prayer had been answered. A voice hailed her from beyond the ditch that bordered the road; she stopped, squinting into the gloom, and saw in a hollow a little off the road several men squatting on their haunches and a number of mules and donkeys, tethered for the night. The beasts did not seem to be carrying loads; either they were returning empty from some trip, or perhaps the government had requisitioned them to help in moving the harvest, which should be beginning about now. The men had lighted a fire. One of them was engaged in roasting, on a spit, some animal about the size of a rabbit, but it wasn't a rabbit. Another was frying meal-cakes in what, by the smell, was a pretty inferior grade of oil, but Leila had not eaten all day and any kind of food smell would have been welcome.

She supposed she ought to go and beg from them, since there was nobody else in sight. But, never having done this before, she felt embarrassed, and hesitated. Fortunately one of the men called out again.

'You hungry, sister?'

She blushed, and nodded, but could not manage to speak.

'Come on over and share with us, then.'

'May I?' she managed.

'Course. We've got plenty. Haven't we, Dogface?' he said to his companion.

'Yeah. Plenty. C'mon, don't be shy.'

What else could she do? She did think, as she descended into the ditch and climbed out the other side, that they were rather a rough-looking lot, but one couldn't be choosy about company in her position or at that time of night, she reassured herself, and indeed oftentimes the poor had a better sense of morality than the rich. They did not stand as she approached, but moved aside to make room so she could sit by the fire. She did so, making a note not to ask what the rabbit-like animal was, for she had decided that she would rather not know.

The meal-cakes were not ready, so the man who had spoken first broke off a piece of bread, added a piece of goat-cheese with his dirty fingers, and handed it to her. She thanked him profusely. It tasted good too, despite the dirt under his nails. 'Where you heading for?' one of them asked.

'I don't know,' she said frankly. 'North somewhere. I come from up there.'

The men exchanged looks. 'Hm. Thought you wasn't from round here. Don't have the accent.'

'Yeah, and if you knew these parts, you'd know there's nothing for...eh, Cadger. How far to the next village?'

'Dunno. Long way. Take you three-four hours, at least. Where was you planning on sleeping, then?'

'I wasn't,' she said.

'You was gonna walk all night? Well what about that

then!'

'Come far?' asked the one they called Dogface.

'From Atripe.' She somehow didn't like to say the White Monastery, because she did not want to get into the tale of her humiliation, but she might just as well have done, for they guessed it immediately.

'One of Father Shenoute's band, then, are you? How come they let you out?'

'I left,' she told them.

'Oh you did, did you! Well, fancy that!'

She started to feel uneasy. A kind of snide, sniggering humor had entered the tone of their voices, it made her uncomfortable, although she couldn't quite have said why. But then the first one who had spoken to her said, 'Meal-cakes ready now. Like one?' She nodded, and he spooned one from the skillet onto a tin plate for her.

'We got some wine too,' the Cadger said.

'Yeah, he boosted it.'

'Shut up, will ya? We got a nun with us tonight.' Again she heard that sniggering laugh. They're just ordinary workmen, she told herself, mule-men and donkey-men, they don't mean anything, they're not bandits like that other time—they have steady jobs and their boss wouldn't like to hear that they'd been rude to a virgin, so they'll behave decently, I'm sure.

'I don't drink wine, thanks,' she said.

It didn't bother them. 'All the more for us,' Dogface said philosophically, and the goatskin began to pass from hand to hand. The man with the rabbit-like creature cut it up with a pocketknife and offered her some, but she refused. She had begun to worry about what she would do when the meal was over. It looked as if the men intended to sleep in the open, by the fire. She could hardly join them. Yet she feared to head into the darkness alone.

'Here, tell us about what it's like in the monastery,' one of them said to her.

'Yeah. We often wondered.'

She began to tell them about the cramped cells, the early morning prayers, the strict discipline, but they did not seem interested. 'You hear all kinds of tales,' Dogface said, 'about the things they get up to. You know—one woman doing it with another, stuff like that. And the old monks sneak across once in a while, I bet you, eh? Human nature, innit?'

Indignantly she denied any such thing. As for the other thing, even though Sansno's unnatural lusts were what had got her expelled, she certainly didn't intend to admit to this lot that such things could happen.

They were incredulous. 'What? You never get any?'

'You a virgin, then?'

She gulped, nodded.

'Wow! The Cadger's partial to virgins, ain't you, Cadger?'

'You can keep 'em, for my money,' Dogface said. 'Too much like hard work. I'll take seconds any day.'

'Yeah, that Cadger. Got a prick like a steel drill, ain't he, the old Cadger, you oughta see it.'

'Seeing is believing.'

'Oh yeah, right, you better believe it!'

She had begun now to feel afraid. Should she run for it? If she had ever had a chance, it was already too late, for during the last few minutes they had moved up closer, casually, one at a time, as if by accident, and they were now sitting around her in a tight circle.

'Time for the entertainment,' Dogface said.

'Yeah, you gonna entertain us, sweetheart?'

'I can't sing,' was all she could think of to say.

They roared with laughter. 'She can't sing! But there's better things you can do with your mouth, though, aint there?'

'Please,' she said. 'There's really nothing I can do to entertain you, I'd just like to sleep, is all.' This set off another chorus.

'Sleep, eh? Who with?'

'Nah, eat our dinner, then don't wanna do nothing?'

'Not fair, that, is it?'

'No, fair's fair, is what I say.'

'Right. One good turn deserves another.'

All of a sudden they started grabbing at her. It was like a game, at first. One would make a grab, and she'd pull away, still refusing to panic, hoping against hope that somehow God would have heard her prayer, but her move would send her into the arms of another one, and he'd try and paw her, and she would pull away again. There was a lot of laughter, a lot of joking insults, directed by one man against another, more than at her. They still maintained the pretense, one that filled her stomach with nausea, that it was all just good-humored fun, that at any minute they might stop and play some other silly game.

But they did not. Without warning, one grabbed her leg and held on, someone else grasped the other leg, and the Cadger, hoisting his tunic, pulling aside his loincloth, dropped to his knees and shuffled in between them. For a moment, before the mass of bodies blocked her view, she glanced back despairingly at the man who had first spoken to her. He had seemed kind. But he was sitting a little apart from the others, his gaze averted, as if he didn't want to know anything about it, as if he could pretend that nothing was really happening at all.

No, there was no Darion here for her tonight.

Chapter Twenty-Eight

It was early June. A horseman was riding north along the road that followed the banks of the Nile. He was a Roman soldier by profession, but he belonged to a specialized cavalry unit, the speculatores, who were used on reconnaissance missions and on long-distance courier jobs like this one that demanded great physical stamina and the ability to travel for long periods with minimal food and sleep. He rode furiously, not worrying about the condition of his mount, for every thirty miles he would reach a government post where a new horse would immediately be made available to him for the next stage. He had started from Elephantis, and he would reach Alexandria, five hundred miles downriver, in less than three days.

In Alexandria, the imperial bureaucracy awaited him impatiently. For the future of Rome itself hung on his news. Rome, stripped of its peasant farmers by centuries of warfare and economic change, was surrounded by latifundia, vast estates worked by slaves, more often than not in the hands of absentee landlords who cared nothing for their land as long as it could support them in luxurious idleness, in the city itself or in the smart beach-resorts that dotted the Italian coast between Rome and Naples. The city, swollen to gigantic size, a seething swarm of many-storied tenements, could no longer live from the produce of these ill-managed lands. If the hordes were to be fed, the heart of empire preserved from famine and revolt, immense quantities of grain had to be imported. One third of Rome's food came from Egypt—if the Egyptian crop failed, the consequences didn't bear thinking about.

So it was vital that the economic planners should learn what to expect as soon as that knowledge became available. And it was vital for the financial bureaucracy of Egypt to know what kind of harvest to expect, for only thus could they calculate what taxes they would realistically be able to levy in the coming year. For since the costs of government were bottomless, and the greed of venial officials deeper still, they would try always to collect as much as they could without actually beggaring the farmers and destroying their source of revenue altogether.

Every year, at the beginning of June, the floodwaters from the south reached the Egyptian frontier. At Elephantis, just below the First Cataract, stood the most southerly nilometer. Cut into a vertical rock that soared out of the river bed were numbered notches a cubit apart. The height the water reached there at full flood could be translated into how far the flood would spread, thus how many arrouras of land would be moistened by its life-giving waters. And that in turn, by intricate calculations, could be translated into how much money the economy would generate, how thick the financial fleece would grow for the tax-collector's shears.

This, then, was the news the courier brought. It was not news that concerned him personally. It was not like bearing the tale of one emperor dead, or another overthrown, or a great victory, or an army in ruins, fleeing the barbarians. The courier was not emotionally involved and he would get paid, and paid well, for this particular job, regardless of whether the Nile rose or not.

But his news greatly concerned the people whom he passed on his way. To them, it could mean the difference between prosperity and penury—even in some cases, between life and death. He did not stop during a stage, and, much as they would have liked to make him stop, to question him and learn his information, nobody tried it, for the severest punishments awaited anyone who interfered with the Courier of the Flood. But when he stopped at a post, waiting while they unhitched his next horse, refilling his water-container or snatching a bite to eat while he stretched his tense, stiff legs, people would approach him, cautiously, with the greatest respect, try to engage him in conversation, if he did not frown at them too threateningly, and gradually steer him around to answering the crucial question:

How many cubits?

At the post just outside Tebtynis, the pagan priest of the village had been hanging around for days, on and off, hoping to see the courier. He was not the priest of any special cult, because a village of that size could not support more than one temple, especially now that this wierd new cult of a crucified malefactor from Palestine had drawn off so many of the old worshippers. That automatically made it an all-purpose temple, nominally dedicated to Isis but serving also for the worship of all the Pharaonic gods, plus the hybrid Serapis, the gods of Olympus, the Roman Emperors, the river Nile, the weather gods, the crocodile god, and any other deity the local population might want to keep on the right side of. Thus the priest, without physical blemish, duly circumcised, shaven of pate, forbidden to wear wool, and with all the other appurtenances of his profession, had no special commitment to a particular deity, but was free to be all things to all men. Even to a Roman who regarded him somewhat sourly over the dried dates he was munching.

'Hot weather for it,' the priest remarked with studied casualness, smiling sycophantically. He needed to know the news because any day now he must initiate the annual festival dedicated to Isis and the rising of the Sacred River. Since the successful celebration of this festival was what made the Nile rise, it was a help if you knew in advance whether the Nile was going to rise or not, and if yes, how much.

The courier nodded, glancing briefly at the priest before looking down to pick over another handful of dates. He did not particularly care for what he saw. He did not particularly like Egyptians of any kind—a mongrel race, vicious, immoral, uncontrollable, it had taken Romans three centuries to stop them from marrying their sisters. But priests! He was a Mithraist himself—most of his unit were Mithraists or Arians—worshipping the sun, the only sensible thing to worship, since it was the source of all life on earth. But those priests! They'd worship anything, bulls, cats, crocodiles, even those disgusting beetles that rolled little balls of shit across their deserts.

'And you've got a long road ahead of you,' the priest persevered doggedly.

The courier grunted, his mouth full of dates. He felt like telling the priest to get lost, but it was hardly worth the effort. If it wasn't him it would be somebody else. They came at you like flies, and in Egypt after a while you just gave up swatting flies, you got inured to them.

'How would you like a little wine to help you on your way?' the priest asked, with a shy, sly glance.

Imperceptibly the courier's expression changed. Drinking and riding wasn't such a hot idea, but with luck he could make it to Alexandria by midnight and it would be nice to have a drink in his belly for the home stretch. Besides, he could cut it with water, half-and-half. 'Is it any good?' he asked.

'The best!' The priest kissed air. 'From my own vineyard. Well, it's my brother's, actually. Exposed, congealed, clarified and put up to age in an underground chamber at a constant temperature.'

'Vintage?'

'Fifteenth year of the holy Emperor Theodosius.'

'Hm.' The courier considered. 'Let me try some.'

The priest sneaked a fat goatskin from somewhere under his linen robes. The courier took a swig.

'Not bad. I'll take it. What do I owe you?'

The priest put on a shocked expression, hands in air. 'Oh, please! I wouldn't dream of it! A gift, I beg you! I get it for free, anyway. It's a pleasure to help a government servant, especially one with a job as vital as yours...No, no, don't thank me,' he went on, if indeed the courier's gruff grunt had been meant as thanks. 'Oh, and by the way—how high was it?'

You transparent son of a bitch, the courier thought. I could see that coming a mile off. Still, a deal was a deal, even if neither had admitted that was what it was.

'Seventeen cubits four palms.'

Nearly twenty-seven feet! The priest all but jumped for joy; what prevented him, even more than the dignity of his office, was the presence of one of his acolytes, a surly youth who stood at a respectful distance, out of earshot.

'Thank you! Thank you so much!'

But the courier had turned already to check the hooves of his new mount, which had just been led out to him. Unabashed, the priest hitched the hem of his robe to keep it out of the summer dust that kept building up, and hurried over to where his acolyte stood.

'How much was it?' the acolyte asked. 'Did he tell you?'

'Nah. You know what they're like,' the priest answered. 'Never tell you anything.'

But the news got out somehow. Maybe the acolyte guessed, or maybe the government groom overheard something when he brought the horse out—you couldn't keep secrets in Egypt. Not the exact figure, but that it was coming and would be a big one, second year running. Prosperity in the land. Within twentyfour hours the rumor had reached the fields where Zachary and Didyrnos were working.

They had completed their liturgy, shovelling, as Didymos had predicted, every conceivable kind of shit into a major breach in one of the big dykes. Then they had cut, bound, stacked, carted and threshed Didymos's barley crop, an early strain that left them free to hire out for the wheat harvest on the village's biggest estate. Now they were sweating through the year's longest days, cutting the wheat with sickles and leaving it to lie so that the binders, toiling behind them, could make it up into sheaves. A field or two back where the wheat had had time to dry, ox-carts and donkeys shuttled to and fro, the donkeys bringing the sheaves to the heavy carts and the carts, as soon as they were loaded, lumbering off to the village threshing floor.

They were a motley crew, the workers. Only a few were employed regularly on the estate, and these gave themselves airs and acted like straw bosses, which most of them weren't. The rest were casual labor, hired for the harvest only. There were people like Didymos, small farmers making a bit extra on the side, and there were landless laborers with no permanent job who starved half the year, and there were drifters, people from outside the village whom nobody knew, who might be anything, tax fugitives, bandits down on their luck, chronic drunks, ne'er-do¬-wells of every stripe. Employers couldn't be choosy when it came to getting the harvest in, but the guards kept a sharp eye out for them.

For the estate had guards too, the big boss could afford that. Their main job was to make sure no rival farmer brought in his carts by night and took off with a slice of the crop, or loosed his livestock to graze the ripe wheat before it was cut. If you came by at night you could see their lamps like fireflies in the dark. But in addition one or two of them hung out in the daytime too, just keeping an eye on things, so that if someone started giving the foreman a hard time, they would have him off the property before you could blink.

And then there were the hermits.

Zachary had a shock the first time he saw the familiar black tunics. Then he remembered how he had been told it was customary for some hermits to hire out for the harvest. They couldn't all make a living all year by plaiting ropes and mats and baskets. Some of the old men frowned on harvesting because it took you into the world with all its temptations, but sometimes your choice lay between that and starvation. You were supposed to maintain extra vigilance, and these hermits were working on that. At the midday break, the hottest couple of hours when everyone sought the shade of a palm or olive tree (thought frankly the olives gave too thin and scattered a shade), they always hung out together, never mixed in with the rest. They would talk little, and in low voices, not like the locals, who exchanged wisecracks, played practical jokes on one another and guffawed like fools at the least provocation.

A couple of times Zachary tried to talk to them but they would barely answer him, saying only yes and no if directly questioned, ignoring other remarks. They were not from Scetis, he found out, Scetis was too far, but he could never find out exactly where they did come from. If pressed, they would gesture vaguely westwards. He did not reveal that he had once been one of them. He suspected they would not believe him, and even if they did, he would not interest them. He was a secular now. The barrier couldn't be breached. If specifically requested to do so, they might advise him, or heal him, or beg alms from him, but they would never accept him as one of them.

Was he regretful or relieved that they would not accept him? Zachary asked himself this question, for he had developed an interest, a very mild and remote interest, in his own reactions. Nothing personal: he might have been studying an alien from another world. But when he asked himself this, the answer came perfectly clearly: neither. I don't care. He had somehow expected to feel that, but he kept checking.

He could understand, though, why they kept to themselves. In eremitic discourse, 'the world' was a code-word for 'women'. There were women working in the harvest, not cutting, that was a man's job, but binding, piling the sheaves, loading them. The women were mostly wives of the male workers, with a few still-¬unmarried village girls. They were not loose in their conduct, with some exceptions, but they were uniformly uninhibited in their speech, giving back as good as they got when the men jokingly propositioned them, making remarks about the dimensions of intimate organs that had the victim covering his ears and grimacing in an embarrassment that was not altogether feigned. You could see why a hermit wouldn't want to listen to that, and still more, why an old man wouldn't want his disciples listening to it.

There was one woman, though, who didn't seem to belong. She had arrived on the job only a day or two before, nobody knew from where. The married women shunned her, as they shunned everyone they hadn't known since they were babies, and the girls shunned her because, although little older than them, she was neither one of them nor a man. So she had to sit on her own, and the men came at her like wasps to an overripe fruit. She acted just like a hermit, ignoring them, trying to pretend they weren't there. She was no great catch, rather mousy-looking, in fact, and some of the men soon got discouraged. Not all, though. On this particular midday break, while most of the workers were talking about the rising of the river, she was being pestered continuously by the one they called Porky, a fat¬faced youth who, if not actually retarded, was at least two bricks short of a load.

'Give us a kiss, then,' Porky was saying, pursing his lips into a ridiculous spout of anticipation.

He hovered over her as she sat in the shade of an olive, hunched up, her knees to her chin and her arms about her knees, as if she was trying to make herself as small as possible and, with luck, disappear altogether. She averted her face and said nothing.

'If you don't fancy it, I've got something that's even better for kissing,' Porky persisted, and with this remark, a witty sally, coming from him, he succeeded in raising a guffaw from some men who were lolling nearby, interested to the extent that nothing really interesting was going on, killing time till the sun cooled a little and they could go back to their backbreaking labor.

'Your ass, Porky?' one of the men ventured, and they all cracked up, rolling on the ground and slapping one another.

'No, this,' Porky said perfectly straightfaced, not getting it, and, pulling his penis from his loincloth, he waved it at the woman like a snake-charmer demonstrating his skill. The mirth redoubled, men clutched their midriffs and bellowed:

'Attaboy, Porky!'

'Show her what you're made of!'

'What are you made of, anyway? Is that a dong or the head of a turtle?'

'Now we all know why they call it a pecker!'

The woman shrank still further into herself, turning

away, refusing to look at the insult offered her, but not responding the way she should have responded, by village standards, with a barrage of obscene and withering invective that would have shriveled the turtle's head and bought the respect of her audience at the same time. Emboldened by her passivity and oblivious to the jeers of the onlookers, Porky leaned down and pushed a hand under the hem of her dress.

For Zachary, strolling past with Didymos at that instant, the gesture unleashed something he had not known existed, something that amazed the new, watching Zachary in his head as much as if it had indeed been done by some alien he was studying. Without thought, to his own astonishment, he seized Porky by the shoulder and spun him around.

'Leave her alone, why don't you? Can't you see she just wants to be left alone?'

Porky wrenched himself free. He was built heavy, in a squat, stolid way, and he knew that even if the guys laughed at him sometimes, they liked him—well, sort of. And here was this weirdo freak, another of those who wouldn't talk to you, challenging him. 'What's it to you?' he asked.

'Nothing. But quit it, anyway.'

'Piss off.' Porky glanced round quickly for approval from the group of expectant males. 'We're just having fun.'

'Are you? Miss!' The woman took no notice, still lost in

her private world. The thought flashed through Zachary's mind that perhaps she too was mentally deficient, but he was into it now, and anyway his dislike for Porky's dumbly obstreperous face mounted every second. 'Miss! Is this man bothering you?' She still didn't answer.

'You see?' Porky exclaimed triumphantly. 'She doesn't fancy you. It's me she fancies.' And, turning his back contemptuously on Zachary, he once again tried to grope her.

Zachary had lost his inhibitions against the use of force at the same time as he lost all the rest of his eremitic habits. He swung at Porky from behind, as hard as he knew how, hitting him on the ear with a blow that would have felled anyone with a higher center of gravity. Shouts of disapproval came from the watching group: 'Hey! No fair! Give the dummy a chance!' Porky turned, half-stunned, but still up and mobile. He paused, thought for a moment, then dropped his head and charged. Except for that one brief episode in the Serapeum (and then he'd been armed with his hermit's staff) Zachary hadn't fought since he was a little kid. He had seen the pancratists, men who fought in a style that mixed boxing and wrestling, a couple of times at city festivals his father had taken him to (much to his mother's disapproval), for whatever use that was. At least he had learned you don't have to stand still and get hit, and his estimate of his own brain as against Porky's assured him he had one advantage at least. He sidestepped the rush, easily, and landed a second one on the damaged ear. Porky roared in pain and humiliation, braked with difficulty, swung around and came in again.

Only this time, not alone.

A man had detached himself from the group, a man with an altogether livelier and handsomer look than Porky, dashing almost, in a raffish, rustic fashion, but yet recognisably of the same blood. 'You leave my fucking brother alone!' he was yelling as he came. Zachary felt suddenly weak and sick. He stood a good chance against Porky, but against the two of them, none. The brother didn't mince matters, he came in obliquely, crouching low with his hands extended, fingers clawed, grabbing for Zachary's genitals. Zachary, fast on his feet, foiled him by a hair, but his sideways move carried him straight into a wild, roundhouse swing from Porky that sent air exploding from his lungs and left him spinning, dizzy, off balance, hopelessly vulnerable.

All this time, Didymos had kept walking. Deep in his own thoughts, he had not even noticed that Zachary was no longer by his side. Suddenly, alerted perhaps by the cries of the spectators, he stopped, looked around, and realized what was happening.

He sighed. Then he started to run. He ran faster and

faster until he was going at top speed. The brother, still crouching, was coming in a second time with his claws out, while Porky wound up for another swing and Zachary, between them, swayed wildly, trying to cover himself. The spectators were all looking the wrong way, at what they thought was the real fight, so they never saw Didymos coming, and then it all happened so fast that they did not even have time to shout a warning.

Didymos, with all the impetus of his speed, planted a flying kick with surgical precision on the brother's tail-bone. The brother did not make a sound, he went heels over head, somersaulted twice before he hit ground and collapsed in a crumpled heap. Hardly breaking stride, Didymos caught Porky's swinging arm in both hands and wrenched it behind Porky's back, leaning over him, bending him double. Then he released the grip of his right hand and gave Porky a rabbit-chop in the side of the neck. Porky collapsed, with hardly even a grunt. It was spectacular but quite a disappointment, the spectators agreed afterwards. No screams, no blood, over almost before they knew it had started.

'Two onto one, you fucks,' Didymos said, sourly eyeing the crowd. He clenched his fists, 'Any more takers?...No, I should think not. You all right?' he asked Zachary.

'Yeah...I guess. Just winded a little.'

'Sit down. Take a breather.' And Didymos sat down beside him, the two of them between the woman and the group, Didymos between the group and Zachary. He knew all of them, of course, he was popular in the village, free with his drinks when flush, a neighbor who would help out when needed. It was only for his sake that they put up with Zachary. Once they had recovered from their shock a couple of them started sucking up to him: 'Wow, you really creamed him, didn't you? Right in the ass! He'll be standing up at dinner-time the rest of the week.' By this time the brother had recovered himself. He looked for a moment like he wanted to make something of it, but Didymos growled and mimed a lunge at him, so he contented himself with muttering vague threats, got an arm under Porky's armpits and hoisted him out of there. One of the sycophants whistled in derision.

'Shut your face,' Didymos said without rancor. 'He's not a bad guy. What would you do if you had a dummy for a brother?' He said nothing to Zachary, then or later, about the fight. He never asked him who started it, or why. That was the nice thing about Didymos. He never asked picky questions, or suggested you might have done things differently. He just accepted what came and did what he thought proper. But he was no fool either, and when he intercepted Zachary's look of proprietary concern for the still silent woman, he grinned to himself, without comment.

Then the bell rang for the afternoon work to start. Zachary hung back until he was sure that the woman would not be molested again. She had not spoken or in any way acknowledged his presence, but as she rose to join the other binders she glanced briefly back at him and for a fraction of a second a faint, shy smile transformed her rather commonplace features. It was gone so quickly he wondered afterwards if he had imagined it. Then she walked away, and he noticed that she was no longer slumped down inside herself, she held herself nicely as she walked, her body erect.

As dusk fell and they were cleaning and sharpening their sickles for the next day, Zachary said to Didymos, 'I may not be home tonight.'

Didymos winked. 'Trying your luck, huh.'

'No, it isn't like that.'

'I bet.'

'No, really.' But Didymos didn't want to believe him, he was only too delighted that his friend was at last showing signs of normal behavior. He himself thought hermits and monks were crazy, swearing never to do it, running away from it, all that juice could only go rotten inside you unless you got rid of it every so often. And to go on that way even when you'd stopped being a hermit...Well, he'd begun to wonder whether

Zachary only liked boys, or sheep, or something, because he'd got too much facial hair to be a eunuch.

Relieved, he set off one way, Zachary the other. Under a palm-branch lean-to the owner of the estate had set up an outdoor kitchen for those field-hands who couldn't or wouldn't prepare their own meals. Zachary saw her, waiting in line there, as he had expected. He joined the line, watching her,seeing where she went to sit; alone, naturally. News of the fight must have gotten around, for no-one seemed to be bothering her.

When his turn came to be served, he took the plate of thin gruel and the small loaf of hard bread and sat down not far from her, far enough that he was no threat to her but near enough to intervene should trouble arise. When she rose to leave he rose also and, after a moment or two, followed her, but at a distance. He had supposed she must be lodging somewhere in the village. He was surprised, therefore, when she turned away at the first crossroads and headed deeper into the country.

By now it was almost dark. In the east, a wafer-thin sliver of moon peered wanly through the horizon mists, less bright by far than the evening star that coruscated with white¬-hot brilliance low in the western sky. Between moon and star they walked, silently, some thirty or forty paces apart, shadows scarcely visible to one another, even had she turned, which she did not. Then she slipped off the road to her left, and he knew where she was headed.

Over there lay the farm of a man who couldn't pay his taxes and who had simply abandoned it, going off to Alexandria or the desert, who could tell? The government would divide his tax liability among his neighbors, thereby ensuring him a warm reception if he were ever fool enough to go back. One of the neighbors had annexed the farmhouse for his son-in-law, but the sty, a solid mud-brick building some distance away, where the former owner had fattened his pigs, had remained vacant. Somehow, though a stranger to the district, she had discovered this place and moved in.

She vanished through the low doorway and he heard her barring the door behind her. He cast about for some straw, made a bed of sorts and lay down in the shelter of the wall. Just before he fell asleep he had a thought and poked in the darkness through a pile of debris next to the sty until he found a stout piece of wood that felt like it might have been the bar of a gate. With this under one hand, he slept.

When he woke it was a brilliantly starry night and the sliver of moon floated high above him. He had the distinct impression something untoward had woken him, and he lay very still, listening. After a while he heard a low murmur of voices and then a drunken giggle. Sounds of clumsy steps drifted to him, then someone lost his footing and cursed. Hissing noises warned him to quiet down. Zachary rose, wooden bar in hand, and slunk catlike down beside the wall of the sty. He waited until they were clustered around the door, three of them, fumbling at it, whispering and giggling about the fun they were going to have.

Then he leapt. Holding the bar waist-high, he swing it viciously, aiming at ribs, kidneys. There came screams, the sound of a fall, then running feet growing rapidly fainter as they receded. In the morning they would tell how demons had attacked them, how the woman was a witch who could summon up demons.

Zachary leaned on his wooden bar, out of breath from the fury of his assault. He was half-hoping he would hear some sound from within, some recognition of his power as a protector. Could it be possible that she had heard nothing?

After several minutes had passed in silence, he lay down again on his straw. But the adrenalin pumped into his bloodstream took a long time to settle, and the stars had begun to pale before he slept again.

He still had no idea why he was doing this.

Chapter Twenty-Nine

It was the day of the great Nile Festival. Every year as the first surge of flood water reached them, inhabitants of all the towns and villages of Egypt swarmed out in procession, following the image of the goddess Isis, the river's tutelary deity, to give thanks for the life-giving waters. So it was in Tebtynis. The image, escorted by the all-purpose priest, borne aloft on a wooden tower by sweating, half-naked men, its face painted, elaborately dressed, wreathed in flowers, was followed by bands of flute-players, bands of drummers, bands of dancers who writhed and twisted, forwards and back, raising from the parched ground clouds of dust that rose and rolled sluggishly away in the all-but-motionless June air. Around them, after them, streamed the rest of the populace, children and all, in their holiday clothes, if they had any, chattering, laughing, passing drinks around, playing pranks, ogling prospective lovers, or just basking in this escape from the diurnal round of grueling labor.

There were Christians among them, too. Not clergy, of course, nor hermits or monks, nor the more serious among the laity, but solid family folk who chose to regard this as a purely secular occasion, a cultural tradition, something the kids could enjoy, something everyone went to, regardless of belief, without feeling it committed them. Lucky for them it hadn't fallen on the Sabbath, or there'd have been tough decisions to make. The worst that could happen to them now was having to sit through an interminable sermon condemning their laxity, while their gaze furtively picked out others they'd seen at the festival, and watched how they reacted.

The procession halted on a low bluff above the river. The previous day the river bed had shown a tangle of shallow waterways crisscrossing among banks of barren sand. Today, a turgid flow reached from bank to bank, submerging every islet, rising by the minute—brown water, laden with the topsoil of land far up-river, topsoil that, when the river finally breached its banks, it would spread generously over the dead-flat fields stretching miles deep along either bank. The bands ceased to play, the dancers stood motionless, the whole crowd fell silent for a few moments while its members stared, as if hypnotized, at the fast-moving whorls of water that revealed, like the rippling moves of a huge serpent, the lethal power beneath its surface.

In that moment of silence, the priest took the golden vase of Isis from his surly acolyte and scrambled down to the water's edge. Balancing carefully on a stone, trying to keep his robes dry, he bent, filled the vase, retreated cautiously, raised the vase above his head and intoned, 'Praise to you, great goddess, Isis the blessed, who has once more brought to us riches and prosperity. Hail, O great river, salvation of Egypt, the farmer's friend. Rise, O Nile, flood our fields, fertilize them with your abundance. I repeat, Rise, O Nile...' and the crowd joined in, 'Rise, O Nile, flood our fields...'

The bands began playing again, the dancers paraded around the wooden tower, which its exhausted bearers had now laid down at the edge of the bluff. Reaching the tower, the priest raised the vase above the head of Isis, seemed about to pour it over her, and then, remembering the expense of all her finery, contented himself with emptying it around her feet. 'Hail, great Isis!' he cried out, and 'Hail, great Isis" the crowd echoed him, while the children, bored by now, chased one another, shrieking, between the adults' legs.

The fields lay deserted. Or almost deserted. One of the guards still patrolled, a conscientious man, loyal to his boss, knowing that some unscrupulous neighbor might still take advantage of the occasion to filch a few bushels or turn his beasts loose for a free meal. He was surprised to see a man and a woman—two of the casual workers, he recognized them—sitting there under a tree. Under two trees, actually. That was the funny part of it. He could have understood it if they had both been under the same tree, having a quickie while their respective spouses enjoyed the festival. 'Must have got separated from you, dear, can't think how it happened, I just looked around and you weren't there.' Risky business, yet folk took that kind of risk all the time.

But these two...They weren't even looking at one another, sitting there several yards apart and kind of staring off into space. He stopped to watch them. Could be up to mischief of some kind. But what? He couldn't think. He didn't feel like asking. They worked there. It was their business if they chose to come in on a holiday. They didn't mean any harm so far as he could see. Let them get on with it, whatever 'it' was.

After a while he moved away.

Zachary watched him leave with relief. For several days now, ever since the incident outside the sty, he had kept watch over the woman, but always from a distance. He still could not be sure what it was about her that moved him. Something about her sheer defenselessness roused in him feelings that he had not known he possessed. He knew that if he did not protect her, nobody else would. He knew that if he were not there she would suffer all manner of vileness and abuse, perhaps even die as a result of it, and nobody would care, her body would be flung into a ditch somewhere, to be torn apart by vultures and wild dogs. It was not that the country people were especially cruel, they simply did not feel for anyone who was not kin to them or at least known for many years. Didymos, good friend though he had now become, would have done nothing for him if some mysterious benefactor had not paid him for it.

But Zachary cared. She was lost, isolated from her own people, just as he was. And the sense that someone needed him, depended on him, even if that person did not acknowledge her dependence, had bound him to her as firmly as any passion of the flesh. Strangely he felt no resentment that she did not acknowledge him. He was not protecting her in order to earn her gratitude. He was protecting her because that was simply what he had to do. He could no more refrain from it than he could refrain from breathing. If she chose not to acknowledge him, that was her choice. She would do so when she felt ready to do so. He could wait for it easily, because he did not regard himself as waiting. He was just living his life.

Now however he felt the temperature changing. Nothing you could point to, no particular look or gesture, but her posture seemed less rigid, her gaze, no longer fixed directly on the ground before her, strayed around, though without ever fixing upon him, She had picked some wild flowers from the bank of a canal too rough and steep for the ploughs to reach, and was absently plaiting them into a string. He noticed that the flowers had already begun to wilt in the heat. She looked down at them, as they lay in her lap, with the faint trace of a smile. On an impulse he rose and moved from the shade of his tree to the shade of hers, squatting down on his heels at the very limit of its shade, still reluctant to trespass within the circle of peace with which she had surrounded herself.

It was close to noon, the air breathless. Crickets chirred so persistently that one ceased to notice them. Directly overhead, in a clear sky veiled by a white haze of heat, a solitary buzzard wheeled, riding an updraft of air from the parched, stripped fields.

'You didn't go to the festival,' he said abruptly. The words surprised him; he had not planned on saying them. He still did not look at her directly, but kept his eyes fixed on a clod of earth immediately in front of him, as if fascinated by the progress of an ant across it.

She smiled faintly, sadly, and shook her head.

'You don't like festivals,' he said. It was a statement, not a question.

'It's a pagan festival,' she said, so quietly that the words were scarcely audible.

'Ah,' he said with a deep sigh. That explained everything. Well, a lot. 'So you're a Christian,' he said, turning to look directly at her for the first time, as if this discovery somehow licensed his looking.

'I'm a Christian,' she agreed.

'Me too.'

The words had come out automatically, from habit. Was he still a Christian? He genuinely didn't know. He no longer knew what he was. But if he did not feel himself to be anything else, then he was, he supposed, still a Christian, of sorts. And in any case, he had been baptized. Baptism, it had always seemed to him, was an irrevocable act. After it, you might be a lapsed Christian, or a sinful Christian, but you were still a Christian. In some sense. So he was not being dishonest, or so he assured himself.

He waited for her to speak. Perhaps he had pushed her too hard, moved too fast. He did not want to put pressure on her, she had had enough pressure put on her. And what did he want from her, anyway? He was not sure he wanted anything from her, beyond having her continue to need him. He felt no lust boil in his veins when he looked at her, though he had to admit that, when that elusive smile touched her face, she was less plain than he had first supposed. He remembered, as if from an immense distance, the ferment Celia had aroused, in his body and his heart, whenever he had seen her, or even thought about her. Nothing like that here. Whatever emotions this woman stirred in him were calmer, quieter, and more reflective by far.

'Is that why you didn't go?' she asked at last, still looking down at the flowers in her lap.

He shrugged. Of course it wasn't. He hadn't gone because she hadn't gone. If she had gone he would have followed her. If she hadn't existed he would have gone with Didyrnos, for no special reason, just out of curiosity. But he knew he could not explain this to her in any way that she would understand. 'I guess so,' he said uneasily.

'Everybody else went,' she said.

'I don't suppose the hermits went.'

'They aren't here, are they?'

'No.' He realized he had no idea where the hermits went when they were not working in the fields. 'They're probably off holding a service somewhere... You know there's a church here, in the village?'

He did not hear her reply, though she had murmured something indistinctly. Glancing at her, he saw tears welling up in her eyes, and that should have warned him. But it did not, for at last he had found something he did want from her. He wanted to know her, know who she was, where she came from, how she had come to be in this condition. So he pressed on, driven by his own want, which had taken him quite unawares, saying 'Have you been to the church here?'

She threw the flowers from her lap, dropped her head and wrapped her arms about it. Her whole body was shaken by her weeping. Instinctively he reached out to her, then quickly withdrew his hand, before it had made contact. Feeling remorse, and an acute discomfort, he squatted there, shifting his weight restlessly from one heel to the other, until her fit subsided. For something to do with his hands, he reached out and picked up the plaited string of flowers that she had discarded, running it absently through his fingers. As she became quiet again, he heard the chirring as if for the first time, and a fugitive flaw of wind that stirred briefly the leaves of the olive tree above him.

'I'm not fit to,' he thought he heard her saying.

'I don't go either, 'he said, wanting to comfort her, not knowing what else to say.

She sobbed, still keeping her face hidden from him in her folded arms. Had she committed some terrible sin? It didn't seem likely, looking at her. But you couldn't know what went on in people's hearts. He watched the patterns of light and shade that the leaves of the olive-tree made over her body. He could observe the minutest changes of that pattern, as the wind again fitfully stirred the leaves. But of the soul within, nothing.

'It's not a question of being fit,' he began awkwardly, when some moments had passed without her speaking. 'At least, that's how I see it. I mean, you can't not be fit...Unless you choose. That's if you truly repent. If you don't repent, of course, it's different. But if you do, it doesn't matter what sin you've committed. You can't be turned away.'

Again she murmured something, something too indistinct for him hear. Was it, 'If only I could believe that!'? Assuming it was, he went on, 'Of course you can believe it! Scripture says so. I should know, I was a hermit once myself.' Yes, he realized suddenly; even he, Zachary, could not be turned away, if he did not want to be turned away. The thing was, he neither wanted nor did not want. In the numbness of spirit that had descended on him when he returned from the brink of death, it was not that he feared he was beyond salvation, rather that he could not bring himself to care whether he was saved or not. But she, whatever had happened to her, still did care, and perhaps enough of his old habits remained for him to care with her, care for her salvation, if not for his own. Or at least not to let her drown in despair.

He had woken her from her trance of sorrow. She dropped her arms, raised her head and looked at him with her tear-streaked face. 'You?'

'Me what?'

'A hermit?'

'Yes, why not?'

She blinked, shook her head slightly.

'Plenty of hermits work the harvest.'

'Yes, but...' He knew what she was thinking. They worked the harvest, but they didn't drink, fight, hang out with the seculars, they kept themselves to themselves, they would not even acknowledge a woman's existence if they could help it.

'Well, it was some time ago. In Scetis. And then in the interior desert.'

'And you...' She seemed to be hesitating, searching for the right word. 'You went back to the world?'

He nodded, still twisting the string of flowers between his fingers; it was beginning to look somewhat the worse for wear now. 'I was very sick,' he said, reluctantly, feeling for the first time the need to defend his action, a need that stemmed from her implied criticism, or what he took to be her criticism. But he was aware of himself enough to realize that this sudden and quite unexpected sense of guilt might spring from deeper levels within him, rather than anything in her mind. 'I almost died,' he felt forced to add.

'I'm sorry.' Her voice was audible now, though he still had to strain to hear her. 'I did the same thing.'

'Nearly died?'

'No. Went back to the world.'

A monastic, then. That made sense. 'Where were you?'

'The White Monastery.' She seemed reluctant even to pronounce the words.

'Shenoute's place.'

She nodded. He had heard of that place, heard little that was good about it.

'And something bad happened in there?'

He regretted the words as soon as he had uttered them, for her face closed up and she turned away from him, as if on the brink of another fit of weeping. But this time she controlled herself, and in a tight little voice said, 'I should never have left it. I thought things were bad there, I didn't know how lucky I was. I should have borne them. Humbled myself. They were right.'

'What happened there?'

'Please.' Her tone pleaded desperately with him. 'I don't want to talk about it. Not now.'

He took that to mean she would want to talk about it, one day. Well, that was fine by him. He could wait. After some moments of silence he began, in a random and discursive way, to speak of his own experiences. Yes, he too had found it hard to bear discipline. He too had been unable or unwilling to humble himself. He told her about Papnoute, about Ibison and the other disciples watching him constantly, trying to trip him up. He told her how he had left that situation, temporarily, as he had then supposed, and on a holy pretext. 'And then I sinned,' he said. 'Mortally.'

He felt it improper to tell her which mortal sin he had committed, but he knew she had guessed from the way she blushed and covered her face. 'I, too,' she breathed.

He did not know whether to believe her. It went against everything her manner told him, but she seemed so naive she could have been tricked into it by some handsome rogue. He wondered whether some monk had fallen, or if it had happened afterwards, after she left the monastery. What she had said earlier suggested the latter.

'I went to the interior desert,' he said, 'to repent. To purge my soul. But the ...I don't know. Things went wrong, somehow. I didn't have any guidance. I guess we're both...' He sought for the word. 'Casualties. Casualties of the Life.'
It was that, he could only suppose, some unconscious realization of that which had drawn them together.

She neither accepted nor denied this, but sat, with her arms around her knees, rocking her body slightly backwards and forwards. He looked up. Through the openwork of the leaves he could see the buzzard still circling above them, drifting, gliding, using its wings only occasionally, to keep airborne, propelling itself across the sky in long lazy arcs as it scanned the ground for something to eat. The patience of it!

Could restless humans, always scratching and scrabbling after some futile purpose, ever achieve such rest, such patience?

The sun burned against his cheek, and he realized that the tree's shadow had shifted—the bird might be holding its position, but even the sun had moved on. He began to feel hungry. Harvesting wasn't like hermiting, you ate twice daily, at midday and at dusk, and needed it, with the heavy labor, even though he had noticed that the hermits working alongside them avoided the noon meal. But today the outdoor kitchen was closed. 'Have you eaten?' he asked, although he knew she had not.

She shook her head.

'There'll be food,' he said. 'At the festival.'

'Food sacrificed to idols,' she said primly.

'So what? If you think you're not fit to go to church, why should you be bound by the church's rules?'

'No,' she said, looking frightened. 'I just couldn't. It wouldn't be right.'

'Come on,' Zachary said impatiently. 'Jesus himself said it. It's not what goes into your mouth makes you unclean, it's what comes out of it. …All right, we'll try and find something that hasn't been sacrificed.'

He rose, and was about to throw away the flowers she had plaited, when a sudden impulse struck him. Twisting them into a circle, he dropped it, before she too could rise, around her forehead. The flowers, limp and withered now, clung to her brow with a rakish air that looked wildly inappropriate and, perhaps because of that, somehow touching. He smiled down at her. Her hands went up automatically to snatch away the garland, then hesitated and fell again into her lap as her own lips cautiously, tentatively, formed themselves into a smile.

'Now you're all ready for the festival,' he said to her, reaching out his hand to draw her to her feet.

They spoke little for the rest of that day, although they remained together, if at a decent distance from one another, until well after dark. When finally they arrived at the abandoned sty, she said to him, 'You can sleep inside if you want to.'

'Do you want me to?' he asked.

'I don't want you to have to sleep out there.' It was the first reference she had made to his nocturnal custom.

'I won't touch you,' he said, anxious that she should believe him.

'I know you won't.'

He brought inside the straw he had collected, laid it out at the farther end of the sty from where she had been sleeping, and barred the door.

For a long time he lay awake, hearing her occasional movements, knowing that she too could not sleep. He wondered if she was staying awake deliberately, regretting her invitation, afraid he would seize and ravish her the moment her vigilance relaxed. He longed to reassure her, but knew that, if she were determined to suspect him, nothing he said would be of any use. But perhaps he was wrong, perhaps she was agonizing over her sins, whatever they were, he could not think they were as serious as she believed. Balanced between these possibilities, shifting back and forth from one to the other, he drifted imperceptibly into sleep.

Chapter Thirty

Her name was Leila, she told him, when they rose the following morning. It was still starlight, but the east had begun to pale when they left the sty. She had been raised not very far away, she said, child of a farmer of some means, but she could not go back, or would not, her story grew confused at that point. She said nothing, then or later, about what had happened to her between leaving the farm and arriving at the harvest.

They were at work before the sun rose, making the most of the hours of relative coolness. The harvest moved at a furious pace now, for the Nile was rising fast and in a few days would begin to flood the fields, ruining any crops that had not yet been gathered in. It would eventually, Zachary calculated, submerge the sty in which they were living. Its former owner must always have marketed his pigs before the harvest ended. He spoke with Didymos, who confirmed his estimate and told him of a house in the village that was for rent. He went with Leila to look at it, after the harvest had ended. It was smaller and cruder even than Didymos's house, a mere two rooms, each no more than nine feet square, mud-floored and walled with plaster. One room had an outer door but no window and the other a single window looking away from the street, into a yard littered with hencoops, broken amphorae, old and unusable tools. But beside the windowless, unpartitioned pigsty it looked like a palace.

'What do you think?' Zachary asked. Leila pursed her lips.

'Well, what's wrong with it?'

'It's not the house. The house is just fine.' She hesitated, biting her lower lip. 'It's just...well, what will people think?'

This puzzled Zachary. 'Think? They'll think we had the brains not to drown ourselves, that's what they'll think.'

'I mean, that we're living in sin.'

He gaped at her. 'What do you suppose they think we're living in now? What difference does it make? Here we can at least have a room each, if that's what you want.'

'No,' she insisted. 'It's different.'

'How?'

'Because out there...Well, nobody really knew. For sure. Nobody saw us there. They might guess—'

'Bet your life they guessed,' he said with a harsh laugh.

'—but they didn't know. But here...I mean right in the middle of the village. Everyone'll know.'

Zachary heaved a long sigh. 'Have we fornicated?'

'No.'

'Have I tried to?'

'No,' she said, turning her face away shyly, 'and I'm deeply grateful, I can't tell you how grateful—'

'Don't,' he said sharply. 'And does God know this?

'Of course He knows. He knows everything.'

'Well then ... What do you care most about, what God thinks of you or what other people think?'

She hung her head. 'What God thinks,' she murmured.

'Listen,' Zachary said, in a firm and reasonable tone. 'You may not know this, I don't suppose it's so common out in the country, but in Alexandria there are lots of people, men and women, good Christians, who live together just like us. And who don't sin.' He did not add that he himself had once longed for that kind of life, with someone else, someone very different from Leila. 'Some folk in the church kind of frown on it, for the same reason, because of what people think. They say it lets us down in front of the pagans. I think it's stupid to worry about what pagans might think. Anyway, we don't have an alternative'

'I could lodge with one of the village women.'

'They wouldn't have you,' he said, more brutally than he had intended. 'They think you're a witch.'

She turned her back on him. Her shoulders heaved. Although she successfully suppressed any sound, he knew that she was convulsed with a fit of weeping, and a spasm of irritation seized him, to be followed swiftly by contrition.

'I didn't say that to hurt you. But it's the truth. We have to face these things.'

Stifling a sob, she said. 'I'll stay there. Out there. You can come here, if you want to.'

He grew angry again. 'Haven't you heard a word of what I've been telling you? It's a seventeen-cubit flood! Water will rise above the roof!' Then he understood. Whatever it was she had gone through had distorted her sense of reality. She had found, with him, in the sty, an island of calm where she no longer had to make choices. Every choice she had made in life had turned out a bad one and she wanted to stop this from happening again. Even at the price of denying the inevitable.

'If you go back,' he said. 'I'll personally drag you out of there. I've never laid a hand on you and I never will, but I swear if you do anything so stupid, I'll just pick you up and carry you, is that clear?'

She nodded, round-eyed, frightened by the unaccustomed violence of his tone.

'That's settled, then. I'll go get bedding from somewhere. Didymos can lend me what I used over there. The sooner we move, the better.'

That left the question of how they would eat, now that the harvest was over. Their earnings would last them through the flood if the flood didn't last too long. But Zachary was a householder now, he did not want to have to depend on casual labor. He went to the estate where they had been harvesting.

After a long wait, and some officiousness from underlings, he was ushered into a large lamplit room with draped windows and heavy, intricately carved furniture. Zachary stared about him almost as if seeing that kind of place for the first time. He had forgotten that there were people who lived like this, who took these material possessions for granted. He saw, half¬-visible in the light of a lamp placed so as to leave the one behind it in shadow, a heavy-set, jowly but not ill-natured man of middle age, the owner of the estate.

'Tell me about yourself.'

Zachary shrugged. 'What's to tell? I worked through harvest for you. Your people know me. I was a hermit once, but what difference does that make?'

'Suggests you might have some glimmerings of morality,' the owner said, grinning at his own humor, although Zachary failed to join him. 'I need that. I'm short a watchman. Nights, I'm afraid.'

Zachary shrugged a second time. It made no difference to him.

'Not from round here, are you?'

Zachary shook his head.

'Don't waste words, do you? That's all right, I like closemouthed men. But you're educated, I think. Read?'

'Yes.'

'Write?'

'Yes.'

'And you want a job as a night watchman?'

'That's right.'

'You're crazy!'

Zachary smiled at last; the lamplight caught the gleam of his teeth. 'Very probably.'

The owner laughed with him. 'Well, it's no business of mine, so long as you do your job. Start as soon as the floods go down.' He waved a hand in dismissal, but Zachary stood his ground.

'You have any work for a woman?'

'No. Sorry. Your wife?'

Zachary shook his head.

'Well, common-law, then.'

'Not even that.'

'Someone you cohabit with, at any rate.'

Zachary hesitated. 'If by that you merely mean "live together", then yes, we cohabit.'

'Aha!' The owner, who until this moment had looked as if he was terminally bored with the whole business, suddenly acquired an immense interest in what Zachary was saying. 'Christians, huh. I've heard of that custom. You live together but you don't fuck, is that right?'

Zachary, his lip curling a little at the blunt word, said 'That's right.'

'And you have all your equipment?'

This time Zachary couldn't help laughing. 'I do.'

'Extraordinary! Couldn't live like that to save my life. Only wish I could.'

My cue to say, 'What about your eternal life?' Zachary thought, but the days when he might have proselytized for the faith were long gone. 'It's not so hard,' he said. 'Once you set your mind to it.'

The owner made a sour face. 'Well, rather you than me, is all I can say ...We may need an extra washerwoman soon. Remind me in a couple of weeks or so.' This time there was no mistaking the finality of his dismissal.

At first, Zachary liked the job. There was no-one watching him, responsible for him, barring the sleepy-eyed foreman who checked him in in the evenings and out again at first light. Between those times he was free to make the rounds of the portion of the estate assigned to him, lantern in hand, a stout truncheon under his belt, and for companion an immense dog, with pendulous, bone-crushing jaws, which he was instructed to retain always on its stout leather leash, except in case of emergency. He could have gone to sleep if he'd wanted to—no bad consequences would have followed, provided the fields and orchards remained undamaged. But that was too great a risk to take, for although in Egypt most workers were legally free men, this fact had never prevented employers from administering savage physical punishment for any dereliction of duty.

He fixed his own schedule, which he took care to vary each night so that no prospective thief or trespasser would not know when or where to expect him. From time to time he would meet up with one of the other watchmen whose territory bordered on his own, but he tended to avoid these encounters, sensing that the others resented him as an outsider. He preferred to remain alone, watching the circling stars, the phases of the moon, learning the sounds and smells peculiar to the night. On top of which, he had time to think—limitless time, or so it seemed.

One consequence of the job was that he saw hardly anything of Leila, for the estate boss, as good as his word, had soon found work for her. He slept through most of the day, leaving about the time she returned, returning to eat the meal that she, rising early, had prepared for him before leaving. His days off were few and far between: on one of these, as they sat on the bank of the now-shrunken river, she finally told him the story of what had happened to her in the White Monastery, how she had come to be expelled and afterwards gang-raped by the carriers.

Zachary was horrified. Not so much by what had happened to her —that was bad enough but no more than you would expect to happen to a woman wandering alone and unprotected—as by her reaction to it. He still could not appreciate that the experience might have been as devastating to her as his own close encounter with death in the desert had been to him.

'But none of this was of your seeking!' he exclaimed, as the memory of it overcame her once more and she hid her face in her hands. She did not dispute this.

'So why do you feel you can't go to church?' It did not occur to him that she, with equal justice, could have asked him the same question, and that if she had asked it, he would not have known what to reply.

'I'm...I don't...'

'Give me one good reason.' Zachary felt smug in his certainty of her female folly. 'You can't, can you? Because you don't have one.' Sometimes, he assured himself, you had to be cruel to be kind.

'I just feel...dirty,' she said at last.

'That's ridiculous Did you want to be raped?'

She shuddered. 'Of course not.'

'Then the sin's on them, them alone. They'll rot in hell for it. For the rest of eternity.' He wished he could have them in front of him for five minutes, he with his dog and truncheon, he'd make them wish they'd never seen her, let alone touched her. Instantly in his inner heart he heard the voices of Scetis: never judge, never give way to anger, still less express that anger in action...Always she had this effect on him, making him want to protect her, even at the cost of violence to others, and he thought, they were wise, then, the old men, telling us to keep away from women, for women carry other dangers besides lust—

He brought himself up sharply. What do you care, what does it matter, he told himself, you're not a hermit anymore, and he felt a delicious sense of freedom and irresponsibility at the thought. He could be and do whatever he wanted, nothing could stop him, not even any part of himself that might still try to.

'You mustn't say things like that,' she said reproached him.

'Why not? It's the truth.'

'That's not the point. We should be looking for our own sins, not the sins of others.' She had been indoctrinated in just the same way he had, he realized, and he all but laughed aloud at the absurdity of them each trying to save the soul of the other while doing nothing at all about their own.

'Look,' he said. 'If we should be doing anything at all we should be getting rid of all this crap they fed to us both.' The vehemence of his own words surprised him. In all the nights he had spent alone, watching the stars, turning things over in his mind, he had never come out as clearly as this against everything he had been taught since childhood. Why now, why like this, in front of her? But he pushed on regardless, saying, 'What good has it ever done, what has it done for us but make us miserable? And all of it's only...only...'

Hovering on the brink of his consciousness was a memory, a memory of something that had happened to him in the desert, in that valley, in that temple—it had something to do with a shouting face, caught in a fleeting moment of life long ago, it was some profound truth about the real nature of things that he had learned and lost, out there, but not lost wholly, something that still clung just out of reach, something which if he could only recapture it would make everything plain...

'Zachary! Please!'

'...hypocrisy! That's all it is. You saw that in the White Monastery. Tell you one thing and do the opposite. Then destroy you if you don't do as they say, not as they do.' He knew, even while he was speaking, that this was not all there was to it. That there was some truth in it, but far from the whole truth. But he blinded himself to that other part of it.

'Please, Zachary!' In her anguish she reached out and clung to him, instinctively, unthinking. 'Please don't say such things! It hurts me so when you say those things!'

'Why? Why? You know in your heart they're true!'

'They're not! They're not!'

'All that happened in the White—'

'Was my fault! All my fault! My pride—'

'Nonsense, woman!'

'It was all because I couldn't humble myself. Wouldn't admit there were others wiser than me. Who knew what was best for me. If only I'd—'

He flung off her pleading hands. 'Leila, you'll never come alive again if you don't throw all this out of your soul. You think—' Suddenly with a flash of intuition he knew what she thought. 'You think,' he went on triumphantly, 'that the rape was God's punishment for your disobedience. Don't you? Isn't that what it's all about? Go on, admit it!'

Her eyes closed, she trembled. Though she said nothing audible, he knew he had hit the mark.

'How could that be the God they told you about—the one so full of love and mercy? Really, Leila! Use your common sense. What kind of a God would do that? That's total nonsense. A God who could do that would be a monster. If God did stuff like that, how could you worship him? Who would worship him, in their right mind?'

'Please!' she cried, flinging herself at his feet, clutching him. 'Please stop! Don't say those things. You'll lose your soul if you say things like that, your eternal soul. Please, do it for my sake if you won't do it for your own, don't hurt me like this!'

Borne along on his own pride and anger, convinced of his own rightness, Zachary had not realized the pain his words were causing her. Now, seeing her prostrate before him, clinging to his legs in a passion of entreaty, his heart was suddenly pierced with pity for her, and for himself, guilt. He, who wished only to protect her, had wounded her as cruelly as those who had despised and abused her.

He crouched, threw his arms about her, raised her up and held her against his chest, embraced her thin and trembling shoulders, stroked her hair with the pure and unselfseeking spirit of comfort that one brings to a hurt child. He held her thus until the tension in her was released and she pulled away from him with a shamefaced look.

'All right,' he said, 'I won't do that again.' Although whether he meant holding her, or speaking blasphemy, or both, he did not make clear, and she did not ask.

They rose and began to walk back along the river bank towards the village. The sun was setting, and under its golden light the fields, deserted for the holiday, slept peacefully before and behind them. Grapes, ready to pick, hung heavy on the vines; blue smoke rose from a forgotten fire somewhere and spread like an evening mist.

'You must forgive me,' she said as they walked slowly, not touching, a foot or two apart. 'I don't want to criticize you, it just frightens me so when you talk that way...And when you've been so kind to me—'

'Me? Kind?' He was genuinely surprised.

'You know you have. And it's because of that...' She broke off. He sensed there was something she both wanted and did not want to say, something she herself perhaps did not yet fully understand or admit to herself. 'I mean, I would feel dreadful if I were to cause you to sin.'

Still more puzzled, he said, 'I don't see how you could do that...It was the things I told you that drove you to anger. Anger on my behalf. Scripture says that anger—'

'I'm not angry any more,' he interrupted her.

'Promise me you won't be.'

'Ever?' he asked, grinning at her.

She flushed, sensing that he was teasing her. 'I meant on my account ...About things done to me.'

'It's hard to promise anything, for ever,' he said, his voice serious again. 'When I hear about all the things they did to you, I just...I can't help myself. You look so helpless.'

'I wasn't,' she said suddenly, with a quickness and spirit he had never seen in her before. 'Once.' After a moment she added sadly, 'Maybe if I had been, none of this would have happened.'

'I think you did right,' Zachary said, truly believing it.

'I was punished for it.'

'You were punished by Shenoute. Not by God. If you truly believe God gave you extra punishment by letting those, those animals—' He broke off, choking. 'Promise me you won't believe that any more.'

She looked up at him appealingly. 'You truly don't think it was God's punishment?' she asked. 'I mean it came so quickly...just hours afterwards.'

Zachary sighed. What does she think I've been trying to tell her for the last hour, he wondered. But he forced his tone down to one of patient reason.

'Quickly? What did you expect? Any woman, alone, out on the road like that, by night, that would have happened to her. I don't care if she was a saint. Or a Mother Superior, come to that.'

'You don't think...if she'd really been a saint...Wouldn't God have protected her?'

Zachary shook his head.

'You hear stories,' she went on. 'About virgins God protected. He turned their ravishers to stone. Or a lion. He would send a great lion to terrify them.' Her eyes rounded in wonder. 'Why, even with me, when I was a virgin—didn't I tell you? Some bandits tried to...to do that to me? And God put it in the heart of one of them to save me! Because I was innocent then.'

'You were still a virgin, the second time,' he pointed out. 'Yes, but I wasn't innocent! I'd disobeyed. I'd given way to anger.'

'Under great provocation.'

'That's beside the point! You're supposed to put up with injustices. And not just put up with them—you should accept them gladly, because they're a test, because that's how you learn humility... And I didn't mean God made them do it. Just He could have stopped them, like He did before. But this time He didn't, and I know why. And even you can't deny that.'

Could he? Zachary wondered. That had been one of the things he thought long and hard about, in the silences of the long nights, as he wandered through the vineyards and olive groves, his firefly of a lantern guttering, the eternal stars his companions. Was God's hand truly in everything? Was everything that happened God's will? He had seen with his own eyes, at the fall of the Serapeum, ignorant and angry men, in the guise of monks and hermits, destroying the learning of centuries, beating and abusing the harmless old men who were its guardians—had God willed this? And if that were so, would we, if we knew all that God knows, perceive and worship the mysterious justice thatunderlay all His acts? Or had He handed over His world to His creatures, after giving them an innocent Adam and Eve for starters, and then His Son as an exemplar, to see what they would make of it? Standing back from it thereafter, in sorrow perhaps, in pity surely, while the good and evil in His children fought out their dark entangled struggles, with evil all too often the victor?

He could not answer that question. Perhaps no-one could. For some reason there came suddenly into his mind the image of a face, the face of the hermit who had cradled his sleeping body on his knee at that first synaxis in Scetis. Poemen. The Shepherd. Perhaps if anyone knew, he would know. Zachary would have liked to ask him those questions, but that was not possible now. He felt suddenly tired of the argument.

'All right,' he said. 'Maybe you're right. Maybe that's how it is...was. But look at it this way. If that was punishment, you've been punished. You've paid in suffering for what you did—if indeed what you did was a sin. So you're clear. You can start over. Begin again.'

'Begin what?' she asked.

He did not answer. He hadn't thought that far.

'I can't go back to the White Monastery,' she said. 'Even if I wanted to, they'd never let me in.'

'You could go somewhere else.'

'And how long would that last?' She gazed off to where the sun had begun to set behind the low barren hills of the western horizon. 'I used to think I had a vocation,' she said softly, as if talking to herself. 'Now I don't think I have any more...And I can't go home. Even if they would have me.'

'Why not?' he asked.

But all she would do was shake her head and say, 'You wouldn't understand.'

They walked back to their cottage in silence.

Chapter Thirty One

One evening Zachary roused himself from sleep to find it had rained during the afternoon. Clouds still hung low over the earth and heavy drops continued to fall from the eaves of houses into the puddles below. A clammy cold seemed to pierce to his very bones.

Few things are more unpleasant than a cold rain in a country built to accommodate neither cold nor rain. Such days were bad enough in Alexandria—he could remember the dank boredom of them from his childhood. But there, at least, the amenities of a great city could do something to palliate them. In the country, there was no relief. On cold, dry nights he could at least warm himself over a brazier from time to time, but now the chill, clammy wind defied any effort on his part. All he could do was shiver and endure.

The thought suddenly occurred to him: why am I doing this?

You can read, and write, the owner of the estate had said to him, and you want to be a night watchman? You're mad! Zachary, jokingly, had agreed with him. Now it didn't seem like a joke any more. Or, if it was a joke, the joke was on Zachary. He had long since abandoned the hermit's way of life. He no longer needed poverty, abstinence, mortification. He could be living in the city, eating delicious gourmet meals instead of lentils and bread, sleeping in down beds instead of hard, chilly cots, washing himself daily instead of letting the filth of weeks encrust his skin. He was sole heir—sole male heir, anyway—to a business grossing countless thousands of solidi a year. His father was aging (he was convinced somehow that his father could not be dead, even if he had had no word in years, his father could surely never have died in his absence, at least it was impossible for him to think of his father as dead). So it would no longer be a matter of stool-in-the-counting-house, learn-the-business-from-the-bottom-¬up. No, by now his father must be already willing to hand over a substantial degree of control, to provide management training for the inevitable day when he would be too old and infirm to run things alone, when he would have to delegate part or even all of his authority to his son.

All of this could be Zachary's. Yet here he was, in a menial job, with long hours and little pay, huddled in a damp cloak that a biting wind cut through, jerked along on the end of a leash by his dog as if the dog were the master and Zachary the beast.

But then there was Leila.

What did she mean to him, exactly? That was another of the questions that had vexed his mind on his long night vigils—

one, like the justice or injustice of fate, for which he had also failed to achieve a satisfactory answer. He had dodged that question when the owner had asked it of him, but it would not go away, indeed it became more pressing the more he considered flight. Could he take her with him? The old question raised itself again in a new form. Take her as what, exactly? As wife? As servant? He imagined explaining her to his mother, for whom rural peasants were somewhat inferior to donkeys. And for that matter, what would the move do to Leila herself? She had never set foot in a city, or even a provincial town. She would be thrown into a way of life that would seem to her an impenetrable mystery, there would be no-one who shared her experiences, no-one she could talk to but Zachary, who would be forced into the position of sole intermediary between her and others just at a time when he needed all his energy to take care of himself .

No, he couldn't take her.

But could he leave her?

They had grown closer as the weeks turned into months. They had exchanged small tendernesses, little acts of kindness: a bunch of late flowers picked by the wayside for her, a pillow discarded by the owner's wife for him. They tiptoed around their conflicting schedules, each waking the other when needful, guarding the other's sleep when not. They spoke quietly and intimately together about things that concerned them while keeping always a thin wall of separation between them. No, he did not love her, he told himself, only to be brought up short by the question, what is love, anyway? There must be more than one kind. Certainly what he felt for her was not what he had felt for Celia, but how disastrous that feeling had been! He might have said he loved her as a sister, except that his feelings about his actual sisters were much more ambivalent. He felt for her, he supposed, as one was supposed to feel about a sister, tender, protective, without any of the turbulence of sexual love.

But also with emotions a sister was not expected to arouse: with pity, and with an occasional irritation, strangely linked to the pity, and brought about by the passivity with which she accepted her fate. He conveniently forgot the long months of equal passivity with which he had responded to his own traumas.

So how could he leave her, bound to her as he was in these ways? He tried, without success, to convince himself that she would soon get over it. He knew she would not. She had made no friends in the village. Despite all he said, she still refused to attend Christian services. She would not even consider returning to her parents. He was all she had. If he left her, it might kill her. Her blood would be on his head—a fine end to all his protectiveness.

He could not stay, he could not take her, he could not leave her. The war between these three impossibilities lasted for hours, making his head ache. No sooner had his mind fixed upon one course than the others thrust their arguments upon him. The pain and the futility of it fueled anger, and the anger focused inevitably on the one who was the unwitting cause of the whole thing.

The wet, cold weather persisted through the next day and night. On the following morning he returned home in a vile temper. Towards dawn, a neighbor had decided to take advantage of the bad weather by slipping a few of his cattle into the newly-growing wheatfields. It happened on another guard's territory, but Zachary heard the sudden shouts, saw the flurry of lights as the other watchmen gathered to repel the invaders. Pulled by his imperious hound, he had run to join them, only to come face to face with a panicked cow that charged right over him, knocking the breath from his body, trampling on his right arm, and smashing his lantern. The arm was still badly bruised and aching, and before leaving work he had had to return the damaged lantern to the storekeeper and secure a replacement for the following night.

When he finally arrived home, his food was cold.

'The food's cold,' he yelled at Leila.

'I'm sorry,' Leila said. 'I tried my best, but the fire just wouldn't draw. I think it's the wind.'

'The wind,' he said contemptuously. 'There's always something,' although hardly ever before had she failed to have a hot meal ready on time.

Stung by the unfairness of it, Leila began to sob.

Her sheer passivity drove Zachary's anger. 'So you're going to weep over me now, are you?' he demanded. 'You realize, don't you, that but for you I could be living in luxury?' The words startled even him, popping out of his mouth without conscious intention. The thought had been implicit in his nightly arguments with himself, but he had never framed it quite this bluntly, even in his own mind. Yet, once clothed in words, it took on a monstrous reality. Right, he told himself, she's all that's keeping you here, in this dumb, cultureless land of ignorant peasants. A woman that for some mysterious reason you attached yourself to. A woman who won't sleep with you, won't bear your children—a spoiled nun, an outcast—and why? Pity, he assured himself. Not love, not responsibility, just pity, that's all it is.

Before he could say more, she rushed from the house.

He finished his unappetising meal and went to bed. He piled every available scrap of material, every piece of clothing on the bed, to no avail. The chilly damp pierced everything. Outside, the sagging clouds presaged another day of rain. He got up and tried to do something about the fire, but she had been right, it wouldn't draw, you could get no heat out of it. He went back to bed, curled himself into a fetal position and at last dropped into an uneasy sleep.

When he woke, some time in the afternoon, he was overcome by guilt. How could he have behaved so vilely to her, she who had never thought of her own interests, who had never so much as raised her voice to him? He thought of her loyalty, her unobtrusive care of him. Was this all she got in return? Someone bawling abuse at her like the village drunk? His anger drowned in an indulgent fondness. He remembered how, most mornings, he felt when he thought of her waiting there in the cottage for his return. The relief he felt that he would not be returning to an empty house, a lonely cell, like he had inhabited in Scetis, with no company but his own thoughts, his own self-accusations. He had come to take that feeling for granted. But how would he feel if she never came back?

He lay awake, worrying about her. When the thought occurred to him, well, if she doesn't come back, you're free to leave, aren't you, he stamped on it viciously—it seemed a betrayal. He rose, dressed, tried to blow life into the sulky embers of the fire. Soon, he would have to leave again for work.

He dreaded having to leave without knowing whether she would return.

Bent over the fire, he heard the click of the latch. He turned in time to see her enter, wet through with the rain that was still falling. She tried to pass through in silence to her own room,

'Leila,' he called to her, and when that had no effect, he caught her by the arm and held her.

She stood, passive still, her eyes downcast, in silence, waiting for whatever it pleased him to do next.

'Leila, I'm sorry,' he said.

'Did you...' she asked hesitantly. 'Did you mean those things you said this morning? About it was only because of me that you were still here?'

'No, of course not,' his guilt drove him to say—even, for the moment at least, to believe.

'Because if you did,' she said, coloring, standing more upright now as her courage returned, 'I don't want you to stay. If you want to go, go. You're educated, intelligent, you could get good work in a city somewhere. I know that. I don't want to be the one that keeps you back.'

He felt a spontaneous rush of affection for her. 'I don't know what I was talking about,' he said earnestly, contritely. 'I chose this kind of life. I did it on purpose. It was nothing to do with you.'

'So do you really want to leave?'

'No.' Something deep in his heart told him, that's not true, but he silenced the voice, willing it to be true, almost believing that if he repeated the denial often enough, passionately enough, it would somehow become true.

'I'm glad,' she said with an unaffected sincerity that sent a pang through his heart.

'Do you have any dry clothes?' he asked. He was still holding her arm, he could feel the flesh, the fragile bone under the damp material that clung to her.

'Yes. I mean, I think so. Everything's so damp.'

'Then go and change,' he said, releasing her arm. And suddenly, without warning, for no reason he could think of—¬perhaps something as trivial as the way the wet clothes outlined her body, or perhaps his mixture of guilt and affection had somehow ignited more violent feelings—he became aware of her as a physical being, a body that could desire and be desired. Out of sheer habit, he automatically and instantly tried to suppress the thought: that was lust, lust was a mortal sin. Then it occurred to him, why shouldn't I desire her? I'm not a hermit any more. It's questionable if I'm even a Christian, in any meaningful sense of the term. I'm free, free to be my normal animal self. Why shouldn't I?

But the reasons were obvious to him, hermit or not. A woman who trusted him, who was under his protection, who had been so abused by others—how would she react if he were suddenly to change the rules of their relationship? She would be shocked, horror-struck, she would automatically repel him. Worse still, she would despise him, His heart withered at the thought of exposing himself to her contempt. He could not bear that.

Luckily, before the turmoil in his feelings could subside, he had to leave for work. He called a brief farewell to her and hurried out into the dripping evening. Immediately he felt the change in the weather—though the clouds remained and scattered drops continued to fall from them, the rawness was gone from the air and the wind had changed, blowing lightly now from the south. Before the night passed, the clouds had cleared, the stars were shining brilliantly, and a balmy air, dry desert air softened by the evaporating moisture of the rains was once again flooding the valley. And Zachary's mood, volatile as the weather, changed with it.

When he returned the next morning, he tried to behave as if nothing had happened, and she in turn made no reference to the events of the previous day. But occurrences cannot simply be erased from the record. It was all there, somewhere: his longing to leave, his anger with her, even his unexpectedly ¬kindled desire. These things might be suppressed, might lie in abeyance for a while, but they had been firmly planted in both their minds. Sooner or later, they would return.

Over his morning meal, a few days later, Zachary confessed to the restlessness that still persisted in his heart. But this time his tone was quiet, reflective, regretful even.

'I can't really see it, you know. Going on much longer as I am now.'

She stopped what she was doing and sat down on a stool, opposite him. He could not meet her eyes. 'What do you mean, exactly?' she asked him.

'It's not enough for me. I can do more than this. I feel like a racehorse that's kept in its stable all day. I want to get out there, in the world, where I can do things.'

'What things?'

He waved his arm imperiously. 'What does that matter? All sorts of things.' He really did not know. Did he want to become a businessman, a soldier. a politician? Nothing so definite as that—all of these too were too constraining, he simply wanted to have a space around him, within which he could feel himself free to act, to do something, it really didn't matter what.

She waited patiently to see what he would say next.

'I want to go to Alexandria,' he said.

He looked up at her now, sharply, as if expecting some reply, but she still said nothing. Her silence was her reply.

'You don't want me to go,' he challenged her.

Her eyes gazed at him sadly. 'If that's really what you want,' she said, 'I won't try to stop you.'

'I almost wish you would,' he burst out. 'I don't think I can stand any more of this Christian forbearance!' Immediately he felt ashamed of himself, and said, 'Leila, forgive me, I didn't mean that. It's just that...I don't know...You act like—¬like it wasn't hard for me, too. Do you think I wanted to just walk out on you, like that?'

'I never said that.'

'You never said it, but you...' He broke off, hopelessly confused. 'Oh, I really don't know! Probably I'm imagining it. You see, Leila—' And then he entirely forgot what he had intended to say, for what underlay his confusion was suddenly revealed to him. 'You see what it is, I just can't bear to think that you might think it was because of something you'd done that I wanted to leave.'

'I didn't,' she protested, surprised. 'I never thought that,' but he ignored or did not hear her, and pressed on:

'Well it's not that, it really isn't, I promise you. You've been good to me. You've done everything you could. It's just something in me. How I feel. I can't help how I feel.' Dimly somewhere in his mind he recalled that helping how he felt, doing violence to his own nature, had been his chosen way of life—he had believed then that it was possible, even desirable. He pushed the memory aside. He needed his own way now.

'I never thought you felt that,' she repeated. 'But I—I felt...'

'What?'

'That I could have been more to you than I've been.' They stared at one another in an awed silence, on the brink of understanding, half aware of what was growing in the air between them but not really yet believing it could exist.

'What do you mean?' he asked.

She lowered her gaze. 'That I could have been...'

'What?'

'A real wife to you.'

He sat there, stunned. 'I never—' he began. 'I would not have asked that of you. I know what you—'

'Please,' she said earnestly. 'Please don't think I said that to try and keep you here. To use it as a bribe. Because if I thought you thought that I'd just bar myself up in my room.

Until you left. It's just... something I've felt for quite a while now.'

'But you never said,' Zachary objected. 'You never gave me any sign that you—'

She smiled. 'Women aren't supposed to, are they?'

'You were sworn to celibacy.'

'When they drove me from the White Monastery they canceled that oath. At least,' she added, a little awkwardly, 'that's how I see it.'

'Leila,' he said, and his voice was harsh, unsteady, as if it cost him an effort to speak. 'There have been times when, yes, I wished you would be more to me than you were. But...I can't now. Not when I feel like this. If it had happened before...well, it's true, I might not feel as I do now. Or again, I might. I don't know. But to begin this now—don't think it's because I don't want to,' he put in hastily, 'but it wouldn't be fair. To you. Unless I could tell you honestly that I was going to stay. And I can't, Leila,' he said regretfully. 'I just can't.'

She reached out and pressed his hand, fleetingly: a sign of forgiveness. 'I understand,' she said. 'Perhaps I shouldn't have said—'

'No, you should, you should.' After a moment's pause he reached out, took her hand and held it lightly, gently in his own. 'I'm glad you did,' he said.

That was all. They sat thus for a while, feeling a deep peace that neither could have explained. Neither one felt the need to say or do more, at this juncture. To do or say anything would have shattered the balance of this fragile moment, forcing them into experiences for which neither was yet fully prepared. In a few more minutes, luckily perhaps, she had to leave for work, She rose, reluctantly, trying to disengage her hand, but he retained it firmly and, leaning forward, placed a single kiss in the center of her forehead. She flushed, averting her head, and then he let her go.

It took him a long time to go to sleep, that morning. He still had to get used to the idea that their relationship could change in this way. Would it make any difference, if it did change? Was his growing restlessness merely the consequence of physical desires that, through sheer habit, he had suppressed, but that were now expressing themselves through other means? If he had a woman to sleep with, to make love to, would that make any difference to how he felt? He would not know until he tried it. But if he tried it and it failed, where did that leave Leila? He couldn't make love to her and then desert her, that would be worse by far than if he had simply left when the restlessness began.

As things were, he could not sleep with her in the fullest sense. All the physical contact they could have would consist of brief, single-minded scuffles in the few minutes together that their opposed schedules permitted. That was not what he wanted from her. Sympathy and affection counted for far more in his feelings towards her than mere physical desire. He needed the long hours of the night to know her in.

By the time he left for work, he was no clearer about what he would do. Whatever course of action he took would have consequences he did not want. But so had inaction. Of all the possible outcomes he could least stand the thought of persisting in this limbo of indecision. He envied the peasants around him their stolid fatalism, born from generations of poverty and arbitrary, absolute rule. He was Greek; he had to have action, even if only to convince himself that he had control of his own fate.

The next morning, the foreman met him, as always, to relieve him of his lantern and dog and to hear if there had been any incident during the night. But this morning, when these formalities were completed, he said, 'The steward wants a word with you.'

Zachary's heart gave a lurch. Normally, especially if you worked nights, you saw no more of the steward than you did of the owner—he managed things through his hierarchy of subordinates, and if he wanted to see you, that was usually bad news, you had been found out in some offence or dereliction of duty. He searched his memory for anything he might have done wrong. Before he could recall anything, he found himself in the presence of the steward.

'You can read and write, I hear,' the steward said, without any preamble.

'Right.'

'Figures?'

'I know arithmetic.'

'See what you can do with this, then.' The steward handed him a roll of papyrus and gestured towards a tall stool at a desk. Zachary sat down. The writing on the papyrus was divided into two columns—debit and credit, he recognized immediately, from memories of documents he had seen, as a youth, in his father's office. He quickly added the two columns, wrote out the totals and the balance, and handed it to the steward.

The steward's eyebrows raised. He glanced at the papyrus and then at the shard of broken pottery that served him as a scratch-pad. What he saw must have satisfied him, for he turned to Zachary and said, 'You're quick.'

'Thanks.'

'Quicker than the last secretary I had. He died of fever last night. You've got his job. Start right a—no, you've been up all night, make that tomorrow morning.'

He jerked his head, indicating the interview was closed.

'But...what about my watchman's job?' Zachary asked, dumbfounded.

'Oh, don't worry about that. I've got a replacement for you. Just make sure you show up this time tomorrow.'

Zachary staggered out into the morning, his head whirling. It had never occurred to him that he might be promoted, or that the owner's inquiry into his education had been prompted by anything more than idle curiosity. But that this should have happened now, of all times! Surely it was the working of providence? Perhaps he had always really been destined for a secular life. Perhaps his belief that he had an eremitic vocation had been mistaken, the fruit of youthful arrogance, perhaps all that he had experienced since his days in Scetis had been calculated to push him in this direction, the pressures becoming firmer and clearer until even someone as obstinate as he felt forced to recognize and accept his fate.

So, he would go home and sleep all day, and all the following night too, if he wanted to. There would be no more cold, lonely vigils in the darkness. Instead, he would be ensconced on a comfortable stool, protected by thick walls from winter chill and summer heat, doing work that engaged his brain, with a strong chance that, if the steward died or retired, he would come to manage this whole vast estate where he had first worked as a humble day-laborer. He could hardly leave, not now that this wholly unexpected change in his life had come about.

He did not, until much later, realize how far his ambitions had been revised downwards. He had forgotten that, a few years earlier, the exact same career—sitting on a stool all day, totting up figures, only in his father's office, not this one—had seemed so repellant to him that he would face all the unknown dangers of the interior desert rather than submit to it.

Leila was, as he had known she would be, overwhelmed with joy at his news. But there was no time to discuss its consequences. The interview with the steward had delayed his homecoming and it was time already for her to leave. On an impulse, he seized her shoulders and tried to kiss her cheek as she left—she dodged his clumsy effort easily, glancing up and back at him with a half-smile in which reproof and promise seemed mixed equally. This sudden animation made her face look almost beautiful, and he felt a rush of pleasure at the thought that, in a few hours, they would be together.

He lay down, hoping to sleep long and deeply so that he could awake, refreshed. when she returned. But his mind remained too active for sleep, and the desires he had suppressed for so long mounted imperiously in his flesh. When he did doze off, his slumber was fitful and punctuated by anxious dreams in which he searched endlessly for objects whose names he could not remember, or was harassed and pursued by creatures he could never identify.

When finally she returned, their speech was hushed, subdued, as if they were both too shy to acknowledge what each of them knew was about to happen. When Zachary took the bedding from their two cots and began to spread it on the floor, she pretended not to notice that anything out of the ordinary was going on. When he came to take her in his arms, she said, with fear in her voice, 'You won't leave me, will you?'

'No,' he said. 'I won't leave you.'

He drew her down beside him on the bedding. 'I'm sorry about this,' he said. 'We should be able to afford something better, now. I'll see to it.'

'Did you ask what your wages would be?' she asked him, and he smiled at the incongruity of her remark, at this moment that should have been one of high passion.

'No. I forgot. I was so stupefied I never thought of it.'

'Please put the lamp out,' she said.

'I was going to.' He had put it ready on the floor, within reach. He would have liked to watch the expression on her face as he made love to her, but he knew that for someone raised as she had been, nothing was possible save in the most absolute darkness. He stretched out an arm and extinguished it.

'Be gentle with me,' she begged him.

He did not answer her, but wound an arm around her while with his other hand he tenderly stroked her hair, her face, her shoulders. He knew that she was no longer a virgin and that the pain she dreaded was not physical pain, but anything that would remind her of the time, or times—she had never confessed to more than once—when she had been violated. But that did not create any problem for him. What he felt for her was so different from what he had felt for Celia. If his passion then had been like a storm that raged around some exposed headland, his passion now was like the tide rising in a sheltered inlet, gently, slowly, but inexorably, filling every crevice of the cliffs, rising and submerging, one by one, the rocks that projected from the sea's bed, until there was nothing but a great shining surge of water, almost silent, all but motionless, yet irresistible.

Aignos Publishing, Inc.

Aignos (pronounced "I-Know" from a German word meaning "Confederates bound by oath") Publishing is an independent, bi-lingual royalty-based publisher. We specialize in experimental and inventive fiction and nonfiction works. We seek bold, boundary-pushing works from today's most exciting authors.

Please check out our other wonderful Aignos titles at www.aignos.com:

Lawyers Gone Bad, Vincent Scarsella
An Aura of Greatness, Brendan P. Burns
Letters, Buz Sawyers
In Conversation, Chris Campanioni
Going Down, Chris Campanioni
Feast of Saint Sebastian, Jon Marcantoni
Nuno, Carlos Aleman
Happy That It's Not True, Carlos Aleman
University and King, Jeffery Ryan Long
John Doe, Buz Sawyers
Anonymous Man, Vincent Scarsella
There's No Cholera in Zimbabwe, Zachary Oliver & Jon Marcantoni
When Angels Fall, Manuel Melendez
Overnight Family Man, Paul Guzzo
Piano Tuner's Wife, Jean Yamasaki Toyama
Covering the Sun with my Hand, Theresa Varela
Dark Side of Sunshine, Paul Guzzo
The Desert and the City, Derek Bickerton

www.ingramcontent.com/pod-product-compliance
Lightning Source LLC
Chambersburg PA
CBHW051430260626
47162CB00001B/35

* 9 7 8 0 9 9 0 4 3 2 2 8 9 *